Death Warmed Up

Admittedly the somewhat suspicious death of a director at Quardon International was due to an electrical rather than a culinary fault, but a catering service suffers by association. And if that were not enough, the food prepared by Executive Meals Service for a charity ball looks like being their ultimate disaster when several guests collapse.

Marian Babson spins a highly original tale of boardroom battles and a gourmet tycoon, taking a knowledgeable and light-hearted look at the pitfalls in wait for those who aim to soothe executive stomachs – and the lethal weapons which lie all unawares to hand...

Death Beside the Seaside

As August Bank Holiday weekend approaches, tension rises in an English seaside town, for one year ago the resort was invaded by motor cycle gangs and the memory of their outrages is still vivid. Will they strike again?

The police are alert, for among the wreckage the vandals left behind a dead girl, her murder never solved. But the delinquent son of one of the boarders at Trudi Kane's lodgings mysteriously disappears, and she experiences unwanted attention from a sinister stranger. And then the body of another girl is found...

MARIAN BABSON

Death Warmed Up

Death Beside the Seaside

Diamond Books
An Imprint of HarperCollins*Publishers*
77–85 Fulham Palace Road
Hammersmith, London W6 8JB

This Diamond Crime Two-In-One edition
published 1994

ISBN 0261 66296 1

Cover photography by Monique Le Luhandre

Printed in Great Britain

Death Warmed Up

CHAPTER 1

The mayonnaise had curdled, the stove had conked out with the meal half-cooked and the soufflé had never had a chance.

I stood in the midst of desolation and silently cursed the day Nick had persuaded me that the path to financial salvation would be lined with deb-types queueing up for special tuition (apprentice was such a down market term) with a first-class private catering service. These days, the smart money no longer went on curtseying to Queen Charlotte's Birthday Cake, but on learning how to make one.

'Oh, Jean! Jean—' Lexie hurled herself at me from the far corner of the room. 'I don't know what went wrong! I only turned my back for the teeniest possible minute—I had to go to the loo—and when I came back—'

Whereas I had been gone for nearly half an hour. I had been on the telephone firming up the details on a Boardroom luncheon for twenty-five in the City next Thursday. It had taken longer than I had expected since every query ('Gas or electricity?') had revealed further problems. ('Well, neither, really—not for cooking. Of course, we have electricity. I mean, we have this super oak-panelled Boardroom, but . . .') More by divination than information given, I had ascertained that there were no cooking facilities on the premises and no means to accommodate any. Therefore a cold buffet would have to be the order of the day. By the time I had settled this, and with the strong feeling that I had just been dragged through a hedge backwards, I had come back upstairs to face chaos.

'All right, all right. No time for that—' I thrust Lexie

away from me. With any encouragement at all, she would have sunk to a shuddering heap at my feet, wailing out her distress. (Really, she ought to have been enrolled in the Royal Academy of Dramatic Art. Except, of course, that cooking was a more demonstrable and marketable skill in this day and age than the mere ability to declaim. Far better to be able to whip up a soufflé than a scene.)

I noted with approval that her friend and co-apprentice, Sidonie, had unearthed an eggbeater, a carton of whipping cream and a half-bottle of brandy from our emergency basket and was eyeing the chocolate *appareil au soufflé* with a determined expression. That girl had the right idea: load the pudding with enough booze and the Board of Directors would think they were getting the real goods. They weren't gourmets—they only liked to think they were.

'Come on—' I rallied Lexie. 'It's salvage time. We'll have the post-mortems later.'

How could I have known that it was such an unfortunate choice of words?

My main concern was to snatch—if not triumph—at least an edible meal from the ruination around me.

It would be putting it too strongly to suggest that the success of the proposed merger depended upon the meal set before Ongar Manganian, but it was certain that he would be better able to judge the quality thereof than any of the whisky-blasted palates possessed by some of the Board of Directors of Quardon International. Behind his back (if gossip columns could be so described), he was often referred to as 'the Starving Armenian', as much because of his gargantuan appetite for food, wine and women as because of his antecedents.

Nevertheless, I had known of at least one promising business deal which had sunk without trace when a short sharp burst of ptomaine had followed immediately upon the presumed-nuptial meal. When the tycoon being

wooed had been released from hospital after having had
his stomach pumped, he had been unavailable to his
suitor-company for evermore.

It was more than that, of course. It was also a matter of
personal pride and a sense of gratitude. Quardon International was our oldest and most reliable client. Their
monthly luncheons helped to balance our books. They
paid promptly and even said thank-you occasionally.

Furthermore, we wished to retain their custom if the
proposed merger with Ongar Manganian's English
company went through.

I lifted the lid of the fish kettle to check on the progress
of the poached salmon; it was now cooling rapidly in its
court bouillon, but appeared to be sufficiently cooked.
Thank heavens for that. Without heat, I could not
transform the court bouillon into the sauce I had
intended but fortunately Lexie had made—or tried to
make—mayonnaise for those who might prefer it. That
could still be salvaged, but did I trust Lexie to do it?

Probably not. I took a clean basin and mixed half a
teaspoon of mustard into a very thin cream with water,
then began adding the curdled sauce, drop by drop.
Lexie watched me closely.

'Are you all right up here?' Edda Price, Tristram
Quardon's secretary, hurried into the kitchen, panting
slightly.

'Yes, fine,' I lied, moving defensively to block her view.
I noticed with approval that Sidonie had also changed
position so that her activities were unobservable.

'You are?' Edda's voice reflected doubt. 'If so, you're
the only ones. We haven't an electric typewriter working
in the building. The lifts are out, too.'

She flicked the wall switch. No lights went on.

'There!' she said. 'I thought so. It's just not good
enough! I shall get on to the Electricity Board
immediately. They really must warn us in advance when

they're planning a power cut!'

I was aware of the swift relieved glances passing between Lexie and Sidonie. It was all the fault of a power cut. They could not be blamed in any way for the oven's having lost heat at a crucial moment.

'How long has the electricity been off?' I asked.

'I've no idea. It's lunch hour for the staff, so no one was trying to type. And the day is so bright and sunny, there weren't many lights on.' She gave an approving glance skywards through the window. 'Spring's coming.'

Fluffy white clouds scudded across a bright blue sky propelled by a brisk wind with a touch of softness in it. I had noticed it myself this morning as I started out and had the same thought. Spring was on the way.

So was Quarter Day and all the bills.

'What time did the clocks stop?' Sidonie spoke for the first time, cutting straight to the core of the situation in her usual incisive way. She was the serious side of the dazzling beauty/plain practical girl combination one so often sees in best friends at that age. She did not, I noticed thankfully, pause in her labours with eggbeater, brandy and cream. Lexie would always try to get round a difficult situation — even a culinary one — by undoing a couple more buttons and breathing deeply. Sidonie knew only too well that a lot more effort would be demanded from her.

'Of course! I hadn't thought of the clocks!' Edda Price darted out into the corridor and we heard her clatter down one flight of stairs. There was nothing so vulgar as an electric clock mounted on any wall in the Executive Suite. If they had attained the cachet of taking lunch in the dining-room up here, they were above mere clock-watching.

'Don't open the fridge!' I warned sharply as Lexie made a move in that direction. It couldn't do the chilled melon any harm, but we'd want to slide Sidonie's confection inside and had better retain as much coldness as possible. There was no telling how much longer the Directors would linger over their drinks or how long the power cut would last. With the kind of luck we were having today, I didn't want to take chances.

'That's all right!' Edda Price bustled back into the tiny kitchen heaving a sigh of relief. 'The power's only been off for half an hour. It must have happened just after the Board meeting broke up. They won't have noticed anything and we won't need lights in the dining-room today. I shall go and complain to the Electricity Board at once! If they restore the power as soon as possible, the lifts should be working again by the time luncheon is over and the Directors want to leave.'

'The kitchen equipment—' I began. But I was speaking to her departing back. She hadn't heard me and it hadn't occurred to her that the oven, the fridge, the dishwasher and all the ancillary equipment ran on electricity. She was worried about the electric typewriters and the lifts; things more immediately concerned with the Directors' interests. I wondered how long it would take her to realize that a ruined lunch might be considered an inconvenience to them.

'That's funny.' Lexie had wandered over and was looking out of the window. 'Everything seems to be working in the offices across the street.'

'So it does.' I joined her and we stood watching the activity within our range of vision. Typewriter carriages moved briskly, computer screens glowed, lights flicked on and off at desks as people moved purposefully, returning from lunch or just leaving for it. 'Perhaps they're on a different section of the grid.'

'Perhaps.' She moved closer to the glass and leaned her forehead against it, twisting to look up and down the street on our side. 'But nothing seems to be happening. I mean, when there's a power cut, staff usually take advantage of it and pop out *en masse* to do a bit of shopping. Nobody minds because there's nothing else they can do. But it's all quiet below and—' She craned for a better view. 'And I'm *sure* I can see the reflection of lights next door.'

'Well, that doesn't help us any.' I moved away from the window. 'Unless you were thinking of popping next door and asking them if we could use their cooker—if they have one.'

'Wouldn't you just know—' Lexie sighed heavily '—that this would happen to *us?*'

It wasn't the worst thing that had ever happened to her—not by a long shot. However, it was interesting to note that she was aligning herself so thoroughly with Executive Meal Service. I had heard her refer to it, when she didn't know I was listening, as 'Meals for Wheels'—a name which was also creeping into occasional business slang. No bad thing, really, to have a catchy nickname. In these sorts of circles, it was half the publicity battle won. But if the meals weren't top quality, no amount of publicity could keep the business afloat.

Sidonie had done a magnificent job. The erstwhile soufflé base was transformed with cream and brandy, topped with whipped cream and sprinkled with crystallized violets. Now we could risk opening the fridge to pop it inside and trust that it would have attained a suitable degree of chill by the time the Directors were ready for it.

What we would do for hot coffee without any electricity, I didn't know. Perhaps, if we were very lucky, the power might be restored before it was time to serve the coffee. Alternatively, I might ring Mona and have her prepare a portable urn of coffee there and send Lexie or Sidonie in the van to collect it.

'Stand by,' I warned Sidonie, picking up her dessert creation. 'Open the fridge door for me—no wider than you have to—and slam it shut again as soon as I pop this inside.'

'Right.' She moved over to the fridge and we executed the manœuvre with perfect teamwork. It was disconcerting to see the fridge dark; one doesn't realize how much unconscious cheer that tiny light at the back radiates.

'I can hear them coming!' Lexie's voice rose on a note of hysteria. 'They're ready to eat! What shall we do?'

'Feed them,' Sidonie said practically.

'Hell!' I dashed next door to the dining-room to check that everything was in order. Lexie had set the table and was sometimes inclined to be a bit scatty about such things, although she could usually be depended upon to pay proper attention to the food itself.

All was well, however. White linen napkins folded into water-lily shapes swam on gleaming plates; the proper place setting was set round every place; the flower arrangement in the centre of the table was fragrant, springlike and, most important, low enough so that they could talk to one another across it.

I lit the candles flanking the flower arrangement, conscious of the voices approaching as the Directors came down the corridor from the Boardroom at the far end. Next to the Boardroom was a small well-stocked bar, to which they adjourned at the end of Board meetings, and for which I was thankful. It kept them out of our hair until they were actually ready to be seated for their meal. In companies without such an amenity, they came directly into the dining-room and served themselves from a bar on a small table set up in a corner, then roamed all over the dining-room with their drinks, getting underfoot while we tried to work.

One final look: everything okay. I dashed back to the kitchen, ignoring the knot gathered outside a small door midway along the corridor, playing their usual game of

'After you, Gaston' and trying to look as though they weren't queueing for the use of the Executive Loo.

Because I was still looking back over my shoulder, trying to see if Tristram Quardon was coming, I collided with the man in the centre of the kitchen. I would have collided with him no matter where he stood. It was a small room and he seemed to fill it, pushing Lexie and Sidonie into corners. He was a great bear of a man, one of those larger-than-life grotesques that life occasionally throws off. They are often to be seen in the most successful ranks of business, politics, or whatever — perhaps in sheer self-defence.

'Oh-ho! little one!' He caught me and held me off at arm's length, which meant I just barely cleared his enormous girth. 'More speed, less haste, no? Or is it the other way around?' His laugh boomed out, shaking the bottles of wine which were open and supposed to be breathing quietly on the sideboard. I could only hope the sediment wasn't stirred and decided that it might be safer to decant it before serving. The Directors were rather more knowledgable about their drink than their food.

'And what do you do here?' A gold tooth glinted in the corner of his smile. His beard was an untidy Van Dyke which threatened, like everything else about him, to burst its bounds at any moment.

'Be nice to her,' Lexie said pertly. 'She's the boss.'

'Oh-ho.' The small shrewd eyes sparkled beneath the shaggy overhanging eyebrows. 'Then it is to you I complain if I do not like the meal?'

'If . . .' I tried to smile. It was not comforting to know that his mind was running along such lines before he even sat down at the table. I wondered how the Board meeting had gone. If they were all in a bad mood, it would be easier for them to blame the food for their discontent than themselves.

'There you are, Ongar.' Tristram Quardon spoke from

the doorway behind me. 'You haven't seen Mark Avery anywhere, have you?'

'Would I be likely to?' Ongar Manganian released me in order to spread his arms wide in a huge shrug. 'That man does not like me, my friend. He does not approve of our deal. There were moments in the Boardroom this morning when I thought he was going to issue the ultimatum that the merger would proceed only over his dead body. I am still not so sure that he will not find some way to block it.'

'You mustn't pay too much attention to what Mark says right now.' Tristram Quardon was patently uncomfortable. He too seemed to wish that Ongar Manganian's mind was running along different lines. 'He's just upset at the moment. He'll get over it.'

'You think so, do you?' One eyebrow quivered and made a sudden leap up to the middle of his forehead. 'I do not. Why is he not here now? Why did he run away as soon as the meeting ended? Why has he not returned—?' He held up a hand, cutting off any reply Tristram Quardon might have made.

'I will tell you why. Because he will not drink with me! Drink occupies a curious place in your English rituals, my friend. In perhaps no other corner of the earth are there so many customs and traditions centring round it. He will not drink with me because he is afraid it might be seen as a gesture of conciliation, perhaps even weakness. And so he has evaded joining us at the bar for drinks. He will not return—if he returns at all—until we are seated at the table. And watch him. Even then, he will only drink water.'

'You're making too much of this, Ongar.' Tristram Quardon protested, glancing at his watch. 'I hadn't realized Mark had been gone so long. Perhaps he went down to his office and got caught by an incoming telephone call—'

'And perhaps he is making a telephone call. Even yet trying to find some way to block the merger. He is implacable, that man.' The booming laugh rang out. 'But so am I, my friend. So am I!'

'I'll have a word with him,' Tristram said unconvincingly. It was patently obvious that he had noted Mark's long absence and had hoped that Ongar Manganian had been unaware of it. Or, at least, of the possible reason for it. 'That's why I was looking for him just now. I thought you might have taken him aside for a word yourself.'

'No, no, not I. He is the sort of man one speaks to only through lawyers. No—' Ongar Manganian looked around the kitchen, bright-eyed and bushy all over. 'No, I am simply inspecting the troops.' He smiled at Sidonie, but his eyes rested on Lexie. 'They are not many, but they are choice.'

Sidonie glowered at him from her far corner. Lexie simpered encouragingly, her hand creeping up to her top button.

I watched incredulously as she toyed with the button. he was not only grotesque, he was at least three times her age. She *wouldn't*, she *couldn't*. Not for *him*!

She did. The button sprang loose from its mooring and a few more inches of Lexie drifted into view.

She couldn't help it; it was born and bred into her. No matter what else he was, he was male and he was a multi-millionaire. The Sloane Ranger rides again!

Nevertheless, I made a grim mental note that we were all going to switch to bibbed aprons. *High*-bibbed aprons. I wouldn't like the clients to get the wrong idea about what was on the menu.

'Lunch is about ready, isn't it?' Tristram Quardon spoke directly to me, but sent a sideways frown to Lexie, reminding her. He might be her uncle and he might have arranged for her to join Executive Meal Service, but she

was still in disgrace. The way she was behaving now
would not get her off probation any faster.

With a pout, Lexie turned away and flounced over to
speak to Sidonie, her back to the room.

'Ready whenever you are,' I assured him.

'Mark probably slipped down to his office for a quick
shave,' Tristram said. 'He's keeping everyone waiting.' It
was well known that Mark Avery had the sort of growth
that required three or four shaves a day if he were not to
look both shady and seedy. He was aware of this and
hypersensitive about it, hence he was always slipping into
the small bathroom attached to his office for a quick
shave whenever he suspected the stubble was gaining on
him again.

'Perhaps I ought to go and get him,' Tristram said.

'I'll go,' I said quickly. Mark Avery's office was two
floors down and Tristram Quardon was not yet aware
that the lifts weren't working. It was not so well known
that Tristram Quardon had had a Pacemaker implanted
about eighteen months ago. That was something else not
particularly confidence-inspiring among the big-business
types who sized up each other's health prospects over the
port and wondered whether Old Smethers would make it
through to the next Annual General Meeting. Those of us
who knew about it did what we could to ease his path.

'Tris—' One of the Directors appeared in the doorway.
'Ongar—' He beckoned to them both. 'Come and settle a
little dispute, would you? We've just made a bet that—'

Tristram Quardon and Ongar Manganian followed
him and their voices faded. I took a final look round
before I went to call Mark Avery to lunch. I noticed that
Lexie had shifted her position—presumably in case
Ongar Manganian had taken another look as he left the
room—and the arch of her back was distinctly
provocative.

I decided that Sidonie and I would do the serving.

There were too many opportunities for brushing and leaning during the course of serving a meal. I didn't want Tristram Quardon to begin wondering what Lexie might be getting up to in other Executive Dining-Rooms than his own. In point of fact, she had always behaved quite properly. But then Ongar Manganian was the first multi-millionaire who had ever come within striking distance.

You can't blame a girl for trying. But she wasn't going to try on my time. No, Lexie would sulk, but she would also stay in the kitchen this afternoon.

As it happened, I needn't have worried. Not about that. By the time the Directors came to their meal, no one had any appetite left . . . for anything.

CHAPTER 2

I tripped—literally tripped—over Edda Price as I entered Mark Avery's office. She was lying, in a neat diagonal line, just inside the door. Not unnaturally, I had entered the room looking around at eye level for its expected occupant. The door had opened easily and I had no reason to expect that a body would be stretched on the floor just a few feet beyond it. I advanced unsuspectingly into the room and nearly went sprawling.

I caught my balance just in time and looked down at the obstacle that had so nearly sent me flying. Edda lay face down and so motionless that I could not tell if she were breathing.

On top of the morning I had just had, it was too much. I closed my eyes and concentrated on deep breathing, fighting off the impulse to faint and thus opt out of any further responsibility in the matter. Joining her on the carpet would do no good at all. Deep breathing while counting slowly to one hundred might not help matters either, but at least it gave me the illusion that I was doing something about the situation. Or rather, that once I had reached my count and opened my eyes, I might be better able to cope with it.

I had reached thirty-three when a faint groan sounded at my feet. I opened my eyes and looked down.

'Where am I?' Edda Price had raised herself up on her elbows and was staring down at the carpet in bewilderment.

'You fainted.' I helped her to turn over and sit up. 'Are you all right now? Would you like a glass of water?'

'Water!' She looked around wildly and burst into tears. 'Mark! Oh, Mark!' She lost all coherence as the sobs increased.

Water. I headed for Mark Avery's private bathroom. I wasn't sure whether to throw it over her or force her to drink it, but water was definitely indicated.

I stopped short in the doorway, swamped by a sense of *déjà vu*.

Mark Avery lay on his back, electric shaver still clutched in his hand. His eyes were wide open, staring at the ceiling. There was a blue tinge to his features which could not solely be accounted for by the stubble he had not had time to attack. I refused to think about the faint smell of something singed in the air.

'He's still there, isn't he?' Edda Price spoke immediately behind me, but I had not been conscious of footsteps. 'It's not a nightmare?'

'It's a nightmare, all right,' I said. 'But it's real.' I turned and the scene took on an even more nightmarish aspect.

Edda Price was still on the floor. Edda Price—the elegant Edda Price—had dragged herself across the carpet like something out of an old Lon Chaney silent film. She huddled beside the desk, tears rolling unheeded down her face, streaking it with mascara.

'Mark,' she said again. 'Oh, Mark! I found him. I tried to go for help, but I fainted. I was useless. And he died. Oh, Mark!'

'There was nothing you could do.' I tried to comfort her. 'If he was like that when you found him, there was nothing anyone could do. It was already too late.'

I shouldn't have said that. With a moan, she lurched forward and began crawling towards the bathroom door to make sure that he *was* the way he was when she found him.

'No, please.' I blocked her progress. 'Come, sit here in the desk chair.'

I tried to pull her upright, but she struggled and I gave up. She was in a state of shock and it was obviously too much to expect her to behave rationally. At the same time, I was quite shocked myself, particularly at her behaviour. I would never have believed that Edda Price could go to pieces so quickly or so thoroughly. I had always suspected her of having a secret passion for Tristram Quardon, but now I wondered whether it might not have been for Mark Avery.

Or was it simply that they had all worked together for so long that the business association had become transmuted into a form of family tie? Mark, Tristram and Edda had started out over a quarter of a century ago in a rickety little office in Long Acre and built Quardon International into a genuinely international company with its own office block in the City. When the first member of a tightly-knit family died, the others were brought face to face with their own mortality.

'Someone will have to tell Tristram Quardon.' The thought followed naturally.

'I can't—' Edda Price turned her stricken face to me. 'The shock might kill him.'

That was a possibility, but he would have to know sooner or later. The demise of so close a colleague was not something it would be possible to keep from him indefinitely. Particularly not in these circumstances.

'And a doctor—' My mind was beginning to function again. 'We must call a doctor. Or perhaps an ambulance.'

'But you said—' She had gained the chair, now she tried to struggle out of it, her face lighting with hope. 'You mean, you're not sure? A doctor might be able to do something?'

'No. I'm sorry.' I pushed her back gently. 'It's just that one has to go through the motions. There has to be a doctor in the case of sudden death . . . accident . . .' The police had to be notified, as well, although I had a vague idea that would be taken care of automatically if we called for an ambulance reporting sudden death.

'It's all so terrible!' But she seemed to be pulling herself together. 'I rang the Electricity Board to complain, but they denied there'd been a power cut in this area. I didn't believe them. I came down here to speak to Mark, let him deal with them. You know what they're like—they'll always pay more attention to a man. And I found him . . . like that.' She closed her eyes briefly.

'Of course, there are things we must do.' She stretched out a hand to the telephone and then seemed to give up on the idea—she wasn't that pulled together yet. She looked up at me pleadingly. 'Send for Roddy.'

I should have thought of that myself. Roddy Bletchley was Tristram Quardon's Personal Assistant. Some people said: heir apparent. Possibly and possibly not. All that was certain was that he functioned as troubleshooter and general dogsbody as well as personal assistant. But he was definitely one of the first who should be told.

After that, the whole mess could be left in his hands.

Automatically, I reached out towards the intercom, then remembered that it worked off the electric mains and so would be out of action. It would alert the switch-

board if I tried to dial an inside number from here and
curiosity might tempt one of the operators to listen
in—then the cat would be well and truly out of the bag.

'Look,' I said, 'we can't call from here. Why don't you
slip upstairs quietly and have a word with him?' I wanted
to get her out of the office before the second shock wave
hit her. Once she began to think about it, she might crack
wide open again.

'Wait a minute,' I said, as she stood up in a daze of
obedience. I couldn't let her walk out of here like that. I
fumbled for a paper handkerchief from the box in the top
right-hand desk drawer, but couldn't face going back into
the bathroom.

'Spit,' I ordered, as though to a child. Like a child, she
obediently moistened a corner of the tissue and I
scrubbed at the mascara streaks.

'All right.' I inspected her without satisfaction. She
would pass muster—but only just. And perferably in a
very dim light. 'Find Roddy and tell him to get down
here. Don't talk to anyone else. If anyone tries to speak to
you, tell them you have to see to the arrangements and go
into the kitchen. Lexie and Sidonie are there. Don't tell
them anything, either, but make them give you a
brandy.'

She gave a wisp of a nod and made her way carefully
and a trifle unsteadily from the room.

Left alone, I closed my eyes and tried the deep
breathing routine again, but it didn't work. As I had told
Edda, there were motions that must be gone through. I
was sure—I was as certain as I would ever be of anything
in this life (or death)—but I had not tried to take Mark
Avery's pulse. I had not held a mirror in front of his
parted lips to see if the faintest trace of breath remained
in his body. These things must be done.

I fought down the impulse to wait for Roddy and
forced myself back into the bathroom.

The beard, hair and fingernails continue to grow until long after death. They're merely extruded protein with no life of their own; the condition of the host does not concern them so long as there are sufficient nutrients to sustain their growth.

I could not get that thought out of my mind and it seemed to me that Mark Avery's stubble was longer, thicker, than it had been when I first looked at him. The damned stuff had a life of its own, quite independent of poor Mark's. He had always claimed so and now the beard seemed intent upon proving it.

I averted my eyes and fumbled for his wrist. Nothing. Perhaps I should have tried the Kiss of Life but I could not force myself to touch the cooling body again.

I lurched to my feet and went to the medicine cabinet, thinking that there might be a smaller mirror concealed inside. As I stood in front of the sink to swing back the mirrored door of the cabinet, I became aware of a strange sensation beneath my feet.

The carpet seemed . . . squidgy.

Already knowing what I must find, I looked down. The carpet was — or had been — sopping wet. It was still wet enough to give me an unsteady feeling, but the moisture was spreading outward into a wider patch of damp, being absorbed into the surrounding dry area. It looked as though someone had splashed a great deal of water on to the floor. Or perhaps the sink had overflowed. But the sink looked perfectly dry . . . drier than the carpet.

When I raised my eyes to the mirror, I did not recognize the pale haunted face staring back at me. The head was shaking faintly in a negative motion, denying the knowledge trying to fight its way upwards from my subconscious.

I stretched out my hand to steady myself against the wall. And then I saw the rest of it: the dark grey-blue scorch marks streaking outwards from the electricity socket into which Mark Avery's electric shaver was still plugged.

No wonder the electricity in the building had failed. Every fuse must have blown with the violence of that sudden deadly surge of power.

I pulled my hand away from the wall as though I had burned it. At that, I suppose we were lucky — everyone except Mark. A fire could easily have started and, with all the executives upstairs and the staff out at lunch, it could have gained a firm foothold and spread out to endanger, if not consume, most of the building before anyone discovered it.

I found that I could not stay in that room another moment. I backed out slowly, abandoning any thought of finding a mirror to hold in front of those bluish lips. With a jolt of electricity like that, resuscitation had to be started at once or it was useless. He had died when the clocks stopped. As I had told Edda, it had already been too late when she found him.

I couldn't remember whether the bathroom door had been open or closed when I went in. Not that it mattered, Edda Price had already been inside and would have opened the door if it had originally been closed. But nothing more should be touched; Roddy would realize that when he arrived.

I glanced at my watch. Just over an hour since all the electricity in the building had short-circuited, since Mark Avery had died.

Upstairs, the Directors would still be boozing merrily, although perhaps beginning to wonder just when luncheon would be served. It was lucky that no one else had decided to come looking for their missing Sales Director and Deputy Managing Director. How much longer could that luck be expected to hold?

Where was Roddy? Had Edda collapsed again on the way upstairs to find him?

'Oh-ho!' The voice from the doorway made me jump.
'So this is where the chef is hiding.' Ongar Manganian
advanced into the office. 'No wonder our meal has been
delayed.'

Where was Roddy? I felt a burst of irritation. Where
the *hell* was Roddy? This was more than I could be
expected to cope with. As Ongar Manganian had just
pointed out, I was a chef. This was none of my business; I
had my own business.

'I'm not hiding,' I said coldly.

'No?' He frowned at me. 'Then why aren't you? I have
just had to walk down to this floor because the lifts are not
working. On the way, I observed no lights in the corridors
and that the electric clocks had stopped over an hour ago.
Surely this means that your cooking apparatus is no
longer serviceable and the meal is ruined. If I were the
chef, I would go into hiding.'

'The meal will be served as soon as—' I caught myself.
'Shortly. If you will kindly return to the dining-room—'

'You were not this pale when I last saw you. Nor did
your hands tremble.' He surveyed me shrewdly. 'Now,
what has happened, I wonder?'

I remained mute. There was no need to speak, he was
working it out for himself.

'You discover that your cooker is not working. You wish
to make a complaint. But quietly, so that it may be fixed,
if possible, in time to place the arranged meal before the
Board of Directors on schedule, or so nearly on schedule
that they will not notice anything has gone wrong.'

In spite of myself, I felt my lips curve in a rueful smile.
He was nearly right. It could so easily have happened that
way. In which case, I would have been the one to discover
Mark Avery and not Edda Price.

'The Directors, however, are celebrating our proposed
merger in the bar. You cannot contact one of them
quietly—the bar is too small. Everyone will overhear your

problem and you do not want that. But there is one
Director who feels he has no cause to celebrate. He has
slipped away from the festivities, back to his own office.
Perhaps to regain his composure, perhaps to begin
regrouping his forces for a final attempt to repel the
enemy. You know that he will be sympathetic to your
plight and will help you—'

The sheer force of that overwhelming personality had
been carrying me along with it, but now I became aware
that I had begun shaking my head very slightly. It must
have been noticeable, for he broke off abruptly and
frowned at me. Still frowning, he looked around the
office slowly.

'But where *is* Mark Avery?' With a swiftness surprising
in so huge a bulk, he crossed to the bathroom and flung
open the door. 'Is he sulking in his tent?'

'Please—' It was too late to stop him from seeing what
had happened, but I put my hand on his arm as he was
about to enter for a closer look. 'Don't go in there. There's
nothing that can be done. We mustn't touch anything
until—'

'Until the police arrive.' He finished the sentence for
me. 'No, no. I see that you are right, little one. But what
a terrible thing to have happened. I would not wish a fate
like this on my worst enemy.'

Nevertheless, an obscure satisfaction glinted deep in his
eyes as he stared at his fallen foe. Mark Avery would do
nothing more to block the merger.

'Christ! It's true!' Roddy had arrived at last. He was
behind me, staring over my shoulder unbelievingly. 'It's
really true!'

'You thought, perhaps, that it was the sort of thing
someone would tell you for a joke?' Ongar Manganian
turned and looked at Roddy without favour.

'No . . . no, of course not . . . It's just—Christ!' He
shook himself like a dog coming out of water and made an

attempt to take charge of the situation.

'You'd better get upstairs,' he told me. 'Edda's
breaking it to Tris. She'll need help.'

He turned to Ongar Manganian. 'I'm sorry, sir, but I'm
afraid you shouldn't be here.'

'Young man—' Ongar Manganian swept him with a
contemptuous look. 'I have not made my fortune by being
in places where I was supposed to be.'

CHAPTER 3

After that, of course, we might as well have been serving
gall and wormwood. The Directors drank more than they
ate, picking at the succulent salmon as though it were a
heap of cinders. In hushed, unbelieving voices, they
discussed the incredible fact that death had crept among
them in the midst of their working day and made off with
one of their number.

In his own office. That had shocked them more than
anything. Business is the bulwark men build against
mortality. They all knew the statistics on death after
retirement. That was to be expected.

But in his own office, in the prime of life. If a man
wasn't safe in his own office . . .

They finished the wine and went back to the whisky.
The brandy wasn't neglected, either. Only the food.
Anyone who had retained an appetite did not wish to
seem disrespectful to the dead by indulging it. Drink,
however, was looked upon as some sort of libation to the
gods to be splashed about in propitiation for their
temerity in surviving when one of their comrades had not.

It was also known as an Irish Wake.

It was a relief to clear up and leave. It was bliss to pull up

in front of the large Notting Hill Gate detached that
served Executive Meal Service as a headquarters and dive
for the warmth and security of the big kitchen. Nick
could unload the trays from the van later.

'You're back late.' Mona looked up from stirring a
large cauldron on the Aga cooker. 'Everything all right?'

'Everything all wrong!' I hurled off my coat and fell into
the comfort of the big welcoming rocking-chair Mona
had insisted no kitchen should be without. 'Couldn't be
worse!'

Lexie and Sidonie rather spoiled the effect of this
announcement by entering on a wave of giggles.

'Yes, it could,' I corrected myself. 'He might have died
of ptomaine after gorging himself on the fish.' A
communal shudder vibrated through the kitchen.
'Instead of which,' I added quickly, 'he died by accident
before he ever got to the table.'

'Who?' Mona advanced on me waving the ladle
threateningly, drops of savoury soup flying from it.
'Elucidate—immediately!'

I elucidated. Gretel crept from her post in the corner to
listen wide-eyed.

Nick wasn't present; that meant he was still out
scouring the highways and byways for the best buys of the
day to bring back for us to build menus around. In
practice, this meant Smithfield, Billingsgate and Nine
Elms, but he often went farther afield, intercepting
lorries of Common Market produce before they reached
their assigned importer, inspecting the early crops in
Green Belt farms to get the prime produce at the best
prices. There was more than a bit of the highwayman in our
Nick. It had served him well during his entrepreneurial days
in an advertising agency and it was now working to our
advantage as he threw his not-inconsiderable energies
into both providing the raw materials for, and guiding
the destinies of, Executive Meal Service.

'Thank heavens—' I was in the process of trying to describe Tristram Quardon's shock and distress when Mona interrupted. 'Thank heavens, he hadn't eaten anything of ours.'

'That's immaterial,' I protested. 'No one could confuse death my electrocution with death from ptomaine poisoning.' Not even the solemn young policeman who had taken my statement before I had been allowed to leave.

'Oh yes they could—and don't you mistake it.' Mona shook the ladle at me. 'People like nothing better than to put two and two together and come up with twenty-five. There are always those who can make two facts equal one wild hypothesis. 'Especially,' she added darkly, 'in the media.'

Gretel was blinking with the strain of trying to translate Mona's English into something that made sense. But there was no time to stop and try to explain to her that incomprehensibility was the point Mona was making.

'Anyway,' I said, 'we have an awful lot of salmon left over. It's all right, it never even went to the table. We served up in the kitchen. The Directors were in such a state they'd have hacked it to pieces and still not got a decent portion.'

'I can imagine.' She probably could. She had worked at director level herself before marrying Nick and retiring, as she had thought then, from the fray. 'Well, we can do a nice salmon mousse for the cold table and anything still left over can go into the seafood vol-au-vents for tomorrow.'

Gretel made a sound halfway between a gasp and a squawk and fled back to her corner. From the odour surrounding her, she had been cleaning shrimp for the canapés and vol-au-vents for tomorrow's reception at a new American bank. They had ordered a substantial finger buffet and specified individual cherry pies for dessert, since the whole thing was supposed to be a slightly belated celebration of George Washington's Birthday.

Mona raised her eyebrows and rolled her eyes upwards. Gretel, I gathered, had been presenting a problem again. I nodded back at Mona sympathetically.

What can you do with the hopelessly cack-handed? Gretel was good-natured, energetic, enthusiastic, eager to learn and willing to throw herself into any task, however menial. Unfortunately, the resulting splash not only ruined the project in hand but meant that everyone in the vicinity had to stop whatever they were doing and help her to clean up. She had obviously been at it again this morning.

Since no one could be sure when Nick would return with his plunder, Lexie and Sidonie went outside and began unloading the van. Trying to appear casual, I got up and strolled around the kitchen, winding up in the corner where Gretel was working at a scrubbed pine side table.

It could have been worse. It often had been worse. This time, it was just a matter of the canapés losing out to the vol-au-vents. Immediately in front of Gretel was the waste bowl of pink and black threads—it was filling rapidly with more pink than black, but that was hardly worth mentioning. More serious was the fact that, of the other two bowls on the table, the one containing fragments of shrimp was nearly full whereas the bowl designated to hold whole shrimp was nearly empty.

Smiling at Gretel, but with an inward sigh, I opened another tin of shrimp and settled down to helping her.

'They are so small,' she said defensively. 'It is not easy to keep them in one piece.'

'That's why we're doing seafood vol-au-vents at the same time.' I tried to cheer her. 'Nothing is ever wasted.'

Perhaps it wasn't, but that wasn't Gretel's fault. I

winced as another shrimp crumbled beneath her too-
eager fingers. It was a pity. Gretel longed to do the really
delicate work: glazing with aspic, piping mayonnaise
scrolls, making confectionery roses, all the little finishing
touches that added so much to a dish. The trouble was, if
we let her near anything, it would be finished, all right.

The outer door crashed against the wall and Lexie and
Sidonie staggered into the kitchen laden with leftovers
from the van. Lexie, carrying the serving platter with
over half a salmon still to be seen beneath the plastic
dome, just made it to the kitchen table where she
deposited the platter with relief. Sidonie carried a large
saucepan in each hand with boxes of mints and glacé
fruits balanced on top.

'I've told you girls before,' Mona scolded. 'Don't try to
unload everything all at once. It doesn't matter if you
have to make several trips — and it's safer.'

'Don't worry,' Lexie giggled. 'There are plenty more
trips to make. This isn't nearly everything. If we'd known,
we needn't have bothered to go there at all today, for all
they've eaten.' She and Sidonie turned and went out to
the van again.

'They have such fun.' Gretel watched them go, then
turned mournful eyes to me, reminded afresh of another
long-standing ambition. 'When do you take me with you
to cook the Boardrooms?'

'Some time,' I said vaguely. *Some time between hell
freezing over and the rivers running dry*. It was bad
enough here where we could keep an eye on her, but what
Gretel might do let loose in unfamiliar territory didn't
bear thinking about.

I realized suddenly that, if she had been with us today,
I should have seriously suspected her of being somehow to
blame for Mark Avery's death. The manner of his
accident had something of Gretel's clumsy incompetence
about it. Imagine a man being killed by a freak accident

with his own electric razor, which he must have used hundreds of times before! I was glad Gretel had been nowhere near the scene. It would have been only too easy to wonder secretly if she had been responsible in some way for that fatal wet patch on the carpet.

'You can do the shrimp flowers for tomorrow,' I offered in apology for my unspoken thoughts. It ought to be all right. They were among our more foolproof canapés: a cracker spread with cream cheese, then one small whole shrimp placed in an upper corner for the flower and a long thin strip of green pepper placed beneath it like a stem, with another shorter sliver of green pepper midway up the first piece like another green sprig. It was simple but impressive, a plateful of them looked like a garden of spring blossoms. Surely even Gretel could manage that.

'Yes?' Her face lit up. She lurched to her feet, rocking the table. 'I start now.'

'No, no, tomorrow,' I said, marvelling at how unerringly she had immediately leaped to do exactly the wrong thing. 'You can't spread cream cheese on crackers and put them in the fridge for twenty-four hours,' I reminded her. 'They'll go soggy. They have to be the last things we make just before we leave for the reception.'

'We?' Her face had been darkening, now it lit up again. 'You are taking me with you?'

Over her head, I met Mona's eyes. There was no help there; she was trying not to laugh. I had boxed myself into a corner this time. Well, I supposed we had to start breaking Gretel in sooner or later. I only hoped the customers didn't break first.

'You'll have to be very careful,' I surrendered. 'Stay close to me and watch what the other girls do.' There wasn't really anything she could do to ruin the reception, was there? And, even if she did, would anyone notice it? Americans weren't used to servants and tended to be touchingly grateful for any service rendered, if not overawed. If the rest of us could keep a straight face, any gaffe might be passed off as some quaint but obscure European tradition. The fact that Gretel had a 'foreign' accent, as opposed to an English accent, would also be helpful. Whatever happened, we might just get away with it.

Lexie and Sidonie burst into the room again on another wave of hilarity. It was sheer reaction to the events of the day, of course. Sudden death took people that way sometimes, especially teenagers who had never encountered death before and who were not closely connected with the departed. Lexie might not find life so hilarious if it had been her uncle who had died rather than one of his business partners.

As it was, they were armoured in their youth and the unexpected brush with mortality had merely given an extra edge to life. Their own deaths were unthinkable, unbelievable, something that could never happen. Surely, long before they were old enough to begin to worry about it, medical science and the advances of technology would have rendered death obsolete. The fact that accidents could happen to anyone was not so much overlooked as ignored.

'That's it!' Lexie dumped a rack of dirty dishes beside the dishwasher. We had only washed up the china belonging to Quardon International when the electricity supply had been restored. We were so anxious to get out of there that we had brought our own dirty crockery back to be washed at home. 'The last trip. The van is empty—we're finished.'

'Good.' Mona began loading the dishwasher. 'Then you can start helping out here. I've hard-boiled the quails' eggs, Lexie, suppose you begin shelling them. Sidonie can start mixing the savoury sausagemeat to wrap around them. We're doing miniature Scotch eggs for the buffet.' She shrugged and we knew what she meant. The small

individual Scotch eggs would be far more expensive than
the regular ones made with hens' eggs, but they were also
far more impressive. The American bank was determined
to impress their guests and it was to be a no-expense-
spared occasion. Not that we were complaining. We
would make a nice profit on it, although not half as nice
as the wine merchant would.

'Scotch eggs!' Lexie giggled wildly. 'Most Americans
have never seen them and don't know what to do with
them.' She giggled again. 'Did I ever tell you about that
time in New York—?' She was overcome by laughter.

We all waited expectantly. We had heard quite a bit
about Lexie's time in New York—although none of it
from her. The newspapers had been full of it when she
eloped to New York with an early boy-friend. No
marriage ever took place and the newspapers had been
far more excited about it than Lady Pamela, Lexie's
mother, who had simply shrugged her shoulders and said,
'They'll come home when their money runs out.' Which,
of course, was exactly what had happened, although the
money might have lasted a bit longer if they hadn't
splashed it about cutting a swathe through the most
expensive places in New York.

The media excitement had died down after her return,
although she was still good for a paragraph or two in the
gossip columns. But that sort of thing didn't ruin a girl's
marriage chances any more. Not in ordinary circles. And
not even the most insanely ambitious mother could have
thought of Lexie as a regal marriage material. Probably
not even ducal. A nice merchant banker, however, or
Something in the City . . . now that was more realistic for
Lady Pamela to pin her hopes on.

But after a year or so, during which there had been a
number of romances—none of them developing into
anything permanent—Lexie had been persuaded to make
a gesture towards a career. She had always been

interested in cooking. Indeed, her only souvenirs from her
fling in New York had been a pile of American cookbooks
and the conviction that she was an expert on American
affairs. Since Executive Meal Service was already working
for Quardon International, Tristram Quardon had
unhesitatingly pulled the right string on behalf of his late
brother's only child and Alexia Quardon was now
working/studying with us. Almost automatically,
Sidonie, her closest friend and some sort of distant cousin,
had come along with her as, I gathered, she had tagged
along since childhood on anything Lexie did. Except, of
course, her wildest exploits, like the New York
elopement.

It had worked out better than any of us had any right
to expect. Both girls were genuinely enthusiastic about
cooking, the fees paid for their tuition went a long way
towards keeping Executive Meal Service solvent, and two
willing assistants meant that we did not need to hire
temporary catering staff for our bigger contracts like
tomorrow's reception. Even on the smaller assignments, it
meant that Mona no longer had to go out with me to help
serve luncheons and could remain behind in the kitchen
cooking towards the next meal, answering telephone
calls, typing invoices and otherwise concentrating on
firming up the business we already had and canvassing
new clients. We were very close to the turning-point, to
the place where just getting by gave way to making a
positive profit and led on to the road to success. Every
little bit helped. Even Gretel.

'Please—' Gretel said, as Lexie fought to overcome her
hysterical laughter. 'The Scotch eggs. You are going to
tell us? Yes?'

'Yes, tell us,' Mona encouraged. While this had been
going on, she had been tossing equal parts of olive oil, soy
sauce and cooking sherry into a large bowl. Now she
added appropriate amounts of garlic and dry mustard

and stirred it all vigorously before going to prepare the
chicken livers. 'We can all use a laugh.'

'My God—we can!' I echoed fervently. In the warm
sheltering kitchen, buttressed by laughter and friendship,
the horror of the day was beginning to recede. I watched
Mona pull a thawed chicken liver from the defrosting
mass and cut away the bits of clinging fat and membrane.
She sliced the remaining liver into bite-sized pieces and
tossed them into the marinade where they would remain
overnight.

'Yes, well—' Lexie took a deep breath and pulled
herself together. 'We were sitting around in a cocktail bar
one night—a whole crowd of us drinking. And, as usual,
there was nothing to eat but salty peanuts and crisps. I
wanted something to eat, but not a full meal. But you
can't get any food in cocktail bars, you have to go into the
dining-room if they're part of a restaurant, or else leave
and go somewhere else. Even then, you have to have a
whole meal.'

'They don't have the law we have here that says any
place that sells drinks also has to sell food.' Mona gave a
faint sigh, perhaps for the days when she and Nick went
on those expense account trips to New York and Chicago.
'They aren't obliged to provide any sort of snacks.'

'And they don't,' Lexie said. 'I started complaining
about it and then I went on to reminiscing about our
English pubs and all the lovely things you could get:
Ploughman's lunch, enormous hot sausages, shepherd's
pie, Scotch eggs, the lot. Oh, I had a real old fit of
nostalgia, I can tell you. Not only that,' she added, not
without a touch of pride, 'I carried all the rest of them
along with me—and most of them had never even seen a
real English pub. But, by the time I was done, they were
all sighing.'

I could well believe it. Even now, we were all hanging
on her words. Lexie could carry anyone along with her.

Even Sidonie, who must have heard the story before.

'Well, naturally—' Lexie gave a dismissive shrug—'I'd forgotten about it by next day. And I never expected anyone else to remember. Then we went to dinner at a friend's—' Every now and again, Lexie let slip a 'we', the only indication she ever gave that she had not been on her own in New York.

'And I found—' she was back on form—'that she'd tried to cook a real English meal for me because she thought I was getting homesick. The only trouble was—' she giggled again—'I must have left something out when I was telling her about Scotch eggs, or she misunderstood completely. You should have seen them! Well, no—' she corrected herself—'they *looked* all right. It was when we cut into them, we discovered what she'd done.

'She'd wrapped the sausagemeat around raw eggs and then deep-fried them until the meat was cooked. At first, we couldn't get the knife through because of the shell, then it sort of *splashed* through. You never saw such a mess in your life!'

'Oh, I don't believe it!' Gretel was whooping with delight at the idea of someone worse in the kitchen than she was. 'Oh, that is so funny! Did it really happen?'

It was never possible to know whether Lexie's stories were actually true, but she told an awfully good story. We were all laughing and relaxed.

'It's true,' Lexie maintained. 'Honestly, it is. Then I had to explain that you were supposed to hard-boil the egg first and take the shell off. But she should have known. Who could ever imagine doing a Scotch egg that way?'

A car horn sounded abruptly outside the house and Lexie glanced at her watch. 'Oh heavens, that's Humpty already! He said he'd pick me up, but I didn't expect him so soon—' She looked at us apologetically, pleadingly. 'And there's still so much to do.'

'He's not all that early,' I said. 'We're running late. Unavoidable circumstances today. You can run along now, but try to be here early tomorrow. There's going to be a lot of work.'

'I will, I promise.' She was half way out the door when she hesitated, as though caught by a sudden thought. 'I know Mona hates the idea,' she said, 'but, honestly, you ought to get a microwave oven. They're all over New York — and they're so fast. We could get everything done in a fraction of the time.'

'And then you need a regular oven anyway,' Mona countered, 'to brown everything. It only doubles the work.'

'Oh, but —' Lexie began. The horn sounded again. She pouted. 'He's in a bad mood tonight.' She waved. 'See you in the morning.' She was gone.

'If the rest of you would like to leave now —' I looked at Sidonie and Gretel.

'I'm in no hurry,' Sidonie said, a trifle grimly. She shared a flat with Lexie, but it was obvious that she wasn't included in Lexie's plans for this evening.

'Nor I,' Gretel said sunnily. 'There! The shrimps are finished. What do we do now?'

'I hate to say this, but — the dishes.' I gestured towards the dishwasher and the remaining jumble of dirty crockery they had carried in from the van. It was an empty gesture, most of them would have to be washed by hand; Mona had filled the machine with the easy load.

Two heavy sighs answered me, but I hardened my heart. The first rule every cook learns is: the person who makes the meal isn't the one who does the dishes. Not if there's anyone else within a two-mile radius who can be conned into doing them. It's a question of self-preservation, which is, of course, the first law of Nature.

Speaking of which, I heard the sound of a car pulling into the carriageway and stopping at the side of the house. Nick was back.

CHAPTER 4

When Nick bounded into the kitchen a moment later, he was looking too triumphant for comfort. *Our* comfort, that is. His eyes were just a little too bright and his smile too charming. There was just a trace of uncertainty in his manner as he looked around the kitchen, rubbed his hands together and said, 'Ah, it's good to be home.'

'Is it?' Mona eyed him suspiciously. 'In that case, why didn't you get here a lot earlier?'

'Ah—' He raised one hand in a defensive gesture, warding off criticism. 'I'll bet you're wondering where I've been all day. You'd never guess. Not in a thousand years.'

'Try me,' Mona said flatly. 'You've been drinking with the boys from the Agency.'

'Only in passing.' He was wounded. 'On the way back, after a hard day tracking down a sensational bargain for you. It's tied to the top of the car—that's why I had to wait until the rush hour was over. I couldn't drive through traffic like that. Wait until you see it! Come and give me a hand getting it into the house.'

Mesmerized, we followed him through the back door and out into the yard, prepared to unload bushels of sprouts, a ton of potatoes, or whatever he had picked up at bargain prices. Then Mona gasped as we saw it.

It sprawled like some giant prehistoric monster, legs in air, all the way across the roof of the shooting brake and jutted out over the sides.

'Isn't it a beauty?' Nick demanded, beginning to unlash ropes. 'Did you ever see anything like it?'

'No,' Mona said faintly. 'What is it?' Since it was obviously a table, she was playing for time with the question. Time to gather her wits about her and decide how best to deal with the situation. Not that she had much choice, Nick had presented us with a *fait accompli*.

'Genuine rosewood,' he misunderstood cheerfully. 'There are three leaves for it inside. One of them's a bit warped, but the boys in the Road ought to be able to give us a hand with that.' He disappeared around to the other side of the shooting brake to tackle some more knots.

'Leaves . . .' Mona murmured weakly. We looked up at the enormous table. 'It's got three leaves.'

'It is magnificent,' Gretal approved. 'You must be able to seat forty around it. You will be able to hold banquets.'

'Banquets . . .' Mona echoed. She raised her voice in a cry of anguish. 'Nick!'

'All right,' he shouted. 'I'm going to slide it off the roof, blanket and all. Stand by to catch it. Lower it to the ground gently and right side up. As soon as it's moving, I'll come round to help you.'

We leaped forward as the table quivered and began to tilt. It slid smoothly and more quickly than we had been prepared for, the blanket protecting its surface accelerated its progress.

My first thought was that I'd rather be unloading a ton of potatoes. Certainly, the table seemed to weigh a ton—and it was all in one piece. Suddenly, we were fighting to prevent it crashing to the ground.

'All right.' Nick arrived to reinforce us. While we tried to hold the table steady against the side of the shooting brake, he turned it so that the legs were where they belonged and suddenly it was standing upright.

'Fine,' Nick said. 'Now let's get it into the house. Gretel, Sidonie, there are three chairs inside the brake with the leaves. One upright and two carvers. Matching. Three trips ought to do it.'

Nick, Mona and I wrestled the table sideways through the door and into the kitchen. It took up most of the room. Sidonie and Gretel staggered in behind us with the two carvers.

'Whew!' Sidonie set down her chair and collapsed into it. She propped her elbows on the arms of the chair and looked down over it approvingly. 'Lovely bit of stuff, this.'

'Rosewood. The original match to the table, I'd say.' Nick shook his head. 'Too bad we couldn't get the full set, but I imagine it got broken up over the years. They probably survived because they doubled as armchairs. Only one dining chair, though. Still, we can find something close enough in the Road and we wouldn't have been able to afford it if it had been complete.'

'What — ?' Mona asked through clenched teeth. 'What are we going to do with it? Where are we going to put it?'

'The dining-room, of course.' Nick looked surprised. 'It's empty. High time we began furnishing it.'

'The table is far too big for it,' Mona said.

'Nonsense. It's just the right size. It's an enormous room. We'll still have space for a sideboard, a couple of wine coolers, the rest of the chairs — when we find them —'

'I mean, it's too big for *us*,' Mona said.

'Ah! Well —' There was a delicate silence.

'Come on, Gretel.' Sensitive to atmosphere, Sidonie got to her feet. 'Let's go and bring in the rest of the things . . .'

'Suppose we carry it through to the dining-room,' Nick coaxed. 'Then we can see how it looks.' He signalled to me and I took my station at the end of the table. Mona stood back and watched us grimly as we managed to shove it out of the kitchen and down the hallway.

'There we are.' Nick positioned the table in the centre of the great empty room. 'Could have been custom-made for this dining-room.'

I had to agree. Large as the table was, there was still plenty of space. The dining-room was in keeping with the rest of the house, a late-Victorian family dwelling, designed in the days when 'family' was understood to mean husband, wife, ten children, grandparents, several indigent relatives and a dozen or so live-in servants to accommodate them all. Not surprisingly, it had stood empty for decades until Nick, in the first flush of being appointed Accounts Director at the advertising agency where he worked, had bought it for rather more than a song and a staggering mortgage. It fitted in with his grandiose ideas of a suitable home for a rising young executive. Once it had been properly done up and furnished, that is.

'Quick—help me to get this off.' Nick began tearing at the string securing the tattered blanket to the table top. 'Before she gets here.' We could hear Mona's footsteps coming slowly down the hallway.

I attacked the string on my side of the table. The knots resisted my efforts. Nick had tied them to stay tied and protect his precious rosewood surface.

'Damn!' I felt a fingernail give, while the knots still held.

'Here—let me.' Nick had untied his side; he came round and began working at the knots with an anxiety bordering on desperation. I knew he wanted Mona to see the full beauty of the table as she came into the room.

'There—' The last stubborn knot gave way and he pulled at the blanket, unveiling the table.

'Oh, Nick! It *is* lovely.' I knew Mona stood in the doorway, but all my attention was for the table. It was beautifully patterned, glowing with the patina of a tenderly polished and cherished piece of furniture. 'Where did you find it?'

'Sometimes you strike it lucky at these country auctions,' he said. 'I was doubly lucky. There was a heavy fog down there and I think some of the dealers who'd ordinarily have bid it out of sight must have got lost or discouraged trying to find the place.'

'How much?' Mona was not going to be sidetracked by minor considerations.

'We'll earn it back in no time,' Nick said. 'With this, we can cater for private parties right here in the house. Just think, no more chasing around with containers, trying to keep food hot or cold, no more struggling in strange kitchens—'

'In the house,' Mona said flatly. The words hung in the air accusingly.

'We'll still be out a lot,' I said quickly. 'There won't be all that many people who'll want to trail way over here for their meal. And I can't see our business clients holding their Board meetings here just to be convenient to the kitchen.'

'Oh, not the City trade,' Nick said. 'We'll just have to continue to cope with that. I was thinking of new business. People who might want to discuss confidential business over a meal and don't want to go to restaurants where they might be overheard. People who want to entertain clients at some place exclusive but undiscovered. Testamonial dinners to departing directors from their colleagues. Oh, we'll find plenty of new business, don't worry. Of course, at first, they'll have to bring their own wines with them—until we can get a liquor licence. But I don't suppose they'll find that any great strain—and it will work out cheaper for them—'

His enthusiasm was mounting. He did not seem to notice that he had lost Mona.

'Liquor licence,' Mona said. 'You mean you're planning to turn our home into a restaurant?'

'More of a private dining club, actually,' Nick said. 'Very private. Reservations only. We pick and choose.'

Sidonie and Gretel had carried in the last table leaves. They looked from Mona to Nick and then glanced at each other. With one accord, they leaned the leaves against the wall in a corner and moved together.

'I'm afraid we'll have to go now.' Sidonie acted as spokesman. 'We'll be here early in the morning. Nine o'clock?'

'Good!' Mona said absently. She probably hadn't heard a word, but the fact that they were leaving had got through to her.

'I say good night then.' Gretel continued to try to observe the amenities, but Sidonie caught her arm and pulled her through the doorway. We could hear their footsteps hurrying down the hallway.

'Good night,' Nick called after them.

'I ought to get back to my quarters,' I said cravenly. 'It's going to be a busy day tomorrow—'

'No hurry.' Nick shot me a betrayed look. 'Why don't we go back to the kitchen and have a drink?'

'—and it's been quite a day today,' I finished firmly. 'It's been a terrible day. Mona will fill you in on it. I just want to go off and collapse. Alone.'

It was the best I could do towards throwing him a lifeline. He was going to have to face Mona by himself sooner or later. Perhaps by the time she had finished explaining—if he could persuade her to explain—what had happened at Quardon International, some of her anger might have been deflected.

'Wait a minute—' Nick began. But I walked out of the room as though I hadn't heard him. I didn't dare do otherwise.

The trouble was that, while I sympathized with Mona, I was on Nick's side. And not just because I was his sister. His idea was good and a logical progression along the path we were travelling. Furthermore, we needed the extra money.

My heart went out to Mona because I could also understand her feelings. The house had been bought to serve as their home. Of course, she wanted to keep it for themselves. It was bad enough that I had already encroached on it. But that was unavoidable—if they wanted to keep it at all.

No one could have foreseen the way the economic climate had changed over the past few years: the rising and falling pound, the shrinking markets, the tightening belts, the closures, the redundancies, the frantic scrabbling to stay in one's accustomed position. Inevitably, advertising had been one of the worst-hit areas; the first thing a tightly-pressed company thought of economizing on. In Nick's agency, the accounts had fallen away or shrunk to a size which made an overall Accounts Director an unnecessary luxury. The regular account executives could easily handle what business there was.

Nick had held out until the Golden Handshake, although 'it was more like tin', was the way he had phrased it. Not enough to pay off the mortgage, let alone keep him in the manner to which he had become accustomed. Nor was anything better in the offing anywhere. There were too many redundant advertising executives chasing too few openings. The smart ones veered off into different fields.

Nick had looked around for a growth industry requiring minimal investment but promising maximum returns. Inevitably, his eye had fallen on me.

I had been back in England for about a year after a stint in Brussels working as a secretary for Common Market Eurocrats. It was the usual dreary story, it bored even me by this time: high hopes, growing disillusionment, a broken romance and the realization that I was getting nowhere and not likely to improve on the situation in an overpriced, overrated job which took more of my time and energy than it was worth.

Back in England, I couldn't seem to settle to anything that appealed to me. I worked as a temp for a while but, despite constant offers to join the permanent staff, I realized that any of the jobs offered would bore me rigid before I'd even learned the names of the upper hierarchy.

I fell into it almost by accident. Prowling the street markets in an effort to offset the dreariness of my tiny room in a shared flat by searching out 'personal touches' to make it 'my own', I began to notice the situation of the stallholders. Stuck behind their counters throughout an endless Saturday, dependent upon friends and fellow stallholders to run errands and/or spell them while they attended to necessities, they were an entire captive market in themselves.

I had always enjoyed cooking and, like Lexie with her American recipes and cookbooks featuring 1001 ways with hamburgers, my main souvenirs from my foreign experiences were sheaves of simple but exotic recipes. I had nothing much to lose and during one week when my flatmates were out at work, I took over the communal kitchen and produced a few crocks of pâtés and several Quiches Lorraines. On the Saturday, it was then a simple matter buying, slicing and buttering several loaves of French bread, loading it all into my little Citröen and setting out to see how I fared.

I was sold out before I was half way down Portobello Road and realized I was on to a winner.

Before long, I had traded in the Citröen for the present-day small blue van, invested in a portable coffee urn and added several more street markets to my rounds. I made a welcome change from the travelling hamburger and hot dog vans and even the ice-cream man. It wasn't much longer before I realized that I could do with some help and Mona began coming along with me occasionally. Gradually, I realized that I could also do with more room, a bigger kitchen and some financial backing in order to branch out and perhaps explore different markets.

It was at this point that Nick and I settled down for a long serious talk.

The result was that we formed an alliance — or, perhaps, simply reinforced the alliance we had had since childhood. Nick turned in his sports car for the shooting brake and began to learn the ins and outs of bulk buying. Mona was another cooking fiend and the kitchen was equipped with the original Aga, still going strong after an overhaul when they moved in. Their freezer compartment incorporated in the refrigerator was too small, so we had invested in a second-hand deep-freeze unit and decided we had the basic equipment necessary.

I gave up my room in the shared flat and moved into the attic flat which had belonged to the original housekeeper and was, therefore, already set up with bedroom, sitting-room, bathroom and tiny kitchenette and in fairly good order — unlike the rest of the house. All I had needed to do was to paint and furnish it and my friends in the street markets had helped me with that. I meticulously paid Mona and Nick the rent I had been paying in the other flat and I knew that it was more of a help than they preferred to admit.

It was not Mona's fault that I sometimes felt like a cuckoo in the nest.

I sympathized, even though I thought it was unreasonable, if not totally unrealistic, of her to expect to have a house of that size just for themselves. Especially when Nick no longer had the wherewithal to keep it going without help.

Naturally, every woman wanted a home of her own. So did I. But a place of this size would be better run as a restaurant or hotel. It was surprising that it had not been bought by a property speculator and cut up into flats or let out as bedsitters.

Even though I occupied the top story, Mona didn't know how lucky she was. Perhaps Nick could persuade her of that. I was too tired to worry about it tonight.

I had a hot bath and went to bed. I fell into an uneasy sleep teeming with nightmares of being chased across a wet and slippery rosewood table the size of a football field, pursued by a buzzing electric razor.

CHAPTER 5

In the morning, it was all hands to the pump.

Nick was shelling almonds when I walked into the kitchen and Mona was making piecrust for the cherry tarts. I helped myself to a cup of coffee from the pot keeping hot at the back of the stove and noted with approval that a big kettle of thick beef stew was simmering away towards lunch-time. It was all very well tasting and nibbling away as one worked, but it was no substitute for a proper lunch. The bits and pieces didn't really fill you up and you soon got bored with nibbling away at the goodies. Apart from which, they were destined for the reception this evening and it would be horrible to run short.

'Something good and hearty, I thought,' Mona said, seeing the direction of my gaze. 'Fill up the little tummies and help keep the little fingers out of the till.'

'Quite right,' I said. We had been working with food for so long that the novelty had worn off, but the girls were still new to it and considered nibbling part of the perks. They had not yet assimilated the basic fact that, in our line of business, food represented money—often quite a sizeable investment. Mona wasn't entirely joking when she talked about keeping little fingers out of the till.

I was delighted to see that Mona was in a joking mood. It meant last night's squall had blown over and we could all work in harmony again. A state much to be desired

when six people were sharing the same kitchen and
working towards a deadline.

No matter how excellent your basic materials, food still
has to be prepared and presented with loving care. I
wouldn't go so far as believing old wives' tales about milk
curdling if the cook gave it a sour look, but there is no
doubt that a pleasant atmosphere added a great deal to
the meal long before it was time to serve it. I had seen
restaurant kitchens where this was not the general rule, of
course—and it was just as well the public never had any
idea of what went on in them.

'Acting on the same theory,' Nick said, 'I thought I'd
get these out of the way before the little darlings arrived.
They're altogether too tempting.' He had a large bowl full
of shelled almonds now and he poured them into a large
strainer and suspended it in a pan of boiling water,
shaking it gently for a few seconds before lifting it out
again. Then he began pinching the skins off the blanched
almonds. A small pan of melted butter was already
nestled on a corner of the stove. Brushed with the melted
butter and popped into the oven on a buttered baking
tray until they were golden and then salted and cooled, he
would produce expert salted almonds at a fraction of the
cost of those bought ready-made in tins. He was right,
they were altogether too tempting to leave around when
the girls arrived.

'There's a side of smoked salmon in the larder,' Mona
told me. 'I think it would be best if you sliced that now.
We'll let one of the girls butter the brown bread and you
can assemble the sandwiches later. That will cut down on
the more expensive depredations.'

'Fine.' I drained my coffee and went into the huge
larder opening off the kitchen. It was a sight to delight
the heart of the original Victorian housewife who had first
lived here.

Strings of onions and bags of drying herbs hung from

hooks in rafters embedded in the ceiling, as did several large smoked hams and strings of smoked sausages. Huge white pottery crocks of marinating chicken livers and drumsticks were ranged along the lower shelves waiting to be transferred to baking pans and the oven.

On the next row of shelves, baked pie cases and vol-au-vent shells waited to be filled with sweet or savoury mixtures and popped into a hot oven. Behind them were ranged jars and tins of luxury items: truffles, olives, pimentoes, maraschino cherries, pickled pearl onions, green peppercorns, foie gras, an assortment of honey, preserves, varieties of olive oil, and all sorts of expensive impulse buys purchased when we were feeling flush and hoarded against the day when they might be just what we needed for some exotic dish.

There was even a joke in (literally) bad taste: a tin of Mexican chocolate-covered ants, donated by Nick on a day when he had returned from an exceedingly liquid lunch with ex-colleagues. Mona and I had vowed that some day we would make him eat them all by himself.

The higher shelves were filled with spices, from allspice and basil through to saffron. In the cupboards beneath the shelves lurked the staples: bags of short and long grain rice, macaroni and pasta shapes, barley, lentils, red kidney beans, dried split peas, whole grain flour, maize, cracked wheat flour, even—whisper it not in the more rarified establishments—enriched white flour.

It occurred to me that I really ought to check with Nick at some point to make sure that our insurance cover took all these comestibles into consideration. They really did constitute a large outlay of capital and, at the current rate of inflation, their replacement value would be considerable.

I picked up the polythene-shrouded slab of smoked salmon and carried it back into the kitchen. I set it down at the far end of the table from Mona and reached absently for a knife.

'Not that one!' Mona said sharply. 'That's the one I'm saving to cut Nick's throat with!'

'Ooops, sorry.' There had been an underlying venom in that joke. Nick wasn't completely forgiven yet; no wonder he was helping out so enthusiastically. 'I'm a million miles away.'

'Your knives are over there—' Mona gestured towards the side table. 'You'd better take what you want and put the rest away before the girls arrive.'

'I'll do that.' Every good cook has her own set of knives; she carries them from job to job; they are as personal as a toothbrush and no one else is allowed to use them. I had nearly committed a cardinal sin by picking up one of Mona's knives. I must pay more attention, my knives had black handles and Mona's had brown handles, so dark a brown they were nearly black, but I was expected to know the difference. Of course, if I had actually started to use it, I'd have noticed instantly that it wasn't mine.

Since the arrival of our apprentices, we had invested in a communal set of knives for them to use. They were good adequate knives and would do for them to train with. Already they were acquiring a dull and battered look, but that didn't matter. Nick could sharpen them up well enough and the girls were learning to take better care of their equipment. Already Gretel was saving up to buy a set of knives of her own. What Gretel might do with a brand new set of razor-sharp knives didn't bear thinking about, but perhaps she would be more expert by the time she actually acquired them.

I selected the knife for the smoked salmon and locked the others away.

Nick winked at me as he shoved the baking tray full of almonds into the oven. 'That's done,' he said. 'Why don't we all take a coffee break now?'

'Because you have to peel the potatoes so that the girls

can make crisps.' Mona was not letting him off easily. 'They can nibble at those, if they want to. It will keep them out of worse mischief.'

'And what about me?' he grumbled. 'Why don't we buy a mechanical potato peeler? We could use one.'

'Because we've got to buy Regency-stripe wallpaper and some paint and do up the dining-room now that you've decided we're going to use that. *And* we're going to do up the hallway properly, as well.'

So that was how he had got round her. Having bought the house originally, they had had little money left to begin making any improvements. They had painted the outside and then intended to do up the rooms they would most use, planning to work their way through the house. Most fortunately, Mona had insisted that the kitchen take priority. They had hardly begun on their living-room and bedroom when the writing began to appear on the walls of Nick's office.

All further renovations had been prudently suspended. It was the sensible thing to do. At the same time, one couldn't blame Mona if it rankled a bit. Here she was, rattling around in an enormous ark of a house, which looked imposing on the outside, but only had two-and-a-half liveable rooms inside. The half was the large drawing-room on the first floor overlooking the front garden and magnolia tree. In fact, it was more like one-third, since there was only a long sofa and coffee table huddled in front of the fireplace and the rest of the room was bare, although freshly wallpapered and painted just before the work had to stop.

I was well aware that the fact that I had done some renovating on my attic flat was the main reason Mona had welcomed me into her home without too much hesitation. Sooner or later, I would want to move out into a larger flat or house of my own and those rooms would revert to Mona and would need only minimum attention

to dilapidations to raise them to satisfactory standard
again. It didn't always keep me from feeling that I was
there on sufferance, though.

'We'll go shopping tomorrow,' Nick promised. They
must have had quite a session after I left last night, he was
not usually so prompt to redeem his promises — especially
where spending money was concerned. Not that he could
be blamed for that. Although the situation was gradually
improving, we hadn't had a great deal of money to throw
around.

'Mind your almonds,' Mona warned. 'They don't take
long.'

'I'll just give them a shake.' Nick swung open the oven
door and did so. 'Another couple of minutes.'

'Too late.' I heard a clatter at the back door. 'Here
come the locusts.'

Nick moved away from the oven hurriedly, but it was
only Gretel.

Gretel was another legacy from my Common Market
days. Her father had been one of the friends with whom I
had kept in contact. When he had heard that I had taken
on Lexie and Sidonie as student/apprentices, he had
immediately written to enroll his elder daughter. She
wanted to try her wings and he did not like the idea of her
going to some strange family as an *au pair*. But, as a
cookery student, watched over by a friend, that was the
perfect solution. The cheque he enclosed had made it a
hard offer to refuse and Gretel had duly arrived and
seemed to be happy, although impossible in the kitchen.

'Just in time,' Nick greeted her. 'You can come and
help me peel potatoes.'

'No, she can't,' Mona said. 'I want her to get some
practice on the mandoline. Give her the potatoes as you
peel them and she'll do the crisps.'

'Oh yes!' Gretel beamed. 'I am so glad I am first today.
I get the peach job.'

'Plum,' Nick corrected with a groan. Peeling the potatoes for her was going to be a major chore.

She would have been given the mandoline anyway. As Mona said, she needed practice. Not that, in Gretel's case, practice was likely to make perfect, but it might reduce her clumsiness a bit. In any case, potatoes were cheap and plentiful just now and we could toss her failures into the stew.

'Do you know—' Gretel accepted a peeled potato from Nick and ground it against the mandoline—'I do not—'

'Gently dear,' Mona said. 'You don't need to saw at it.'

'Yes.' Gretel modified her stroke. 'I do not think Sidonie is happy.'

'Everyone can't be happy all the time.' Nick might not have been aiming his comment solely at Gretel. He tossed another peeled potato into the bowl beside her.

'No,' Gretel frowned. 'But she came back to my flat last night and she was in a very strange mood. Not happy.'

'She'd had a hectic day,' I said. 'It was rather awful at Quardon. I shouldn't think anyone was happy yesterday.'

'It was not that,' Gretel said. 'I fixed us a meal and she was very quiet. I think something was bothering her.'

If she'd eaten the meal, it was probably nothing that a little bicarbonate of soda couldn't take care of.

'Nick—the almonds,' Mona said quickly, before he could voice the thought in all our minds.

'What did you give her?' I asked curiously.

'Something simple, I plan, after such a day. I do soup and nice little sandwiches.' Gretel paused thoughtfully in her labours. 'But they were not so nice. Is a very confusing language, English. I want nice sandwiches like you make with the meat paste and the fish paste for tea. But I want something a little different. The soup is too bland, so I make sandwiches with curry paste. It was not the same thing at all. Sidonie explained to me after we throw them away. She says there is even a paste for artificial jewels.'

Gretel sighed deeply. 'This, I do not understand.'

Nick managed to keep a straight face until his back was turned. He removed the tray of almonds, but Gretel was too absorbed to notice. The circles of potato had not yet achieved uniform thickness and often fell away from her mandoline in chunks and incomplete circles.

'Straight through to the larder, Nick,' Mona directed. 'Salt them there and leave them to cool. I hear the others coming.'

'Mmm — something smells good!' Lexie burst into the kitchen, followed closely by Sidonie.

'Everything smells good,' Mona corrected. 'Or soon will do. Into your aprons, quickly! This is our busy day.'

'Panic stations!' Lexie giggled. 'Which one is mine?'

'I want you on the blender,' Mona said. 'They've ordered dips. We'll give them bowls of onion, devilled ham and sherried crabmeat dip. That ought to keep them happy. Gretel is making the crisps for the dips.'

'Perhaps we ought to give them crackers, too,' Sidonie said, doubtfully eyeing Gretel's struggles with the mandoline. Her fingers twitched. She was obviously longing to take the mandoline away from Gretel and slice the potatoes herself. Her crisps would be wafer-thin and perfect. But Gretel had to learn and she was paying for her course, too.

'It doesn't matter.' Lexie shook tabasco sauce into the first blender bowl with lavish abandon. 'Americans don't pay that much attention. Just make the dip spicy enough and you can give them bits of old horseblanket to dip into it and they won't know the difference.'

'We'll stick with crisps,' Mona said. 'And perhaps cheese straws,' she conceded to Sidonie. 'But watch that tabasco — there's a difference between making it spicy and burning their palates out.'

'Don't worry.' Lexie poured in more sour cream and splashed in cooking sherry. 'They'll never notice. They'll

eat anything—especially the men. One of the worst things
I ever tasted was some chocolates made to what they
claimed was an Old American recipe. They had *winter-
green* filling!' She grimaced. 'It was like eating chocolate-
covered toothpaste.'

'Sidonie—' Mona distracted the girl's attention: she still
seemed perilously close to snatching the mandoline from
Gretel and doing the job properly herself. 'Sidonie,
perhaps you'd do the cheese straws. You'll find some puff
pastry on the shelf in the butler's pantry. I took it out of
the deep-freeze hours ago, so it should be defrosted by
now. And bring in the crabmeat for Lexie, would you,
please?'

The butler's pantry was next door to the larder, a long
narrow room, again with plenty of shelves—well, he had
to have somewhere to stack the silver plate, didn't he?
Those were the days. We found it ideal for the deep-
freeze locker. There was also a lock on the door, which we
never used but always felt that it might be useful some
day—just in case we were ever able to afford any of those
silver serving dishes.

Sidonie returned and silently handed the packet of
crabmeat to Lexie, then settled to rolling out the pastry
for the cheese straws at the large Victorian washstand
with a marble top which we used especially for pastry. I
knew she found it a boring job, but this time it seemed to
send her into a trance. She sprinkled the pastry with
grated sharp cheddar cheese, folded it over, rolled it out
again, sprinkled, rolled, sprinkled, rolled—far too many
times.

'All right, that's enough,' I had to say before she
stopped. 'You can cut it into strips now.'

She blinked and seemed to shake herself. 'Yes, of
course.' She gave a half-hearted smile. 'Sorry, I got
carried away.'

You see? Gretel met my eyes and gave a meaning nod. I

just kept myself from nodding back. There was more than indigestion bothering Sidonie.

But it was not just Sidonie. Even Lexie had slipped into a solemn mood, attending to the blender mechanically while her mind appeared to be elsewhere.

'There!' Nick tossed a last potato into Gretel's bowl with an air of finality. 'That's done!' He rose, stretched and began sauntering towards the door.

'*Now*—' Mona's voice stopped him—'you can bring in the crock of chicken livers, blot them on the kitchen towels, wrap them in bacon and skewer them with cocktail sticks.' Her tone brooked no argument. It was a messy, fiddly task—and it was his.

Gretel beamed. It was the sort of chore that usually fell to her. Lexie and Sidonie were still oblivious. I began to get a bit worried.

'Lexie, that's blended enough. Turn it off.'

'Sorry.' She snapped it off and stood staring into space. Sidonie went on slicing the pastry into oblong strips, using an unnecessary amount of violence.

'Lightly, Sidonie. We don't want the marble carved, you know.' Mona shot me an anxious glance. Something was wrong.

'Sorry.' Sidonie flushed. It was seldom necessary to correct or reprimand her; she wasn't used to it as the others were. She bent again to her work, cutting lightly.

I wondered if she and Lexie had had a quarrel. Yet they had seemed perfectly amicable as they arrived together. Whatever the problem, they seemed more preoccupied than seriously upset.

'Wakey, wakey!' Nick rushed in where Mona and I were pussyfooting around. 'You're both asleep on your feet. What's the matter, Lexie—too much partying last night?'

'I didn't sleep much,' Lexie admitted. 'Uncle Tristram rang last night just before I went to bed. I've been wondering how to tell you. It's all so awful.' She shuddered, more serious than I had ever seen her. Lexie usually took life very lightly.

But not, perhaps, death. I knew instantly what she must be talking about. Only one really awful thing had happened lately.

'Mark Avery,' I said.

'Yes. Uncle Tris said the police were there all day—long after we left—going through Mark's office, examining everything, inspecting, measuring . . .' Her voice faltered. 'And—and—that's what makes it so awful. Even worse than it was.

'Oh, Jean, the police aren't sure it was an accident. They think someone might have tampered deliberately with the wall switch. They found the cover plate had been removed and the wires inside messed about so that too much current went through the electric razor when he switched it on—'

Gretel gave a horrified gasp. Nick turned pale green—he used an electric razor himself.

'And so,' Lexie finished miserably, 'Uncle Tris asked me to speak to you. He doesn't think the police will want to see any of us again, we were too far out of the way upstairs there—and besides, we only go there once a month to cook. But Uncle Tris wants us to try to remember if we ever noticed anything out of the ordinary at any time. If we did, we're to tell him.'

CHAPTER 6

'No,' I said, fighting sudden dizziness. 'I didn't see anything. All I saw was Mark Avery.' I had to cross abruptly to the rocking-chair and sit down while they clustered around me making soothing noises.

It was all right for Nick and Mona and Gretel; they

hadn't been there. It wasn't even so bad for Lexie and Sidonie; although they had been with me at Quardon International, they hadn't seen the body.

But I had looked on Mark Avery lying dead in his office. I realized now how fortunate I'd been last night. Some self-protective mechanism had operated to blot out the memory and let me get a good night's sleep. I doubted that it would work tonight. Not now that I knew it hadn't been an accident; that, incredibly, one human being had done such a thing to another. And deliberately—that was the worst part. An angry blow might have been under-standable, forgivable. But this had been cold-bloodedly planned in advance, prepared for; a deadly trap set and waiting, while somewhere a stealthy killer mixed with other men, laughing and joking—and waiting for his victim to walk into the trap.

Mark Avery was inextricably in my mind now and remained there, haunting me for the rest of the day. For the first time, I wished that I did not have to work with food. Suddenly, I did not even want to look at it or think about it, far less concern myself with its preparation.

But, if I were feeling sick, how much sicker must they all be feeling at Quardon International?

By the time we arrived at the United Boroughs of New York Bank premises, my mood had improved. Mona had insisted on my taking a couple of aspirins and a rest that afternoon. I was ready to stop worrying about something I could not change and begin worrying about the reception.

'Now, remember, Gretel.' I concentrated on the chief cause for concern. 'Move slowly and smoothly. Don't overload your serving tray. Pay attention to what you're doing—'

'Yes, yes.' She was radiant, an understudy being given her big chance because the star had broken a leg. All we could do was hope that Gretel wouldn't break anyone's leg.

'I will be very careful.' She smoothed the frilly white apron tied over the black uniform. 'I will watch you and do everything you do.'

'Yes, well . . .' That idea made me slightly nervous, but I hesitated to give her *carte blanche* to use her own judgement. In the past, her judgement had not been particularly good. 'Just do your best.'

Lexie and Sidonie exchanged amused glances and fell in, one on either side of Gretel. 'Come and take a quick look round with us,' Lexie said. 'We'll want to know where everything is, in case anyone asks us for directions.'

'Everything?' Gretel was puzzled. She turned to watch Nick and Mona unpacking our containers. The food was here — what more could anyone possibly want?

'Cloakrooms, telephones, exits, parking lot — if any — all the usual offices.' Lexie prodded her forward. 'Come on, we haven't much time. The guests will be arriving.'

'Go with them, Jean,' Mona said softly, as they left the room. 'I don't trust Lexie's sense of humour.'

'Oh, but she wouldn't dream of doing anything to spoil this.' I was certain of that. 'It's a new account. She knows how important it is to us.'

'She wouldn't think of it as having anything to do with us,' Mona corrected me. 'She'd think of it as a good joke on Gretel. Just keep an eye on her, I'll feel safer.'

I moved off gratefully. Did Mona realize that the sight of food still made me feel faintly queasy? I'd be all right once the reception was in full swing and I had other things to think about. For the moment, I welcomed the excuse to get out of the small claustrophobic kitchen.

I caught up with them half way down the corridor. Innocent as lambs. Not quite gambolling, but ready to at any moment. Lexie and Sidonie enjoyed the occasional receptions we catered for—the atmosphere was less formal than the luncheons and the eavesdropping usually a great deal more amusing—and Gretel was in the seventh heaven at being allowed to participate at last.

The Bank had a maisonette-type arrangement, sub-letting the ground and first floor of a business block in Knightsbridge. The ground floor housed the cashiers' desks and usual arrangements; the first floor was given over to the offices of the officers of the bank. Presumably, there was a vault or safe somewhere around the premises, but that was none of our business. We were only here to provide the buffet on the ground floor.

The buffet. That reminded me. I glanced nervously at Lexie. *Not* the floor show. But all appeared to be well. Which is to say, her uniform was buttoned demurely all the way up to the neck. I didn't bother to check the other two; I knew they'd be all right. It would not have occurred to them that we were in the heart of Millionaire-land and were about to mingle with some of the most influential people in international finance. If it had, they would have dismissed it with a shrug, unimpressed. It would be more important to them that the food was served at the right temperature and—in Gretel's case—did not slide off the serving tray to the floor just as the most important person in the room reached for a devilled drumstick.

We located and inspected the major points likely to be of interest, all of which appeared to be without surprises. Before returning to the kitchen, we tied a black bow around Gretel's right wrist so that she could remember which was left and which was right when she was giving directions.

Several bank officials stood clustered together waiting to greet the first arrivals. They nodded amiably to us as we passed.

Nick and Mona had set out shallow dishes of salted

almonds, small bowls of dips and large bowls of crisps at
strategic points around the room. Several desks had been
pushed together and covered with tablecloths to form the
bar. Again, salted almonds, dips and crisps were spaced
at intervals along the length of this.

My eyes narrowed as I noticed a young man methodi-
cally walking along the impromptu bar and sampling our
offerings with a pseudo-connoisseur's air of being able to
tell the country of origin of the salted almonds and the
vintage of the dips. Only a wine merchant could carry off
such a farce.

'I hope you like it,' I slipped up behind him as he was
trying not to choke on the dip Lexie had overdosed with
tabasco. 'It's only a naive little chilli grown on the North
Slope of the Napa Valley during the dry season, but I
think you'll be amused by its presumption.'

'Really?' Eyes watering, he swallowed hard and tried to
focus on me. 'The caterer, I presume?'

'Mr Stanley,' I replied. I did not offer my hand.

'Uccello, actually,' he said. 'Aldo Uccello.' Despite his
name, his accent was impeccable. Second or third
generation, presumably, and graduate of a very good
university. Why did I find him so annoying?

'Couldn't the bank afford French wines?' I asked. 'They
didn't warn us they were doing this on the cheap.'

'No need to be snobbish.' His vision cleared and he
beamed down on me. 'We're all in the Common Market
now.'

'But some are more common than others.' I turned and
crossed over to Nick and Mona. Annoyingly, I could hear
what sounded like a chuckle following me.

'Everything all right?' Mona greeted me.

'Yes, fine,' I answered automatically, trying not to look
back over my shoulder. 'Why shouldn't it be?'

'Easy,' Nick intervened. 'Calm down. You don't have to
snap Mona's head off. We're all on edge.'

'I'm *not* on edge,' I snapped.

'Look out!' Nick stiffened to attention, staring over my shoulder at something happening behind us. 'Here come the first guests!'

After that, it was modified chaos. Mona remained in the tiny kitchen, heating up the canapés to be served hot and filling the serving trays which we ran in and snatched up, swapping our empty trays for the full ones. It added to the awkwardness that the crew from the wine merchant's had set up shop on a table just outside the kitchen door and were juggling full and empty trays, as well. I narrowly averted collisions several times and the situation seemed to be so fraught with peril that I made Gretel remain in the reception area and took out her empty trays for refilling myself.

I was not particularly surprised to see that the wine merchant was not bothering to make any trips, or doing much of anything; he left all that to his minions. I only hoped it didn't give Nick ideas. One tradesman — however high class he considered himself — mingling with the guests instead of attending to duty was enough.

I was not consciously watching him, but I could not help noticing that he had stationed himself close by a large, vaguely familiar figure. They both had their backs to me and I caught my breath as Gretel approached them, balancing her tray carefully and offering it to them with a smile.

While the large man examined the tray closely, the young man helped himself to a vol-au-vent. Almost immediately, the large man transferred his attention to his companion and watched him pop the vol-au-vent into his mouth, chew and swallow. After a judicious moment, he helped himself to three vol-au-vents and seemed to murmur something to his companion. The young man took a devilled drumstick and bit into it while the other was still working his way through the vol-au-vents.

Gretel looked puzzled, but kept smiling. Even when the large man began denuding the tray of all the drumsticks. She glanced around uncertainly, as though she would move away, but I caught her eye and shook my head, motioning her to stay where she was.

Ongar Manganian was not to be discouraged. If he wished to eat everything on Gretel's tray, the bank officials would not thank us for trying to stop him. There may have been guests present who were potentially more valuable clients for the bank, but there would not be many. This was no time to spoil the ship for a ha'porth of vol-au-vent. There was plenty of food and enough of us serving it. Let Ongar Manganian monopolize as many trays as he liked; the bank officials would just smile benevolently. This was why they were setting out the sprats to catch the mackerel, or, in this case, the whale.

Fortunately, I had recognized him in time. He had half-turned as someone had passed him and I was able to make the identification.

Gretel watched in fascination as he cleared her tray. I could see that she was struggling to keep from making some comment and I made my way hastily towards her. She had done awfully well so far and it would be a pity to blot her copybook now. Especially in front of Ongar Manganian.

Across the room, I spotted Lexie determinedly forging her way through the crowd in the same direction. Worse, she was not pausing when people indicated that they'd like something from her tray; in fact, she was pulling it away from them. Was it a coincidence, or had she sighted her quarry?

She had. As she came closer, I saw that her two top buttons were undone and she was wearing her most seductive smile. In the distance, I noticed Sidonie frowning.

Lexie was so intent upon projecting charm, personality—and availability—at Ongar Manganian as she approached that she didn't notice me until it was too late.

Gretel, on the other hand, was delighted to see me. Her tray was empty and she had been standing her ground in some confusion since I had plainly ordered her not to move.

'Gretel—' I took the empty tray from her hands and replaced it with my full one. 'Take this—and circulate.' I gave her a tiny push, sending her back into the crowd.

'Lexie—' I greeted her as she came up to us. 'Take this—' I shoved Gretel's empty tray at her and removed her own tray from her hands—'and get it refilled. Hurry now—the people over in that corner haven't been attended to for quite some time. When you come back, start over there.'

Looking daggers at me, she moved sullenly away. I knew that when she got to the kitchen Mona would take up the matter of the undone buttons. It wasn't going to be Lexie's evening—not if I could help it.

'Ah yes—the boss.' Ongar Manganian said affably, to my surprise, recognizing me instantly. 'You cover a great deal of territory in your endeavours.'

'So do you,' I said. Perhaps it was not so surprising. Although it seemed a much longer time, we had met only yesterday—and the events of that traumatic day were likely to be seared across all our memories for quite some time.

'And, once again, it is to you we are indebted for all this most excellent food.' His eyes appraised my tray greedily.

It was enough to inspire greed in even a lesser man. There were plenty of marinated chicken livers wrapped in crispy bacon, hot and savoury; interspersed with these were hard-boiled eggs cut into thirds lengthwise, the yolks devilled with a pinch of curry and each one topped by the tiniest of parsley sprigs; for additional colour, as well as taste, there were pickled baby beets, cut in half and filled with softened cream cheese before being speared back together with the ubiquitous cocktail stick.

'How delicious it all looks,' he murmured, making no effort to select anything, although his eyes sparkled. He turned to the young man beside him with a meaning look. 'Does it not?'

'It does indeed.' With elaborate casualness, the young man leaned across and took a chicken liver from the spot on the tray nearest to Ongar Manganian, the one I would have ordinarily expected Manganian to take. It struck me as slightly odd. Certainly it was peculiar, not to say rude, behaviour on the part of a wine merchant co-catering this reception.

'It is good, yes?' Ongar Manganian did not appear to take the behaviour amiss. He watched intently as the young man savoured the delicacy, rolling it around in his mouth like rare wine. I was relieved when he finally swallowed it instead of spitting it out.

'Very good,' the man pronounced. He smiled into my frown. 'And I'm rather by way of being an expert on the subject. My family run a restaurant in Soho.'

'Really?' I said icily. It was surprising that he had not tried to arrange for them to do the food while he sewed up the liquor concession.

'I'm the black sheep of the family.' He seemed to answer my unspoken thought. 'One of them. Poor Mama and Papa—three fine sons and not one of us has followed them into the business. My eldest brother turned out to be an electronics wizard—I studied it for a bit, but it hadn't the fascination for me it had for him. My youngest brother went into education and is Deputy Headmaster of a Comprehensive now. That didn't interest me either, but I found I had my own talent. We've all gone our separate ways.'

Ongar Manganian had been watching his face intently

as he spoke. Now he nodded and helped himself to a chicken liver . . . and another . . . and another. As he chewed approvingly, he gave the young man that meaning look again.

'I'm afraid—' Once more, he leaned across and selected one of the egg sections from a spot awkward for him but within easy reach for Ongar Manganian. 'I'm afraid the young lady doesn't approve of me. She thinks I was critical of her dips. I was not—' He chewed, swallowed and continued. 'They are excellent dips. The eggs are very good, too.'

'Dips are sloppy food,' Ongar Manganian said, a crumb of bacon clinging to his beard. 'I do not like them.' He frowned at the tray and picked up a curried egg. He nodded approvingly and began alternating the eggs with the chicken livers.

'I can assure you,' the young man said, 'you don't know what you're missing.'

'I intend to miss nothing,' Ongar Manganian said.

The young man grinned indulgently and took a beet-ball from beside Manganian's elbow. 'Or perhaps she is old-fashioned,' he said, 'and thinks we should be properly introduced. Perhaps you might oblige. You seem to know her.'

Ongar Manganian considered this proposition while his companion finished the beetball, then turned to me. 'I am afraid I do not know your name.'

'I'm Jean Ainley,' I said. 'Executive Meal Service.'

'Excellent.' Ongar Manganian took another beetball abstractedly. 'Then I have much pleasure in introducing you to a rising young man in my employ. He is a financial genius and I am training him properly. Aldo Uccello—' He paused to chew and swallow.

'For now, Aldo is my right hand. My . . .' He groped for the more formal expression. 'As Rodney Bletchley is to your Tristram Quardon. Aldo is my Personal Assistant.'

'How do you do?' There was still something odd about this. Aldo Uccello was no Roddy Bletchley. But neither was he what I had originally concluded. 'I'm sorry I seemed rude,' I said. 'I thought you were the wine merchant. I mean, I thought you should be on duty and not roaming around sampling the refreshments.'

'A wine merchant he is not.' Ongar Manganian spoke with authority. 'But I can assure you he is very much on duty. I could not function without him.' Having said which, he turned his full attention to my tray, depleting it rapidly and uninhibitedly.

Meanwhile, Aldo Uccello stood back and watched, making no move to take anything else. I realized abruptly that he had eaten one of everything offered, while his master watched intently. After Aldo had eaten with impunity, Ongar Manganian had then helped himself freely.

Personal Assistant, was he? Not so many centuries ago, in the land of Ongar Manganian's birth, there had been another and more realistic title for his post: *Official Taster*.

CHAPTER 7

'Special instructions.' Released, but only on parole, I reported back to the kitchen. 'More chicken livers, vol-au-vents and devilled drumsticks. Lots of them—he eats like a vacuum-cleaner.'

'I don't know—' Mona wore the expression bordering on panic that usually set in at this stage of a reception. 'I'm afraid we're running low—'

'Then several other people will have to go short. This is for Ongar Manganian. The bank won't thank us if we neglect *him*.'

'Well . . .' Mona began to refill the tray reluctantly. There looked to be enough food still on hand. Inevitably, the less favoured items abounded. There were quantities of beetballs and stuffed eggs and pints of dip still left. Although we were getting low on the choicer items, I judged that we would have enough to see us through. The reception was at that full flood just before it starts to recede as people go on somewhere for dinner or depart for the theatre. But, just in case, it was time to give it a gentle push.

'Start sending out mostly cherry tarts from now on,' I told Mona. 'That ought to give them all a hint.'

'Everything going well here?' One of the bank officials put his head round the door. 'No problems?'

'Everything's fine.' I told him what he wanted to hear which, in this case, was the truth. 'I'm just getting a refill for Ongar Manganian. He asked for more of these especially.' No harm in letting him know that one of his best prospects was enjoying the food enough to request more of special items.'

'Oh, good, good!' He beamed approval. 'That's the right idea. Keep him happy. He's a very important man.'

'I know,' I said, but he was gone. I smiled and shrugged at Mona, who finished filling up the tray with a more cheerful expression. I was just about to pick it up and depart when there was a rush of movement behind me.

'I think it's rotten of her! *Rotten!* Sidonie slammed down her empty tray. 'I'm sorry, Jean, Mona. I couldn't stop her, but I told her I wouldn't stand for it!'

'What's the matter?' I took a tighter grip on my tray, beset by visions of Lexie doing a striptease to attract Ongar Manganian's attention or, alternatively, of pouncing on him and—My vision gave out there. Not even my direst forebodings could imagine Lexie physically budging a bulk like that, far less dragging him off to her lair.

'Where's Nick?' Sidonie looked around wildly. 'He's got to do something. Before it's too late!'

'He's just stepped out for a minute,' Mona said, using the popular euphemism. 'What's wrong? Has Gretel—?'

'No, no. It's Lexie. Lexie and her beastly Humpty. He's gate-crashed! Lexie's smuggled him in—I *told* her not to do it—and he's eating and drinking everything in sight. Someone from the bank is going to notice any minute. He stands out like a sore thumb—he's about twenty years younger than anyone else in the place. Nick's got to throw him out—fast!'

'Oh no! And just as everything was going so well!' I set down my tray, then remembered that Ongar Manganian was waiting for it.

'Here—' I caught it up again and thrust it at Sidonie. 'Take this and go and dance attendance on Ongar Manganian. Let him eat it all—even the tray cloth, if he feels so inclined. But *don't* let Lexie near him!'

'I understand,' Sidonie said unexpectedly. She gave me the sort of look to make me feel that she did understand. I wondered how much she had to put up with from Lexie along those lines. It couldn't be easy to be the plain flatmate, dragged along as part-chaperone, part-companion for the sake of whatever passed for propriety in their circles and standing by ignored while Lexie turned full voltage on any eligible males in the vicinity.

Sidonie took the tray and whisked away, leaving me staring blankly after her for a moment.

'Lexie—' Mona broke the spell. 'If we ran a genuine school, we'd have to consider expelling her.'

'But we don't,' I reminded her. 'And we can't.' We would not only lose the money pouring into our coffers for Lexie's tuition—and possibly Sidonie's—but we would risk antagonizing our oldest and best client, her Uncle Tristram.

'I know,' she sighed. 'You'd better go out and see what you can do. I'll send Nick out to help you as soon as he comes back.'

I nodded and returned to the reception. I had no trouble spotting Lexie's Humpty, although I had never met him. As Sidonie had noted, he was at least twenty years younger than most of the other guests. He was also the second largest male in the room; second only to Ongar Manganian himself. Looking at the large ovoid shape, one immediately saw why his given name of Humphrey had been transposed so aptly into Humpty.

And he was heading for a fall.

Automatically, I scanned the room as I moved across it. Gretel, frowning with concentration, had not dropped anything, spilled anything, or collided with anyone—yet. A quiet pride was beginning to radiate from her as her confidence grew. If she got through the rest of the evening without mishap, we would have to consider letting her help at Directors' Luncheons. It might not be a bad idea. A spell in the kitchen after this escapade might even get it through to Lexie that she had gone too far. Letting Gretel replace her would underline her disgrace.

Sidonie, as instructed, was standing before Ongar Manganian while he systematically depleted her tray. I noticed that a couple of bank officials had joined him, but they were wise enough not to get between him and the refreshments, nor to take any themselves. Although she maintained a professional smile, Sidonie's worried gaze followed me as I advanced on Humpty.

Lexie was watching from a far corner, half-hidden behind a cluster of guests. When she saw my head turn in her direction, she moved to one side so that she was completely concealed. I knew that she was still watching, though.

Humpty was unaware of my approach. He had marked

out a corner of a desk for himself with a bowl of dip,
crisps, celery and napkin containing four drumsticks. By
his elbow, there were three empty glases. He was holding
out the empty glass in his hand to one of the wine waiters
for a refill as I reached him. I stood there silently for a
moment, looking at him.

The Hon. Humphrey had some double-barrelled name
I had never quite caught. Lexie invariably referred to
him as Humpty. He was one of her regular escorts. Too
impecunious to be of any real interest to her, he was the
one she fell back on when there was nothing more
promising in the offing. Although financially ineligible,
he amused her. There was another fairly regular escort,
too—what was his name? I glanced around, but Humpty
seemed to be the only intruder and Sidonie hadn't
mentioned anyone else.

One was enough. Too many. Clients weren't going to
patronize a catering service which ran in its own
freeloaders at their expense. It was time to get rid of
Humpty—and quickly. I looked back, but there was no
sign of Nick. It looked as though I was going to have to
throw him out by myself. There was no more time to
waste, he was already beginning to attract some curious
glances.

He turned his head suddenly and we were eyeball to
eyeball. Furthermore, he knew it. I could see it in the way
his face changed. The slack-lipped grin gave way to
something more truculent.

'All right,' I told him. 'Out! The party's over!'

'I beg your pardon?' He tried to bluff it through.

'Out!' I repeated.

'Me? Are you talking to me?' His voice began to rise. He
looked around for support, but Lexie wasn't going to
show herself until the crisis was over. 'Do you know who I
am?'

'Yes,' I said. 'And that's why you're leaving.'

'Now see here—' he began to bluster. 'I'll have you know—'

'Spot of bother?' a quiet voice asked at my elbow. I turned gratefully, but it was not Nick. Ongar Manganian's personal assistant had come up behind me and it looked as though he were going to lend me some of his assistance.

'Gate-crasher,' I said briefly. 'I've asked him to leave.'

'Very wise of you.' Aldo Uccello ran an expert eye over Humpty. 'I wouldn't say he was adding anything to the tone of the occasion.'

'I don't know who you think you are—' Humpty glared at him wildly. 'But—'

'Aldo Uccello.' Aldo extended his hand and Humpty automatically took it before realizing what a bad idea that was. He was drawn forward inexorably.

'Suppose we step outside and I will explain further.' Aldo dropped his arm casually around Humpty's shoulders, the grip of his hand changed slightly and Humpty gasped with pain. It was smoothly—expertly—done. No one else at the reception was aware that anything was happening except that two of the youngest guests were strolling out of the room in a friendly manner.

Except for Ongar Manganian, that is. I saw the slight turn of his head and knew that he had missed nothing and was unsurprised by the turn of events. Possibly it was he who had sent Aldo Uccello to my aid. Just in case, I sent him a fleeting smile of gratitude, which was half-acknowledged by a nod before he returned to his conversation with the bankers.

His personal assistant was a man of curious talents. There had been an unnerving expertise in the way he had removed Humpty. It was obviously not the first time he had performed such little services. I trusted they stopped short of taking Humpty for a ride—his transgression had not been that serious. But it shed an interesting new light

on Aldo Uccello: as well as Official Taster, it seemed that
he was also a bodyguard.

I hoped that he didn't include acting as a hit man
among his many little chores.

CHAPTER 8

It was generally agreed that the reception had been a
success, but the next day was Saturday and there was no
time to rest on our laurels. It was the busiest day for
Portobello Road Market and we had many good
customers among the stallholders who would be looking
for us. Apart from which, there was always a goodly sum
to be scooped up from the casual trade. It was a major
tourist area and, while the faces were constantly
changing, they also got hungry and had full pockets. A
few hours on duty there did wonders for our cash flow
problems.

Nick occasionally grumbled that we ought to give up
the Portobello route now that we were moving up into the
more rarified strata of City Boardrooms. But we hadn't
risen high enough yet to be above the need to pay our
suppliers and it could take a long time for our invoices to
be processed through financial departments before clients
eventually sent out payment to us. A Saturday working
Portobello provided the financing for most of the
luncheons we would serve the following week.

Today, however, Nick was not only helping to unload
the van, he had offered to come along with me. It wasn't
quite unheard of, but he usually avoided this duty for fear
of being seen by one of his advertising friends. Being
Director of Executive Meal Service carried snob appeal;
being caught filling pitta bread pockets for the queue at the
tailgate of a van was too down-market to be contemplated.

'Are you sure this will be enough?' Dubiously, he surveyed the crocks of pâté, the large bowls of egg mayonnaise, chicken salad, tuna salad, the piles of pre-sliced meats and loaves of buttered brown and white bread and stacks of halved pitta bread.

'If it isn't, we can always come back for more.' I wrestled the tub—light but awkward—of green salad (shredded lettuce, endive and fennel) into its place at the rear of the van.

Mona came out carrying a large plastic container of grated cheese. 'Don't forget this.' She handed it to me and stepped back, looking at Nick accusingly.

'I'll just go and get the coffee urn,' he said. 'Then we should be ready, shouldn't we?'

'I thought,' Mona said coldly, 'that you and I were going in to town to look at wallpaper samples and choose the paint today.'

'You don't want to go into the West End today,' Nick protested. 'It will be too crowded. Everyone will be trying to get at the sample books, the salespeople will be rushed off their feet and won't have time to attend to us properly. No, we'll go on Monday when it's quiet and we can take our time choosing what we want.'

'Well . . .' Mona was clearly wavering.

'Besides—' He spoiled it by adding: 'Today I've got to see a man about some chairs.'

'I might have known it!' Mona exploded. 'All your promises never—'

'The coffee urn—' Nick disappeared at high speed, voice trailing over his shoulder. 'I'll be right back.'

'Your brother!' Mona turned to me for support. 'I don't know how you ever put up with him for a lifetime!' Her face changed in a way that made me suddenly nervous. 'I don't know how much longer I'm going to be able to.'

'He's very keen on the idea,' I defended. 'I don't really see that it matters whether you get the wallpaper or the chairs first. He'll carry through and finish the whole project as soon as he can.'

'It's not that,' Mona sighed. 'It's just that he's always promising more than he can deliver. Half the time, he has no intention of doing whatever it is, but he promises anyway. Just to keep people quiet. I wish he wouldn't, but I can't break him of the habit.'

'He was always like that.' I remembered the occasions as a child when I had waited for my elder brother to come home from school and take me to the cinema or down to the shops for an ice-cream, or whatever it was he had promised to do. Waited and waited, while the shadows lengthened and the sick feeling in my stomach grew as I gradually realized that he had forgotten all about me and gone off on some more interesting concern of his own. Inevitably, I had learned that 'promise' was only a word to Nick, not a concept as it was to other people. It made for a bumpy childhood, but had been good basic training for adult life. Mona, however, had been the only child of an adoring father. She was learning her lesson about male promises comparatively late in life.

'I suppose it's just the way Nick is made.' I sighed, too.

'Here we are.' Nick returned, wheeling along the large coffee urn on its metal trolley. 'I'm afraid I'll need a hand getting this into the van,' he said to Mona.

She turned on her heel and stalked back to the house. The door slammed behind her.

'What's the matter with her?' Nick looked after her with a surprised expression.

'You *did* promise.' That was all I was going to say; it brought back too many reminders of my childhood.

'I meant at the first opportunity,' Nick said. 'This isn't an opportunity, it's a working day. Mona ought to be more reasonable.'

Nick joined me on my Saturday round so infrequently that it was quite reasonable of Mona to expect him to go with her instead, but I forbore from pointing this out.

'You know—' He frowned abstractedly at the wheels of pizza and quiche lorraine in the makeshift rack hung from the back of the passenger seat. 'We ought to have a different type of van if you want to operate a mobile canteen. Something more professional—with cooking facilities. We could do hot sausages, toasted sandwiches—'

'Let's leave that to the pubs,' I said. 'The customers are quite happy with things the way they are.' I slammed and latched the rear door and went round to the front. Nick was already in the driver's seat. 'Besides, I thought you wanted to give up this side of the business and concentrate on the executive meals.'

'Yes, but we ought to be sensible.' He drove into the road and headed towards the market. 'I mean, this brings in quite a decent whack each week, doesn't it?'

'It helps to keep us solvent,' I admitted.

'There you are!' He lifted one hand from the wheel in an expansive gesture. 'And that's just one van. Think what we could do with two.'

'What I'm thinking,' I said truthfully, 'is that Mona would kill you. You promised her that the next car you bought would be a saloon. You know she hates the shooting brake.'

'But we need it,' Nick said plaintively, quite as though I had ever argued that fact. 'You know we do. Mona would hate even more—' he gave a short laugh—'climbing over sacks of potatoes and onions piled into a saloon.'

'I know,' I said. 'But you can't blame her for being upset at times. This business has rather taken over her life. She wants something of her own. Something that isn't tax deductible or off the expense account.'

'Mona never complained about the expense account when I was at the Agency.' Nick sounded a trifle bitter. 'She still wants all the luxuries, but she's got to learn that she can't dictate her own terms any more.'

'I'm just warning you,' I said.

'She won't leave me,' Nick said confidently. 'Besides, what I have in mind might be something she'd approve of. We could use it for holidays and save on hotel bills. If we had one, we could make a few ferry trips over to France and combine a short break with loading up with cheeses and delicacies and our duty-free allowances. She'd like that, all right.'

'Just the same . . .'

'Ah, she'll come round.' He had no doubts. 'And it wouldn't be all that expensive. A second-hand motor caravan. If you know what you're doing — and I'll take old Pete with me, he's an expert mechanic — you can pick one up at a good price. Sunday morning, down Kingsway around Australia House. All those Aussies who've been over here doing Europe and want to go back home are lined up with their motor caravans trying to sell them off to the newest contingent of Aussies who've just arrived. They don't mind if the occasional Pommie steps in — as long as he's got the ready. We ought to be able to pick up something decent at a knockdown price. Then we can just convert it a bit, make more room to carry food and cook it, perhaps another cooking unit and a second tank of Calor gas—'

'That would mean you had to take out the bunks.' I brought him down to earth. 'Then you wouldn't be able to sleep in it when you went to the Continent.'

'We could re-convert it,' he said testily. 'It would be quite simple, really. Don't make mountains out of molehills.'

'Think of it as a dress rehearsal for explaining the project to Mona,' I told him. 'She'll think of all these objections, never fear.'

'Ah, Mona.' He sighed heavily. It began to sound as though the bloom was off the rose for both of them.

'Mona . . . well, Mona will just have to adjust to a few things. *You* think it's a good idea, don't you?'

I could not deny it. I was in favour of anything that would help Executive Meal Service to grow and expand. I was especially in favour of something that would mean consolidating and enlarging our already lucrative cash trade. With two vehicles, we could cover a second string of street markets, those usually serviced only by the ubiquitous hot dog and hamburger vans. Our experience had already proved that stallholders and public alike were delighted to be offered a better variety of more expensive and flavourful foods.

'Don't you?' I had not replied quickly enough.

'I think it's a super idea,' I said. 'I just can't help thinking about what Mona will say.'

'Leave Mona to me,' he said shortly.

On Sunday morning, Edda Price rang up. She had my private telephone number, which was not the one printed on the Executive Meal Service business card, but the separate telephone in my upstairs flat.

'I'm sorry to disturb you,' she said, sounding crisp, efficient and not at all sorry. 'I wouldn't have done so if it weren't urgent.'

'Of course.' I tried to sound sympathetic and alert. It took a moment before I could focus on my watch. It couldn't be eight-thirty! Perhaps I'd forgotten to wind it. I held it to my ear, where it ticked relentlessly.

'I was sure you wouldn't mind.' Equally relentlessly, Edda Price thrummed into my other ear. 'I thought it best to get this settled as soon as possible.'

'Yes.' I stifled a yawn. 'What is it?'

'It's terribly short notice, I know, but it can't be helped.' That was obviously as much of an apology as I was going to get. 'Tomorrow. We're having a Special Board Meeting to . . .' For the first time, her voice faltered. 'To settle the question of who's going to take Mark Avery's place on the Board.'

'Already?' The word slipped out before I could stop it, I was so startled.

'I agree,' she said. 'I think it's in the worst possible taste. I want to assure you that Quardon International had nothing to do with it. It has been *forced* on us by our new . . . associate. Mr Manganian has to go out of the country on business and he wishes to leave his own nominee on the Board. Some Italian man, although I believe he was born in this country—'

'Aldo Uccello,' I said. 'His personal assistant.'

'Personal hatchet man!' For a moment, the old Edda spoke. 'You know him?'

'I've met him,' I said. 'They were both at the reception at the United Boroughs of New York Bank the other night.'

'*Were* they?' I could almost hear the click as the information registered and was filed away for future reference. 'Then you can see it wouldn't do at all. Tristram Quardon is going to fight it—he wants Roddy on the Board instead. *Much* more suitable. Oh, but it's all so appalling—' Her voice cracked and once again I glimpsed the broken woman sprawled on the carpet in Mark Avery's office. '*Squabbling* like this when . . . when Mark isn't even in his grave yet!'

'I imagine the funeral will be private,' I said.

'Yes. Yes, just the family—his wife and two sons—and a few close friends . . . Tristram . . . myself . . .' I heard her catch a deep painful breath and blow her nose.

'And tomorrow—' It wasn't quite changing the subject, but it brought it back to a less emotive level. 'How many for lunch?'

'Yes, the Board,' she said gratefully. 'I'm not sure how many will be there. Not all of them. The meeting was called so suddenly. Some of them had other engagements—'

And some of them didn't want to get caught in the middle of a power struggle between Tristram Quardon and Ongar Manganian. They couldn't be blamed for that—it was a no-win situation.

'*About* how many do you expect?' I prompted, beginning to do a little mental arithmetic on my own. Certainly Tristram Quardon and Ongar Manganian would be there, also Roddy Bletchley and probably Aldo Uccello. That made four, and Edda to take the Minutes made five . . .'

'There may be twelve,' she said uncertainly. 'Or thirteen.' She gave a sort of cough that was meant to pass as a laugh. 'With the things that have happened lately, that would be apposite, wouldn't it?'

'What would you like for lunch?' I ignored the rhetorical question and asked a more practical one of my own.

'I don't know,' she said. 'I don't care. I doubt if anyone else will. Food isn't very important at a time like this. Except—' there was an abrupt jarring viciousness in her tone—'to Ongar Manganian!'

'Something simple,' I said, calculating rapidly. Simple enough to be reassuring to the others and not make them feel guilty because they were living high when Mark Avery had been struck low . . . but something that would be impressive to Ongar Manganian.

'Steak-and-kidney pie?' I suggested. Oysters could be added, as in the Old English recipes, without detracting from the security food aspect for the English Directors, but the touch of luxury would serve to signal to Ongar Manganian that he was getting a dish slightly above the ordinary. Mashed potatoes could be stretched out if more than expected arrived and were thus safer than new potatoes. Spring greens were at their best now and would also be reassuring as well as delicious.

'Oh, I suppose so,' she sighed. 'They won't want anything elaborate. It wouldn't seem right.'

'No sweet, but a good cheese board,' I said. The lack of a sweet would provide a touch of austerity, tempered by a lavish cheese board, which most of them would prefer in the circumstances.

'Yes, yes.' Her heart wasn't in it. 'I'll leave it to you. So long as you can do it, that's all that I was worried about.'

'We'll fit you in,' I said diplomatically. No point in letting her know that we had nothing else scheduled tomorrow. 'Of course, as it's such short notice, we may not be able to bring our usual waitresses—' This would be the ideal opportunity to slip Gretel into the active team and leave Lexie back in the kitchen doing the donkey work. The fact that it was Quardon International would emphasize to her that her wrist was being well and truly slapped for Friday's escapade.

'That doesn't matter,' Edda said. 'Who's going to notice?'

She had a point. Despite Lexie's fond hopes, the servitors were, for the most part, the original invisible people. There was the classic story, which surfaced at intervals with only the name of the world-famous actor changing, of the actor who disappeared from the table during a formal dinner, borrowed the waiter's jacket and served the next two courses to his friends without being noticed. No one ever paid any attention to the form hovering over one's chair dispensing the food.

'We'll be there early,' I said. 'Just in case there are any problems.'

There was a short silence and I wondered if I had been tactless. After the last luncheon at Quardon, there was little that could be considered a problem.

'That's fine . . .' Her attention seemed to have wandered elsewhere. I remembered that there was supposed to be an invalid husband in the background; one of the reasons she had done so well at Quardon. A

person who is not too anxious to go home doesn't mind
long hours of overtime.

'Just do as you think best.' She rang off.

CHAPTER 9

Everyone was in the kitchen when I returned from the
fishmonger's with the oysters in the morning. The
fragrance of toasting sesame seeds hung in the air and
Gretel was in her accustomed corner grating cheese. We
used the days when there were no luncheons scheduled to
catch up on all the little tasks that would expedite our
work when we were busy. I knew Mona had planned to
cook for the freezer today and so I had left a note telling
her of our change of plans.

She had found the note. Two large pans stood waiting
to be filled while she cut up and mixed the steak and
kidney.

'Here you are.' I dropped the parcel of oysters on her
table and went to wash and change.

When I returned, Nick was struggling with the oysters.
He was getting to be quite expert; furthermore, I had a
sneaking suspicion that he enjoyed it all far more than he
admitted. It was one thing to be theoretically knowledgable about a field and quite another to roll up your
sleeves and earn your expertise. I also suspected that he
played up this angle for all it was worth when he met his
old advertising colleagues for the occasional pub crawl.
Not that anyone—except Mona—could blame him for
that. It had been traumatic for him to have been
suddenly declared redundant, although it was happening
all around him. Not all his friends had fallen on their feet
in the catlike way Nick had. But not all his friends had
obliging younger sisters already self-employed in a

promising business that needed only a fresh infusion of
capital and labour to expand and flourish.

By this time, Nick's friends had probably forgotten that
he had waited to collect his golden handshake—and he
wouldn't be reminding them. It made a better story that
way. Everyone knows the secret of success in business lies
in the ability to move up to a better job one step ahead of
being given the push at your old company. If any of them
remembered, Nick had probably convinced them that he
had actually started me off in business and had been
biding his time in order to collect his golden handshake
before joining me.

It was too bad that Mona couldn't enter into the spirit
of the project as wholeheartedly as we had. She was
dealing with the oysters now as though they were personal
enemies who had done her an unforgivable injury. I
restrained a wince as she hurled them into the pie mixture
and looked away. It would be both pointed and insulting
to offer to take over from her at this stage. I would just
have to place my trust in the fact that her end results were
almost always perfect, despite the way she occasionally
treated the ingredients.

'Gretel—' I turned thankfully to someone whose only
problem was trying to grate the cheddar without also
grating her fingernails into the bowl. Gretel might be
clumsy, but at least she was uncomplicated.

'Gretel, would you like to come with us to Quardon
today? You can start learning the Boardroom luncheon
routine.'

'Me?' Gretel's face lit up. '*Me*?' (Would Cinderella like
to go to the Ball?) 'Today? So soon?'

'You did very well at the reception Friday evening.' I
hoped that didn't sound too patronizing, but Gretel
seemed to be taking it in the spirit in which it was meant.
'It's time you began getting a bit more practice.'

'I would love this!' Gretel attacked the grater vigorously

with the remaining nub of cheese. 'Oh!' She gave a sudden scream of dismay. 'My fingernail!'

'It's all right.' Restraining a wince, I spooned up the nail fragment and surrounding shreds of cheese. 'You can borrow my nail file. Leave the rest of the cheese, someone else can finish up, and go and change into your uniform.'

It was really too early, Mona was just putting the pies into the oven, but Gretel needed to calm down before she would be of any more use in the kitchen. I glanced at my watch as Gretel left the room. Where were the other girls? It was past their usual arrival time. Had they run into a traffic jam along the way?

Outside, the day was grey and chill. Last week's brief promise of spring had disappeared as though it had never existed.

The mood of the Quardon Directors would be about as bleak as the weather. Oxtail soup, I decided, taking the containers from the deep freeze. No frills, all security food today. It might provide some obscure comfort after what sounded as though it were going to be a very sticky Board meeting. No one was going to be anxious to welcome Ongar Manganian's representative on to the Board. At the same time, not everyone would welcome Roddy Bletchley, either. Oh, why did Mark Avery have to die just when things were going so well?

Mark Avery had had to die because he was in someone's way. The grim answer came unbidden and I shuddered convulsively.

'Careful,' Nick warned. 'You could catch pneumonia bending over an icy deep-freeze all day.'

'It's not that icy.' His words pinpointed the vague unease I had been feeling before the thought of Mark Avery had crowded it out. It returned in full force now. I pinched the polythene bag anxiously, but the soup seemed solid enough. Nevertheless . . .

Food poisoning is the nightmare threat that must

always lurk at the back of the minds of anyone dealing with food, whether they be professional caterers or hostesses in private homes. Odourless, colourless, tasteless, silent . . . sometimes deadly. Undetectable—until the first victim collapses.

'It's all right, isn't it?' Anxiety, fuelled by guilt, propelled Nick and Mona to my side instantly. We needed a new freezer; that should take priority over a second van or even doing up the dining-room. We had bought this one second-hand, as a stopgap measure, and had been nursing it along ever since. It was a dangerous thing to do, but we had got away with it . . . so far.

'I think so.' Mona moved her hand around inside the cabinet, testing the temperature. 'But, just to be on the safe side . . .' She lowered the thermostat another notch.

We could not go on like this much longer. The risk was too great. Harmful bacteria could form and grow too easily. Constant vigilance was necessary. In Great Britain alone, about five thousand cases of enteritis are notified each year caused by *Salmonellae*. Even though few of those cases are fatal, that's an awful lot of discomfort—which can last from one to eight days—and a lot of lost reputations among the people inadvertantly responsible.

Rarer in occurrence, but producing one of the most poisonous toxins known, is *Clostridium botulinum*; the neurotoxin acts on the central nervous system and the effect is usually fatal. The victims can take from twenty-four hours up to eight days to die. The lucky ones can take over eight months to recover. That one didn't bear thinking about. Nevertheless, there were occasional outbreaks.

'I'm sure it's all right,' Nick said positively. Mona and I exchanged glances. He knew less than either of us about the dangers, nor had he ever taken any trouble to learn them, as we had. He was still immersed in his advertising world when we had taken the necessary courses and had never bothered to remedy his deficiencies along those lines.

'Is anything wrong?'

We looked up to find that Lexie and Sidonie had entered silently while we had been bending over the freezer cabinet. A vaguely familiar figure lurked behind them as though trying to hide.

'Nothing.' We moved away hastily. At some point, it would be proper to give the girls a lecture on bacteria and the dangers of food poisoning, but discretion demanded that we wait until we were beyond stone-throwing range ourselves. After we had bought our new, first-class freezer, we could be sanctimonious about the problem.

'Never mind.' Sidonie shrugged out of her coat, unexpectedly taking charge. 'Humphrey has something to say to you. And so has Lexie.' She turned to face the culprits. 'Come along, now.'

'Like to apologize . . .' Humphrey shuffled forward, mumbling. 'No harm intended . . . Just a joke . . .' He ran out of steam and threw Lexie a look of desperate appeal. He was not accustomed to apologizing for his actions.

'Really,' Lexie pouted. 'I don't know why Sidders—'

'Sidonie!' Sidonie corrected sternly.

'I don't know why *Sidonie*—' Lexie sighed deeply and started over—'is making all this fuss. Humpty was *my* guest the other night and—'

'When you're paying the bill, you can invite the guests.' It might sound harsh, but it was time to make the position clear. Lexie had too many impecunious friends to be allowed to get away with ideas like that.

'All right, I'm *sorry*,' Lexie said grudgingly, one eye on Sidonie. 'How was I to know everyone would be so *stuffy* about it?'

Common sense should have told her; but that was not a commodity Lexie had ever felt the need of. She had other ways of getting what she wanted. She left common sense to plain practical people like Sidonie.

'We've picked up an unexpected assignment for today—' I spoke across Lexie to Sidonie. 'Quardon International are having an unscheduled Board meeting. I thought we'd take Gretel along and give her some practical experience. She did very well the other night. Lexie—' I answered the unspoken question—'can stay here and help Mona this afternoon.'

'Oh no!' Lexie cried. 'It's not fair! Uncle Tris will be expecting to see me. Besides, Gretel will just make a mess of everything, you *know* she will. It was only a fluke that she didn't do anything wrong the other night.'

There was a suppressed snort of laughter from Humpty. He had been wandering about the kitchen as we talked, his greedy, gleaning eyes alert for anything he could nibble. I had watched as he had dipped his fingers into the bowl of shredded cheese, but was too busy dealing with Lexie at that moment to take on Humpty as well.

'I don't know why you think it's so funny!' Lexie whirled on Humpty and then saw that he was not reacting to her plight; in fact, he had been unaware of it. His attention was elsewhere.

Pinned up over Mona's workplace were some old American cartoons, yellowing with age, which Nick had brought back from one of his trips to New York. One depicted a hostess at a dinner-party passing round a dish to her bemused guests. The caption read: '*I'll never forget the last time I served mushrooms—ambulances all over the place!*'

I gave a last worried look at the freezer and moved away. This was one of the days when the cartoon failed to amuse me.

Another drawing showed a salesman handing over a new pressure cooker to a male customer and saying: '*A*

*word of warning, lest you forget the instructions and blow
your fool head off.*' There was also one of a man who had
got his necktie hopelessly entangled in an eggbeater, with
his wife commenting: '*Oh, fine. I must call on you for
help more often.*'

Humpty stopped snickering, puzzled by Lexie's abrupt
attack. He had been reading the cartoons, not listening to
our conversation and the nuances of Lexie's situation had
escaped him.

'It was *your* fault, anyway!' Lexie had realized her
mistake and her fury increased, still directed at a
bewildered Humpty.

'It was *his* idea—' She appealed to me. 'He thought it
would be fun to sneak in and get a free feed. Oh, *please*,
can't I come with you today?'

I might have weakened but just then Gretel returned,
neat and tidy in her uniform—with every button firmly
done up. No nonsense there. 'I am all ready,' she said
proudly.

'So you are.' I met Lexie's eye and she saw that her
cause was lost.

'Oh, all right,' she said sulkily, dividing a glare between
Gretel and Humpty. 'But Humpty can stay here with me
and do his share of the work. Nick—' she added
nastily—'will be glad to have someone else to peel the
potatoes.'

Humpty didn't seem to mind. He had resumed his
wandering and was bearing down on the larder like a
homing pigeon.

'We can always use an extra pair of hands.' I moved to
cut him off before he reached the larder door. 'Why don't
I find you a spare apron and you can sit over here.'

'Yes. All right. Yes.' Humpty allowed himself to be led
to Gretel's empty corner. He inhaled deeply as the aroma
of steak-and-kidney pie began floating through the room.
One could almost see his salivary glands working.

'Never mind the potatoes,' Mona said briskly. 'He can peel apples. I thought we'd do a few deep-dish apple pies for the freezer this afternoon.'

A glazed smile spread over Humpty's face. I began to suspect it might be easier to co-opt him than get rid of him.

Perhaps Lexie suspected it, too. Her baleful expression deepened. She had intended Humpty to share her disgrace and sense of punishment; instead he was beaming with delight. He had obviously deduced, correctly, that he was in line for a working lunch and would have the added perk of dipping into any food that came his way.

Mona and I exchanged glances and she nodded. She'd keep an eye on Humpty and make sure that he sang sufficiently for his supper. Nick was transparently amused by the situation and turned away before Lexie noticed it and transferred some of her fury to him.

Sidonie had disappeared to change into her own uniform. It was still a bit early, but Gretel was in hers and I suspected that Sidonie was not above wishing to underline Lexie's disfavour.

I removed a selection of cheeses from the fridge so that they could begin warming up to room temperature in good time for serving, and started collecting the things we would need for the luncheon. Gretel carried the serving board and cheese wire out to the van; even though she seemed to be improving, there was no point in tempting fate by letting her carry anything breakable or spillable.

Mona opened the oven door to check the progress of the pies. Nick would load those into the van in about another half-hour; the crust was already turning a delicate golden brown. I glanced at my watch, everything was moving along in perfect timing.

'That smells good.' Sidonie came back into the kitchen, looking crisp and efficient but with an air of suppressed excitement.

'Good enough to eat,' Nick said cheerfully. 'Pity it's destined for the Boardroom bellies, I could do with a bit of it myself.'

Humpty's face fell. Up to then, he had obviously thought it was on his luncheon menu.

'Perhaps there'll be some left,' I said. 'We're not sure how many will turn up, so we may have overcooked.'

'I thought we'd have sukiyaki ourselves.' Mona slammed the oven door shut. She got a chunk of rump steak from the fridge and carried it back to her table. Humpty watched the swift, sure movements of her gleaming knife in fascination as she expertly slivered the steak into thin strips. He was making heavy weather with the paring knife allotted to him and someone else was going to have to core the apples if we wanted anything left of them at all.

'Never mind that for a moment,' Sidonie said. 'Mona, Jean, Nick—' She darted a sudden suspicious glance at her cousin. 'Lexie hasn't told you our news, has she?'

Lexie wasn't telling us anything. She had withdrawn into a fit of smouldering sulks and hunched in her corner moodily stabbing at a large potato.

'It's *so* super.' Reassured, Sidonie continued. 'I didn't want to tell you before because I didn't want you to get your hopes up, but it's all right now. We've brought it off! We've got you the catering contract for the Charity Ball next month!'

'Marvellous!' I cheered before Mona could speak. I could see her opening her mouth to ask, '*What charity ball*?', but that was irrelevant. I knew that Sidonie worked for several charities in her spare time and one thing might lead to another. I discounted entirely her polite '*we*'. Lexie might have been dragooned into an occasional appearance at a committee meeting or a minimal subscription, but Sidonie would have been the moving spirit for anything actually achieved.

'I had to give them an estimated quotation, since we wanted to surprise you. But you can confirm it now—' Sidonie pulled a folded piece of paper from her pocket. 'I don't think I was too far out.'

'It looks bang on.' I studied the scribbled figures. Sidonie had been learning far more than I had thought.

'What precisely—' Mona came round to read over my shoulder—'does this entail?'

'Oh, you know the sort of thing,' Sidonie said airily, forgetting that everyone wasn't familiar with her world. For a moment, she bore an uncanny resemblance to Lexie. 'Everyone will be going to private supper-parties beforehand. The Ball will start about 9 p.m. There'll be lashings of champagne and they'll expect sandwiches and strawberries and cream around midnight. Then they'll draw the prizes, more champagne and dancing, and perhaps half of them will go home. The main thing is the buffet breakfast at about 4 a.m. or so.'

'Buffet breakfast . . .' Mona murmured thoughtfully. 'Country-house style, I suppose . . .'

'That's it,' Sidonie said. 'Lots of chafing dishes set out along a trestle table. Probably about a hundred and fifty or so will stay on for breakfast.'

'A hundred and fifty,' Mona echoed weakly, but rallied almost immediately. 'Scrambled eggs, I suppose. Masses of scrambled eggs . . .'

'Sausages, grilled mushrooms, devilled kidneys,' I took up the refrain, thinking aloud. 'And kedgeree . . . lots of kedgeree. Yes, we should be able to manage.'

'Don't forget—' Lexie interrupted nastily. 'You'll have to hire some extra people to help with the serving. This time, Sidonie and I will be *guests*.'

CHAPTER 10

I was shocked at the sight of Tristram Quardon. He was pale and gaunt, as though layers of flesh had melted away collapsing his skin back on to the skeleton frame, emphasizing the skull structure just beneath the surface.

Alas, poor Yorick . . . alas, poor Mark . . . alas, poor Tristram. Everyone was a loser at a time like this.

He popped his head round the door and gave a wan smile at the preparations going on. He nodded briefly to me, looked at Sidonie and Gretel, and disappeared again. If he had noticed Lexie's absence, he had evidently decided not to remark on it. He had enough problems today.

Hard on his heels—as was only to be expected—came Edda Price. She was looking better, but she could have hardly looked worse than the last time I had seen her. As though aware of this, she was almost aggressively efficient.

'We're going in now. We shouldn't be long. The only item on the agenda is . . . is Mark's replacement. There'll be seventeen for lunch. Not all of them,' she added disapprovingly, 'members of the Board.' Of course, they would have to feed the unsuccessful candidate—that ought to make for an interesting lunch.

'Lunch will be ready when you are,' I said as soothingly as I dared. 'It won't matter if it takes longer than you think, or if they linger over drinks afterwards.'

We put the pies into the oven at a comfortable temperature and the pot of soup on top of the stove to simmer. The spring greens could be put on to cook as we served the soup.

Everything was under control in the kitchen; I

wondered if the same could be said for anywhere else in the building. There was a feeling of sickness, of muted hysteria, in the air. Secretaries and typists still gathered in gossiping knots in the hallways, looking over their shoulders and jumping at sudden loud noises. As I passed the typing pool on my way in, an ambulance had gone by outside, klaxon wailing. There had been abrupt silence in the typing pool; it was easy to visualize the hands suspended above the keyboards . . . waiting. Gradually, as the sound of the ambulance died away in the distance and the typists realized that Quardon International had not been its destination, the typing started again and the crescendo of sound returned to normal. Until the next ambulance or police car was heard approaching . . .

I had Sidonie set the plates and glasses round the table while Gretel arranged the silverware and napkins. It seemed safer that way. True, the napkins drooped a bit, resembling water-lilies in the last stages of dissolution, but no one was going to be in a critical mood after this Board meeting if, indeed, they noticed anything at all.

Meanwhile, I found I had a worse awkwardness to deal with. Both nominees for the so forcibly vacated Director's seat were prowling the corridor outside, trying to look as though they were not waiting for a summons to the Board room. They kept passing the kitchen door and I could hear the occasional scraps of conversation between them.

Aldo was disposed to be friendly, but Roddy could not decide whether his dignity and possible about-to-be-exalted position would be impinged by fraternizing with the enemy. On the other hand, Ongar Manganian might win and Aldo would ascend to the Boardroom heights, in which case it would not be safe to have shown open enmity. It made for a very scrappy, nervous interchange of remarks on the weather, the state of the country, or anything except what was going on in the Boardroom.

Inevitably, the kitchen became a neutral refuge for them.

'Hello, everything all right here?' Roddy had been the first to utilize it as a temporary bolt-hole. After all, he could disappear into the Gents only so many times before it would begin to look as though he were either in a state of extreme terror or had something seriously wrong with him.

'Just fine,' I said with a sinking heart as he leaned against the door jamb, obviously prepared to stay for a while. From that vantage point, he had a clear view of the corridor by just turning his head slightly.

'Fine, fine,' he said vaguely. 'Everything looks—and smells—very good. But then, it always is. You do a very good job.'

'Thank you.' I knew he wasn't really listening, either to what he was saying or to my replies. All his attention was concentrated on the closed door at the end of the corridor.

'Yes. Er . . . excuse me. I think I hear . . .' His voice trailed off as he disappeared from view.

'Something is wrong?' Gretel frowned at the abrupt exit and looked around guiltily to see what new mistake she had made. 'He is displeased?'

'He has troubles of his own,' I said. 'Hello, Mr Uccello.'
Box and Cox. One went out, the other came in.

'Aldo, please,' he said. 'I'm not the formal type—and I don't believe you are, either.' He lounged in the spot just vacated by Roddy, giving a more superficial impression of being at ease, but I noticed that his attention was equally attuned to the happenings at the far end of the corridor.

'Everything looks good—' he gave a perfunctory glance round—'and smells good.'

It seemed to be the only thing anyone could think of to say around a kitchen. I'd have expected a more original comment from him, if his parents genuinely ran a restaurant of their own. I suddenly remembered that he had also said that he had a brother who was an electronics wizard and he had started out that way himself. Electronics—electricity, the two were very close, weren't they? Had he been in the building last week? I hadn't seen him then, the first time I had seen him was at the reception with Ongar Manganian—and that reminded me of something else.

'Perhaps you'd like to taste everything,' I said. 'Just to be sure.'

'You caught that, did you?' He was amused. 'I thought you did. You looked quite shocked for a moment—before you pulled yourself together.'

'It *was* a shock,' I said. 'I couldn't believe my eyes. It's—it's so archaic! How could you?'

'Oh, I don't mind humouring the old boy.' He shrugged. 'He imagines he has enemies everywhere. Mind you, he probably has. I'm not saying I'd be happy playing his little game in some corners of the world, but it's probably quite safe here in England.'

'Probably . . .' I let the word trail off. No one could ever be certain about anything concerning Ongar Manganian.

'And I'm safer than most,' he said firmly. 'Don't forget, I've been familiar with all sorts of flavourings and spices since childhood. If there was anything off about any dish, I'm far better able to spot it than most.'

'Just the same . . . in this day and age . . .'

'People don't change that much,' he said. 'There's never been a time when certain types wouldn't act to get someone out of the way.'

Was he speaking from experience? Suddenly, graphically, the picture of Mark Avery rose in my mind. Mark—sprawled on the carpet—out of someone's way for good. I felt myself sway, my eyes closed . . .

'Here, sit down.' He moved quickly, pushing the kitchen stool under me. 'I'm sorry, I shouldn't have said that. I wasn't thinking. You found him, of course.'

'Along with Edda,' I said. 'She was there first, but she fainted, and then I came along.'

'Edda, yes,' he said thoughtfully.

'Have a drink of water.' Sidonie thrust a glass at me. Gretel watched anxiously.

'I'm all right.' I drank some water, then handed the glass back to Sidonie and slid off the stool. The memory of last week was still so strong that I reached out my hand and flipped the light switch on and off in a sort of nervous twitch just to make sure that the electricity was still working. It was.

'Lightning doesn't strike twice in the same place.' Sidonie was trying to be encouraging. I smiled wanly.

'The police don't believe it was lightning,' I reminded her.

'Furthermore, the belief is a popular fallacy. I myself have seen lightning strike again and again in the same spot.' Ongar Manganian stood in the doorway behind me. He had come down the corridor silently. 'Not always during the same storm, it is true. But one storm follows another and some places seem to have a fatal attraction for the bolts. They are the magnets in the electro-magnetic field.' He spoke with authority. How much else did he know about the subject?

Gretel whimpered and stepped back.

'That is right.' He looked at her impassively. 'It is best not to stand near such a place. Not if you value your safety. Of course—' he turned his head to encompass Aldo—'some people like to live dangerously.'

'Is the meeting over?' Aldo met his eyes with equal impassivity. 'That didn't take long.'

'Not over, no.' Ongar Manganian shook his massive head. 'Suspended, temporarily, for what they call a corridor conference. Tristram Quardon confers with his minion and—' he jerked his head towards the corridor—'I wish to confer with you.'

'Charmingly phrased,' Aldo murmured. 'Obviously an offer I can't refuse.'

'You would be wise not to. If you will excuse us—' He sketched a bow. 'Much as I regret leaving you lovely ladies—'

Gretel cringed another step backwards, smiling nervously. The movement left Ongar Manganian with a clear view of the working counter. His gaze roved over it automatically—it was the food he regretted leaving, not us—and he stiffened suddenly.

'What are you doing with *that*?' he demanded. 'Who sent you?' He whirled to face me. 'What are you doing here?'

'We're doing the lunches.' I looked at him blankly. 'We always do. You know that.'

'Lunches—hah!' He swooped past me, snatching up something on the counter. 'You lie! Who has subverted you? Whose pay are you in? Tell me! I will find out anyway!'

Gretel cowered against the farther wall, taking deep sobbing breaths, hands half hiding her face. I hoped she didn't think our business luncheons usually proceeded along these lines.

'I don't know what you're talking about,' I said flatly. In the doorway behind me, help was at hand in case Ongar Manganian passed from merely raving to outright homicidal. Tristram Quardon, Roddy Bletchley, Edda Price and a good selection of the Board were crowding the doorway, drawn by the shouting.

'This! This!' He was shaking something under my nose, his hand such a blur I could not see what he was holding, what had enraged him so. 'How do you explain this? What are you doing with a garotte? For whom was it destined?'

'Ongar—' Aldo said softly, warningly. 'Ongar, take it easy. What have you got there?' He reached out and stopped the fist in mid-shake. The shape in it began to take form.

'The cheese wire,' I said, looking at the coil of wire with a handle at each end. 'We're having a cheese board instead of a sweet this afternoon. That's only the cheese wire to cut the cheese smoothly. What's the—' I broke off.

What's the matter with him? was not a tactful question.

'Cheese wire?' Ongar Manganian repeated wonder-ingly. He looked down at the object in his hand, examining it as though he had never seen such a thing before. Perhaps they didn't have them in the parts of the world he normally frequented. 'Cheese wire?'

'Cheese wire,' Aldo said firmly. 'You hold one end down, straighten the wire and pull it through the cheese.' He tried to take it away from his employer to demonstrate, but Ongar Manganian held on to it stubbornly.

'Cheese wire?' He was still incredulous. 'Where I come from, it is a garotte. Ready-made. Ready for—'

'In England,' I said, as firmly as Aldo, 'this is a cheese wire. You can buy it in any kitchen equipment shop for less than a pound.'

'In England!' He shook his head. 'Only in England would they dare!' In a swift, serpentine movement, he shook out the wire, uncoiling it, one handle in each hand. 'Less than a pound! A deadly weapon: secret, silent, infallible and so cheap. Less than a pound—available at your friendly kitchen equipment shop. Only in England could this be possible!'

'It's a cheese wire,' I insisted. 'Let me show you—' I reached out for it.

'Let *me* show *you!*' Suddenly, the wire looped around my neck and was drawn snug, but not too tight . . . yet. A wire noose that could cut through the soft flesh as easily as through the yielding cheese. It could cut my head off. I caught my breath and stood silent, not daring to move.

For that terrifying endless moment, no one dared move.

Ongar Manganian's face swung close to mine, his eyes burning, hypnotic. 'So easy,' he said. 'Silent as a knife, final as a bullet—and so disposable. At such a price, anyone can afford to murder. To strike and move away, leaving the garotte embedded in the throat—' The wire began to tighten.

'All right, Ongar, that's enough.' Aldo touched him on the shoulder. 'You've made your point.'

'Cheese wire!' Abruptly, Ongar Manganian chuckled. 'To cut the cheese!' He released his hold at one end and the taut wire relaxed. With one quick—expert—flick of his wrist, he pulled it free and tossed it away from him, back on to the counter where it re-coiled like a waiting snake.

The group in the doorway melted away like witnesses at the scene of an accident fearful of being asked for their names and addresses. I found I was breathing deeply, unable to look at anyone.

'You wanted to talk to me.' Aldo led Ongar Manganian from the room. There was a further relaxation in the atmosphere without his presence.

'He is mad!' Gretel sobbed. 'Insane! It is not safe to have someone like that abroad in the streets!'

'He's paranoiac, certainly.' Sidonie tried for a dispassionate assessment, but she was pale. 'He thinks the whole world is plotting against him. I've heard of people like that—' She shuddered, her precocious maturity slipping away. 'I've never seen one before. Not in action. Are you all right, Jean! Are you sure you're all right? He looked so—so *mad*.'

'That is what I said.' Gretel dabbed at her eyes, recovering now that a second opinion endorsed her own. 'He is mad!'

'I'm fine.' I fingered my throat uncertainly. It seemed

that I could still feel that wire tightening around it but, so far as I could tell, there was not even the faintest indentation to mark the spot where it had been.

'Are you all right?' Roddy Bletchley echoed the question from the doorway.

'Fine, thank you,' I repeated automatically.

'You weren't frightened, were you?' He came into the room, trying to appear cool and in control of the situation, but tiny beads of perspiration bedabbled his forehead. 'We wouldn't have let anything happen. I was all prepared to step in—' He pulled out his handkerchief and mopped his brow.

'Fine.' There must be something else I could say. I turned away, busying myself at the stove. 'I'm quite all right.'

'The man was out of control!' Mop, mop, mop, but his forehead was still damp. 'I've never seen anything like it. He's a danger to the civilized community.'

'That is what I say!' Gretel moved forward eagerly. 'He is mad! He should be shut away!'

'Er . . . yes,' Roddy agreed uneasily. He seemed to be recollecting that, mad or not, Ongar Manganian was allied with Quardon International now and anything that happened to him might rebound on them. 'He got carried away for a minute, that's all. Foreigners . . .' He trailed off, belatedly recognizing that Gretel had an accent herself.

'They've gone back to the meeting, have they?' I brought the conversation back to a businesslike level.

'Yes, yes,' he said. 'It shouldn't be much longer now.'

'Just a question of a rubber stamp at this point,' Aldo agreed, appearing in the doorway.

Did he sound too happy about it? Roddy shot him a suspicious look.

'You handled that very well.' Aldo turned to me. 'The old boy was most impressed.'

'I didn't do anything,' I said. 'I was too stunned to move.'

'But you didn't show fear. That's the main thing. He has his little ways of testing people. You needn't worry, he'll never try anything like that again. You've passed the test, you're in his good books now.'

'Well, he isn't in mine.' I turned away to see to the greens. 'I can do without that sort of nonsense.'

'It won't happen again.'

'It shouldn't have happened the first time!' Roddy took up the cudgels on my behalf. I'd have been more impressed if he'd taken them up when Ongar Manganian had the wire around my neck. 'The man's a savage. Unfit for civilized life.'

'He had to claw his way up out of the gutter.' Aldo's face hardened, his eyes were flint; he looked as though he might have done some clawing himself. 'It's all right for people who've always lived off the fat of the land to criticize, but you don't get very far if you try to keep to civilized rules where he came from. Once you've escaped, you can begin to learn the niceties of social life.'

'I haven't had that sheltered a life,' Roddy protested. He tried to look tough, but only succeeded in looking as though he hadn't a claw to his name. He was a fixer, not a fighter; that was why he was so useful to Tristram Quardon.

'Comparatively speaking, you're bound to have had.' Aldo, too, was useful to his master, in his own way. Also, it seemed, loyal.

Which one was going to be rewarded by a seat on the Board?

The door at the far end of the hall opened and they both went silent, ending what had threatened to degenerate into a childlike squabble. They waited for the summons.

'Oh dear.' Edda Price came into the kitchen, looking

quite dazed. 'They asked me to tell you. They'll be ready
for lunch in about half an hour. They're only going to
have a quick drink first.' She rubbed her forehead. 'I've
got to get back. I'm going to have a drink, too. I need
one.'

Aldo moved forward as though to open a door that was
already open. She started and looked at him, then at
Roddy . . . almost guiltily.

'Come on, Edda,' I said. 'Put them out of their misery.
Who's the new Board member?'

'Oh dear!' She darted through the doorway into the
safety of the corridor before turning to answer. 'It was all
so confusing. No one could seem to agree. They went on
and on. Then Mr Manganian suggested a compromise
candidate and—' She stopped and gulped.

'And—?' I prompted.

'And . . . well . . . they decided on *me*.' She turned and
vanished, leaving a thundering silence behind her.

'Yes, I can see it,' Aldo said slowly. 'It's a clever move.
He's off to the States and Womens' Lib is riding high
there. It will be to his advantage to say that he's just
appointed a woman to the Board. He thinks of every
angle.'

'You're taking it very calmly, I must say.' Roddy wasn't
doing so badly himself. The reason became apparent as
he continued musing aloud. 'Of course, it won't be for too
long. She must be coming up to retirement soon—'

'Old directors don't retire as early as the staff.' Aldo
was amused. 'They're beyond the level where the rules
apply. I wouldn't be too sure you'll get rid of her so easily.
She's got a lot of expertise. It was a good choice.'

'Yes. Oh yes!' Roddy seemed to decide that enthusiasm
was his best line. 'I couldn't be more pleased—' He broke
off, perhaps realizing that that was going too far. He'd
have been a lot more pleased if he'd got on to the Board
himself.

'We ought to go along and offer our congratulations,' Aldo said. 'Join in the festive drink. It might look a little pointed if we didn't. We wouldn't want to be thought poor losers, would we?'

'No, no, never.' Roddy followed him from the room.

'I think it's marvellous,' Sidonie said firmly. 'Edda should have gone on to the Board long ago. Mark and Tristram both wanted her to, but she had this silly idea that she shouldn't rise too far above her husband. As though he was going to do any rising at all! All he ever wanted was nice comfortable invalid's life and she let it hold her back.'

It was odd to be occasionally reminded that both Sidonie and Lexie knew more about Quardon than I did. Because I was working there first, I tended to forget — and they never stressed — the family links that both of them possessed with Tristram Quardon.

'I'm glad it's happened at last,' I said. 'It's a shame Mark Avery couldn't be here to see it —' Too late I remembered that, if Mark Avery were still here, it wouldn't have happened.

I wasn't the only one to remember that. The thought stopped all conversation abruptly and we turned silently to our tasks. . . .

The Directors were soon assembling in the dining-room and there was no more time for idle chatter anyway. I still deemed it safer to leave Gretel in the kitchen doing the preliminary dishing up rather than the actual serving, so Sidonie and I kept busy dashing in and out with loaded trays.

The meal went quickly, conversation was subdued and no one seemed disposed to linger over food. I received a congratulatory nod from Ongar Manganian as he discovered the oysters in the pie, but no one else noticed.

During this time, Gretel appeared to be in a state of increasing agitation. I began to wonder if the pressure was too much for her and whether she would last through the luncheon. Several times she seemed close to tears.

It was not until the end of the meal that I discovered what was wrong. Sidonie had gone ahead, carrying the basket filled with water biscuits, cream crackers, bran and wheat biscuits and oatcakes and I picked up the cheese board to follow her. Then I halted and looked around.

'I am sorry,' Gretel sobbed. 'I have lost it. Everything was going so well and now it is ruined. You will never take me with you again. I have looked everywhere but I cannot find it. Oh—' Her voice rose in a wail. I hoped the Directors couldn't hear her.

'Never mind,' I said. 'Never mind that now. Quick, give me a knife!' I snatched a knife from her and hurried towards the dining-room, trying to keep possible implications out of my mind.

The cheese wire-garotte was missing.

CHAPTER 11

After the Directors had departed, we turned the kitchen upside down, but there was still no trace of the cheese wire.

'Perhaps someone thought it was too dangerous to leave around,' I suggested, 'and impounded it.' I thought of the crowd scene in the doorway as Ongar Manganian had given his little performance with myself as his unwilling assistant. Everyone had been standing there . . . watching. Had it given anyone ideas?

Perhaps someone had taken it for future use. The use Ongar Manganian had so ably demonstrated.

We looked at each other without comment and returned to our search with renewed vigour, but without

success. The cheese wire had not fallen behind any of the
appliances, had not been tidied away in an unthinking
moment into one of the cupboards, nor been absent-
mindedly placed at the back of the fridge or stove. The
cheese wire had definitely gone missing.

*The next time anyone saw it, it might be embedded in
someone's throat.* The throat of one of the people who
had been present today as its possible alternative function
had been so vividly demonstrated.

Edda! I saw again that brief flash in Aldo's eyes before
he smiled. Fury . . . or comprehension? The realization
that his master had pointed out the method and the
weapon for removing the next obstacle from their path.
Edda, the compromise candidate, who wasn't expected to
occupy the seat on the Board for long.

'It is not here—' Gretel looked up in despair. As a last
desperate resort, she had burrowed to the bottom of the
waste bin. 'It is not anywhere. I have lost it!'

'It's not your fault,' I said. I did not add whose fault I
thought it was. 'Come on, we can't waste any more time
looking for it. Let's get back to Notting Hill Gate.'

'But,' Gretel protested, 'we cannot go away and leave it
unaccounted for. It—it is a dangerous weapon.'

'So is practically anything, if used in the wrong way:
the kitchen knives, a gas oven, kebab skewers—' I
stopped, reluctant to carry the thought through. *An
electric razor.*

'Besides,' I added, 'anyone can buy a cheese wire. They
needn't steal ours. It isn't like buying a gun or poison; the
sales person wouldn't even notice.' They were also readily
available to anyone who had access to a kitchen,
especially a restaurant kitchen. The thought cheered me.
Aldo had no need to steal ours—unless he had sentimental principles against using family utensils for
murder. If he did, he was one of the few; most murders
happened in families.

'Go on,' Sidonie urged. 'What else were you thinking just then? There was a very interesting expression on your face. A penny for them—'

'They're worth more than that,' I said. If I uttered what I had just been thinking about Aldo, it would be slander of the most serious sort. Actionable in the High Court, where it could cost me a pretty penny for those thoughts.

'Is everything all right?' Roddy Bletchley stood in the doorway. 'I—I mean—' He recoiled before our combined gaze. 'You're usually gone by now. I came up to get some papers Tris left in the Boardroom . . . Well, I only thought I'd ask,' he finished limply.

Send for Roddy. Roddy the Fixer. Could he fix this?

'I'm glad you did,' I said, choosing my words carefully. 'I'm not sure whether everything is all right or not. I rather fear not. Our cheese wire is missing.'

'Missing?' Roddy recoiled even farther, looking as though it would be the last time he ever asked us if everything was all right. 'Are you sure?'

'Positive,' Gretel said, in a tone that brooked no doubt. 'It was here earlier when—when—we all saw it.'

'Yes.' Roddy blinked, obviously seeing the same thing the rest of us were seeing: the cheese wire tightening around my neck in Ongar Manganian's hands.

'He tossed it on to the counter.' I found myself imitating the expert dismissive flick of the wrist. 'But when we went to put it on the cheese board, it was gone.'

'I noticed you weren't using it,' Roddy said. 'But I thought you didn't want to bring it to his attention again, not knowing what he'd do. The man's unstable. He must have taken it again and—' He broke off, looking ill.

'*Someone* took it, I'm afraid.' That was as far as I was prepared to commit myself.

'He's left the building,' Roddy said. 'I don't know what we can do about it now.' He sounded relieved. Perhaps he thought I'd insist that he face Ongar Manganian to demand the return of the cheese wire.

'Uccello's driving him to Heathrow to catch the New York flight,' Roddy continued. 'It's quite brilliant, really,' he added thoughtfully. 'He'll be able to walk on carrying an offensive weapon and no one will ever know. A little bit of wire like that won't show up on the metal detectors the way a knife or gun would. It probably wouldn't register any more than a foil-wrapped packet of aspirins. He'll be able to land in New York all equipped and unsuspected.'

'Equipped for what?' I asked. Roddy was letting his imagination—and his dislike for Ongar Manganian—run away with him. 'At that level, they don't need to do their own killing.'

'No, no, I suppose not.' Roddy abandoned the idea reluctantly.

'It's more likely to be used around here.' I underlined it for him. 'So just keep your eyes open.'

'You don't mean—?' He went a pale green. 'You don't think—?'

'Just keep your eyes open,' I repeated.

The house was empty when we got back. My first surprise gave way to the realization that Mona had been in a mood to drag Nick forcibly into the West End for the afternoon to choose wallpaper and paint as he had promised. They would not have left Lexie and Humpty alone with all the food, so those two must have left earlier.

'I suppose we ought to do the dishes,' Sidonie decided regretfully. Everything else seemed to have been taken care of before the others left.

'That's all right,' I said. 'I'll do them. You two can run along now.'

'We're in no hurry.' Sidonie began stacking the dishes in the dishwasher. 'It isn't fair to dash off and leave you with all the dirty work.'

'That's right.' Gretel moved impulsively to join her, knocking a pan off the edge of the sink as she did so.

Sidonie and I exchanged glances as Gretel stooped to retrieve the pan. At least it hadn't been something breakable and the pan was a good heavy duty one; it wasn't even dented.

But it wasn't a good idea to let Gretel help with the dishes, no matter how willing she might be. I cast about frantically for an alternative occupation to suggest.

'Jean,' Sidonie said hesitantly, interrupting my own thoughts, 'you *are* pleased, aren't you?'

'Pleased?' I echoed, watching Gretel move purposefully towards a rack of glasses Mona had left draining on the sinkboard. She was plainly determined to polish them and return them to their cupboard shelf. No prospect could have been less pleasing.

'About the Charity Ball? I thought you would be. You . . . you don't *mind* my going ahead and setting it up without consulting you first? I didn't want to disappoint you, in case I couldn't bring it off.'

'Oh, Sidonie!' I realized guiltily that I had not thanked her properly. In fact, I hadn't referred to the matter all day. Of course, there had been other things to worry about and I had forgotten it. And all this while, poor Sidonie had been brooding over my lack of response.

'I'm delighted. Really, I am. There just hasn't been time to settle to discussing it properly.'

'And you're not upset because—?' She was looking slightly more mollified. 'Well, because Lexie and I will have to be on the other side of the table instead of helping you with the serving?'

'Good heavens, no!' Such a thing had never occurred to me. 'Of course, you'll be out front with your friends—'

'*I* will help you behind the table,' Gretel said proudly.

'Now I am getting good experience, you may not need more people.'

Sidonie and I exchanged thoughtful glances. 'It's true,' Sidonie said. 'There'll be you and Mona and Nick and Gretel. Since it will be a buffet, four of you ought to be enough.' She sounded relieved. 'It will mostly be a case of keeping the serving dishes filled and seeing that everything is going smoothly. Perhaps, if you got really pushed, I could slide behind once in a while and—'

'No, I'm sure we'll be able to manage,' I said. 'It will be *your* night. You just concentrate on having fun.'

'Ye-es.' She sounded dubious and I remembered that Lexie was going to be at the ball as well. I wondered again just how much fun Sidonie was able to have with Lexie always around, always more vivacious, always ready to deflect the attention of any male. I had seen it happen at some of our luncheons. A man might start out talking to Sidonie, but before either of them realized what was happening, he wound up in conversation with Lexie. It was as well that Sidonie was so sweet-natured, and also that she had other assets—such as a large inheritance due to her from a legacy when she became twenty-one. A fact Lexie was not above hurling at her during one of their infrequent quarrels, as though it were somehow derogatory. Sidonie always reacted as abjectly as though it had been.

And yet, it was Sidonie who paid the rent for the flat they shared. If Lexie thought everyone wasn't aware of that, she was deluding herself. I also suspected that, when they went on their shopping expeditions, Sidonie wound up paying for most of Lexie's clothes . . .

A car door slammed outside, abruptly derailing my train of thought. The noise was followed almost immediately by clatter and commotion at the back door, then Nick and Mona burst into the kitchen carrying rolls of wallpaper, buckets, brushes and boxes of paste.

'There you are—' Nick greeted us. 'Or almost all of you. Isn't it lucky we don't have any luncheons scheduled for the next two days? All hands to the pump and we can have this job just about finished by then. It will make a nice break for you from all that cooking.'

'*If* you wouldn't mind, that is.' Mona was more cautious but equally enthusiastic. The prospect of finishing another room had brightened her eyes and lightened her steps. The idea of having a couple of days free from cooking wasn't doing her any harm either. She looked years younger.

'We will help, *ja*!' Gretel's eyes gleamed. 'I *love* the paste and paint—nearly as much as cooking!'

I choked back a laugh at Nick's expression. What it would mean to have Gretel stumbling among the paint pots had obviously not occurred to him before. He would not have spoken so quickly or so carelessly if it had.

'Well . . .' Mona shot Nick an anxious glance. 'We'll see, Gretel. We'll have to be very careful. This is very expensive wallpaper.'

'Nothing but the best for our home,' Nick said, perhaps too quickly. Mona didn't notice, but I had known him long enough to know that it was suspicious. He was up to something . . . again.

'I will be very careful,' Gretel promised. 'And,' she sighed, 'Sidonie is always careful.'

Which left Lexie. She might be perfectly willing to help out in an extra-curricular activity, or she might be quite caustic about it. That would depend on whether she was still sulking over her slapped wrist.

'We could start with the withdrawing-room, I suppose.' Mona was still considering the earlier problem. 'We could practise in there and get into the swing of things before we begin on the dining-room.'

'Oh, I don't think we need to bother about the with-drawing-room.' Nick was elaborately casual. 'It isn't important whether we get that done up.'

'Why not?' This time he had aroused Mona's suspicions. The withdrawing-room was at the far end of the dining-room and had once been used as a small parlour to which the ladies could withdraw while the gentlemen passed round port and cigars. Mona had long wanted it as a morning-room for herself, despite the fact that a later occupant of the house had demolished the wall separating the two rooms and replaced it with sliding doors so that the withdrawing-room was an extension of the dining-room. Mona had ambitions to rebuild the inside wall, but it would be some time before they had enough money for a luxury like that.

'Well . . . we won't be needing it immediately . . .' Nick was obviously aware that he was treading on dangerous ground. He was treading on her dreams—and he had already trampled over too many of them.

'How do you know? We might book a big party straightaway. We'd need to use it as an extension then. Of course it should be done up—and to match the dining-room.'

'Our first bookings won't be for big parties,' Nick said confidently. Too confidently. 'I promise you.'

'I see,' Mona said evenly, beginning to get the picture. 'Then suppose you tell me what our first bookings *will* be. You've already made them, haven't you?'

'Why don't you girls—' Nick glanced uneasily at Gretel and Sidonie—'take this stuff through into the dining-room? We'll be along in a minute.'

'*Haven't* you?' It was just short of a scream.

Sidonie and Gretel gathered up rolls of wallpaper and hurried from the kitchen. They had no wish to be involved in a family scene. I felt like going with them, but I had to know the answer to Mona's question myself. I stayed.

'It was while I was having a few drinks with the old

chums at the Agency the other week,' Nick began, with every appearance of frankness. 'The subject happened to come up. They've bagged a new account: introducing a range of gourmet foods. The cupboard store type; no tins, no freezing, just the special foil packets with extra-long shelf life. They're going to pull out all the stops on this one—' His voice was rising enthusiastically. 'Top billings, sky-high budget, television ads, poster campaign, double-page spreads in all the glossies and Sunday supplements—'

'And where do we come in?' Mona asked coldly. 'I presume we *do* come in somewhere—or have they offered you your old job back?'

Nick winced at the low blow, but Mona was right. Nick would not have been so enthusiastic if he had not found a way to deal himself in on it. I began to have a glimmering of what was coming.

'We got to discussing the shooting—' Nick went on resolutely. Having started, he was going to have to tell her the whole story. 'They wanted something better than the usual studio set-up, something on a long-term basis since, if everything goes well, they'll have to film several series of commericals over the next few years—'

'The dining-room,' Mona said flatly.

'It's perfect. Plenty of space, the french windows opening out into the garden, the chandelier, the big rosewood table. Best of all, they can set up the cameras in the extension and do fourth-wall shooting from there without any crowding.'

'My dining-room,' Mona said. 'In my home. Splashed over every hoarding, in every magazine I pick up, on everyone's television set. You've given away my privacy!'

'*Our* dining-room,' Nick corrected. '*Our* home. And I haven't given anything away. They're paying rather well for the privilege.'

'Yes,' Mona said. 'I wondered why you were being so

generous in the shop. You were positively urging me on to choose the most expensive wallpaper. I thought you were trying to impress the sales clerk, but that wasn't it, was it? It was because you weren't paying for it yourself. The Agency has bought my wallpaper and paint!'

'Of course.' Nick seemed surprised that she could ever have doubted it. 'They wanted the place to look opulent. I told them to leave it to us.' He gave her a crafty smile. 'Once we get the papering and painting out of the way, we'll talk to them about a carpet.'

It was the wrong thing to say. Even Sidonie and Gretel, who had returned to hover in the doorway, knew it.

'We will say good-night now,' Gretel said firmly. She took Sidonie by the elbow and began backing away.

'See you first thing in the morning,' Nick called after them. 'We've got a busy day ahead of us tomorrow.'

'Oh yes,' Mona said. 'We're in a rush, aren't we? How soon does the filming start?'

'Plenty of time,' Nick said serenely. 'A couple of weeks. We'll have the work all done and the paint dry before then. It will work out perfectly.'

'Oh, perfect,' Mona said. 'Perfect! Everything is perfect for you—as long as someone else is paying for it!'

'I don't know what you're upset about. You know we couldn't have afforded this on our own. Perhaps not for years. You're the one who's always on about getting this place finished.'

'But I wanted it for ourselves. Not for everyone who feels like coming in and using it as their own. Not for your film crews, not for your old buddies—not even for your sister and her apprentices. I wanted it for *us!*'

She burst into tears and rushed from the room. We heard her stumble on the stairs and I started forward.

'Better not.' Nick caught my arm. 'It didn't sound as though you were particularly in her good graces either. Just leave her alone. She'll come round, she always does.'

'Some day you're going to push her too far,' I warned him.

'I doubt it,' he said. 'But we'll let her cool down for a few days before I tell her the rest of my plans.'

'The rest? Oh no, Nick! What else have you done?'

Upstairs, the bedroom door slammed. Nick winced.

'I haven't done anything else . . . yet.' He gave me a cheeky grin. 'It's just a brilliant idea in the back of my mind. When the crew gets here and they see the kitchen—'

'Not the kitchen, Nick!' For a moment, I felt murderous. All my sympathies shifted over to Mona. 'We *need* the kitchen for cooking. *That's* our livelihood. We can't have film crews and actors underfoot there.'

'Not actors,' Nick said. 'That's the beauty of it. Just Mona.'

'Mona?'

'She's a good-looking woman. You may not have noticed it, but she is. With just enough maturity to inspire confidence in consumers. And the way she handles the food and equipment: that sureness of touch, the no-nonsense way she can decapitate a carrot. They'll love her. A few subtle words in the ear of the director and producer, and you wait and see. They'll have her dishing up the sponsor's product in no time.'

'Oh no. You'll never be able to talk her into that one.'

'And no reason why it should stop there,' he went on dreamily. 'She'd be a sensation in her own cooking series, using her own recipes. I can see it all—' He stretched out a hand, unrolling a glorious future. 'Today, dunking the new product in boiling water; tomorrow, the new Fanny Cradock!'

'But you're no Johnnie! She'll never do it. She'll see you in hell first!'

'Don't bet on it,' he said smugly. 'She's putty in my hands. Just let me work around to it in my own time and my own way. You'll see. And then you can call me Svengali.'

'I wouldn't dream of it,' I said. 'If Svengali had only had your nerve, he'd have been Emperor of Europe.'

CHAPTER 12

It was more than a week before Mona began to thaw out and return to a state approximating pleasant. During this time, Nick walked on eggshells and acted the part of the model husband. He stayed close to home, never suggested dropping down to have a drink with the boys, and gave no indication that he had any plans for the future beyond getting the dining-room into the best possible order.

It was too much to hope that he had abandoned his idea. The occasional glint in his eyes as he surveyed a particularly photogenic moment in the kitchen (Mona removing a tray of muffins from the oven; Mona stirring a steaming cauldron of soup and testing the flavour by tilting the hollow-handled wooden spoon so that the soup ran down from the large bowl at the stirring end to the small sipping bowl in her hand) betrayed him.

All the world's a stage. And Nick was more than willing—he was eager—to turn his entire home into one great big stage-set.

Some women would have relished the prospect. Lexie would have revelled in it. But Mona was a private person by nature and she had been raised in the old-fashioned tradition: a lady gets her name in the newspapers on only three occasions in her life; when she is born, when she marries and when she dies. Anything more was vulgar and ostentatious.

Mona cherished her privacy; she wanted her home and her life to belong to herself—and Nick. Now Nick was destroying the privacy of their home. Just wait until she discovered that he planned to strip away her personal privacy and turn her into a public figure! I wouldn't be surprised if she sprinkled ground glass over the crunchy breadcrumbs and chopped almonds of his apricot crumble some night. I wasn't sure I'd blame her if she did.

Meanwhile, the dining-room was nearly finished. Nick had done the ceiling first, inexpertly and by himself, but it hadn't looked too bad after the second coat. The rest of us took turns painting the woodwork, alternating with the necessary chores in the kitchen. Sidonie had worked with her usual calm competence, although her heart was obviously in the kitchen. Lexie had been surprisingly co-operative and cheerful, if a bit slapdash. Gretel had amazed us all.

For the first time, we had discovered something Gretel could do without constantly putting her foot wrong. She handled paintbrushes with ease, almost with skill; but it was when we reached the delicate task of matching and hanging strips of wallpaper that she really came into her own. She scampered up and down the stepladder, patiently adjusting the long strip of wallpaper by fractions of an inch until the pattern matched so exactly we could not see the join after we stuck it down. She was laughing and exultant when she realized she could do something better than the rest of us.

Unfortunately, *her* heart was still in the kitchen, too.

'I have been finding some wonderful old English cookbooks in the Portobello Road markets,' she confided to me. 'You must come to dinner, Jean, and let me show you. Such recipes you never have seen!'

That was what I was afraid of. Some English cookbooks, even in recent times, had been published with deadly errors in them. Every now and again one saw a desperate plea from a publisher asking for the return of all copies of a certain cookbook and added that, if you did not wish to return the book and receive another, for God's sake, do not attempt the recipe on page such-and-such.

Most recently, an enterprising cookery writer (who clearly did not test all her recipes or the publication would have been posthumous) had included a recipe for a delicious dish of cooked rhubarb leaves—the part you normally throw away. (*Why just cook the rhubarb stalks and waste all those lovely green leaves?* she had asked. 'Because they're loaded with deadly oxalic acid and can kill you, that's why,' someone had answered.) Erratum slips had gone flying, presumably to good effect, since there had been no subsequent reports of deaths and lawsuits.

I decided it was my duty to have dinner with Gretel and check out those cookbooks. Murphy's Law ruled when Gretel stepped into a kitchen: if anything could go wrong, it would. Getting hold of one of those misprinted cookbooks would be typical of her.

'Just something very light,' I had insisted, vestiges of self-preservation clinging to me. 'I'll be having a hearty lunch with a prospective client earlier. I couldn't possibly eat much.'

'A light supper,' Gretel had promised. 'That will be easy. You will see.'

'It smells delicious,' I said as I entered, uncomfortably aware that this might be the only genuine compliment I could bestow during the course of the evening. Gretel's creations often looked and smelled delicious—but, as some sage had observed, the proof of the pudding was in the eating.

'Thank you. Let me take your coat,' Gretel said, beaming. 'Come and have a drink.'

We moved out of the diminutive hallway into an almost equally tiny sitting-room with a table and two straight chairs in one corner. 'You will have sherry?'

'That will be fine.' I sat in an armchair while Gretel carried my coat through to the small bedroom. I had seen her flat before; it was a single flat like thousands of others in London, rebuilt to squeeze too many rooms into too small a space, in not very good repair, and renting for an iniquitous sum. The alternative was a huge mansion flat, shared with several other people—some of them strangers—and renting for a hugely iniquitous sum.

Behind me, I could hear Gretel fussing around in the kitchen, then she reappeared with glasses of sherry and a dish of salted almonds which she set by my elbow.

'There,' she said, sitting down. 'This is so nice, *ja*?' She looked around with dissatisfaction. 'In so small a flat, one should not feel sometimes lonely. Sidonie and Lexie are so lucky to share a flat. They have such fun. And you, in the big house with your family. There is always someone to laugh with.'

'Yes,' I said doubtfully. There hadn't been many laughs with Nick and Mona lately.

'I have sometimes thought,' she confided, 'of asking Sidonie and Lexie if they would have room for me. It is such a big flat. Do you think they would mind?'

'I don't think they'd mind your asking,' I said cautiously. 'But I don't know if they *do* have so much extra room. The flat belongs to Sidonie's family and I think they have to keep a spare bedroom available in case her parents want to stay in town at any time.'

'Oh,' she sighed. 'I was hoping, perhaps, they might like to have another there to help with the bills.'

'You can try.' I dipped idly into the salted almonds—they seemed to be rather unevenly toasted. 'It can't do any harm to ask.'

'Perhaps I will try,' Gretel said with an air of decision. 'As you say, it cannot— What is the matter? Are you all right?'

I couldn't answer, I was choking. I had the feeling that

something had exploded in my mouth and was taking the top of my head off. I gagged, choked and managed to expel the contents of my mouth into the tiny paper cocktail napkin Gretel had provided. Then I lay back, gasping for air, eyes watering.

'What is wrong?' Gretel bent over me anxiously. 'Is it a fit? Should I call a doctor?'

'Gretel,' I said weakly. 'Gretel, what did you *do* to those almonds?'

'I do them just the way I learn from you,' she said. She paused and sniffed the air as I inhaled and exhaled rapidly several times. 'Oh dear . . .'

'Yes,' I said, a trifle grimly I sat up and wiped my eyes, then cautiously opened the paper napkin for a closer inspection. '*Oh dear!*'

'So that is where they went,' Gretel said with an air of enlightenment. A mystery had been explained. 'I know I have peeled more garlic cloves, but when I go to press them, they are not there.'

A peeled garlic clove and a blanched almond; two gleaming white ovals, almost indistinguishable at a quick glance. When you considered Gretel working with both raw materials at the same time, there was an almost fated inevitability about the whole thing.

'I must have dropped some garlic cloves into the almonds when I am placing them in the baking tray.' Gretel was still working it out. 'So that is why some of them came out a funny colour. I thought it was that the oven did not heat properly.'

'Yes,' I said. I should have been more careful. Everything Gretel attempted in the culinary line required close inspection before commiting it to the palate.

'Oh, Jean, I am so sorry. Is it awful?'

'It *is* rather ghastly.' I sipped at the sherry and made a face. Everything tasted of garlic. 'Could I have a glass of water, please?'

'Yes, yes!' She dashed to get it. I heard the clink of ice tumbling into a tall glass and wondered wryly if she could manage to ruin *that*.

She had done her best. There were tiny flowers embedded in the centre of the ice cubes. Since they resembled no known blooms, I had to assume they were some plastic fantasy. They looked pretty enough suspended in the ice, but were going to look pretty dispiriting slumped at the bottom of the glass when the ice melted. They were also a trap for any unwary drinker who might drain the glass without due care and attention.

I wasn't going to linger over my drink that long. I gulped it greedily, letting the icy water anæsthetize my taste-buds. Gradually the aftertaste of garlic began to fade.

'You are all right?' Gretel asked anxiously. 'I must go now to cook the meal—'

'Please,' I said. 'No garlic. I've had enough to last me a long while.'

'No, no,' she assured me. 'No garlic. It is mushroom omelette. With herbs. Very delicate flavour—garlic would kill it.'

It had nearly killed me, but I allowed myself to relax. The proposed dish sounded harmless, except—

'Where did you get the mushrooms?' I asked cautiously. 'You didn't pick them yourself, did you?' With commercially-grown mushrooms available at all times in shops, Gretel might not realize that the season for wild mushrooms was between late July and late September. It would be only too like her to have noticed and picked any mushroom-like fungus she had found growing in a park or garden.

'No, no,' she laughed. 'When would I have the time? Where would I go to do so? No, I buy these in the market early this morning.'

I relaxed again. That should be all right. 'Is there anything I can do to help?'

'No, no. You sit there and finish your drink. Everything is under control.'

If it was, it was the first time. I leaned back and sipped at my sherry again. It tasted less obnoxious this time; almost like sherry, in fact. Another few minutes and my sense of taste might return.

There were clattering sounds from the kitchen, but I forced myself to remain seated. I tried to occupy myself by attempting to identify the various noises emanating from the kitchen.

Crack—that was obviously a knife breaking an egg. *Clack*—that was an empty eggshell hitting the floor. I hoped it was empty.

Butter began sizzling and spitting in the frying-pan while Gretel beat the eggs vigorously enough to chip the bowl. I hoped she hadn't used so much butter it would splatter on to the gas flames and set the frying-pan alight.

There was too much to worry about. The kitchen was fraught with peril when someone like Gretel was working in it.

There was a final explosion of sound: the hiss as the mixture was poured into the hot frying-pan; a long triumphant sigh of relief from Gretel; and then the steady bubbling sound as the mixture settled down and began to cook—too rapidly and at too high a temperature, but a leathery omelette was something I could manage.

'Very soon now—' Gretel whirled back into the room, tossing dishes and cutlery on to the table and setting our places with more enthusiasm than care. She should not have left the omelette unattended, but I didn't feel that I ought to sound too much like an instructor since this was a social visit. Apart from which, I had the fated feeling that nothing was going to save the omelette, anyway.

'Sit there! Sit there!' Gretel protested as I made to get

up. 'There is nothing you can do. I have done it all.'

That was what I was afraid of. I settled back in my chair and tried not to look at the plastic petals beginning to protrude from the melting ice cubes.

I heard the gurgle of wine running into tulip-shaped glasses, a further jangle of cutlery, then Gretel's footsteps returning to the kitchen. 'You can sit up at the table now,' she called. 'I am coming right in.'

I dutifully took my place. Gretel re-entered in a triumphal rush and plonked a heated plate in front of me. I stared down at the food, bemused, trying to think of a polite comment. I had never seen a rigid omelette before.

'It smells delicious.' That much, I could manage with perfect truth. I probed delicately at it with a fork—and encountered firm resistance.

Surely she hadn't booby-trapped the omelette with plastic flowers? No, nothing so grand. I probed a little further and dislodged a small twig. After a moment of intensive study, I identified it as something in the dried herb line. I couldn't say what without tasting it and, somehow, I wanted to put off that evil moment.

'Well—' Gretel lifted her glass. 'Cheers, you say.'

'Cheers,' I responded, thinking I could say a lot more than that if I let myself go. But how can you convince someone that she's set her heart on the wrong line of work?

She set down her glass, picked up her fork and dug into her omelette with gusto. I followed her example with a great deal less enthusiasm.

After fighting a fragment of omelette free of the whole, I discovered the reason for its rigidity. The egg coating encased an entire saucer-sized open-cap giant mushroom. While cooked on the outside, the egg mixture that had dribbled into the open gills of the mushroom was still runny. The most charitable thing I could think about

Gretel's use of dried herbs was that she had inadvertently spilled a packet into the omelette while working. Surely she couldn't have used that much deliberately?

I looked up and saw Gretel watching me anxiously. There was nothing I could do but smile and try to eat the concoction. It was like trying to munch one's way through a compost heap.

'I'm afraid I'm not very hungry,' I murmured, leaving as much as I dared.

'Ja.' She gave a resigned nod. She had not been able to finish hers either. 'Perhaps next time I should cut the mushroom up into small pieces?'

'That would help,' I agreed. 'Also, perhaps, a lighter hand with the herbs. And use fresh herbs, if possible.'

'Ja.' She sighed and cleared away the plates, then brightened. 'Now comes dessert,' she announced.

I braced myself.

The refrigerator door opened and shut. There ensued a long silence. Then came a series of clinking sounds and dark Nordic mutterings. I began to grow unnerved.

I bit down a renewed offer of help and crossed to the bookshelves on the other side of the room. I had intended to vet Gretel's choice of cookery books and this seemed as good a time as any. I had the feeling that there was going to be a considerable delay before the next course.

Looking over the miscellany of cookery books ranged along the bookshelves, I realized that Gretel had been speaking loosely when she described them as English cookbooks. They were printed in the English language, but not all of them could be correctly classed as English.

There was the obligatory Mrs Beeton's—one of the later versions, not featuring the apocryphal '*First, catch your hare*'. Which was a shame—I would rather trust Gretel to catch a hare than to cook one.

This edition contained other choice items of shopping advice, however, which gave a fascinating picture of a vanished world of autocratic housewives and long-suffering shopkeepers. I hoped Gretel never attempted to utilize any of these hints; I could not see a modern merchant standing by calmly while his prospective purchaser tested his merchandise for freshness and quality according to Mrs Beeton:

'*In selecting nutmegs, prick them with a pin; if good, the oil will instantly spread round the puncture.*' . . . '*To choose a ham . . . run a skewer in close to the bone in the middle of the ham.*' . . . '*Dip a bright steel knitting needle into the milk . . .*' . . . '*Plunge a knife into the butter . . .*' . . . '*Macaroni, when good, breaks crisply.*'

I had a brief unsteadying vision of Gretel—or anyone else—rampaging through a shop selecting her purchases according to Mrs Beeton's recommended methods, pursued by one of today's shopkeepers who object even to a gentle squeeze of a tomato. These days, it's the consumers who are downtrodden.

I replaced Mrs Beeton and continued along the bookshelf. There was a strange American tome featuring such hackle-raising delicacies as Cranberry-Horseradish Mousse and Peanut Butter Aspic. (On the whole, I was beginning to feel that I had got off lightly with tonight's menu.)

Yet another proclaimed itself 'An American Cookbook for India'. Entranced, I read its opening homily: '*Finding your cook is the first step towards having good food and serving it well, for your dinners will be no better than the man who makes them.*' Oh, that was the right cookbook for Gretel! If there was one thing she needed for perfect meals, it was someone else to cook the food.

She had also unearthed a couple of strange little books about cooking in wartime, so I supposed I could only be thankful that she hadn't tried to feed me Woolton Pie. As it was, one of them strongly advocated something called Hay Box Cookery and gave minute instructions for con-

structing a hay box, suggesting substitute materials in
case the reader could not acquire either asbestos sheeting
or hay. Since the substitutes advocated were, respectively,
many layers of newspapers and small balls of newspaper,
and I had always understood that there was a shortage of
newsprint at that time, I replaced the book on the shelf
marvelling at the resourcefulness of an earlier generation.

However, the cookbooks Gretel had acquired seemed
safe enough. Although some of the recipes struck me as
decidedly eccentric, there was nothing in them that could
actually kill one. Not even one so unwary as to dine with
Gretel.

'Yee-an . . .' A wail of distress came from the kitchen.
'Come and help me, please. I am in trouble with my
yelly!'

'Coming.' She was also in trouble with her 'j' which had
a tendency to slip under stress. It had taken me some time
to grow acccustomed to being called Yean, although she
was improving lately.

I entered the kitchen to find her struggling with a jelly-
mould. Whatever she had put in it seemed determined to
stay in it and she was on the verge of tears.

'Wait a minute,' I said. She had upended the mould
over the serving plate and was shaking it furiously. 'You
won't get far that way. You want to dip a knife into warm
water, dry it, and then run it around the inside of the
mould.'

'I have tried that already!' She gave the mould another
ferocious shake. 'It does not work!'

'Then set the mould in warm water for a minute.'

'I haff tried that, too. It does not work!'

Too late, I remembered hearing the sound of an
electric kettle reaching full steam just before it clicked
off. I glanced at a basin from which steam was still rising.

'We'll try again,' I said encouragingly. 'Keep calm.'

'*Ja*.' With a sigh of exasperation, she plunged the

mould back into the basin of boiling water.

'No, wait a minute—' I rescued the mould and set it down on the table. 'Let's try the knife again first.'

I dipped the knife, dried it and worked it around the inside of the mould. It seemed to encounter sporadic resistance: perhaps there were lumps of fruit in there? I could not discern through the murk.

'What is it?' I asked, hoping I did not sound too dubious.

'It is called Bavarian Fantasy,' Gretel said proudly. 'In three layers; lime chiffon, almond cream and raspberry cream.' She reached for the mould possessively.

'How ambitious.' I let her take the mould with a gloomy certainty that we were heading for disaster. Gretel always wanted to try the most ambitious recipes when she had not yet conquered the basic principles.

'We try again!' Before I could intervene, she upended the mould over the serving plate again instead of putting the plate on top of the mould and then turning it over.

Plop . . . plop . . . swoosh.

The first two layers fell out separately. The final layer, dissolved by the boiling water in the basin, poured green foam over the other two, flooding the serving dish and slopping over on to the table.

'Well, back to the old drawing-board,' I muttered.

Gretel said something explosive in her own language. It was probably just as well that I could not translate.

'Never mind.' I tried to be soothing. 'We just eat the two good layers.' But I had fresh qualms as Gretel poured off the green liquid. The remaining jelly seemed curiously immovable. I began to suspect that we were going to have to cut it with a knife—possibly a carving knife.

'Perhaps we'd better dish up here.' I picked up the serving spoon and, under the guise of passing it to Gretel, managed to tap it experimentally on the raspberry cream. It bounced off.

'*Ja.*' She attacked the jelly with a vigour that suggested she had made jelly—although not in this particular form—before. The serving spoon cut firmly through the resilient mass.

For a moment, I thought she had won—and then I saw the long stringlike threads clinging to the spoon, like tentacles, as she lifted the jelly and tried to deposit it in a dessert dish.

Gretel gave a wordless cry and hurled the spoon, milk jelly and all to the floor. I could not help thinking that that was the best place for it. But Gretel was genuinely upset, hovering between hysteria and tears.

'Never mind,' I said quickly. 'How about some cheese and crackers instead?'

She wavered for another perilous moment, then we met each other's eyes.

It was impossible to say which of us giggled first. Suddenly, we both exploded with laughter, the dangerous moment passed and disappeared. We carried cups of coffee back into the living-room and sat down, still giggling weakly.

At some future point, however, I was going to have to suggest to Gretel that she might do better by switching to a career in interior decoration.

CHAPTER 13

One interesting side-effect of the forthcoming Charity Ball was that Sidonie began to overshadow Lexie for perhaps the first and only time in her life. Neither of them seemed consciously aware of it, but it was happening. Sidonie was more quietly confident, absorbed in committee discussions and arrangements when she wasn't on duty, no longer such a satellite of Lexie's, her own interests becoming paramount.

'Sidders and her stupid old charity work!' Lexie was restive and jeering. 'I don't know how she can bother wasting her time like that.'

'Mm-hmm,' I said absently, spreading pâté on the toast rounds for the Tournedos Rossini. No one would ever have to worry about Lexie wasting time on something that did not benefit her directly.

'But it isn't *fair*,' Lexie complained. 'Sidders's family have more money than God—and she doesn't even *care*. She's more interested in things like this stupid cooking lark. Catch *me* doing it if I didn't have to!'

'You'd better not let her catch you calling her Sidders,' I said. 'You know she doesn't like it.'

Lexie's declaration did not surprise me. I had always known her heart wasn't in her cooking—which was rather a shame. She was quite good at it when she paid attention. It was no secret that she would prefer to be a social butterfly, fluttering from one chic restaurant to another, sitting out front consuming delicious meals rather than being back in the kitchen creating them. Unfortunately, like so many of us, she couldn't afford it. That was what she found so rankling about Sidonie's attitude. Even without coming into her inheritance, Sidonie had enough money to lead the sort of life Lexie longed for, but that life didn't attract Sidonie at all. Sidonie was genuinely and increasingly absorbed in her cooking studies and in her work for charity. Perhaps it was the absorption Lexie envied as much as anything. What Lexie needed was a subject of her own she could immerse herself in—or, perhaps, the ability to do so.

'I'm sorry, Jean.' Belatedly, Lexie realized that she might have been offensive. 'I don't mean there's anything *wrong* with cooking for a living. I'd just rather not, that's all.'

'Then you'd better find a rich husband.' (As though the

idea hadn't been drilled into her from earliest childhood.)

'You sound like my mother.' Before, Lexie had just been rebellious, now she turned bitter. 'She's always going on about it. But it's not all that easy, you know, not when you don't have any money yourself and everyone knows it. They're all looking for heiresses, even if they *are* rich themselves. Two fortunes are better than one. And if you've got land as well . . .'

She let the thought trail off. The air between us was suddenly electric with rancour. I knew she was thinking of the rich acres of Gloucestershire where Sidonie's family farmed and lived in a Queen Anne manor house. Yet another part of her heritage Sidonie did not appreciate enough, for a small portion of which Lexie would have given her eyeteeth.

Really, from Lexie's point of view, it was hardly surprising that she let Sidonie pay so many of her bills. In some obscure corner of her mind, she must feel that it was owing to her. And when Sidonie came into the bulk of her inheritance and was no longer protected by the Trust Fund . . .

'If only my father had lived—' Lexie was suddenly wistful. 'He was brilliant, you know, really he was. Everyone said so. He'd have built up a business of his own—just like Uncle Tris. Bigger. Better. I *know* he would have. But *his* heart was faulty, too—and the doctors didn't know so much about Pacemakers in those days. Uncle Tris was lucky, his trouble didn't develop until much later in life and medical science was so much more advanced. I suppose it's lucky for me, too. If it runs in the family . . .'

Her hand fluttered to her blouse again, but not to undo any button this time. Her fingers slipped between the buttons, pressing against her flesh, testing the beat of a heart that might someday prove treacherous.

'Come on,' I said briskly, trying to conceal a sympathy which might send Lexie from an unconscious concern

into a full-scale dramatic scene if she noticed it. 'The
Board meeting will be breaking up any minute now. We
don't have time for iffing around.'

'All right.' Lexie gave a reluctant laugh and shrugged
her shoulders dismissively. 'My mother married the wrong
brother, that's all. Not that she'd have had much of a
chance with Uncle Tris—he's married to his business. No
woman ever had a chance.'

She was certainly right so far as Lady Pamela was concerned. I had seen Tristram Quardon's face once when a
telephone call had come through from her when I was in
his office. True, no one likes a begging call—and I had
the impression Lady Pamela didn't make any other kind,
at least not to her wealthy relative—but there seemed to
be a more personal dislike behind his cold expression.
Edda had told me that one of the main things he disliked
about Lady Pamela was the way she had raised his
brother's only child—but he had not been fully aware of
that until Lexie had decamped on her ill-fated New York
escapade.

'There, that's done!' Sidonie came back into the
kitchen. She had been setting round the smoked rainbow
trout in the dining-room. The idea was to speed things up
when the Directors finally got round to the thought of
food by having the first course waiting for them. Edda
had suggested it, in the hope of getting them back to work
a bit sooner. We doubted it, but were willing to let her try
the experiment.

Lexie had been spreading the thinly-sliced brown
bread wih unsalted butter and arranging the triangles on
small plates. She held two of the plates out to Sidonie who
took them automatically, but paused before returning to
the dining-room.

'Has Lexie told you the good news?' she asked.

'No.' Nothing Lexie had said so far could possibly be
construed as good news. 'What is it?'

'I was going to let you tell her,' Lexie said. 'It's *your* news.' She began to butter more bread, although we already had enough.

'My birthday present.' Sidonie's face was aglow. 'My father is giving me a microwave oven for the flat. Lexie suggested it to him. Isn't it super? And, Jean, he's letting me have it early so we'll be able to use it at the Charity Ball.'

'How nice,' I said. We could handle the refreshments perfectly well without a microwave oven, but Sidonie was so pleased I hadn't the heart to say anything to dampen her spirits.

'Isn't it?' She beamed. 'I'll be able to cook meals for the freezer and then we can have them as soon as we want them, whatever time we come in.'

'That was what sold your father on the idea,' Lexie said. 'He's the one who arrives unexpectedly at all hours. He's just looking after his own comfort.'

'Pay no attention to her,' I told Sidonie. 'It's a lovely birthday present.'

'Wait until *next* birthday,' Lexie said softly.

Sidonie flushed guiltily and I realized that her next birthday must be the crucial one.

A familiar babble of voices began at the end of the corridor and snapped us all back to attention.

'Here they come,' Sidonie said gratefully.

'Not for ages yet,' Lexie said. 'They're only just out of the meeting. They'll be an hour yet in the bar.'

'Take the bread through, anyway, Sidonie,' I directed.

Roddy nearly collided with her as she dashed past him. 'Is everything all right?' He gave his characteristic territorial call. I could visualize him as one of the not very adventurous feathered species, with drab camouflaging plumage, head ducked low against possible predators, but determined to preserve his nest and nestlings.

'Why shouldn't it be?' Lexie snapped. 'Really, Roddy!'

But it had not always been. It had not been so very long since the worst possible thing had happened in this building. Was Lexie so deep in her own concerns that she had forgotten already?

'What's happening with the investigation?' I asked. 'What are the police doing now?'

'Nothing.' He seemed surprised at the question. 'What should they be doing? The Inquest decided it was all a terrible accident. Misadventure. The building had been renovated before Quardon International took it over and someone botched the wiring. At this point in time, no one could even say who the electricians were or whether they're still in business. It must have been some cowboy outfit. Impossible to trace them now. Amazing something didn't happen before. Of course, Mark didn't use that switch a great deal. He usually used a battery-operated razor, but the batteries had worn down so he reverted to the mains razor he kept in his desk for emergencies. It would probably have been all right even then—if he hadn't spilled that water.'

'Roddy!' Sidonie returned just in time. I was feeling distinctly queasy and I noticed that Lexie had gone a pale green. But Sidonie had not heard the conversation and was intent on her own preoccupations. 'Roddy, *you'll* buy a ticket, won't you?'

'What?' Roddy turned, blinking at this sudden distraction. 'What ticket?'

'For my Charity Ball,' Sidonie said. 'Come on, Roddy, it's in a good cause.'

'Tell him how much it costs,' Lexie jeered. She had regained her colour and was enjoying Roddy's discomfiture.

Sidonie told him and Roddy went green in his turn. 'Come on, Roddy,' Sidonie said again, while I marvelled silently. Once—and not so long ago—she would never have thrust herself forward like this. Now she advanced on Roddy, gently bullying, brandishing the ticket. 'You know you can afford it. Just one ticket—you don't even have to take anyone. Lexie and I will be there and we'll dance with you. Just one ticket—'

'Ticket? Ticket? What is tickets?' Ongar Manganian was suddenly in our midst. I had known he was back in town, but I hadn't been certain that he would be at Quardon today. Just in case, though, I had prepared Tournedos Rossini.

'For my Charity Ball—' Lexie turned to him. 'Next week. Would you like one?'

'An English Charity Ball—' Ongar Manganian advanced into the kitchen, Aldo right behind him, and removed the printed card from Sidonie's fingers.

'I was just buying one myself, Mr Manganian,' Roddy said quickly. 'It's a very good cause.' He fumbled for his chequebook.

'And you think I will enjoy this?' Ongar Manganian brought a fierce gaze to bear on Sidonie.

'I'm sure you will,' she said pertly, almost flirtatiously. Perhaps she had been getting more than it seemed out of her association with Lexie; perhaps she had been studying Lexie's methods of handling men. 'You see,' she added, with the air of one producing an ace of trumps, 'Jean is doing the catering.'

'Ah!' He gave her an approving nod. 'You know your best selling point. You are a clever young lady. It does, indeed, make a difference that Jean is doing the cooking. It is always valuable to know that a trustworthy cook is in charge.'

He glanced keenly at Aldo and a silent message seemed to pass between them. 'We will have two tickets,' he decided.

So he didn't trust me enough to come without his official taster.

'I'm sure Mr Quardon will want a ticket, too,' Roddy said.

'Don't worry.' Sidonie was triumphant. 'I've already got him. Two tickets! He's bringing Edda Price.'

'That is well.' Ongar Manganian nodded again. 'I have the feeling that she is a lady who could do with more festivity in her life.'

'You needn't feel sorry for *her*—' The words seemed torn from Roddy. 'She gets what she wants—in her own quiet way.'

And now did she want Tristram Quardon? Something in his tone brought that suspicion to mind. But if so, what about that invalid husband lurking in the background? I saw Lexie catch the implication. Her head snapped up and turned briefly in Roddy's direction.

The nuances appeared to have escaped Ongar Manganian. He crossed the room in pursuit of his major interest and began browsing among the saucepans on the stove.

'Ah, asparagus tips,' he approved. He had already given a happy smile to the Tournedos Rossini as he passed them. He lifted the lid of another saucepan. 'And new potatoes.' He replaced the lid and looked around. 'And for dessert?'

'In the fridge,' I said resignedly. He opened the door with the air of a child trying not to tear too greedily at his stocking on Christmas morning.

'Ah, crème caramel. Excellent! Splendid!' He straightened and beamed down at me. 'I shall now join the others for an apéritif in blissful anticipation of the feast awaiting me.' Still beaming, he left the room, Aldo following closely at his heels as though to guard him from a sudden stab in the back.

'You certainly know how to please the old boy, Jean.' There was an edge to Roddy's voice which made the remark more of an insinuation than a compliment.

'Anything edible would please him,' I said and, wanting to retaliate, added, 'But what have you been doing since we last saw you? Have you found our cheese wire yet?'

'Cheese wire?' He looked at me blankly, as though I had suddenly lapsed into Sanskrit.

'The garotte,' I amended nastily. 'The one that went missing from our supplies the last time we were here.'

'Oh yes, I remember. The thing that foreign girl kept rabbiting on about. If you ask me, she lost it and was afraid to admit it. Probably let it fall out of the window or something and didn't want to tell you.'

'Gretel wouldn't do that,' I said.

'No? I notice you don't have her with you today. Got rid of her, have you?'

'Gretel is working with Mona today,' I said coldly. 'You aren't our only client, you know.'

Actually, we had no other assignment today. Gretel and Mona were cooking in anticipation of the first photographic session in the dining-room tomorrow. We were expected to provide all the frills and garnishes for the products they would be photographing. A subdued Gretel had volunteered to remain with Mona today.

I think Gretel was still feeling abashed at her failure to set the perfect meal before me, flawlessly cooked, which she had so obviously planned in her imagination. She now dogged Mona's footsteps, watching every move, as though she might discover the secret of perfect cooking if only she paid close enough attention. I knew that she was beginning to get on Mona's nerves, but everything was getting on Mona's nerves these days. It was safer to leave her with Mona today than to take her along where she might wreak more havoc.

'Poor Gretel,' Lexie said. 'You shouldn't be so hard on her, Roddy. Just because you've fallen down on your job.' There was a challenge in her voice. 'Finding the cheese wire, I mean.'

'It's nowhere to be found.' Roddy almost snapped at

her. 'I've told you. Either your foreign girl lost it, or
someone else —' he glanced over his shoulder — 'carried it
out of the building with him.'

I remembered Roddy's slanderous earlier theory that
Ongar Manganian might have taken it to New York for
dark purposes of his own. I didn't blame Roddy for being
reluctant to repeat it if Ongar Manganian was on the
premises and possibly within earshot.

'Here's your ticket, Roddy.' Sidonie gave it to him with
an air of faint disapproval and stood waiting while he
wrote out his cheque.

CHAPTER 14

Nick was playing with fire again.

Mona had been in a bad mood when we returned to the
house yesterday afternoon and she was in a worse mood
this morning. It didn't help that the hallway was cluttered
with camera and lighting equipment and criss-crossed
with cables. Strangers tracked mud through it and into
the dining-room. It was as well that the decorating hadn't
extended to a carpet or she really would have been
hysterical.

As it was, she went about the kitchen tight-lipped,
except to snap at Gretel when she found her too close on
her heels. Lexie and Sidonie kept well out of her way.
Nick was in the dining-room, reliving past glories with his
old colleagues and taking bows on his perspicacity in
getting out of the rat-race in time and setting himself up
in such a thriving new business where he was his own boss.

Of necessity, I was acting as liaison between the dining-
room and kitchen. Mona wasn't speaking to Nick, and
she wasn't saying very much to me. I knew that Nick had
not yet approached her with his ideas for making her rich

and famous—and I wasn't looking forward to her reaction when he did.

They were shooting stills for magazine ads today and for the next few sessions. I knew that by the time they were ready to start filming, Nick hoped to have manipulated them into using Mona instead of a professional model. To this end, he had already started making leading remarks.

'I must show you round after we've got this set up,' Nick said to the clutch of Directors (Creative, Photographic, Product, Sales and Unidentified) surrounding him. 'Wait until you see the kitchen!'

I shook my head vehemently at him. Mona had ruled the kitchen out of bounds. If any of them showed his head round the door, she was likely to start throwing things.

'After lunch,' Nick said blandly. 'We can't intrude on them right now—Mona's fixing something special for our lunch.'

'Oh, super!' one of them said, the others made enthusiastic noises. 'I'd hate to have to eat the product.'

I backed out of the room hastily and made for the kitchen. If Mona was expecting to feed them it was news to me. She was practically on strike, doing the absolute minimum at the slowest pace possible. The only time she had shown any animation was first thing this morning when she had come down to the kitchen carrying her handbag and placed it conspicuously on the table in the far corner. She had then insisted that the girls do the same. ('We want to be able to keep an eye on them. We don't know what sort of riff-raff we'll have tramping through the place today!') The handbags huddled on the table and Mona ostentatiously moved to block them from view whenever any of the crew walked past the doorway. It did not augur well for future relationships.

Nevertheless, Nick had plainly announced to everyone that we were going to provide lunch and it would be fatal not to, whereas to do so would be good public relations for the private restaurant service we hoped to inaugurate in the dining-room after the filming had finished.

'Does this look all right, Jean?' As I entered the kitchen, Lexie thrust a colourful platter under my nose. Tomatoes were cut into water-lily shapes and filled with hardboiled egg yolks mixed with mayonnaise; the egg whites had been cut into star shapes, one of which perched neatly in the centre of the egg mayonnaise, the rest were scattered over the bed of lettuce leaves on which the tomatoes nestled.

'Very nice,' I approved absently. Perhaps a trifle gaudy, but doubtless very photogenic. 'Take them through, will you, dear?' If they weren't what was wanted, let Nick tell her. I had other problems.

Mona faced me almost as though she knew what was coming. She probably did. Nick must have mentioned it at some point if he thought she was going to do it. My dear brother had not yet assimilated just how opposed his wife was to his bright ideas.

'About lunch—' I began hesitantly.

'Yes?' There was a dangerous light in Mona's eyes.

'Er . . . Nick is expecting us to give them lunch . . . you know?'

'I know.' Her tone was too pleasant, it didn't match her expression. 'That's all in hand—' She gestured. 'Gretel is making one of her special ragouts for them.'

'You wouldn't!' I gasped. She knew how much might depend on it. 'You couldn't!'

'Couldn't I?' She gave me a small deadly smile and turned away. The subject was closed.

'It's all right, Jean.' Sidonie was at my elbow. 'We're keeping an eye on her.'

I moved cautiously towards Gretel's corner and was not reassured to find her with mortar and pestle crushing juniper berries. I had the distinct impression that the only form in which Nick's mates favoured juniper berries was distilled. They were going to wish they had stuck with the product.

I wondered if I ought to warn them. But then I carelessly allowed myself to meet Gretel's glowing eyes. Her self-confidence was restored; her pride redeemed.

Had I the right to destroy that for what might turn out to be just more of Nick's problematical pie in the sky?

'In two hours,' she promised me. 'Such a meal as you have never seen!'

That was what I was afraid of. Especially considering what I had already seen.

'It's all right,' Sidonie murmured again; she was still at my elbow. 'I'll keep a close watch.'

'Fine!' I hoped I said it heartily. I smiled impartially at both of them, but put my trust in Sidonie. She had been working with us long enough to be able to spot anything potentially disastrous. Although, with Gretel, one could never be sure. She never made the same mistake twice— but she had a gift for discovering new mistakes.

I tore my gaze away from Gretel's table. She obviously considered this her big chance and was seizing it with both hands—and every condiment in the kitchen. Heady fumes arose from a large bowl in which unidentifiable cubes of meat were steeping in an alcoholic brew. (Well, she had the right idea there.)

Mona stood at the sink, her back to us, listening but unhelpful. She was hoping something would go so wrong that it would drive the interlopers out of her house for good. She did not quite dare to sabotage the proceedings herself, so she was using Gretel as her catspaw.

I moved towards the door, Sidonie moving with me. 'Try to keep things under control,' I said. 'See that she doesn't swamp it with spices. Don't let her use too much—'

'Don't worry,' Sidonie said. 'She can't do much harm

with that lot—and there isn't any rat poison in the house, is there?'

'If there were,' I said, 'Mona would have put it in Nick's coffee this morning.'

From the dining-room, I heard Nick calling me. I hurried through to face whatever molehill his colleagues had blown up into a mountain, if not a smouldering volcano.

'Mashed potatoes!' Nick greeted me as though the fate of the world depended upon instant obedience to his command. 'Pyramid shape—done with the ice-cream scoop.'

I froze a smile on my face as I looked around the room. The arc lights were in place, the cameras trained on a bone china place setting flanked by shimmering silver and crystal glasses. A serving dish full of the Product glittered suspiciously just modestly off-centre, not so much preserved in aspic as immobilized with varnish.

Lexie, surrounded by advertising executives, was unbuttoned to the limits of decency and laughing extravagantly at some remark that had just been made.

'Right!' I said crisply. 'Mashed potatoes. Lexie, see to it! And quickly, please!'

She stopped laughing and gave me a poisonous glare. But she should have returned to the kitchen as soon as she placed her platter of tomatoes on the table. I had her dead to rights and she knew it.

Breathing deeply with indignation—a touch wasted on me—she brushed past me, ostentatiously neither speaking to me nor looking at me. From this blow, I could recover. The men watched her leave with regret.

'You've got a lot of hungry men working up an appetite here—' Nick was in the wrong for not having despatched Lexie back to the kitchen and he tried to cover it by blustering at me. 'How is the lunch coming along?'

'Just fine, thank you.' Revenge was sweet and

instantaneous. 'Gretel is taking care of it.'

Nick lost colour, his jaw dropped and he closed his mouth again with a visible effort. His eyes pleaded with me to tell him I was joking. I shook my head.

'Excuse me.' He gave his colleagues a sickly smile. 'There's a technical detail I ought to check—'

Cravenly, I remained in the dining-room patiently moving serving dishes around the table while the camera crew decided on the most flattering angle. I kept one ear cocked towards the kitchen, but heard no major explosion. After a while, Nick returned, looking wan but not entirely desolate. Apparently some sort of compromise had been reached.

Sidonie had done an excellent job of curbing Gretel's contemplated excesses—perhaps she had tactfully taken over the cooking itself in the final stages. The meal was quite tasty, if something short of gourmet standard.

However, Nick had taken the precaution of lavishing pre-luncheon cocktails upon his friends, as well as providing several bottles of good wine with the meal. By the time they arrived at the coffee and brandy, they were decidedly mellow and just short of falling off their chairs. Which was exactly the way Nick wanted them. If any of them felt unwell later in the afternoon, they would attribute it to overindulgence in the alcoholic refreshment rather than suspect the meal itself.

By the time we had cleared the dishes away and they had reeled back to the business end of the table, we had three bookings for private parties and a preliminary enquiry about catering for the agency's next Christmas party.

So far, so good.

Nick was bustling about trying to look more sober than the others and be helpful while they went on shooting. I realized that he was trying to keep their minds off the

promised tour of the kitchen until the girls had had a
chance to finish the washing up and the place did not
look quite so sordid.

The afternoon's shooting proceeded at a slower pace
than the morning's since the technicians were no longer so
sure whether it was the cameras or their eyes which were
out of focus. It couldn't move slowly enough to suit me; I
hoped that they would reach the hour at which some
fervid union member would call 'time' and they would all
depart so swiftly that Nick would have no chance to
further his Machiavellian schemes.

It was a vain hope, of course. Nick had never in all his
life let his eyes waver from the main chance and he was
keeping watch on the clock, too.

'Tea-time!' He struck just as the clock struck four.
'Suppose we pop into the kitchen and see if we can
organize a cup of tea?'

I had been waiting for something like that. I backed
out of the doorway as Nick and his executive chums
started forward. I was in the kitchen well before they
could get there, ready to try one last gambit to keep the
peace.

'Mona,' I said, 'I'm sorry, but I'm terribly tied up with
this lot. Do you think you could nip up to my flat and get
me my—?'

'I will go!' Gretel was still aglow with her triumph. I
shook my head at her, but she was beyond signals. 'Was it
not wonderful?' She started for the door. 'Every scrap off
their plates, they eat! She did not have triumphs like that
often. 'Nothing was left! They truly enjoyed it!'

On a wave of euphoria, she sailed through the doorway
and up the stairs without having noticed that I had not
told her what I wanted fetched. Mona remained by the
stove, watching me suspiciously. Lexie and Sidonie
paused by the cupboard where they were stacking the
dishes away, looking at both of us warily, as though

conscious of a gathering storm.

'Mona, dear—' I began again, but too late.

'Hello, my loves.' Nick stood in the doorway, the various directors massed behind him. 'What about a spot of tea for some parched throats?' He led the others into the kitchen.

'We're busy,' Mona said abruptly. 'We can't have people underfoot.'

'We'll make it ourselves.' He smiled ingratiatingly. 'You girls gave us a magnificent meal, we ought to be able to make a pot of tea for ourselves. Just carry on with what you were doing—don't let us disturb you.'

Stepping forward, he put an arm around Mona's shoulders and moved her to one side. 'We can manage,' he said reassuringly. 'You just take it easy.'

Behind him, one of the directors gasped. 'Look at that!'

The Aga was in plain view now, a cauldron bubbling at the back, a kettle humming on a front hob. On the wall behind it, a range of copper-bottomed utensils shone in the artificial light. Bags of dried herbs, suspended from the ceiling, swayed gently from the motion of bodies moving past. Strings of onions, garlic, red and green peppers, sausages . . .

Even I had to admit that the effect was supremely photogenic, although I noted that most of the more picturesque items had been moved into the kitchen from the larder at some time when I hadn't been paying attention and, obviously, neither had Mona.

'What a scene!' the man (was he the Artistic Director?) said. 'What a fantastic setting!'

'Is it?' Nick blinked with surprise. As though viewing the kitchen for the first time through different eyes, he stepped back, raised his hands in front of his eyes, making a frame of them, and peered through it intently.

'Yes,' he acknowledged slowly, as though bowing to superior wisdom. 'Yes, I suppose it is.'

'No!' Mona hurled herself forward to stand in front of the Aga, arms spread out defensively, as though protecting it from vandals. 'Oh no you don't!'

'Your soup is boiling over, dear,' Nick warned mildly.

'Oh no!' Mona whirled and dashed to bend over the steaming cauldron. It was nowhere near boiling over, of course, but she gave it a precautionary stir and then automatically lifted the sipping spoon to her lips to taste it, presenting them with just the picture Nick had been angling for.

'Bloody marvellous!' one of them said. 'Nick, you craftly old sod, how long have you been keeping this one up your sleeve?'

'She *is* good, isn't she?' Nick said modestly. 'Just looking at her, you *know* that soup is going to be perfection itself.

'Bloody marvellous!' the man said again, pivoting slowly to take in all the aspects of the kitchen. He raised his voice. 'Bert! Come through here a minute, will you? Bring a camera!'

'No!' Mona stepped forward, facing Nick as though she might spring at him like a tigress. 'Not *my* house! Not *my* kitchen?' All that saved him was that she hadn't realized yet that he was planning to use her, as well.

'It's my house, too,' Nick reminded her unforgivably. 'And my kitchen.'

'Oh!' That did it. She struck so swiftly Nick had no time to dodge. The wooden spoon she was still holding broke with the force of the blow and Nick went reeling.

Mona ran from the room, grabbing blindly for her handbag from the table and pushing past the men clustered around Nick. We heard the front door slam behind her.

'Poor girl.' Nick smiled weakly, nursing his jaw. 'She's overwhelmed, that's all.'

The men nodded, accepting the explanation. In their world, people queued up—on their knees, if necessary—

for the opportunity to become a public figure through television exposure. They could not imagine that anyone might find it repugnant.

Nick didn't deserve sympathy. I let the men struggle to lift him into the rocking-chair and crossed the kitchen to join Sidonie and Lexie. Sidonie was holding a handbag in her hands—it was Mona's.

'She went off with mine,' Sidonie said. 'She couldn't see what she was doing, she was crying so.'

'She'll be back as soon as she's calmed down a bit,' I heard Nick assuring his colleagues. I looked across the room at him.

'Don't bet on it,' I said.

CHAPTER 15

We decided to let Nick stew in his own juice for a while.

Sidonie had called me on my private line much later that night. 'It's all right, Jean. Mona's here.'

'Thank heavens!' Of course, I had been fairly certain that Mona wouldn't do anything desperate—she wasn't the suicidal type—but it was a relief to know where she was and that she was safe.

'I'm afraid she doesn't want to speak to you,' Sidonie said hesitantly. 'In fact, she doesn't know I'm calling, but I thought I ought to.'

'Quite right,' I said. 'But it might be better not to let her know that you've contacted me until she's—er—less upset. She *is* still upset, I suppose?' It was an unnecessary question; if Mona wasn't still upset, she'd have come home.

'I'm afraid so,' Sidonie said. 'Oh, not with you, especially, but with Nick . . . and the way things have been going.'

'I know,' I said.

'It was quite sensible of her to come here,' Sidonie said. 'Of course, as soon as she realized she had my handbag, she wanted to return it. And it had my keys in it, so we found her waiting for us when we got back. I don't think she quite knew where else to go.'

'I suppose she didn't.' Most of Mona's old friends—the ones she hadn't shared with Nick and who could be trusted not to give her away—lived up near the Scottish border. It was one thing to take Sidonie's handbag in honest mistake for her own, but it would have been beyond Mona's sense of propriety to use money from it.

'She can stay here with us for a few days while she cools down,' Sidonie said. 'There's plenty of room. And we'll be able to smuggle whatever she needs to her.'

'That's a good idea,' I approved. It was certainly a lot better than having Mona wander off again and disappear to heaven knows where. 'Do you think she'll agree?'

'I think so,' Sidonie said. 'So long as we promise not to let Nick know where she is.'

'That's fine with me,' I said. 'Let him squirm a bit. He has it coming!'

For the remainder of the week, Nick went not-so-quietly to pieces. In front of his advertising chums, who were still cluttering up the dining-room, he maintained the pretence that Mona had been called away to care for her sick mother. At the end of the day, when they had all gone, he paced the kitchen, raging.

'Where *is* she? Where can she have gone? I've rung everyone we ever knew and none of them have seen her. She can't just have vanished off the face of the earth!'

'People do.' Lexie twisted the knife with concealed glee. 'You hear about it all the time. They're never found again. That's because most people disappear to escape from an intolerable situation. The police know that,

that's why they don't break their necks to find anyone
unless it's someone under age, or they think there was
something suspicious about the disappearance.' She
smiled sweetly at Nick. '*Have* you gone to the police, yet?'

'No!' She knew he had not. He was terrified of the
possible publicity, of all his friends finding out that his
wife had left him. Unless or until Mona was found
floating in the Thames, Nick would keep the police out of
it.

'Oooh,' Gretel mourned. 'It is so sad, so terrible. This
was always such a happy place and now . . . now . . .' She
broke off, choking back sobs. We had decided that it was
safer not to tell her that Mona was all right. In the
kindness of her heart, she might have blurted it out to
Nick and put him out of his misery. As it was, Gretel's air
of being in a house of bereavement was undermining
Nick's nerves far more effectively than any sniping we
could do.

'You should not stand here and do nothing.' Gretel
appealed to Nick with desperate earnestness. 'You should
call for Scotland Yard — if it is not already too late!'

'Oh no!' Sidonie said quickly, as Nick looked irresolute.
'It's much too early to think about the police. I'm sure
Mona will come back as soon as she's had a bit of time to
cool down.'

'Perhaps she's got amnesia.' Wickedly, Lexie stirred it
up a bit more. 'The way she rushed out of here, she might
have tripped and fallen and hit her head. She could be
wandering around somewhere, not knowing who she is or
where she belongs—'

'Oh, that is terrible!' Gretel gasped. 'It cannot be
allowed. You *must* go to Scotland Yard!'

'We have no reason to believe anything of the sort has
happened.' I divided an icy look between Gretel and
Lexie. 'I suggest we keep calm.'

'That's all very well for you to say.' Nick was perspiring

visibly. 'You aren't lying awake most of the night thinking about all the terrible things that might have happened to her. And when I do sleep,' he brooded, 'I have nightmares.'

'Oh, poor man!' Gretel said. If she had known the truth, she would have blurted it out at that moment. The rest of us were made of sterner stuff.

'You've always been subject to nightmares,' I reminded him. I could remember many childhood nights disturbed by Nick's sudden shouts of rage or alarm. 'You've even had nightmares when an advertising campaign was going badly.'

'Little sister—' he glared at me bitterly— 'you were ever such a comfort to me.'

'You brought this on yourself,' I said. 'You know Mona never wanted any part of turning her home into a three-ring circus.'

'It's my home, too,' he muttered sulkily.

'*And* you've pointed that out once too often. You should have known better.'

'I'm *sure* everything is going to be all right.' Sidonie intervened hastily, unwilling to be witness to what was devolving into a sibling squabble. Lexie snorted with suppressed laughter; a family fight was her idea of light entertainment. 'Mona is bound to come back soon.'

'She'd better hurry. Perhaps you've forgotten—' Nick had a try at spreading the alarm and despondency. 'Your Charity Ball is next week and we're short-handed as it is. if Mona doesn't come back, you're going to have to pay for extra help, she does as much work as two or three people.'

'I'm *certain* she won't let us down.' Sidonie was in danger of giving the game away by being too unworried. She seemed to realize this just in time. 'And anyway,' she added, 'Lexie and I can slip behind the scenes and help out, if necessary. No one will mind if we do.'

'*I'll* mind!' Lexie protested. 'You may enjoy playing High Priestess of the Pantry, but I'm looking forward to being one of the guests for a change. It isn't fair if you're going to make me work. It's my evening off!'

'You needn't worry.' Sidonie gave her cousin a cold look. 'I'm *sure* Mona won't let us down.'

Spring flowered abruptly that week. It might not last but, for the evening of the charity ball, it was present in all its glory. The marquee crouched in a field of daffodils rippled by the mildest and warmest of breezes. Rush torches flamed on both sides of the curving carriageway.

'But how funny!' Gretel exclaimed. 'I did not expect a tent — even such a big one. Why do they not have the ball indoors?'

'It's a charity ball,' Nick said. 'Not a private party.'

'And so?' Gretel was unenlightened.

'The trouble with a charity ball,' I explained, 'is that anyone can buy a ticket and come. There's no control over the guest list. People who have houses big enough to hold a ball in don't like the idea of a lot of strangers roaming through their house and noticing what valuables they have and where they're kept. There's too much danger of an uninvited return visit some night.'

'People would do this?' Gretel sounded aghast.

'They do it all the time,' Nick assured her. 'Burglars even read the glossy magazines devoted to beautiful homes. That's why so many of the photographs are so lifeless. The collections of snuff-boxes, the antique silver service, the Old Masters, have been removed from view before the photographer is allowed to start work. These days people have to be very careful about giving the impression that they have anything worth stealing.'

Inside the marquee, the polished wooden floor was beginning to sound less hollow and strange as more people crowded in. Long wooden tables ran the length of

the far side, set with clusters of champagne-filled glasses
at intervals. The hum of talk and laughter grew; the band
tuned up their instruments.

'The weather could not be more perfect!' Gretel
babbled. 'Oh, Sidonie, you are so lucky!'

'Yee-es,' Sidonie said dubiously, her gaze roving up and
down the table and across the tent. I knew the feeling.
Sidonie was not going to enthuse—or even relax—until
the evening was safely over. 'So far, so good,' was as much
as she would admit at the moment.

Later in the evening, we would take over the long
trestle tables and set out dainty sandwiches and the
obligatory strawberries and cream. I had spent the
morning carefully hulling the fiendishly expensive
hothouse strawberries and had not been pleased to find
that—even at the price we paid—some of them were
already turning soft and squishy. It was as well we were
using them tonight.

So far as I was concerned, I would be happy to see
strawberries lose their reputation as a luxury food. It was
not generally known that strawberries contain a toxic
agent, cocemarin, which holds back the clotting of blood.
People recovering from coronary thrombosis are often
treated with the chemical. If they were to eat strawberries, or any food to which cocemarin had been added,
hæmorrhage could result. It was an obscure worry,
perhaps, but in these days when doctors did not always
think to warn their patients of the side-effects of new
drugs—if, indeed, they were aware of them themselves—it behooved caterers to be aware of the more
obscure dangers of otherwise innocent foods. Almost
anything could be deadly—if the wrong person ate it. But
how did you know who the wrong person was? You
couldn't stand at the door handing out questionnaires
about allergies.

I returned my attention to the present situation. Later

still this evening—or, rather, tomorrow morning—we would serve breakfast to the dawn patrol. Chafing dishes were primed and waiting in the van. Sidonie's early birthday present, a large microwave oven, already occupied pride of place at the far end of the table and several of her friends had been admiring it. Strong hints were obviously going to be dropped to other fathers as gift-giving times approached.

'And oh! you look so beautiful, Sidonie,' Gretel said.

It was true. Sidonie was radiant in a shimmering gold and aquamarine gown that brought out unsuspected green highlights in her eyes. For once, she was the centre of most of the attention and beginning to allow herself to enjoy it. Lexie, in a demure, improbably virginal white gown, seemed to be in a self-effacing mood—which was most unlike her. Perhaps she felt that this was so much Sidonie's night that there was no point in trying to compete. Although her colour was high and there was a glint of devilment in her eyes to signal that, at any moment, her mood might change.

There was little hope of that with Mona. Although she had arrived shortly after the rest of us and donned her uniform, she was making it very clear that she was neither forgiving nor forgetting. She was keeping as much space as possible between herself and Nick, ignoring smiles, waves, and anything that might be classed as an overture.

It was going to be a long hard night. Sidonie and Lexie moved away to mingle with the guests and I realized just how much I was going to miss their familiar moral support.

Gretel was humming under her breath and moving restlessly in rhythm with the music; the dancing had now started. I sent her out to help Nick carry in things from the van. That would work off some of her energy.

I moved towards Mona, who had stationed herself as

far away from the rest of us as possible, but she gave me a
cold blank look and turned away. Obviously, I was too
much my brother's sister to be welcome company. I
hoped she would thaw out as the night wore on. We were
going to have to work together as a close team when the
serving started.

Right now, it was the turn of the wine waiters. They
were circling the tables armed with champagne bottles,
topping up glasses. As I looked around the tent, I began
to pick out familiar faces.

Roddy had just led Lexie out on to the dance floor,
watched sullenly by Humpty, who was sitting at a nearby
table with a couple of Hooray Henrys who were holding
out their glasses as the wine waiter approached, obviously
determined to get as much as possible of everything
going. At these prices, one could scarcely call them
freeloaders and I suspected a large part of Humpty's
sullenness was due to the fact that this was one party he
had had to pay for instead of crash. Sidonie would have
seen to that.

Tristram Quardon and Edda Price were prowling the
periphery of the tent looking for their table. Both
appeared rather strained and weary. I wondered if there
were more trouble brewing back at Quardon International.

I became aware of Ongar Manganian, followed by his
Italian shadow, walking towards me. He was frowning as
he surveyed the array of glasses ranged on the pristine
white tablecloth, unmarred by any suggestion of food in
the offing.

'You are here,' he greeted me. 'So presumably we will
eat at some time.'

'Not for a while yet,' Aldo said with a lazy grin. 'You're
supposed to dance first, you know.'

'In all the time I have known you—' Ongar glowered at
his aide—'this is the first time I have detected a taint of

madness. Are you truly insane—or do you think I am? In any event,' he added, 'there is no one here I wish to dance with. Not on the right side of the table. Is that not true?'

'Quite true.' Aldo gave me a look which was obviously intended to be flattering. I began to edge away. Sidonie might not mind, but other people might take a dim view of the help fraternizing with the guests, much less monopolizing the lion of the evening. And Ongar Manganian was very much the lion of any occasion he chose to honour. Already there were several pretty little vultures circling their intended pray.

'*There* you are, Ongar—' While the younger ones were still circling, a more experienced one swooped. 'Now come along. It's time you took your place on the dance floor.'

'Don't worry.' She gave me a bright unseeing look and a blank dismissive smile which put me in my place. 'I'll bring him back when you start serving the food.'

She wouldn't be able to keep him away when we began serving the food—and she knew it.

'Lady Pamela,' I explained to Nick, who had just come up behind me. 'Lexie's mother.'

'Like mother, like daughter.' he shrugged. 'That's a nice dress she's almost wearing.'

It was fair comment and also, possibly, the reason Lexie was dressed with such unusual demureness. Not because of any deference to Sidonie's position tonight, but because she didn't want to compete with her own mother. Word had it that Lady Pamela was a Tartar when crossed.

Of course, Lexie was rather like that, too. I caught a glimpse of her face over Roddy's shoulder as she watched her mother coax Ongar Manganian on to the dance floor. For a split second, just before Roddy murmured something to her and she turned back to him, her face was murderous with rage.

Did she really imagine she had a chance of snaring Ongar? Or that her mother did? I felt certain the wily magnate was more than a match for both of them— although not in the way they hoped. He had escaped ladies of higher rank and greater fortune in his time.

Although, to be honest, he had also succumbed with enough frequency and unexpectedness to allow any woman, of whatever station, to hope. And he was reputed to be generous— very generous— when the fancy took him. Perhaps Lexie and Lady Pamela were not so far out in their ambitions, after all.

Tristram Quardon and Edda Price had also been watching the by-play. I wondered how Tristram would like it if his sister-in-law were to become the wife— or mistress— of his latest associate. Edda looked worried, but Tristram's face was expressionless. He would probably prefer to see Lady Pamela in that position than Lexie.

Despite the currents swirling beneath the surface, the evening went well until we served the strawberries and cream while the band were taking their midnight break. Then the trouble started.

The champagne had been flowing a little too freely. There were always a few who would take advantage. It was not inevitable that something should happen, but the odds were heavily in favour of it.

I was aware of a growing disturbance, which seemed to centre around Humpty's table and to be spreading outwards from there. I couldn't see what was happening, though, and remained puzzled until a strawberry suddenly struck my cheek splattering cream over my uniform.

I dabbed at the cream with a napkin and looked around. Suddenly the air was full of flying strawberries trailing droplets of cream like the tails of comets. There were shrieks and scuffles as those caught in the crossfire tried to get out of the way.

'Oh, really!' Edda Price had just taken a dish of strawberries and cream from the table in front of me. 'This is disgraceful! So—so juvenile!'

What did she expect? It was the younger ones doing it. I heard Lexie's shrill giggle just a split-second before a squishy strawberry exploded against Edda's elaborate coiffure, dripping red juice and cream down her face and on to her black velvet gown. It seemed as though a few grudges were being worked off tonight. My own strawberry had told me that Humpty had not really forgiven me for throwing him out the time he had gate-crashed.

'Here—' I handed Edda the napkin I had been using.

'It's no use—' She tidied herself as best she could. 'This will have to go to the cleaners. Oh, why are people so thoughtless?'

'It's a form of upper-class insolence.' Tristram Quardon had joined us. 'If you can't afford to have your clothes ruined at one of these affairs, then you can't afford to attend at all and shouldn't be here. I've seen it before, but not in a good many years.' His lips tightened. 'The Bright Young Sods at play! There was a lot of it at one time, but it died out when life got tougher. I'm sorry to see it coming back again. I'm sorrier still to see Lexie out there with them.'

With them? She was one of the ringleaders. Crimson-splattered, she and Humpty appeared to be leading one group against another, none of whom were familiar to me.

The floor had been cleared of all except the combatants now. Several of the older people were shouting vainly for order.

'Oh, they are not nice!' Gretel wailed. 'They should not behave so at such a lovely party. Look at poor Sidonie—they are ruining her evening.'

Pale with fury, Sidonie was skirting the edge of the

battle, waving frantically at Lexie and Humpty, trying to restore some sort of order. She was having no more success than her elders. She seemed to realize that it was going to take more than her efforts and slipped out of the tent for reinforcements.

As I watched, a girl dashed up to the table, exchanged an empty dish for one full of strawberries and dashed back into the fray.

'Right!' Nick said grimly. I had not noticed him come up behind me. 'That does it. Let's withdraw the ammunition. That will put a stop to it.'

We swiftly began to remove the strawberries from view, working together as a team again. Mona was handing dishes to Nick without seeming to notice it. Our one concern was to clear the table before anyone else could come and collect more ammunition. When they had used the last of their own strawberries, the battle would be over.

Out of the corner of my eye, I saw Sidonie leading the band back into the tent. They took in the situation and went quickly to the bandstand, taking up their instruments.

As quickly as it had begun, the battle was petering out. As the band began to play again, a few brave couples got up to dance, keeping well to the edge of the floor.

'I'm sorry about this,' Tristram Quardon said to us. 'I'll speak to Lexie about it.'

But Lexie had noticed our heads turning in her direction and was bright enough to guess the gist of the remarks being made. One moment she was there, the next moment she had disappeared. Probably gone to clean up—and hide out—in the rest room until she though the coast was clear again.

If she was smart, she'd stay there a long time.

CHAPTER 16

'Fools!' Ongar Manganian was shaking with rage. 'Wicked, stupid fools!'

'Should they be dancing so soon?' Gretel worried. 'The floor is slippery. Someone may fall and be hurt.'

'Serve them bloody well right,' Nick said, still grim. 'Except that it's always the wrong ones who get hurt.' Lexie was still missing.

'It's all right.' Sidonie was still upset, but trying to smile for the benefit of any onlookers. 'We're insured for that. For all sorts of contingencies. And people will be careful. As soon as this set ends, we'll have the floor cleaned and then it will be perfectly safe.'

'Wicked!' Ongar raged again. 'It should never have happened. Such wickedness! Such stupidity! Such fools!'

'Oh, nonsense!' Lady Pamela said lightly. 'They're just high-spirited. We were always larking about like that when I was a deb. You're making far too much of it. You were young once yourself, weren't you?'

'Young, yes. Stupid, never!' The look he turned on her must have told her that she had just blasted any chance she might have had with him, even before he continued speaking.

'When I was young,' he said softly, bitterly, 'when I was a little boy, we never play with food. There was famine in Armenia. You know what that means?'

'I'm sorry.' Lady Pamela stepped back involuntarily, as though physically shoved by the intensity of his rage and contempt.

'It means no food. No play, even. It means crawling in the gutter, picking up and eating the grape pips the rich have spat out. Eating them, maybe with the dirt and spittle still on them—yes, and fighting other scavenging children for the privilege—because we were starving. Because there is a little nourishment in them that will help us to survive maybe one more day.'

Lady Pamela shuddered and stepped farther back.

'But here—here they make games with food. Throw it at each other. Splash champagne like sea-water. And laugh. Laugh! They do not know—'

'I'll speak severely to Lexie—' But Lady Pamela might as well have not spoken.

'They laugh at me. I know it. They call me "The Starving Armenian" because I like to eat. But they do not know how right they are. I starved once, yes. But never again. I make a vow when I am a little boy. I will grow up and never again will I be hungry. I make millions— billions—and I tell you, if necessary, I spend every penny of it on food—

'*You*!' He whirled on me. '*You* understand what I mean!'

'Yes.' I shrank back before the burning intensity of his gaze, but he was right. I did know what he meant. Working in catering, surrounded by food, experimenting with it, trying new ways to prepare it and present it, the essential nature of it was rarely considered.

With food, you lived; without food, you died. It was as basic as that.

You could chop it, mince it, spice it, colour it, shape it into unlikely forms, try to disguise it any way you please. You could fry it, boil it, bake it, grill it, sauté it,' flambé it—as though all your preoccupation with the processes could mask the real reason for it.

Diet faddists carried on as though there were no need for people to indulge themselves in it at all. Psychologists further obscured the issue with various theories that food was love, or an anodyne for boredom. But the truth remained.

'Food is life.' Ongar Manganian nodded at me. 'In this country, you have not learned this the hard way. To treat food with disrespect is to mock at life itself. You should not be surprised that there are many peoples who despise you for it. And if, some day, the tumbrils roll, you will have only yourselves to blame!'

If Lexie could have heard that conversation, she wouldn't have returned to the ball at all. As it was, she remained in her retreat for at least half an hour before she ventured into the marquee again.

I spotted her deep in conversation with Humpty in a shadowed corner. Both of them were suspiciously animated and unsubdued by the disapproval they had generated earlier.

Her mother and Tristram Quardon spotted them just then. From different points, they moved to converge on Lexie, but some sixth sense warned her in time.

Once again Lexie did her disappearing act, leaving behind, not a puff of smoke, but a blinking bewildered Humpty, looking around for the companion he had been talking to just a split second before. Then he realized that the enemy was still advancing, determined to create an unpleasant scene with him in lieu of Lexie.

He wasn't as fast as she was, but he was just as determined. He lumbered away, putting several dancing couples between himself and the Quardons before he found a loose flap in the tent and slipped through it to safety.

Lady Pamela and Tristram Quardon suddenly became aware that they were heading for a direct confrontation with each other, with the reason for it no longer in sight. They locked hostile implacable glances for a moment, then averted their eyes and returned to their respective tables.

It was some time before I saw either Lexie or Humpty

again. Not until we were starting the preparations for breakfast. By then, the crowd had thinned considerably. Most of the older generation had left, as had the younger ones who had to think about getting up and reporting for work later that morning. Only the diehards were left.

We had decided to cook the sausages on the spot in the microwave oven, browning them in a chafing dish before serving. We had Gretel working at the microwave oven since the sight of sausages emerging seemingly as raw as when they had entered would be less unnerving to her than to the rest of us. She was accustomed to mishaps like that and, once we had assured her that the sausages were truly cooked, despite appearances, she accepted our word happily. Cooking was largely an act of faith with her at the best of times.

I set containers of cold scrambled eggs and another container of toast behind Gretel in readiness. For those who wanted it, she could heap the cold scrambled egg on the cold toast and then pop it into the microwave to heat in seconds. We were fairly certain she could handle that safely.

Just in case, Mona was stationed next to her, between the chafing dishes of browning sausages and devilled kidneys. She could quickly lend a hand if problems developed.

I would take care of the kedgeree and creamed mushrooms, while Nick manned the coffee urn beyond me. Mona had gone back to keeping him as distant as was possible. We had set out a tray of Danish pastries on the other side of the coffee urn in the hope keeping the queue moving so that they wouldn't congregate around the coffee urn and create an obstruction.

It was ironic, in the light of what had happened earlier, that we had vetoed serving bread rolls on the grounds that they were the traditional weapons when a youthful gathering got rowdy and began throwing things.

At a nearby table, Ongar Manganian was watching our preparations intently. So was Aldo, but without the intentness, and giving us an occasional approving nod. I wondered if his family catered for many outside functions or whether they confined all their efforts to the restaurant. Perhaps someday I would lunch at that restaurant and have a quiet look round—if I could find it, if one word of the story he had told me was true.

Roddy Bletchley had drawn Tristram Quardon aside for what looked like one of those corridor conferences. Unfortunately, there was no corridor available and Roddy was obviously feeling the lack. He glanced around unhappily and settled for guiding Tristram over to the corner where Gretel was working. He frowned at Gretel, but she was too intent on her relays of sausages to notice. This seemed to reassure Roddy—or perhaps he remembered that Gretel wasn't English and decided that the nuances of an involved business conversation conducted in lowered tones would escape her. He began talking earnestly to Tristram Quardon.

From her table, Edda Price watched them as though wishing she could lip-read.

That was when I saw Lexie and Humpty re-enter the marquee. They split up almost as soon as they were inside and moved off in different directions. Lexie was still obviously trying to avoid an encounter with either her mother or her uncle, but she seemed to have recovered some of her assurance. She joined a group of friends and, very shortly, her laugh was ringing out.

Meanwhile, Humpty was circling the marquee moving ever closer to the buffet table, as though stalking game. His eyes were every bit as greedily intense as those of Ongar Manganian, but he had not the excuse of childhood starvation.

'Are you ready?' Sidonie came up, glancing at her watch. 'If we start soon, we might have a chance of clearing this lot before dawn.' She stifled a yawn. 'I'm beginning to feel that I've had enough of them all.'

'Ready any time you are,' I agreed. Those watching must have seen my head nod. There was a sudden stampede.

Humpty beat Ongar Manganian by a short head, snatching the first serving of scrambled eggs from Gretel. He then preceded Ongar the length of the table, heaping his plate, taking more than his share from every serving dish.

Fuming, Ongar followed Humpty, but not taking quite so much. 'I will come back,' he promised. Behind him, Aldo carefully duplicated—in smaller portions— everything his master had chosen.

The others crowded along then and we were so busy that I had no time to notice anything more until the first rush was over.

'Kedgeree, please.' The voice was familiar and I looked up to find Roddy holding out two plates. 'I thought I'd get them both something to eat,' he explained, gesturing. 'It might help to ease the situation.'

I followed the direction of his gesture and saw that Tristram Quardon had cornered Lexie at last. Neither of them looked happy about it, in direct contrast to Gretel, who was ecstatic at having such a promising conversation within earshot. I hoped she wouldn't drop any dishes while trying not to miss a word.

'Tris is pretty upset,' Roddy confided. 'Not that I blame him. Lexie is a bit much sometimes.'

As he spoke, Tristram Quardon shook his head in exasperation and seemed about to abandon his niece, perhaps for all time. Lexie stretched out an imploring hand and caught his sleeve. She began talking rapidly, earnestly, head dipped like a penitent. Tristram's face remained stern but the atmosphere between them seemed to be lightening.

Roddy hurried back to them with the kedgeree and they accepted the plates gratefully, taking the opportunity to declare a tacit truce. Roddy returned for a plate for himself, looking as though he had just accomplished a good day's work.

I was beginning to feel that way myself. Everyone had been fed and we had plenty in reserve for second helpings. They were all seated at tables and the hum of contented conversation was rising.

Sidonie spoke to the band and they rose and came over to the buffet. We had another brief flurry of activity. When it was over, I approached Nick at the coffee urn.

'I think we all deserve a cup of coffee,' I said.

'Before the second wave hits us,' he agreed. 'Our Starving Armenian looks just about ready for more.' He filled a cup and handed it to me. 'Anyway, they seem to be enjoying—'

At that moment, Humpty lurched to his feet, gave a cry of agony and, clutching his stomach, pitched to the floor.

All conversation stopped abruptly.

'I'm dying!' Humpty howled, rolling about on the floor. 'I've been poisoned!'

Ongar Manganian stopped eating abruptly and pushed his plate away. It was an historic sight to witness, but I would have given anything not to have seen it. Not when Executive Meal Service had been doing the cooking.

'Dying . . .' Humpty had a penetrating whine. 'Poisoned . . .'

Aldo gave me an encouraging nod and determinedly— ostentatiously—continued eating.

No one else was prepared to be so sporting. The band members hurriedly deposited their plates at their feet and took up their instruments, looking around uncertainly, waiting for some signal from someone.

'I hope they're not thinking of playing "Nearer, my

God, to Thee",' Nick muttered between clenched teeth. 'That would be all we needed.'

'Those sausages!' Mona was beside us, all differences forgotten, joining forces against a common danger. 'Nick, has the deep-freeze been working all right?'

'The deep-freeze is all right!' Nick snarled. 'This has nothing to do with us. He brought it on himself. Did you see the way he loaded his plate? That fellow eats like a hog at swilling time!'

'Of course,' I said with relief. 'That must be it.' Humpty's overburdened stomach had rebelled at last, presenting him with a richly-deserved bout of indigestion. It was simply unfortunate that it had had to happen here.

I turned just in time to see Tristram Quardon sway and fall.

Nick vaulted the table, then hesitated. But Tristram Quardon lay quietly, while Humpty was howling his head off. Nick took a deep breath and advanced on Humpty.

I dashed up to the end of the table, ducked underneath, and knelt beside Tristram Quardon.

'I did not do anything,' Gretel whimpered, cowering behind the microwave oven. 'It is not my fault.'

'Shut up, Gretel,' I said absently. 'No one is blaming you.' He lay there, preternaturally still, and I had to steel myself to reach for his wrist and try to find his pulse.

Mona, with her customary presence of mind, had dashed off to telephone for an ambulance. Sidonie, wringing her hands, had gone first to Humpty, and was now hovering over me. Lexie was pressed back against the table as though trying to dissociate herself from everything.

'Is he all right?' Sidonie wailed. 'First Humpty, now Tristram? What's happening?'

'Nothing.' I fought a grim, defensive battle. 'They've just been taken ill suddenly, that's all. It's been a long

night — and Tristram wasn't in the best of health to begin
with.'

'No! No, you must not deceive yourself.' Ongar
Manganian had hurried to his fallen colleague's side, but
his eyes still watched Humpty. 'It was intended for me,
the poison. He pushed ahead of me . . . took my place . . .
took the food intended for me . . .'

'Don't be absurd!' I pulled myself upright, forgetting
Tristram Quardon momentarily. 'There was nothing
wrong with the food!'

'Oh, Jean —' Lexie, in her turn, was swaying. 'Jean — I
hate to tell you this —' Abruptly she sank to the floor,
knees drawn up in a foetal position.

'Jean — I'm afraid I'm not feeling very well myself.'

CHAPTER 17

The waiting-room of the nearby hospital was overflowing
by the time we had all crowded into it. It was as well they
had no other emergencies on hand. We must have looked
like ghosts from the proverbial feast as we paced the floor
awaiting news of our fallen ones, who were upstairs
having their stomachs pumped.

Ongar Manganian stroked his stomach thoughtfully,
his eyes darting from side to side as though some unseen
enemy might suddenly launch an attack.

Aldo had taken advantage of the situation to put an
arm round me. In just a few more minutes I was going to
pull away and give him an icy look, but not quite yet. I
rested my head against his shoulder, trying to think.

It must have been the fish . . . it *had* to be the fish.

Humpty had eaten generous portions of everything,
but Lexie and Tristram had eaten only the kedgeree. But
Roddy had eaten it, too, and he seemed to be all right.

And what about all the others? Surely, if the fish were tainted, many more guests from the ball would be upstairs having their stomachs pumped.

Perhaps the fish was like the curate's egg, only parts of it were bad . . .

'I don't see how it could have happened,' Sidonie said. 'We were always so careful.'

'Please, my friends, you must not blame yourselves.' Ongar Manganian tried to comfort us. 'I have enemies. This could have happened anywhere, at any time. I have always known that.'

'Do you mean—' Nick spoke with dangerous quietness— 'because *you* have enemies, *our* reputations have been blasted into oblivion?'

Ongar shrugged. 'It is entirely possible,' he admitted.

'By God,' Nick said, 'If I thought that, I'd murder you myself!'

Aldo stirred uneasily and I found myself restraining him. 'No, no,' I murmured. 'Nick doesn't mean it. He just talks for effect.'

Ongar Manganian seemed to realize this. 'I will make it up to you,' he promised, unworried.

'Make it up to us? How can you?' Nick choked with fury. 'You have no idea what we stand to lose. The business we've built up, the plans for the future. If this gets into the newspapers, we won't even be used for photographic sessions!'

Sudden hope flared in Mona's eyes. One person's hell was someone else's heaven. But why did they always have to marry each other?

'We don't know yet—' Aldo spoke cautiously—'that the food was responsible.'

'We will before long.' I refused to admit false hope. 'They took away samples of everything. We ought to have the laboratory reports in a day or so.'

'Sooner than that!' Ongar Manganian was indignant.

'You do not imagine I would leave something of such importance to your public health authorities? I have made my own arrangements with a private laboratory! Even now, they are conducting their tests. The instant they have finished, I will have the results. Then we may know with whom we are dealing. And—' his expression was grim—'I will take steps!'

'We should also get a report from the hospital authorities here,' Aldo reminded him. 'As soon as they've analysed the stomach contents.'

'My poor, poor little girl.' Lady Pamela gave a long, shuddering sigh. Roddy Bletchley, who had been hovering like a dragonfly between Lady Pamela and Edda Price, darted to comfort her.

'It is unfortunate.' Ongar gave her a cold look. 'But your daughter is receiving the best of care. They all are.'

That much was true. Motivated as much by guilt as by genuine concern, Ongar Manganian had ordered private rooms for the victims, disturbed the slumber of his Harley Street specialist and had him rushed to the hospital to take charge personally, and it appeared that he had a toxicologist and laboratory on tap. It was one way of making sure he was kept informed and with a minimum of red tape.

Perhaps we should be grateful, but I found that I could not believe in some mysterious enemy who had set out to poison Ongar Manganian and struck down innocent people instead. I wished I could believe it. It was a more comforting theory than the possibility that some negligence in our kitchen was responsible for the outbreak. If that were to be proved, how sympathetic would Ongar Manganian be then?

I shuddered. If only Mona had been supervising the kitchen for the past week, I would feel on surer ground. But Nick and Gretel had been holding the fort while I was in and out attending to the business luncheons with Lexie and Sidonie. There was no way of telling what might have happened behind my back.

Nick, preoccupied with his own concerns, might not have noticed the deep-freeze acting up again until it was too late and the defrosting process had already started. It would be entirely like him then to readjust the thermostat and leave everything to re-freeze without bothering to mention it to me.

And Gretel — who knew what Gretel might have done as she blundered helpfully about the kitchen? Gretel was surely the weakest link in our chain. Anything was possible with her. *Had* she made some deadly mistake? She was acting as guilty as Typhoid Mary about to be unmasked yet again. Why were people who could have such a devastating effect on food so irresistibly drawn to it?'

Gretel was sobbing in a corner now. Edda Price stood over her uneasily, her thoughts obviously elsewhere. Somewhere upstairs with Tristram Quardon, who had been the worst-hit of the trio.

And yet, that in itself was odd. He and Lexie had been almost the last to eat. What sort of micro-organism could act so quickly? Humpty had been the first to collect his food and wolf it down, it was not so surprising that he might have succumbed.

But what of all the other guests who had eaten in between the first and the last to be served? I pulled away and studied Aldo. He looked fine. So did Ongar Manganian. Yet they had been immediately behind Humpty in the serving queue.

'How do you feel?' I asked Aldo.

'Absolutely fine.' He knew what I meant. 'Not a quiver or a collywobble. Don't worry.' He patted me reassuringly. 'The food was delicious and I don't see how there could have been anything wrong with it.' He frowned. 'But there's something wrong with the pattern of the attacks—'

'Unless—' The first numbing shock was wearing off now and I was beginning to think more clearly. 'Humpty *did* push in front of you, otherwise the first serving would have gone to Ongar Manganian, just as he said. And then later, just as Roddy collected the servings for Lexie and Tristram, I noticed that you two had nearly finished. I was expecting you to come up for second helpings momentarily—'

'So you think someone could have tampered with the food, not once, but twice?' He shook his head. 'The only one who could have done that was someone behind the table, serving . . .'

'No!' It was impossible to believe. Gretel could have made one mistake of some kind, but would she have repeated it later that same evening? It was in Nick's best interests to see that everything went smoothly. And Mona? No, angry and upset though she had been, Mona would never deliberately poison the food. Not even to get even with Nick.

'No,' I denied again. 'It couldn't have been one of us.'

'I agree.' Ongar Manganian had come up behind us. 'My enemies could not have suborned one of you so easily. There must be another explanation. Perhaps when we are allowed to visit the patients and question them—' He glared around unhappily. 'Why are we being kept waiting for so long?'

'It takes time to pump out three stomachs,' Aldo said. 'And the patients are going to be rather weak and unhappy for a while. I shouldn't imagine they'll feel much like talking.'

'And the laboratory? Why have we not heard from them? They know where to reach us?'

'It takes time.' Again Aldo tried to soothe him. 'They don't know what they're testing for. Unless something shows up right away, it will mean a long series of tests to work through all the possibilities. It could take all night. All morning,' he corrected himself.

Already, dawn was streaking the sky and birds were fluttering and chirping in the trees of the square outside the hospital.

'Call them and ask for a progress report,' Ongar ordered. 'The very poisons that have been ruled out may tell us something.'

Aldo tensed. For a moment, I thought he was going to tell Ongar to do it himself. Then he shrugged and smiled down at me. 'I'll be right back,' he said. But before he could leave, a nurse entered.

'If you'd like to see your friends—' Without hesitation, she marched up to Ongar. She had obviously been briefed as to who was paying the bills. 'You can go up for a few minutes now. But you mustn't stay long. They're still quite weak.'

We wheeled in a body and rushed for the door.

'I didn't mean *all* of you—' The girl tried to block our exit, but she hadn't a chance. Ongar Manganian shouldered past her with a grunt. Aldo caught her as she stumbled and set her to one side.

'I will speak to the doctor!' Ongar thundered back over his shoulder. 'Have him come to me!'

We crowded into the lift and Aldo pushed the button for the third floor, where our casualties occupied adjoining rooms. We faced the front, silent and grimly attentive as the lift trundled upwards, not sure what we'd find when we got there.

Lexie and Humpty were together. Humpty lying back in bed; Lexie, obviously visiting, huddled in a hospital blanket in the chair by his bedside. They looked at us accusingly as we burst into the room.

'My poor, poor darlings!' Lady Pamela swept forward. 'How *are* you?'

They ignored her. Humpty looked from Nick to me and drew a deep breath.

'You might as well know,' he said. 'We intend to sue!'

CHAPTER 18

That froze any expression of sympathy on our lips. There was no question now of sympathizing, far less of apologizing. I stared at them incredulously. I knew Humpty didn't like me, but . . .

'Lexie,' I said faintly. 'Lexie, you can't mean it!'

'I'm sorry, Jean.' She wriggled uncomfortably, clutching the blanket more tightly round her as though she would like to pull it over her head and disappear into it, but the set of her jaw was stubborn. 'Humpty thinks we ought to.'

'Humpty—?' But he was still settling his grudge against us for ejecting him from the reception he gatecrashed. There was no quarter there.

'It's just not good enough.' He glared back at me implacably. 'You can't do this to people and expect them to take it lying down.'

'Oh, really!' Sidonie strode forward, looking as though she would like to shake sense into them both. Nick put out a restraining hand. 'You can't *do* this!'

'We can, you know.' Opposition seemed to be strengthening Humpty. 'You can't go around feeding contaminated food to people and expect them not to mind. We've been *suffering*.' He looked around. 'We're in *hospital*.' He shuddered. 'We've had our stomachs pumped!'

I looked behind me for support, but Aldo had vanished. Ongar Manganian crossed to the bed, walking delicately, as though it might do further harm if he jarred

Humpty or Lexie. He stood looking down at Humpty thoughtfully.

'I think you're rotten!' Sidonie was close to tears, her Charity Ball ruined, her first attempt at trying her wings dashed to the ground, and now a lawsuit pending, so that anyone who might have missed noticing what had happened would see it all rehashed in the scandal sheets. 'Both of you!'

'See here—' Humpty blustered. There was getting to be too much opposition. 'You can't talk to us like that!' He looked from Sidonie to Ongar Manganian, who still had not said a word. 'See here—we have our rights.'

Nick's fists clenched and this time it was I who put out a restraining hand.

'These people are your friends.' Ongar switched his scrutiny from Humpty to Lexie. 'Would you do such a thing to them?'

'They're not *my* friends,' Humpty said. 'People who purvey poisoned food aren't anyone's friends. They're a danger to the community. And,' he added righteously, 'the community needs to be protected from them. The public has a right to know what they've done.'

'What does Tristram Quardon have to say about this?' Ongar demanded. He looked around. 'Where *is* Tristram Quardon?'

'Yes,' Lady Pamela said. 'Where is your uncle?'

'He—' A tear formed and rolled down Lexie's face. 'He's very bad. The worst of any of us. They're still working over him. They've transferred him to Intensive Care.'

'Oh no!' Lady Pamela looked more thoughtful than shocked. 'That's terrible!'

Humpty cringed as Ongar Manganian bent over him abruptly. He snatched up Humpty's bellpush signal to call a nurse and began jabbing it repeatedly, his face grim.

'What is going on?' he barked at the nurse who appeared in the doorway, out of breath from her dash down the corridor in response to the urgent signals. 'What are you doing with Tristram Quardon?'

'I don't know,' the nurse gasped. She settled her cap and went on more decisively. 'I thought there was an emergency.' By now she had spotted the bellpush in Ongar's hands and frowned disapprovingly. 'I thought the patient rang.'

'There *is* an emergency,' Ongar snapped. 'I want to know what is happening to my friend.'

'It's all right,' Lady Pamela intervened. She was standing behind Lexie's chair. 'It's perfectly in order to tell *us*. We're his closest relatives. We have a right to know.'

'But I don't—' the nurse began.

'Enough!' Ongar interrupted her. 'I will speak with someone in authority. Get me the doctor.'

'Doctor is busy with his patient.' The nurse was on surer ground. 'He can't be disturbed.'

The doctor was busy with Tristram Quardon. Fighting for his life. We digested the realization in silence for a moment.

'Very well,' Ongar said. 'Have him report to me as soon as he is able.'

The nurse vanished and Ongar dropped the bellpush back on to Humpty's pillow. We were all lost in our own thoughts. I moved closer to Nick and Mona. If Tristram Quardon died . . .

Edda Price began to sob quietly. Roddy patted her arm awkwardly. There was nothing to say. Her world was crumbling around her for the second time in as many months.

'We'll be ruined,' Mona chocked. '*Ruined!*'

'I don't see what you're getting so upset about.' Humpty was increasingly on the defensive. 'After all, the insurance will take care of everything.'

'It won't take care of our reputation!' Nick snapped. 'You're putting us out of business.'

'One moment!' Ongar Manganian held up a hand. 'What is this about insurance? How much are you carrying?'

'We're not,' Nick said. 'I don't know where he got that idea—'

'*We* are,' Sidonie said quietly. 'The Charity Ball. We have the customary comprehensive cover. We're insured for everything from having to cancel because of bad weather, to someone's having an accident while on the grounds, to—' Her voice broke. 'To an outbreak of ptomaine poisoning among the guests due to the catering.'

'And you say this is usual?' Ongar frowned.

'Yes.' Sidonie seemed slightly surprised that he should question it. 'It's a standard cover offered to charity organizers for garden parties, fêtes, balls, gymkhanas—'

'And how many people knew of this?'

'Why . . . why, everyone. There was no secret about it.' Sidonie's eyes widened. 'Lexie and I were laughing about it when I got the proposal form to fill out . . .'

'I see,' Ongar said softly. The silence deepened.

There was movement behind me. Someone entered the room, closing the door firmly behind him. I turned to find Aldo by my side.

'I've just been through to the laboratory.' He reported to Ongar Manganian. 'They've run all the preliminary checks for all the obvious things and found nothing. They're still testing, as per orders, but they're willing to give you odds that there's nothing wrong with the food.'

Lexie disappeared into her blanket, but Humpty's mattress wasn't so obliging.

Mona hurled herself into Nick's arms, laughing in relief. He swung her around, lifting her off the floor, then

set her down again and turned to face Humpty, his eyes
blazing dangerously.

'See here—' Humpty pressed back against his mattress,
trying to brazen it out. 'I'm willing to be reasonable. I'm
perfectly prepared to settle out of court.'

'*Oh!*' Her burst of indignation carried Sidonie across
the room. She tore at the blanket cocoon sheltering Lexie
and pulled it away. She managed to get in one rousing
slap across her cousin's face before Lady Pamela caught
her hand.

'That will be quite enough,' she said coldly. 'I think it's
time Lexie went back to her own room and rested now.'

'Yes.' Lexie struggled forward, trying to fight free of
the twisted blanket. 'Yes, I'm very tired. And—' she tried
for pathos—'I feel terrible.'

Her bid for sympathy was wasted on the rest of us. We
watched her coldly and she seemed to shrink back from
the combined force of our gaze. Lexie never could stand
disapproval and now she was facing open hostility for
perhaps the first time in her life.

'I believe the young lady has some explaining to do
before she leaves us,' Ongar said. 'It would be better that
she begin now. Or—' He turned to Humpty, who was
eyeing Lexie with no more fondness than the rest of us.
'Or perhaps *you* would tell us?'

'Let Lexie tell you herself,' Humpty said sulkily. 'It was
all her idea. Everything,' he added bitterly, 'was her
idea.'

'Everything?' Ongar seemed momentarily at a loss. He
looked at Humpty uncertainly.

'There you are, Manganian!' The door flew open and a
tall, thin man in a white jacket charged into the room.
Two nurses hovering nervously in the doorway bore
witness to his credentials—unnecessarily. Only someone
at the top of his field would have the arrogance to savage
the hand that fed him so lavishly. 'What the hell are you

playing at here?'

'Playing at?' Ongar swung to face the consultant. 'What do you mean?'

'What do *you* mean?' the doctor countered. 'I've just had the report on the stomach contents. They were all perfectly innocent. What devious game are you—?'

'We know that.' Ongar sounded almost apologetic. 'There has been a terrible mistake.'

'There certainly has. We've wasted valuable time and, worse, weakened a man who was in no condition to be weakened, before we discovered what was actually wrong with him.'

'Tristram Quardon—' Aldo stepped forward. 'What *is* wrong with him?'

'We're preparing him for emergency surgery now,' the doctor said. 'But he should never have had to go through the ordeal of having his stomach pumped. Who was responsible for giving us false information? I shall hold him personally responsible if the operation is unsuccessful!'

'What's the matter with Tristram?' Lady Pamela's voice rose unsteadily.

'His Pacemaker has failed.' The doctor swung to glare at her. 'We're replacing it immediately, but he's been put through added and unnecessary stress. He's not in the best of condition for surgery—'

'*Pacemaker*?' Ongar Manganian said unbelievingly. 'Tristram Quardon has a Pacemaker?'

'Doctor—' One of the nurses spoke timidly from the doorway.

'Coming—' The doctor turned towards her, then swung back to glare at us all impartially. 'I'll have words with you later, Manganian. Don't go away!' The door snicked shut behind him.

'Tristram Quardon has a Pacemaker?' Ongar repeated, still incredulous. 'Why was I not told?'

*Because Tristram Quardon was afraid it might count
against him. Because he was afraid you might use the
knowledge to further undermine his control of Quardon
International.*

'We . . . we didn't think it was important, Mr
Manganian,' Roddy Bletchley spoke as timidly as any
student nurse. 'We didn't think it made any difference.'

'*We* didn't think,' Ongar Manganian mimicked him
cruelly. '*We* didn't—!' Who knew of this?' he demanded.

'Everyone,' Roddy said. 'Everyone who was around at
the time,' he qualified. 'It happened nearly two years ago.
He's been getting along so splendidly we'd practically
forgotten it by this time. He was his old self again.'

'*You* knew.' Ongar glared at him. 'And *you*.' He
switched his glare to Edda Price. 'And—'

'We *all* knew,' Lady Pamela cut in impatiently. 'What
difference does it make, for heaven's sake? Some people
can go on for decades with their original Pacemaker. Tris
has just been unlucky, that's all.'

'Is it?' Ongar met Aldo's eyes. 'But there are
occasions . . . and places . . . that *do* make a difference
when a man carries a Pacemaker within him. It is
dangerous for him to enter an electronic field . . . to
linger near a microwave oven . . .'

'Microwave! Oh no!' I felt dizzy, but there was nowhere
to sit down. I would *not* sit on the edge of Humpty's bed. I
leaned against Aldo instead. 'I can't believe it.'

'It is true,' Ongar said. 'In the United States,
restaurants must now display signs: '*Warning. Microwave
oven in use*.' I had already noticed that such warnings
were not required here. Perhaps because the microwave
oven had not reached such a peak of popularity. Or
perhaps because there are not so many Pacemakers. Over
there, the operation has replaced the appendectomy as a
surgical moneyspinner. Better, because the appendix can
only be removed once, but a Pacemaker can be

implanted and replaced several times.'

'The United States . . .' I echoed faintly. Automatically my eyes turned to Lexie. Lexie, who had learned so much on her famous trip to New York. Lexie, who had kept insisting that we really needed a microwave oven . . .

She was huddled back in her chair, the blanket clutched around her again, but she could no longer escape by withdrawing into it. Her face was pale and frozen, her eyes burned, defying us to prove anything.

'*Lexie* . . .' I whispered. '*No!*'

Sidonie shrank away from her, no longer ready to do battle with her, not willing to touch her at all now. Even her mother stepped back. Lady Pamela, who had earlier insisted, 'You can tell us . . . we're his closest relatives.'

His next-of-kin. Lexie, his heiress.

Once again, I saw that scene by the microwave oven. Tristram Quardon, frowning and uncomfortable, trying to move away. Lexie, putting her hand on his sleeve, not letting him go, holding him in range of the deadly microwave emissions . . . until the damage was done and he collapsed.

Then, coldly and callously, she had tried to throw the blame on us. She had claimed to be sick herself, thus setting the seal on our growing conviction that something was wrong with the food. She had carried through with the charade to the point of having her own stomach pumped in order to keep the doctors from discovering the real trouble with Tristram Quardon. The fact that they had pumped his stomach as well was an added bonus, further weakening him and endangering his chances under the surgeon's knife. With just a little more luck, they might not have learned about his Pacemaker until it was too late.

'I can't believe it,' Edda Price said slowly. 'Not Lexie! Why, from the time she was a little girl, she adored her Uncle Tris—' Her voice wavered and broke.

'But they grow up.' Ongar Manganian sighed heavily. 'Some grow up hungry; some grow up wicked.'

Lexie had been hungry in a different way: money-hungry. She had grown up surrounded by friends who all had more money than she had and overshadowed by the knowledge of the inheritance due to her cousin. She must have watched Tristram Quardon with secret anticipation, especially over the last few years when it had become apparent that only a few beats of a faulty heart had stood between her and Quardon International. But her uncle had gambled on having a Pacemaker implanted and the gamble had paid off. Until now.

Lexie always had been impatient.

'Don't admit a thing, Lexie,' Humpty warned. 'Don't say a word until you have legal counsel. I'm not going to.' He pressed his lips together tightly and glared at us.

But he had already said too much. Earlier, before the full extent of the scheme had been realized. '*It was all her idea. Everything was her idea.*'

Edda Price was still shaking her head unbelievingly, but Roddy, I noticed was quietly backing towards the door.

'Well,' he said defensively, as he caught my eye and realized that I had seen him. 'Someone has to do something—'

And Roddy was always the person called upon to do it. Roddy, the troubleshooter. But need he rush so enthusiastically to do something about this situation? The rest of us were only just coming to terms with the enormity of it. It had not yet occurred to us that the proper authorities should be called in to deal with it . . . with Lexie.

'That's right!' Lexie gave an abrupt reckless giggle that owed more to hysteria than to mirth. 'Roddy will fix it, won't he? Roddy fixes everything!'

Aldo caught her meaning faster than the rest of us. But

then, Aldo had not known Lexie as the rest of us had. He had never worked beside her . . . . laughed with her . . . been charmed by her . . . even against our better judgements.

And there had always been an underlying enmity between himself and Roddy. He deserted me to block Roddy's line of retreat.

'That's right.' Again, Lexie gave that shrill mirthless laugh. 'Don't let him get away. Roddy fixed more than you know.'

'Mark Avery.' Ongar Manganian made the connection. Like Aldo, he was less blinkered than the rest of us.

Roddy always took care of everything. He would be able to cross the wires of an electrical connection, for instance. And he had free access to all the offices. No one at Quardon International would have given it a second thought if they had seen him emerging from Mark Avery's office — after having left Mark Avery's battery-operated shaver to run its batteries into uselessness and splashed a pool of water where Mark Avery would have to stand to use the mains-operated shaver.

'I did it for you.' Roddy looked at Lexie with something less than devotion. 'For us.'

But he had not acted alone; there was no question of his trying to shoulder all the responsibility. Although it was Roddy who had initially decoyed Tristram Quardon into the deadly microwave field, it was because of Lexie that the microwave oven was there. It was also Lexie who had come along to take her turn at keeping her uncle in the fatal area until the damage was done.

'*You* were lucky —' Lexie turned her malevolent gaze to Edda Price. 'If Jean and Gretel hadn't made such a damned row about the cheese wire going missing —'

Edda retreated, one hand rising protectively to her throat. So she had been the intended victim. No wonder Roddy had tried so hard to convince us that Ongar

Manganian had taken the cheese wire. With Edda dead, there would be that seat on the Board to fill again. This time, Roddy might have a better chance.

Also, with both Edda and Mark dead, Tristram Quardon would have first call upon their shares in the business. He could buy them at a preferential price and thus a great deal more control of Quardon International would pass to Lexie . . . after his death.

Aldo had Roddy in a firm grasp now. Lexie sank back in her chair, exhausted.

Humpty had begun shaking uncontrollably as the realization of the true state of things swept over him. He had been the real catspaw tonight. He had been promised a quick and easy profit for a feigned fit of food poisoning. He was not terribly bright and had no idea of the darker forces operating behind the cover he was providing. How could he, any more than the rest of us, have suspected the evil behind Lexie's laughing face?

'So . . .' Ongar Manganian sighed deeply and looked to his lieutenant. 'There is nothing more we can do.' He reached for the private telephone beside Humpty's bed. 'It is time to set the official wheels in motion.'

CHAPTER 19

There was too much oregano in the spaghetti sauce. Other than that, the meal was close to perfect. The best part of it, of course, was that I hadn't had to cook it myself. There is nothing quite so soul-satisfying as hearing crashes, screams and curses emanating from the kitchen and knowing that, whatever has gone wrong, you are not going to be expected to cope with it.

Not that there had been an inordinate amount of disruption; possibly the sounds I had heard were just part of the everyday routine in an Italian kitchen. No doubt I would become accustomed to it in due course.

'More Grappa?' Aldo enquired solicitously of the table at large.

'No, thank you.' My eyes were still watering.

He poured more anyway and went round the table, his mother following him with the coffee-pot while they replenished glasses and cups.

'I'll burst if I have one more mouthful,' Mona declared and indeed the seams of her dress were already straining. The meal wasn't entirely to blame, however. She and Nick were reconciled and blissfully happy, although not for the same reason. Nick was certain that Mona had capitulated completely and would now fall in with his plans, little realizing that she had stopped taking the Pill during her absence. ('By the time they're ready to start shooting,' she had confided to me, 'I'll be too big to fit in the frame. Nick will have to find someone else.')

'A toast.' Ongar Manganian rose to his feet, holding his glass aloft and catching my eye. For a moment I thought he was going to say, '*To the happy couple*', which would have been too premature by half. I gave him a baleful look.

'To our enchanting hostess, who has provided such a delicious meal.' He finished quickly, drained his glass and sat down again.

I relaxed. That had been about the only toast we could all drink to happily. With Roddy in custody pending trial, Lexie on remand and Humpty out on bail and waiting to be called as Queen's Evidence, the situation was still too fraught for too many of us for the merriment to be unrestrained.

Sidonie, I was glad to see, was looking better these days. Without the insidious undermining of Lexie's constant presence, always forcing a comparison between them, Sidonie was quietly blossoming. She might never be

a beauty, but she would someday be a force to be
reckoned with. Antonio, Aldo's electronics-wizard of a
brother, was keeping close to her side, looking as though
he would be happy to do the reckoning. She could do a lot
worse.

Gretel was sparkling at the end of the table, laughing
with Papa Uccello. The discovery of Lexie's perfidy,
although shocking her, had upset her less than the rest of
us — she had quickly discovered compensations. Within a
short time of a tight-lipped Lady Pamela's removing
Lexie's things from the flat, Gretel had moved into the
vacant room. We had encouraged the move, for we knew
Gretel would pay her fair share of the utilities and provide
company for Sidonie and keep her from brooding too
much. The arrangement was working splendidly. In the
kitchen, too, she had improved almost beyond
recognition as her confidence grew.

I had recently received a lyrical letter from Gretel's
delighted father after she had been home for a weekend
and proudly demonstrated her new-found ability. He had
always known that apprenticing her to me would be far
better for her than working as an *au pair* for unknown
strangers and I had proved him triumphantly right. His
little girl was now an accomplished lady, a perfect cook, a
sparkling conversationalist — the stories she could tell! (I
winced at that one.) And she had made so many fine
friends! He added, in closing, that his other daughter
would soon be old enough to continue her studies in
England and was already looking forward to joining
us.

'Please —' Edda Price pushed back her chair and
helped Tristram Quardon to his feet. 'We don't want to
break up such a lovely party, but I think we ought to be
leaving now. He won't admit it —' she smiled fondly at
him — 'but Tris still tires easily.'

That precise situation was still anyone's guess, but I

wasn't going to worry about it. I had problems enough of my own.

'Gina—' Mama Uccello sank into the chair beside me and beamed at me. 'It is so nice to see you, at last. I have heard so much. All the time, "Gina, Gina, Gina" from my Aldo.'

'Jean,' I corrected weakly, sensing that I was fighting a losing battle, It seemed I had an all-purpose name which could be adapted to any nationality.

'Gina,' she agreed happily. 'My boys—they are useless in the kitchen. All the hopes we had of them—pfft! They go their different ways. But—' she smiled lovingly at Aldo, then at Antonio—'but they are good sons. They find the right girls. Our restaurant will flourish.'

'Excuse me.' Ongar Manganian leaned across me. 'I do not think your son is so wonderful. He tells me he cannot travel with me so much any more. It will interfere with his courting!' A warm squeeze of my shoulder told me that he was not angry with me.

'Aldo is right,' Mrs Uccello said. 'When you find a good girl, you do not leave her for someone else to find. You are big man, big money—is easy for you to find another assistant.'

'Perhaps, perhaps.' Ongar nodded. 'But where do I find one who will—' He broke off just short of indiscretion. While Aldo had maintained an amused and tolerant attitude towards his employer's gustatory paranoia, it was more than possible that Aldo's mother would not take kindly to the realization that her son had been used as a guinea-pig for suspect food.

'It is true,' Ongar went on thoughtfully, 'that I need someone here in England permanently to keep watch over my interests—and for this I have trained Aldo well. But perhaps . . .' He nodded sagely again. 'I have been considering. The young Humphrey—he is not really bad, I think. Misguided, ill-advised, but there is something I find not entirely unlikeable about him—'

Perhaps he reminded Ongar Manganian of himself. He was big enough. I did not voice the thought.

'Not beyond redemption,' Ongar decided. 'When this is over, I have the notion to take him in hand. I believe he can be taught . . . moulded . . .'

Poor Humpty. From Lexie's catspaw to Ongar's. At least, the pay would be better. Also, a few years of testing food which genuinely might be poisoned ought to give him a more respectful attitude towards it. What was it about the punishment fitting the crime . . . ?

'That's *my* chair—' Aldo lifted his mother to her feet. 'Suppose you go rescue your husband from the Nordic charmer. You know he was always a fool for Marlene Dietrich.'

'Hah!' His mother aimed an affectionate cuff at his ear. 'I Dietrich him!' She moved off resolutely towards Papa Uccello and Gretel, while Aldo took his place beside me.

'Now—' Aldo caught up my hand complacently. 'As we were saying—'

I found myself smiling back at him, while my mind continued along another path.

Before too long, I really must take up with the Uccellos the matter of the amount of oregano in the spaghetti sauce.

Death Beside the Seaside

CHAPTER 1

He was a Saturday-night Starer.

I can't help it, they frighten me. There's no way you can reach them. You can smile sweetly at them, send them a chummy wink, offer them a request number — but it doesn't work. They won't meet your eyes, they won't give any sign that they recognize you as a human being, or even that they're human themselves. If you persist, they slide away, dissolving into the shadows they sprang from.

Then, just when you're beginning to relax again, you suddenly feel those eyes boring into you from some far corner of the room and you don't have to turn around to know that your Starer's back. Staring.

They're always in the far corner of the room, always in the shadows, always alone. Naturally. They're born loners, the Starers. If they could make any kind of contact with another human being, they wouldn't be lurking in a corner, nursing their drink and staring, would they?

I pressed down on the loud pedal, beamed my brightest smile towards that corner, and said cheerily, 'All right now, it's time for special requests. Who'd like to hear a favourite song? How about that handsome gentleman over in the . . . ?'

He was gone. Drifted away like smoke in the way they always do. So insubstantial that, after a few moments, you couldn't swear that they'd been there at all. As for ever describing one of them, forget it. How do you describe a swirl of smoke in a smoky room? He was a Saturday-night Starer, that's all. You run into them every now and again. Sometimes, like tonight, they show up on other nights of the week, as well. They're an occupational hazard. I just hadn't expected to run into one over here, that's why he jarred me so. Silly of me. It's the same all over the world, we all know that. Or we would, if we let ourselves think about it at any length.

The less inhibited were shouting out their requests now and I let my fingers rove over the keyboard plinking out encouraging chords. They were the more usual weekend audience: friendly, relaxed, out for a good time. Easy to please, willing to meet you half way to be entertained. So nice, so normal.

I brightened my smile to disguise the fact that I'd never heard of half the numbers they were calling for. I was still fairly new here. But I'd learn, I'd learn . . .

The room hushed abruptly and I realized that I'd unconsciously slipped into Rimsky-Korsakov: *Scheherazade*. Probably the effect the Starer had on me. My subconscious identified with the frightened girl keeping death at bay by the flimsy power of her ability to keep a capricious tyrant entertained . . . entranced.

How Freudian can you get?

My fingers faltered and stumbled as I tried to segue into something more suitable for a cocktail-bar audience on a Bank Holiday Friday night. But they wouldn't let me.

'Keep going, lass,' a voice roared out. There was a spattering of applause. Incredibly, they were enjoying it. They didn't want anything I might consider more suitable. They wanted *Scheherazade*.

I went along with it for a while, the music soothing me as much as them. As I came towards the end of the movement, I leaned forward into the microphone.

'You know,' I said chummily, 'you may not believe it, but there are lyrics to this. No, honestly,' I answered the ripple of laughter. 'We used it for a Television Spectacular once. Oh yes, I can just hear you saying, "Those Americans would do anything . . ."'

It got another laugh. But suddenly, I wished I hadn't said it.

He was back. I could feel those eyes boring into me. Without looking up, I knew which corner he was in. Staring . . . and listening . . . and staring . . .

Staring with those ice-cold impersonal eyes. What was going on behind them?

God knows what they imagine themselves doing with you. Or to you. But, whatever it is, it's a pretty safe bet that you're not going to enjoy it.

But that doesn't matter. Because you're not human. You're the cut-out doll from the centre-page spread, the plastic body without any feelings, the inflatable rubber doll from the sex shop. He's the only one in all the world who can feel anything—and you wouldn't want to know what he's feeling.

It was time for another vocal, but I didn't think my voice would stand up to it. Even my fingers stumbled over the intro. I flashed a smile and started again.

'It's all right, Trudi.' Ted was beside me, setting a glass of chilled white wine on top of the piano for me. 'I've spotted him. I'll go over and tell him to hop it. We don't want his sort around here.'

Ted moved off purposefully and I half-turned on the piano bench to follow his progress. But the Starer was gone again. There was just an empty seat in the corner from which I had felt those eyes boring into me.

It was unlikely that he'd be back tonight. Not now that he knew Ted would be watching out for him.

But would he be waiting outside when I left for the night?

'*Bless Them All!*' Someone called out the title and, since it was a number I knew, I swung into it. Voices joined in from all over the room. There was laughter and the bustle of waitresses serving fresh drinks. Everything was the way it ought to be again. Inside here.

'Sorry about that.' Ted was back. 'He got away, but he won't get in here again. I'll see to that.' He hesitated. 'I'll see you home tonight, too.'

'Thanks.' I turned off the mike and pressed down on the loud pedal while I kept playing to cover our conversation. 'I'd appreciate that. I . . . I feel a bit silly, but he really spooked me.'

'Nothing silly about it,' Ted said. 'You can't be too careful this weekend. There's a lot of riff-raff about.' He ran a gloomy eye over his customers, most of whom, although spending money like drunken sailors, failed to find favour with him.

'You've heard our expression, "Where's there's muck, there's brass," ' he said. 'Well, you can turn it round the other way and still be right: "Where there's brass, there's muck." ' Again he surveyed his customers with distaste. 'Muck!'

I looked around the room myself with what was becoming an increasingly expert eye. They weren't that bad. They weren't the regulars, of course. Not tonight. This was the Friday-night start of the long August Bank Holiday weekend. The regulars would all be keeping their own places open, tending to their own hordes of tourists down spending money on the last big holiday of the year until Christmas. Something else that was the same all over the world.

There were a few of the two-week holidaymakers, winding up their yearly holiday this weekend. The rest were strangers, people down from London for the long weekend; perhaps some of them starting their own two-week holiday a bit late in the year. All perfectly respectable people, so far as I could tell.

But Ted was viewing them all with a jaundiced eye. In fact, the whole town was. Everyone feared a recurrence of the events of last August Bank Holiday, when marauding gangs of motor-cyclists had invaded the seaside resort, fought among themselves, vandalized the shops and terrorized the townspeople until, finally, they receded like the tide. Like the tide, leaving bits of flotsam and jetsam to mark their passage: empty beer cans, splintered shop-front windows, a few of their number marooned in hospital with knife wounds and broken bones, and the naked body of a young girl lying on the beach just by the Grand Pier.

She had never been identified. Only last week, the local newspaper had run a series of follow-up articles on the events of that Bank Holiday weekend, pointing out—unnecessarily—that such things must never be allowed to happen again in Our Fair City. The final article had dwelt sadly on the idea that such a young girl—surely someone's daughter, sister, cousin, friend—could disappear from what must be her accustomed haunts and never be missed.

No one had been able to identify her from the published photograph and the police had come to the conclusion that she had come down to the seaside with the motor-cycle gangs, probably as a pillion passenger, and been abandoned either when her dead body had been discovered (but not reported) by the gang, or when she had failed to turn up at their rendezvous for the return trip to town.

There had been further speculation that she might be a foreigner, some little *au pair* who had perhaps quarrelled with the family where she was supposed to be living and had taken herself off with some exciting boy-friend. Her erstwhile employers would assume that she had returned to her native country; her family would assume that she was still living happily in England and learning to speak the language like a native, although not a good correspondent in any language. Either way, it could be several more months—or years—before anyone thought to institute the enquiries that would eventually lead to the discovery of her fate.

I was glad I hadn't been here at the time. My piano bar was situated at the long floor-to-ceiling window overlooking the Grand Pier with a fine view of the beach—if I turned round. There were moments when it was dis-

turbing enough just thinking about what had happened
without actually having been here to see it then. No
wonder the town was tense tonight, with people jumping
at the sound of a car backfiring. I'd jump myself at
anything I thought was a motor-cycle and I'd only
experienced the whole thing second-hand, through the
newspaper articles and the stories and remarks of the
people who'd lived through it.

Ted was still glowering around the crowded room,
looking out for trouble. He'd even have welcomed a
return of the Starer, I suspected. It would give him someone to challenge. He didn't like a waiting role and that
was all any of us had right now. Waiting for trouble we
hoped wasn't going to come. There was no reason why it
should.

The police were waiting, too, and the gangs knew it.
They had descended on other seaside towns during this
long, if not hot, summer. Always a different town, always
over a weekend — but there was no record of their having
gone back to a place a second time. Not that that signified
anything. The very unpredictability of their manic forays
meant that nothing could be foreseen about their behaviour. Weeks would go by peacefully and then some quiet
resort would be descended on and devastated before the
police could call in enough reserves to get the situation
under control.

It wasn't a new phenomenon. It appeared to have occurred periodically over the past twenty-five years or so,
but it always took the authorities by surprise because it
skipped generations. Just as they thought the rivalries and
gang warfare had died out, suddenly there were new gangs,
new rivalries and new raids on unsuspecting towns, arbi-
trarily chosen as battlefields, well away from their own
territories. In the beginning, they had made their way to
the battlegrounds by train and bus, now the standard of
living had risen and they had their own motor-cycles, thus

expediting their getaways and making it harder to catch them.

'Right . . .' Ted said, in reluctant admission that things were probably as peaceful as they seemed. He turned and looked through the big plate glass window behind me, checking the beach, the Grand Pier, the trippers promenading along the sea front. I turned and caught him staring out to sea.

'*I saw the harbour lights . . .*' The song seemed to ripple from my fingers and throat of its own accord and I continued with it. It was gently nostalgic, sad and haunting, but peaceful. I stole another glance at Ted and saw a smile tugging at the corner of his mouth. It was soothing him, as I had intended it to. The customers seemed to be enjoying it, as well. But they were an undemanding bunch, on holiday, they'd have enjoyed anything.

Then Ted glanced down and the smile was wiped away. I knew that he was looking at the foreshore, where the body had lain. Right across from his pub.

It was a posher pub now, trying hard to be a high-class cocktail-bar with entertainment along American lines—a new departure for the English seaside, I gathered. Ted called it The Phoenix because it had risen from the flames and wreckage of the old pub. The insurance had paid for most of it and a fresh infusion of money from a new partner had taken care of the rest.

'Tomorrow, they'll likely start coming.' Ted turned back to me. 'Or Sunday, that's when they can raise the most hell. Because some of them have to work on Saturdays, but they've got Sunday and Monday clear. Sunday . . . that's when they came before.'

He rubbed his left arm thoughtfully, the arm that had been broken that night.

The crowd was thinning out now, it was close to closing time. There was no one left sitting around the piano, not that there had been many earlier. The regulars weren't

here tonight and the arrangement always came as a shock
to new people who had never seen such a thing before. By
tomorrow, they'd be used to the idea and I could count on
a full house. Right now, I could talk freely, so long as I
kept playing and leaned away from the mike.

'They won't come back,' I said. 'They never do.'

'They might.' He flexed his fingers. 'And this time, I'll
be ready.'

They could never do so much damage again, in any
case. The Phoenix was on the first floor. Ted would never
operate anything at ground level again. You can't ride a
motor-cycle up a flight of stairs.

The ground floor had been taken over by the local
Chamber of Commerce as a Tourist Office. It was open
from 9 a.m. to 6 p.m. and sold maps, postcards, tickets to
the shows playing on the Grand Pier and at the other
theatres around town. They also offered bus tours to the
local attractions: The Stately Home with the Safari Park
in the grounds (combination ticket available); the local
Freak of Nature; the surrounding Beauty Spots (picnic
lunch included); and the side trips to neighbouring towns
and shopping centres. They also gave advice, provided
lists of Bed and Breakfast accommodation, arranged rail
travel and acted as agents for the day trips to France running from the neighbouring port.

The Tourist Office's chief virtue in Ted's eyes was the
hours it kept. Open during the day and closed at night, it
provided no competition and offered no distraction. To
the contrary, trippers visiting it during the day would
often take advantage of the proximity of The Phoenix to
nip upstairs for a quick one before catching their bus or
going out on the Grand Pier; while, dark and shuttered at
night, it presented no temptation to the most determined
tearaway to smash his way inside and start trying to van-
dalize a rack of travel brochures.

Ted had always firmly denied the occasional accusation

that the fact that his brother-in-law, Albert Tiverton, was a Councillor had had anything to do with his having rented the ground-floor accommodation so fortuitously. Thousands wouldn't have believed him—including many of the townspeople—but I did. I knew his brother-in-law.

Oh, not well. No better than you would wish to know a beefy, beery man who pinched your behind upon introduction and made ponderous *double entendres* about the Special Relationship. Only one thing could be said in his favour: he wasn't a Starer. His eyes just plain lit up and read 'Tilt!'

It had taken some fast and fancy footwork over the next few weeks, but I thought that Councillor Tiverton was finally getting the message. He hadn't dropped in for some time now.

Of course, it was the height of the Season and he had his own interests. Foremost among them was an amusement arcade called (wouldn't you know it?) The Fun Palace, which bestrode the entrance to the Grand Pier. You couldn't get out on the pier without passing through it. It was a combination penny arcade and hall of mirrors with a joke shop specializing in whoopee cushions, fur spiders and plastic dog dirt tucked away in one corner. It was very popular with the visiting children and the more immature specimens among their parents.

I had met his wife, Milly, Ted's sister, even more rarely. She seemed a docile, downtrodden, rather discouraged woman who would have profited by having been introduced to Women's Lib at an early age. Or, even now, being introduced to a sharp double-bladed axe with the firm assurance that no jury on earth would convict her.

'Right, that's it,' Ted said, as a few more stragglers got up and headed for the exit. He raised his voice. 'Time, gentlemen, please!'

'*Good night, Ladies*' . . . I began playing as the lights dipped. I had learned that song beat even the calling of

'Time' as a notice of dismissal from which there was no appeal.

Glasses were emptied hastily, goodbyes called out, the room began emptying. I kept playing until the last of them had gone and then I turned to look out of the window.

The lights on the Grand Pier had dimmed for the night. The moon had disappeared behind a cloud. It seemed later and colder than it really was. The crowd along the promenade had thinned; those who remained no longer seemed so cheerful and innocent.

It reminded me that there was a Starer somewhere out there. Perhaps staring at the last of the customers drifting out of The Phoenix . . . waiting . . .

'Get your coat, Trudi,' Ted said. 'I'm seeing you home tonight. Aye, and the rest of the weekend, as well. You'll be all right with me.'

CHAPTER 2

The town rose up from the sea front in tiers, like a wedding-cake. At sea level, there was the Lower Town, a flat basin stretching back for half a mile, heavily built up with hotels along the sea front, fish and chip shops, fancy restaurants, catchpenny stalls and places of amusement featuring every possible permutation of dream, fantasy or nightmare which might be reckoned to extract a few more pence from the pockets of indiscriminate tourists. It had taken me a while to get used to it. I think they call it culture shock.

Even the sea itself looked alien to my eyes. Accustomed as I was to the open sea and sky and rolling sand dunes of Long Island and Cape Cod, the English seacoast looked miniature and claustrophobic, enervated and overcontrolled, subdued—not to say, beaten into submission.

Instead of a wide unbroken stretch of sand, this was a mile-long stretch of shale, lightly powdered with imported sand, bounded at one end by the Grand Pier, a Victorian extravaganza extending an endless length straight out to sea, with more shops and stalls along its length and the Grand Theatre marking the end of it. At the other end of the beach was the Minor Pier, smaller in every way, decommissioned now and totally given over to the Yacht Club belonging to the Marina on the far side of the Minor Pier. The Marina was a new development. An artificial harbour had been dredged out, a sea wall erected around it and, ashore, a number of blocks of flats had been ranged along the front and were already changing hands at prices way beyond the original purchase price. Already, too, small new shops were clustering around the original grocery store and ships' chandlers. In time, the area would undoubtedly become known as the New Town, and the Upper and Lower Town be relegated to the status of Old Town.

The first tier of the Lower Town was given over to lodging-houses, antique shops, more restaurants, and shops for the practical necessities of life, like chemists, shoe repairers and newsagents/tobacconists. There was also the inevitable proliferation of charity second-hand shops. On a wet day, the sea front was deserted while the trippers browsed for hours through the cast-off delights offered in the side streets and winding passageways of the first tier.

The second tier was the point at which the Lower Town and Upper Town met, although no one ever referred to it by anything so Transatlantic sounding as Mid-Town. This was where the foresighted Founding Fathers had placed the Town Hall and various public amenities, such as the library and sports field, high enough above sea level to be beyond the reach of a flood tide. This was also where you found the Sainsbury's, the Woolworth's, the Marks and Spencer's, and those other ubiquitous chain stores which dominated every High Street across the land.

The third and fourth tiers were residential, where the people of the town actually lived, retreating up there after they had spent a busy day earning money down on the sea front. The schools, both of them, were tucked away here, too.

The final tier was the great plateau that levelled off and rolled back across green acres to become part of the agricultural inland, linking up eventually with the motor-way leading to London.

At the top of this plateau, looking out over town and sea, huddled the nursing homes and sanatoria, strategically placed by their Victorian builders to allow invalids the benefits of the sea breezes, while discouraging all but the hardiest and nearest-mended from descending to the town and dissipating their feeble energies on the frivolous amusements it offered. Tradition dies hard and the nursing homes and sanatoria endured to this day, sheltering the elderly, the convalescent, those recovering from operations and, in at least one sanatorium, the mentally disordered.

Which reminded me of the Starer again. Had he come from up there? I shuddered.

'Bloody weather,' Ted grumbled. 'I'll turn on the heater.' He leaned forward and did so. 'End of August and you couldn't tell the difference from bleedin' February. Except it was warmer in February.'

'Thanks,' I said gratefully. There was no point in trying to explain. Besides, it *was* cold. Not that it discouraged the holiday throngs. They seemed to just throw on another sweater and continue what passed for merrymaking with them. 'At least it isn't actually raining.'

'Better if it was,' Ted grunted. 'Bit of rain and the wrong sort might stay at home. Seaside's not much fun in the wet. Wouldn't hurt business, either. Those already here would just take their pleasures inside. Plenty to do in the arcades and shops and pubs.'

'More than enough to do indoors,' I agreed. There had better be, if this was a typical English summer.

The car laboured up a final hill, turned and drew to a stop. I was home—or what was passing for home these days. It would have been too expensive to stay in one of the hotels and too depressing to stay at one of the boarding-houses on the lower level. Fortunately, Ted had arranged for me to stay in what he called 'theatrical digs' in a house on the third tier, just comfortably above the noise and crowds of the Lower Town.

'Don't get out,' I said, as he began to move. 'I'll be all right now.'

'Ah well.' He settled back, rubbing the arm that had been broken. 'I'll wait and see you safe to the door. I don't like all those bushes there by the gate. Bloody daft place to have them, if you ask me. I'd cut them all down if they were mine.'

'Oh, but lilacs are so beautiful in the spring,' I said unconvincingly. Spring was long past, the scented purple blossoms had faded and gone, leaving dark clumps of shadowed rustling leaves behind which anything might be lurking. I shuddered again.

'Get inside,' Ted said. 'There's a mortal chill in the air tonight. And don't worry about anything. I'll make sure we don't have that one hanging about again.'

'Thanks.' I smiled feebly as I got out and slammed the car door behind me. I went up the path, not looking left nor right, but glad I had Ted waiting behind me, keeping watch.

The hall light was glowing and I was uneasily aware that I was silhouetted—a perfect target—as I turned to wave reassuringly to Ted from the doorway. I had shut the door and locked it behind me before I heard the car motor starting up again.

*

The Prime Minister of Mirth was sitting on the finial of the stair rail as I turned. He yawned a greeting, tail twitching.

'Good evening, George,' I said.

I got a double answer. Robey snorted, twitching his whiskers this time, and Formby appeared from nowhere to curl around my ankles, chirruping.

'All right, all right,' I said. 'Wait a minute, can't you?' I hunted for the plastic bag of leftovers which had slipped, as usual, to the bottom of my handbag. 'Where's Gracie?'

There was another answering chirrup and a marmalade shadow slid into the hallway from the dining-room, followed by another, altogether bulkier, figure.

'You spoil them, you do,' Daisy Dayton said in the gratified tones of a pet-lover who quite understands that her darlings are irresistible. 'Spoil them rotten.'

I found the bag of leftovers and brought it out. With a yowl of approval, Robey leaped to the floor, stretched, and led the procession to the kitchen.

'Slim pickings tonight, kids,' I shook the bite-sized pieces of cocktail sausages and cheese into the three bowls, trying for an equal division. 'The customers were hungry.'

'Trying to save themselves the cost of buying a meal later, more likely,' my landlady sniffed. 'You don't get the best sort on Bank Holiday weekends. I'm surprised Ted put out the good bits tonight. Peanuts and crisps are good enough for *them*.'

'It wasn't a bad audience,' I defended. 'Except for—'

That pair of burning eyes surfaced in my memory, cutting me off. I couldn't say what colour they were, nor could I bring into focus the nebulous white blur of a face surrounding them. He might pass me in the street tomorrow and I would not realize it—not so long as he kept his eyes lowered. But if he were to raise his head and look into my face—'

I shuddered again.

'One of those, eh?' Daisy Dayton had been in The Profession herself, touring the Provinces in a dance troupe coyly called The Daisy Chain between the Wars and then as a member of ENSA ('Every Night, Something Awful, that's what they used to say,' she had confided cheerfully) during the war. She had had her share of experiences, good and bad, before the late Mr Dayton had detached her from The Daisy Chain and they had retired to the seaside. She had not lost contact with her former colleagues, however, and from putting up a few chums when they appeared at local theatres, she had passed almost imperceptibly through the stage of putting up friends of friends until she found herself a fully-fledged theatrical landlady whose 'digs' were prized as one of the better billets on the circuit.

'You mustn't let it get you down, dear,' she said. 'There are always some of those about.'

'I know,' I said. 'I guess I just wasn't expecting it here, that's all. It got to me.' I shuddered again and added apologetically, 'There've been some nasty cases in the States . . .'

'The world isn't what it used to be, dear.' She sighed. 'Things are getting nastier everywhere.'

Fields, too, was of this opinion. Formby, having gulped down the contents of his own dish, had sidled round to hers and helped himself to a piece of sausage. Fields laid back her ears and smacked him across the chops. Formby clenched his teeth in his prize and backed out of range. Fields crouched over her dish, her high-pitched growl rising threateningly.

'Sing it, Gracie,' Daisy cheered, diverted. 'Oh, you should have heard her in the old days!'

'Really?' I was momentarily startled. Fields could not be much more than three or four years old. And she sounded in fine voice to me.

'The *real* Gracie, I mean. Sorry, dear.' Daisy sighed again. 'I get carried away. I know they're not really their namesakes, really I do. But I like to pretend sometimes. It's why I named them the way I did, to begin with. Because I couldn't stand to think of people like that being gone from the world. This way, it seems as though they're still with us, almost. You don't mind, do you, dear?'

'Of course not,' I said. 'Why should I?' It was a fairly mild eccentricity, compared to some I had seen. If she could extract a degree of comfort from it, who was I to object?

'That's all right, then,' she said. 'Some people don't like it, you know. They say it gives them the creeps. As long as you don't mind — ?' She paused delicately.

'I don't,' I affirmed. I had just had an encounter with something that genuinely produced the creeps. Innocent little Robey, Formby and Fields weren't even in the running with that.

'I didn't think you would.' She was obscurely satisfied. 'You're not that sort.'

Robey sat back on his haunches and looked from his empty dish to his two companions. Fields was the only one still eating and she gave another warning growl. Formby had begun circling her plate warily again. Robey decided it was all beneath him and settled back to wash his face majestically.

'Am I the last one in?'

'That's right, dear. I'll lock up for the night now. No one wants to be out late at a time like this. You never know . . .'

Ye shall know not the day nor the hour. It was not a comforting thought. It was not intended to be. But, for all the dark Testament echoes, she was right. No one was going to linger on the slopes of Town late at night this weekend.

Not unless they were tourists and didn't know any

better. But the occupants of this house had been here long enough to share in the general paranoia of the townspeople. They were going to lock the doors, batten down the hatches and keep the lowest of profiles until the danger of marauding invaders was over. I supposed it must have been like this in early times when Viking raiders were a constant threat to those living along the coastline. Vikings had receded into historical perspective and now the new danger came from within; from the young and bored who found their amusement in preying upon their own country.

'The Great Dandini came in just before you did, dear.' Daisy Dayton shot home the bolts with decisive clicks. 'I'd thought he might stay out a bit later, being a man and all, but he takes good care of himself.' She sniffed. 'Wants to live to be a great big star with his own show. But he'd better put in more rehearsal time. His act is getting slack, dear, very slack. He might think it doesn't matter, out there on the end of the pier, but the Public notices these things, dear. Even if they applaud just to be polite.'

'It's the end of the season, nearly.' I felt obscurely moved to defend the little man in the basement bedsitter. 'He's probably tired and gone a little stale.'

There were times enough when I found my own audiences exhausting. A sensitive performer doing three shows a day, trying to satisfy an audience of both adults and children must be close to the breakdown point by the end of summer. His audience-participation segment alone — with a myriad grubby little helpers trooping onstage to rap on the walls of his magic cabinet, look up his sleeves to assure themselves he concealed nothing but his arms, pull strings which turned into endless streamers of flags, and all the rest of the participation stunts — would have driven me out of my mind if I had to do it. However, the Great Dandini was an expert at coping with awkward little customers bent on either showing off or exposing the mechanics of his tricks. But just keeping that smile on his face at such times must have taken its toll.

'Of course, Norma and Little Johnny went up to bed ages ago.' Daisy continued counting her chickens. 'They must be well into the Land of Nod by now. Poor things.'

I nodded without comment. Certainly, Norma Handel would be asleep. She seemed to spend an inordinate amount of time sleeping. As to what Little Johnny might be doing while his mother slept, I wouldn't like to speculate. On at least three occasions, I was fairly sure I had spotted him flitting along the promenade at an hour when everyone would have thought him fast asleep. I'd never mentioned it, of course. Why add to Norma's troubles? If she didn't already suspect it, she'd find out soon enough that her son was uncontrollable. He wasn't particularly likeable, either. There was something sly about his eyes. I had also noticed that none of the cats remained in a room once he had entered it.

'There now!' Daisy splashed milk into each of the three bowls on the floor. It seemed to remind her of something. 'Are you sure you wouldn't like a little something yourself before you go upstairs, dear?'

'Quite sure, thanks,' I said. 'I'm just very tired. I think I'll go straight to bed.'

'You do that, dear. It doesn't pay to get overtired. An *artiste* lives on her nerves. Oh, *I* know . . .'

I smiled and slid away, escaping whatever reminiscences might be in the offing. Usually these glimpses of a lost world fascinated me, but tonight I was genuinely exhausted. I could feel the ache between my shoulder-blades and at the back of my neck, brought on by tension.

Daisy Dayton was partially right. Tonight, at least, my nerves had taken a battering.

Nor was the situation likely to improve all weekend. Even if the dreaded motor-cycle invasion never came, I still felt threatened on a more personal level by the Starer.

Where had he come from? Where had he gone? Would he come back?

Probably he was nothing more than some dull little clerk in some grey anonymous firm, who would be horrified — and perhaps a bit flattered — to think that he could appear sinister at all.

The twinges between my shoulder-blades began to subside and I yawned as I neared the top of the stairs. Any danger was over, for the time being. I was back in my own digs, safely locked in for the night, surrounded by friendly people. I could relax.

CHAPTER 3

As usual, the floorboard creaked on the first-floor landing. I never seemed able to avoid it and it always startled me more than anyone else. Norma Handel would be sunk in slumber at this hour — at practically any hour — in the large front bedsitting-room overlooking the street. The other large room on this floor, occupied by Henry Parsons, the Punch-and-Judy man, was also dark and silent. He was another who had to pander to the caprices of a juvenile audience: perhaps that was what made him so aloof and morose when he was out of his sheltering booth.

The door at the far end of the hallway opened. I had a glimpse of a pale secretive face and a baleful eye, then a small hand shot out to close around a long handle attached to a flat disc and pull the whole thing into the safety of his room. Little Johnny was taking no chances that anyone might run off with his newest toy, a metal detector. But why had he left it out in the hallway in the first place if he was so concerned about it?

Shrugging, I climbed the final flight of stairs to the top floor, where I had the back room. The front room was

occupied by Kate Carter from the Mad Manic Music Hall.
Daisy Dayton did not entirely approve of Johnny's having
a whole room, even a small one, all to himself. However, I
quite saw Norma Handel's point. I wouldn't care to share
a room with Johnny myself. It was also kinder to the
child, since Norma only wanted to spend her time
sleeping, to let him have a place where he could watch
television, play records and entertain his friends — if he
had any. Although I doubted that Norma had been
worrying about Johnny's comfort.

'Oh, it's a sad thing, dear, very sad,' Daisy had confided to
me, soon after introducing Norma Handel and her young
son. 'She isn't one of us, of course, but I'm not prejudiced. I
don't insist on theatricals, although I'd rather have them.
Well, you know where you stand with your own, don't
you, dear? But I had to take them in, it's so sad. Besides,
she's a long-term boarder. That's not to be sneezed at,
these days. And she's warm, dear, very warm.'

I must have looked puzzled, for Daisy elucidated.

'Money, that is, dear, bags of it. Although not hers, not
yet. That's why she's got to toe the line — her mother-in-
law's line. She can't help it. The old lady has the money.
Norma's husband is *up there*, you see —'

My face must have shown that I didn't see. I glanced
heavenwards involuntarily, but Daisy Dayton hadn't been
referring to anything that high.

'In the Nursing Home — although I don't reckon *he's* con-
valescing. He's there for the rest of his days, if you ask me.
Just sitting in a chair staring into space, they say. Doesn't
recognize her or the boy when they visit him. Doesn't talk,
doesn't move. Oh, it's terrible, dear, terrible. And she's
still a young woman, she should be out enjoying herself.
But she never will — that mother-in-law of hers will see to
that. She's got to behave like a proper wife, even though
the man she married doesn't exist any more. But she's got
to live near by and go up and visit him twice a week, taking

the boy with her. It's not good for either of them, dear, not good. The only one it can't harm is the husband himself because he's beyond it all. But if Norma doesn't behave the way her mother-in-law thinks she ought to, she'll never get any of the money. No, nor Little Johnny, either. Oh, it's wicked, dear, wicked.'

I was inclined to agree. But I didn't feel that Norma Handel's attitude was helping. This was obviously the biggest crisis she had ever faced in her life — and she was coping with it by trying to sleep her way through it. At the cost of ignoring her son. It did not appear to have occurred to her that she might be laying the groundwork for another serious crisis in the future . . .

As I entered, my room was lit briefly by the sweeping beam from the lighthouse at the end of the marina. I didn't bother to put the overhead light on, but crossed to the desk at the window looking out over the back garden and the town. I stretched out my hand to switch on the desk lamp and hesitated, caught by the feeling that something was vaguely wrong and trying to identify what.

The bulb was still warm. The lamp had been switched off only recently. Someone had been in my room. *Perhaps he still was.*

I snapped on the light quickly and whirled around. The room was, of course, empty. If I hadn't been over-wrought already, I would have known who the intruder had been. Realization came to me as I turned back to my desk and saw the untidy pile of unopened letters beneath the desk lamp.

Dear Little Johnny had been on the prowl again.

I crossed the room and opened my closet door. Sure enough, my suitcases were no longer quite as I had left them. Doubtless Johnny had moved them, the better to run his metal detector over them in search of hidden treasure. Why go to the effort of combing the beach when he might find something exciting closer to hand?

I slammed the closet door shut, certain that Johnny
would be listening and get the message. If the noise disturbed anyone else, it was just too bad. It was high time
something disturbed Norma and brought her back to
reality; trying to join her husband in his catatonic state
wasn't doing anyone any good.

I went back to my desk and took up my letters. There
was a scorch mark on the back of one envelope where
Johnny had pressed it against the light bulb too closely
and too long as he tried to read its contents. I opened it
and was pleased to see that it was a lined envelope — no
wonder Johnny had been trying so hard to read through
it. He must have thought it was something particularly
juicy. In fact, it was a rather boring missive from my mother
relating the uninteresting adventures of distant relatives I
could barely remember.

The rest of my afternoon post consisted of letters from
friends, a small cheque from a recording company for the
one and only record I had ever cut, and an assortment of
junk mail my mother had inexplicably forwarded, each
enclosed in a fresh envelope, by air mail.

I set aside the only letter I felt like answering, took my
keys out of my handbag and went back to the closet with
the other letters. I used my empty suitcases as repositories
for items I didn't care to leave lying about the room.
Which meant practically everything — especially personal
mail. I had learned about Little Johnny fairly early on in
my residence here.

Daisy Dayton was aware of the problem and usually very
good about locking up behind her when she had finished
cleaning the rooms and making the beds. Unfortunately,
she was easily distracted and an unexpected telephone
call could bring her flying down from another floor; a
prolonged conversation could disrupt her schedule so that
she tended to rush on to the next task, neglecting to go
back and clear up any unfinished items — like locking doors.

I opened the nearest suitcase and threw in the opened
letters with unnecessary force. There was nothing in them
that anyone could not have seen. They would have been a
bitter disappointment to Johnny had he been able to read
them. No secrets, no scandals, not even anything of any
particular interest. All he could have learned about me—
already visible from the address on the envelope—was
that my real name was Gertrude Candowski. I had
shortened it to Trudi Kane for professional purposes—a
common practice. Nothing I could possibly be black-
mailed over.

I wasn't sure where that thought had come from, or
when that suspicion had begun to grow. Perhaps it was
those sly watching eyes; perhaps it was the fact that Johnny
always seemed to have so much money to play with. More
than even the most doting mother might think fit to lavish
on him. Not that I was certain that Norma had that much
money to throw around. The general impression was that
her mother-in-law, who *did* control the family money
supply, kept her on a pretty short leash.

I relocked the suitcase and placed it in the far corner of
the closet. I'd have another word with Daisy about
keeping my door locked. My life might be an open book,
but I reserved the right to be choosy about who turned the
pages.

I went back to the desk and sat down to read the letter
from Marge, who had taken over on the piano bar for the
summer at Sandy Acres Bay. It was full of local gossip,
bringing back familiar scenes. For a moment, I was looking
out on the wide sweep of sea and sand dunes, seeing the
familiar faces gathered around my piano. The 'summer
people', who came back year after year; the wives and children moving into rented beach houses for the summer
while their husbands sweltered in the steaming cities,
working during the week and getting away at weekends to
join them by the sea. They had been doing it for years,

would continue to do it until the children were old enough to disappear into worlds of their own, leaving their parents free to make that trip to Europe—or get a divorce.

It was a way of life, if only for the time being. And I had watched them sitting around the bar in the evenings, the women in whatever was fashionable that particular summer, the men in their standard seaside uniforms, either jeans and T-shirts or Bermuda shorts and Bleeding Madras jackets, staring into their drinks and wondering where all the bright promise had gone. Where had Camelot disappeared to? How had the Sweetheart of Sigma Chi evolved into the Battleaxe of the Leavittown Estate? Would a new job, a new house, a new wife, bring back the magic?

I'd been on the gin-mill circuit for five years and there were times when I felt the general disillusionment was beginning to get to me, too.

Then, right at the end of the summer season, Ted had come along. His arm still in a plaster cast from the August raid, he had come to the States for a short holiday while his pub was being rebuilt. He'd wandered into the cocktail-bar where I was appearing one night and we'd started talking.

On the whole, I had no regrets. I was seeing a bit of the world; I got up to London about once a week and took in a matinee; I had even made a few day trips to France, although I had not got as far as Paris yet.

For the rest of it, I was an entertainer and a job was a job. I might just as well be playing the eighteenth chorus of 'Maybe it's Because I'm a Londoner' of an evening as the eighteenth chorus of 'The Whiffenpoof Song'. On the whole, the English were a more cheerful audience, less introspective and more genuinely out to have a good time. Cheerfulness breeds cheerfulness and I was finding renewed enjoyment in my chosen profession.

Also, I was a novelty here and that helped. If there

were any piano bars in England, they were few and far between. Ted had immediately recognized that I could be the starring attraction The Phoenix needed to become the most popular Lounge Bar on the Coast. He had arranged a Work Permit for me and imported me, piano bar and all. He was right.

At first, the customers had found it strange, and perhaps a little alarming, to be so close to an entertainer. The curved padded counter built around the piano had been deserted more nights than not while the customers had huddled at tables at a respectful distance. But gradually they had grown accustomed to it and begun to sidle into seats at the far end of the keyboard, until finally every seat was filled—even the ones right beside me.

After that, I found I could chart the progress of their holiday. The newcomers sat timidly at the rear tables watching the drill. As the incumbents around the piano rounded off their holiday and disappeared, I noticed that the others crept forward; from the rear tables to the front, from the front tables to the seats round the piano bar— giving every indication of enjoying themselves hugely at their own daring.

Apart from this principle, which I had learned was called 'Buggins's Turn', they behaved generally much as an American audience. They sent over drinks for the pianist and I always had a row of glasses ranged above the keyboard. Luckily, I also had the usual arrangement with Ted so that, despite the appearance, few of the drinks were actually alcoholic.

They also learned the method for requesting special numbers and I was soon swamped with the customary snow-drift of cocktail napkins and beer mats, sent up from the floor, with favourite song titles scrawled on them in ball-point, Pentel and even lipstick.

It began to seem almost like home, except for the vari-ation in titles and the fact that a few of the cast of

characters were missing. I still got the amateur vocalists—
some of them very good—who joined me at the microphone
to sing their theme songs, but the amateur musicians were
missing. Perhaps they were all working in groups over
here, or perhaps rock backgrounds had left them unequipped to cope with arrangements that depended on
melody. At home, there was always a drummer. Some
managements even kept a set of drums behind me so that
punters who fancied themselves as Gene Krupa or Ringo
Starr could have a go. Sometimes they showed up with
their own drums. I didn't mind. They were usually content
to thrum out the beat quietly in the background and it
takes a lot to put me off. It hadn't happened here yet.

Anyway, Ted was pleased and talked of extending my
engagement through the winter. Even better, interested
parties from London had been down and were making
discreet noises about London appearances in the Lounge
Bars of exclusive hotels. It was too early to tell whether
that would come to anything, but I smiled, nodded and
trilled out with the fancy bits whenever I suspected someone had slipped in to look me over.

So far, nothing had happened, but it was early days
yet. A lot of the relevant people were still on vacation,
flinging themselves as far afield as Inland Revenue were
likely to countenance, heedless of talent right under their
noses, if not exactly local.

Meanwhile, *The Stage* had mentioned me approvingly
and the *Variety* correspondent had been close to lyrical.
My future prospects were looking a lot brighter than the
view had been from Sandy Acres Bay. Whatever else disturbed me about this engagement, I must remember that
and hang on until something solid actually materialized.

I made a mental note to have another chat with Daisy
Dayton about keeping my door locked at all times. I
would stress again the undesirability of leaving anything
unguarded with Little Johnny in the house. Daisy already

knew this, but had an ostrich-like ability to hide herself from unpleasant facts. I suspected that Norma was paying rather over the odds for her accommodation — and for the illusion that her son was being safely looked after while she slept her life away. She was old enough to know that nothing was as easy as that and money couldn't buy quite everything. But that was Norma's problem, not mine.

I unlocked a desk drawer which bore telltale scratches around the lock and dipped into my stock of incredible seaside postcards which I had bought in an unbelieving daze when I first arrived. There was no need to keep them under lock and key, of course; similar examples were displayed in every shop along the front, but I still had the double-standard feeling that an innocent child should not be exposed to them. Of course, an innocent child shouldn't be rummaging through my room, either.

I chose one of the boldest and addressed it to Marge at Sandy Acres Bay, scrawling an indecipherable signature on it. If the US Postal Authorities let it through, she would know the source. If they didn't, they could never prove it was me sending such material through the US mails. Nations had double standards, too.

Just before I turned in, I drew the curtains, although the beam from the lighthouse was already blurred by the encroaching mist. The foghorn had started up, as well. A lot of people would be sleeping easier tonight when they heard it. It portended just the sort of weekend they had been hoping for: wet, murky and very discouraging to trippers.

I found that I, too, was feeling more relaxed as I drifted off to sleep with the foghorn still hooting direfully in the distance.

CHAPTER 4

Traitorously, Saturday morning dawned bright and beautiful. I was awake early and the first one down to breakfast — apart from Little Johnny, who had already eaten and gone out. I silently thanked heaven for that. Little Johnny Handel was not a person I wished to see across the breakfast table first thing in the morning. In fact, I could face it with equanimity if I never saw him again in my entire life.

At least he was out of the way this morning. For such small mercies, I was duly grateful.

'You're down early, dear.' Daisy Dayton hurried in with a pot of coffee and a guilty look, although it was I who should feel guilty for disturbing her early-morning session with the radio and the morning newspaper. 'I've just put your egg on to boil.'

'That's fine, thank you,' I said resignedly. I had long since given up trying to peruade her that I didn't really want an egg, only coffee and toast. I was paying for full board and full board I would have — if it killed me. We had compromised on a boiled egg and extra toast for breakfast, although Daisy still seemed to feel that she was cheating me because the others had what she called 'a proper fry-up', which consisted of various combinations of bacon, eggs, tomato, mushrooms, sausages and fried bread. To placate her, I managed the full breakfast on Sundays but, during the week, even one boiled egg was more than I felt like eating. Fortunately the cats were friendly and obliging; they didn't even fight over who was going to get the egg, but queued up to take a spoonful of egg in turn.

But we were all foiled this morning. Daisy brought in a

cup of coffee for herself, along with my breakfast, and sat down opposite me. Perhaps it was just as well. It would give me the chance to discuss our joint problem — even at the price of eating my own egg.

'Daisy—' I said, giving the importunate Formby a surreptitious push under the table with my foot; Robey and Fields had got the message when Daisy sat down and had retreated across the room to gaze benignly at the table with apparent unconcern— 'Daisy, I'm afraid you're going to have to do something about Johnny Handel. He's been in my room again.'

'Oh no,' Daisy sighed. 'No.' She seemed to be denying the need to take action more than the news that the brat had been on the prowl again. 'I'm so sorry, dear. He didn't take anything, did he?'

'Not so far as I can tell,' I admitted. 'I don't seem to have anything he likes. Fortunately.'

'He's never taken anything yet.' Daisy was more prepared than I to look on the bright side. 'It isn't as though he's a sneak thief—'

'Just a sneak.' I was not going to let her off the hook. 'He's been through my things. I don't happen to have anything worth stealing. But someday—'

'I know, dear, I know.' Daisy shook her head. 'That boy will come to no good end!'

'And the sooner, the better,' I said grimly. 'I won't have it, Daisy. You've got to keep my door locked—'

'It was!' she wailed. 'I've kept *all* the doors locked all summer — even on the hot days when I'd ordinarily leave them open to air the rooms properly. But it's no good. He's got hold of some sort of master key somewhere — and I can't be in the house every minute. I have to go out and do the shopping.' She seemed on the verge of tears.

'I just don't know what to do, dear. Honestly, I don't. There's no use changing the locks. It would cost a fortune and I couldn't afford it. And it wouldn't do any good as long as he's got that master key . . .'

'And it's no good talking to Norma, I suppose. Even if you could shake her out of that stupor.'

'She doesn't want to know, dear. She never did. And I hate to worry her, she's having a hard enough time.' Daisy looked at me fearfully, as though I might issue an ultimatum she didn't want to hear.

'I don't usually take non-pros, dear, you know, but this was different. They came personally recommended — just the way you did. Of course, you're a pro. But you know what I mean, I can't turn them out. It wouldn't be wise to upset Councillor Tiverton. He isn't a nice man when he's crossed, not nice at all.'

I could well believe it. He wasn't a particularly nice man even when he was trying his best to be charming. If crossed . . .

'Yes,' I said, 'I see what you mean.'

I wondered if I saw more than that. Councillor Albert Tiverton had never struck me as the type to take a disinterested attitude to damsels in distress. If he was prepared to do anything to alleviate their present distress, it was a pretty safe bet that they could look forward to a more personal distress in the future, when he presented his bill. If there wasn't anything in it for Our Albert, he wasn't going to play. The fact that Norma was able to lose herself in the sleep of the just for at least eighteen out of the twenty-four hours merely indicated that Albert Tiverton had not yet put in for payment.

'He's an old friend of the family, dear,' Daisy said defensively. 'Well, through his wife, that is. I've known Milly and Ted for more years than I like to recall. Naturally, I wanted to do them a favour when I could.'

'Naturally,' I agreed, giving Formby another push.

'Poor Milly,' she sighed. I thought for a moment she had homed in on my suspicions about the Councillor, but she was off on a tangent of her own. 'She thought she was doing so well, marrying a politician, but it just goes to show, doesn't it, dear?'

'That's right,' I agreed absently, lost again. I usually got lost at some point in any conversation with Daisy. Eventually, I either caught up with her or she moved to another subject; either way, it could be a merry chase. But I was still too annoyed this morning to play that little game.

'But the problem under discussion —' I called her back to order sharply — 'is Johnny Handel. Little Johnny Handel,' I added, just in case she might think I had someone else in mind.

Formby gave a sharp, despairing howl of frustration as he watched me swallow the last morsel of boiled egg. Daisy looked as though he had expressed her sentiments exactly.

'Oh yes, dear,' she said unconvincingly. 'Yes, of course. I'll do something about it, dear. I'll speak to him, I'll speak to him severely.'

That and ten pence would get her a ride on any bus in town.

'You do that,' I said uncompromisingly. 'I don't want him in my room again. There's no reason why he should even be on the same floor as my room. If I ever again find that he has been —'

'I'll take care of it, dear. I'll see to it.' She cut off my abortive threat hastily, which was just as well. I'd had no idea how I was going to end up. It was one of those sentences which, once launched upon, seems to carry its own momentum until, suddenly, you realize there's nowhere for it to go.

'See that you do,' I said darkly and stood up before I could get further embroiled. 'I'm going out now —'

'Going anywhere nice, dear?'

It was the sort of inane inquiry that always made me want to reply, 'No, I'm going somewhere nasty.' Where did they expect I'd be going?

'Shopping,' I said weakly, and fled the room with her words of encouragement winging after me.

'That's right, dear. You want to get to the shops before the trippers get there and pick everything over . . .'

Actually, I was only heading for Marks and Spencer's to pick up an attractive lambswool cardigan I had mentally earmarked for myself a couple of weeks ago when the new line had gone on sale. Daisy's warning was timely; I had already noticed how quickly popular lines sold out. There was something about the seaside air which caused the visitors to snap up items they could equally well find in their chain stores at home.

My stroll down to the shopping centre of the town was slowed by the constant flow of traffic which meant that I had to go out of my way to a corner where there were traffic lights before I could safely cross. I had never seen such a snarl of bumper-to-bumper traffic. And it was still quite early—not ten o'clock yet. By mid-day, the flood would have assumed terrifying proportions.

This was the last big weekend of the year. August Bank Holiday. The end of the summer school holiday for the kids, which is the reason the seaside is always so crowded for the month of August when parents take their holidays to fit into the school holiday. This weekend was the end of holiday for them and, for the trippers, a long weekend and the last chance for a whoop-up and knees-up between here and Christmas. They were all determined to make the most of it.

Inevitably, there were motor-cyclists among the crowd, but they seemed to be arriving singly or in pairs. Unless they were going to link up to form that terrorizing gang later. Townspeople on the pavement watched them suspiciously, which was hardly surprising. Their very uniform, especially the ominous hooded crash helmets, dehumanized them, turning them into robotlike creatures from whom anything might be expected.

I was nearly at the intermediate level containing the shops now. As I waited to cross the last street, the coaches began rolling past, placards in their windows identifying them so that their parties could recognize them easily in the coach park.

With eyes as mistrustful as any of the townspeople, I watched them roll past, mentally assessing their potentiality for carrying trouble. Three had parties of children who looked inadequately supervised. That meant the possibility of shoplifting and hooliganism. The more exclusive shops had already posted notices reading: 'Children not admitted unless accompanied by an adult'; but the shopkeepers along the promenade, specializing in sweets, ices and small portable novelties, were just going to have to take their chances with sticky little fingers.

Another coachload proclaimed itself The Darby and Joan Club, while another was a Senior Citizens' Outing. They seemed unlikely to get into any punch-ups although, these days, one could never be sure.

The traffic lights changed to red and the traffic growled to a reluctant standstill. The little green man flashed on and I started to cross the street. I was only half way across when he began to flicker warningly. I increased my pace and just made it to the kerb as the front line of cars leaped forward with an impatient roar. I hoped the older day trippers were pretty nippy on their feet, or there would be carnage of a different sort than expected this holiday weekend.

The shops were full of familiar faces as the townspeople did their shopping early to get in supplies, for the next two days when food stores and chain stores would be closed. I saw Milly Tiverton pushing a wheeled basket full of vegetables and salad greens. Ted walked beside her, carrying his own shopping which seemed to have pretty much duplicated hers. Although the deep-freeze for The Phoenix kitchen was always well-stocked, I knew that he considered it an admission of failure to have to dip into it for his own personal supplies. He had been a widower long enough to insist on demonstrating his ability to survive and live well without a woman in the house. I suspect that it was partly reaction against his sister's matchmaking attempts, which had never produced a female he considered satisfactory.

('Lame ducks, every one of them,' he had confided to me once. 'Speaks well for Milly's tender heart — she'd like to see the poor things with a happy ending. But she never seems to think what it would be like for me. I'm the one she bloody expects to live with them, as well as support them! Maybe she thinks it doesn't matter to me. Maybe she thinks I'm past it. Ah, well,' he had sighed deeply. 'Never mind. Let it be . . .')

It had crossed my mind even then that the reason all of Milly's friends were lame ducks might be because they were the only ones it was safe to have around with a husband like Albert Tiverton, but Ted had obviously never thought about that. If he had, he had ignored the thought. Perhaps he thought Milly was 'past it'. Siblings were never very good judges of each other's attractiveness or emotions.

Fortunately, they were on the other side of the street, so conversation wasn't required. I waved cheerfully and dodged into Woolworth's. I could use some toothpaste and soap.

What I couldn't use was a meeting with Little Johnny Handel. We realized simultaneously and with apparently equal horror that we were on a collision course in the toiletries aisle.

We both swerved abruptly, avoiding each other's eyes, and continued on our separate ways. He was heading for the door and I stopped in front of the toothpaste display to browse and try to decide whether I wanted to stick with an American brand I knew or try one of the unknown English quantities. It was the sort of decision I could normally spend a happy quarter-hour over, but now I could not settle to enjoying it. I had the uneasy feeling that Little Johnny might double back on his track and re-appear at my elbow momentarily.

I glanced over my shoulder and saw him, just as he was glancing back over *his* shoulder. He hesitated in the door-way, his expression both furtive and triumphant, then his eyes met mine and his face went blank. He turned and rushed out of the store, leaving me oddly disturbed.

Of course, Little Johnny always looked furtive. Usually with good reason, I suspected. Especially this morning — and not just because I had so nearly caught him going through my room last night.

I realized suddenly that, as he had come down the aisle towards me, I had received the distinct impression that he was stuffing a small unwrapped object into his pocket.

Perhaps I was wronging him and he had actually paid for it. But I didn't think so. This store usually put every item — no matter how small — into a paper bag. That, with a sales slip, was the customer's proof of purchase. I doubted that Johnny could produce a sales slip for what-ever he had put into his pocket.

There was nothing I could do about it. He was already out of the store and probably half way across town by now. Even if I reported my suspicion — and it *was* only a suspicion — he could have disposed of the evidence before anyone caught up with him. I also had the suspicion that he had had plenty of practice.

Nor was there any point in trying to talk to Norma about the problem. Even if she believed me, she wouldn't thank me for that sort of information. It wasn't what she wanted to hear. More probably, she wouldn't hear it at all. She would listen sleepily, not really assimilating any-thing that had been said to her, then yawn and go back to her room and her bed. To sleep some more, to while away the hours, days, weeks of waiting. Waiting for what?

Sleeping Beauty was traditionally awakened by a kiss from Prince Charming, but Norma had already found her Prince Charming, married him, and lost him to a deep trance of his own in one of the nursing homes on the top of the hill. Did she think that another one might come along if she retreated into the classic role? She forgot that fairy tales strictly rationed Prince Charmings: one per Enchanted Princess, till death do them part.

But Life was real, Life was earnest — and Norma was due for a rude awakening some day. Perhaps some day very soon. Police in the parlour . . . Little Johnny, tearful and protesting improbable innocence . . . Norma, blinking and yawning and wondering what had gone wrong with the script . . . none of the bit players knew their proper roles — and Prince Charming was nowhere in sight.

I hoped I wouldn't be there to see it, but I was dreadfully afraid that I would be. Life was surging on much too swiftly, as it always did. Only Norma seemed to have the gift of sleeping it away.

But the Summer Season was ending; the Pantomime bad spirits were gathering, snarling and snickering in the wings, ready to snatch away the gifts bestowed at the christening by the good spirits. If Norma didn't wake up soon, it would be too late.

Perhaps it was too late already.

CHAPTER 5

It hadn't been much of a day to begin with, and now it was well-nigh ruined. Before noon, even. Perhaps Norma had the right idea: it didn't pay to get up at all.

Thoroughly dispirited, I made my purchases at Wool-

worth's and plodded along towards Marks and Spencer's.
It simply confirmed my gloomy loss of confidence in the
entire day that the next person I ran into was Kate Carter
from the Mad Manic Music Hall playing at the Grand
Theatre at the end of the Pier.

Don't get me wrong. Kate is a darling, really. It's just
that one gets the feeling she's typecast in her show—
'manic' is the word for it. After a while, one begins to
hope for the depressive phase to set in, but it never does.
There are a lot of them in show business and sometimes
they make it big—very big, indeed. But, after the first
half-hour, they can be very exhausting company.

'Trudi!' She hailed me from a drugstore, waving wildly—
not so much to attract my attention as to dry the nail
polish, a different colour on each nail of her left hand.
'Come and tell me what colour suits me best. I can't
decide!'

'They all look marvellous.' I wasn't going to be drawn
into that one again. I'd fallen for it before. Under the
guise of soliciting advice, Kate managed to give herself a
free coating of nail polish from the tester bottles—right
under the eyes of the sales staff—in different stores about
once a week. 'Why don't you buy the lot?'

'I might, at that,' she said, then hesitated. 'But which
one should I *wear* tonight?' Abstractedly, she started on
the nails of her right hand.

'Wear them all,' I advised recklessly. She usually
wound up with a few mismatched nails, anyway. It wasn't
easy to keep dipping into the same bottle with a salesgirl
watching. 'Who's going to notice? You're up on stage.
Your audience is far enough away for anything subtle to
be lost beyond the first few rows.'

'Yes, you're right.' She sighed heavily. 'Oh, Trudi, you
don't know how lucky you are, not having to work
matinees.'

'I've got a pretty good idea,' I said. Since I didn't go on

duty at the piano bar until six — half an hour after opening time, in order to give a bit of an audience time to assemble — I had dropped in and sampled some of the matinee performances of the Summer Shows on offer. I'd found them pretty incredible.

A lifetime of summers heretofore exposed to the Straw Hat Circuit had left me totally unprepared for what the British considered suitable summer entertainment. Whereas America was dotted with Summer Theatres who vied with each other from June to September to bring the best available theatre to summer residents, the British seemed to consider that none of their audiences had an attention span beyond the traditional twenty minutes allotted to primary school children. American offerings varied from the tried-and-true old standards to pre-Broadway tryouts of new shows. The British Summer Shows were mostly revues, largely consisting of the kind of acts that killed vaudeville.

After viewing a couple of them, I began to long for the sophistication of *Springtime for Henry*. Not to mention the weary expertise of whatever superannuated actress was currently touring in *The Glass Menagerie*. I even longed for the gaucheries of the no-hoper tryouts allegedly bound for Broadway, even though everyone knew they'd never get any farther in that direction than the Manomet Playhouse. At least, these all presumed an audience willing to engage themselves for the evening through two acts and an interval. Another plus was that you seldom saw children at these performances. An American summer audience wanted to escape from its brats for an evening, not drag them along with them.

'*And* your audience is over eighteen!' Losing interest in nail polish, Kate replaced the last bottle in the rack. She now had a complete manicure, albeit a somewhat eccentric one. It went with her image, though, and she seemed quite happy about it. 'You don't know what an advantage it is not to have to pitch your act towards the dear little kiddies, as well as their Mums and Dads.'

'I've got a pretty good idea,' I said again. Most of the acts I had seen flop did so in the no-man's-land between the generations. Some 'artistes' just about ruptured themselves trying to get the jokes blue enough to make an X-rating, in the hope that the adults would laugh, while the reason for the laughter went over the heads of the little darlings in the audience. Few succeeded. Most limped offstage to reluctant applause, leaving behind a strained atmosphere as parents hoped the kiddiewinks would forget to demand an explanation of the jokes later.

'Not while you're protected by the Licensing Laws, you haven't,' she said bitterly. 'You'll never know what it's like until you get Our Own, Our Very Own, Little Johnny Handel in the audience heckling you. He'll probably be there this afternoon. God! Someday I'm going to murder that little bastard!' She flexed her multi-hued talons wistfully. 'I'd be a public benefactor. They'd give me a medal.'

'Every performer in town would contribute to it,' I assured her. I had heard Little Johnny's lovable habit discussed at length over the supper table. The Great Dandini dreamed of getting him onstage to help with the Sawing-the-Lady-in-Half routine and bundling him into the box instead of the lady, and then forgetting the part of the routine essential to the safety of the body in the box. The Punch-and-Judy man favoured the simple blunt instrument technique and swore he kept an iron bar in reserve inside his booth, ready to use it at the first opportunity and lay the blame on Punch. But Little Johnny was too clever for any of them and remained out of range, yodelling catcalls and bright remarks from the back of the audience.

'Never mind.' She was still gloomily contemplating the prospect of this afternoon's matinee and I tried to cheer her. 'The Season is coming to an end. This is the last big weekend of the year. He may get bored with that amusement when the audiences aren't so big.'

'It's not so good for us, either, when the audiences shrink.' Kate helped herself to a generous dollop of hand lotion from another tester. 'It means they may not bother to keep us going until the end of September if the returns aren't worth it.'

'Surely they wouldn't close it down. Anyway, you've got a contract—'

'Run of the Season,' she said gloomily, massaging the lotion into her skin, giving the impression of wringing her hands. 'I didn't like that wording to begin with. It doesn't define the length of the Season. If the Corporation decides the Season's over, there we are. They'll close the show on the grounds of saving the ratepayers' money and we won't have much comeback. Oh, we'd get Equity to fight it out with them, but it would probably end in a compromise. Meanwhile, we'd be out of work. And it's a long time until the Christmas Pantomimes go into rehearsal."

'It may not happen.' We left the counter and moved out into the street. I headed towards Marks and Spencer and she came with me, obviously having attached herself to me for the rest of the morning.

'On the other hand, it may be on the cards now.' She was determined not to be cheered. 'Councillor Tiverton has dropped a few hints, you know.'

'I'll bet that's not all he hinted.'

'You're right.' She grinned suddenly. 'Isn't it too bad he isn't as important as he thinks he is? I don't want to be caught within ten miles of him when his balloon bursts.'

'What do you mean?' This was the second time this morning I'd heard strange intimations about Councillor Tiverton. I couldn't decide whether it was a matter of general knowledge I'd missed out on because I hadn't been in town all that long, or whether it was something peculiarly English, the nuances of which would for ever escape an American.

'Oh, nothing.' She shrugged restlessly. 'He's not worth worrying about. To hell with it! To hell with everything!' She straightened her shoulders, her chin shot up defiantly. 'I've come to a decision. Do you know what I'm going to do? I'm going to put the Massage Parlour Skit into the show this weekend!'

'You can't!' I gasped. She had performed it for us on Sunday evenings at the digs. It was killingly funny, but awfully close to the knuckle. And, for a seaside audience, with children included . . . 'You'll never get away with it. They'll ring down the curtain.'

'I'd be well into it before anyone realizes — and then they won't dare.' She laughed aloud. 'Just watch me! I mean it, Trudi. Come along to the matinee and witness the Great British Premiere.'

'I'll do that,' I said. It would be interesting and instructive to see how the sketch played before a mass audience. And she might just get away with it. After all, the show was called the Mad Manic Music Hall — and I'd never seen anything as mad and manic as that skit. Also, Kate was shrewd enough to temper her material to the mood of her audience. She had never played the skit in exactly the same way twice, even for us; it was bound to change and improve if she could work in front of a live and critical commercial audience.

Kate had several sketches she had devised and written herself. They were sharp and funny — perhaps too sharp; they seemed to stir the audience to uneasiness as much as to laughter half the time. She had begun by using 'Air Hostess' in the Music Hall ('I'm sorry, the wing seems to have fallen off. But don't worry . . .') It brought instant identification with everyone who'd ever been on a package tour. When she had realized this, she had immediately begun work on 'Tour Leader' and introduced it.

('Your husband went off to find the Black Market to change some money and hasn't come back yet, Mrs Badger? Three days ago? . . . Of course we'll look into it. Meanwhile, let me introduce you to Mr Henley. His wife went round to the kitchen last week to complain to the chef about the food. He hates being on his own . . .')

Her other sketches were too sophisticated for her present audiences. She'd do well in cabaret or supper clubs, perhaps even better in a one-woman show. The problem, as with all of us, was making the breakthrough.

'Be careful!' In her abstraction, Kate had nearly stepped out into the stream of moving traffic. I pulled her back. 'Watch where you're going!'

'Sorry,' Kate said. 'I was lost in thought,' she added, unnecessarily.

'This is no place and no time to think,' I scolded. 'You'd better stay on your toes this weekend. The town is full of strangers who don't know where they're going but don't want to waste any time getting there. It's dangerous.'

'I know.' She shuddered and looked around, taking in the hordes of holidaymakers crowding the street, their voices raucous and complaining, already looking for places to eat. 'I hate it when the town is like this. Too full, too crowded with people just down for a day or the weekend. I suppose it's good for business, but I still hate it.'

'So do I,' I agreed. There was something unnerving about so many people milling about without any purpose except the vague amorphous one of having a good time. It gave a curiously rootless feeling to the whole town: all these people, surging through, determined to enjoy themselves, as though they were making a smash-and-grab raid on happiness.

And sometimes it was other people who got smashed.

DID YOU SEE THIS GIRL? The police poster shrieked from shop windows, from the Tourist Attractions Bulletin

Board, from lamp-posts and hoardings. The face of the dead girl stared out with blank sightless eyes betraying the fact that it was a death photograph. Perhaps somewhere she had featured on holiday snapshots, live and laughing.

But not here. Here, she had been the 'August Nude', the body on the beach after the August Holiday tide had receded. She was 'This Girl', still unidentified after all these months. The police had obviously rushed through this batch of new posters in the hope that someone who had been here last August Bank Holiday might be paying a return visit. Probably their hopes didn't extend to the murderer's returning to the scene of the crime; they would be satisfied with any fragments of information which might help them to construct a picture of her last day on earth. Someone who had glimpsed her on the promenade, or buying something in one of the shops, or perhaps exchanged a few words with her and had noticed whether or not she had an accent, either foreign or regional. Perhaps, if they were very lucky, a witness who had seen her with someone else and could describe that companion. The odds were astronomical, but the chance had to be taken. Meanwhile, the blank eyes stared out at the passing throngs, most of whom just glanced at the poster and glanced away again. It was nothing to do with them.

'Ugh!' Kate followed the direction of my gaze and saw the police poster. 'That was a nasty do. Why do they have to drag it up all over again? And on a Bank Holiday week-end, too!'

'Because it's still unsolved, I suppose. They think someone might remember something. Another Bank Holiday weekend — it's a psychological time to joggle memories. You were here then, weren't you?'

'Yes.' She gave a sharp, almost hostile look, obviously reading more into my innocent question than I had intended. 'But all I know about it is what I read in the papers. We were breaking in a new act in the Mad Manic Music Hall that weekend, so we had enough troubles of our own. Then, when the motor-cycle gang arrived—' She broke off and shuddered. 'I don't *want* to remember that weekend. No one does. Why can't they let it be?'

I had already answered that question. I remained silent.

'We were *all* here then,' she said defensively. 'All except *you.*' She made it sound like an accusation. Tit-for-tat, I suppose. She seemed to think that I had been blaming her in some way. 'It was the last big holiday weekend of the Season. That's why the town drew so many visitors.'

Two motor-cycles roared past us, snorting defiance at the world. Kate flinched visibly.

'Sorry,' she apologized, 'but I hate those things. I wish they'd never been invented.'

'That's hardly surprising. Most of the town feels that way. And yet, it's only a minority who misuse them. Most of the cyclists are decent, law-abiding people who can't afford to run motor-cars.'

'Then let them stay home!' Kate spoke savagely. 'Or at least use public transport.' She shuddered again. 'I'm sorry, Trudi. But you don't know what it was like that night.'

'I've heard quite a lot,' I said, and I had. From Ted, nursing both his broken arm and his drink as he sat beside me at the piano bar, telling me of the horror, but trying to persuade me that it was unlikely to happen again and I ought to come and spend a season working at his new pub.

From Daisy, who had sat in her own living-room watching with incredulity as the television set relayed the incredible scenes of vandalism and devastation from the sea front just a few hundred yards below. ('I didn't let the cats out for a week after that, dear.')

From the townspeople and shop owners, who had made Ted's new pub their gathering-place in a gesture of solidarity with the local resident who had suffered most during the invasion. Also, of course, The Phoenix was the newest, brightest and best pub along the promenade. They seemed to like my act, too.

From the other performers, who had been caught in the midst of the violence and looting as they tried to make their way back to their digs after their shows had ended. I knew for a fact that several of the more high-strung had already provided themselves with tranquillizers in dread anticipation of this weekend.

Like the survivors of earthquake, blizzard or other natural catastrophe, everyone had their own story of that weekend. Where they were, and what they were doing when the motor-cycle mob struck; the narrow escapes, the bruises, the insults, the terror. One and all dreaded a return engagement.

'We were lucky,' Kate said. 'Dandini and I were still in the theatre at the end of the pier. We just stayed there all night — the whole cast. When the first motor-cycles began to race each other along the pier, the manager pulled up the drawbridge. They didn't expect that — most of them didn't know it existed. A couple of them shot right off into the water — *that* cooled them off. And ruined their machines, too, I sincerely hope!'

'Served them right,' I applauded. 'Too bad the shop-keepers along the promenade weren't so well fixed.'

'We stood at the end of the pier and watched the fires they set. It was unbelievable, like something out of a night-mare.' Kate was shivering, despite the heat of the sun. 'They were savages — from another world, another time. You could *feel* the hatred. Especially after they lost those four machines. They splashed around in the water, cursing us. And you should have seen the faces on the others as they climbed down the pilings to help them salvage the machines.' She gave another deep shudder.

'That's why I'm afraid they'll be back. They want revenge.'

CHAPTER 6

It had developed into one of those rare days when an English theatre could have done with air-conditioning. Such days are few and far between — and so are English theatres equipped with air-conditioning, although the heating systems are usually adequate. They need to be.

In the afternoon heat, the audience had been uncomfortable and restless, myself included. Released now from the matinee performance, I breathed the cool salty air gratefully. The length of the pier stretched out before me, leading back to the promenade and I decided to let the crowd go ahead of me. I sat on one of the free benches (there was a charge for using the deck chairs) and relaxed.

The crowd headed for shore as eagerly as their Victorian counterparts must have done. The difference was that they had approached this end of the pier from the shore, whereas the Victorians had arrived by pleasure steamers from the great smoky cities, disembarking with gratitude at the end of the pier. With gratitude, because the steamers were unable to sail in close to shore and, prior to the building of the long proud piers the length and breadth of the English shoreline, disembarkation at the seaside resort of their choice had meant that they had to climb down into smaller boats that would take them in closer to the shore; the final stage of their landing being accomplished piggyback astride porters who carried them on to the beach safely and reasonably dry. Small wonder that vaporous ladies and their stiff-necked escorts soon opted for those resorts which built landing piers jutting out into the water to meet the steamers half way. Before long, every seaside town had boasted its own pier and the great Victorian exodus to the seaside had begun.

It continued to this day, but now by dry land all the way. From my vantage point, I could usually see the day-return coaches discharging their passengers at the bus stop just beyond the pier. It was too late in the day for that now, of course, it was nearly time for the coaches to begin picking them up for the return journey home.

Those around me were already demolishing the last of their picnic lunches. Along this end of the pier and at the back of the theatre, fishermen hopefully dangled their rented lines in the deep water, waiting, with a patience that bordered on coma, for a bite. Seagulls wheeled above, ready to swoop on any crust that might be thrown away.

The tide was going out and the foreshore seemed to lengthen every time I looked at it. Some people were still swimming, but more were paddling, trouser-ends rolled up, splashing in the shallows. Children were still building sand castles or playing with frisbees; most of them. I spotted one who was intent on more serious things.

Little Johnny Handel was sweeping the shore with his metal detector. That child had a one-track mind—and profit was the track. Yet, according to Daisy, there was no lack of money in that family. Obviously, he felt that enough of it wasn't filtering through to him.

I was too far away to hear the buzzer go off, but I saw him halt abruptly, then slowly and meticulously swing the metal detector around in a long arc. Several of the other children abandoned their games and sidled closer to him, watching intently.

Johnny raised his head to glare at them and they fell back. Not far enough. He waited, pulling the metal detector close and clutching it to him. His lips moved. Whatever he said could not have been pleasant. The children moved farther back.

Still not far enough. Johnny remained motionless, glaring. They all held the tableau for another minute, then, suddenly, the children broke and scattered, fleeing back to the safety of sand castles and frisbees.

Johnny watched them go, waiting until they had resumed their games. When they were all occupied, not even glancing in his direction any more, he began to move slowly. In his own way, he was as patient as the fishermen along the pier. But there was something unnatural about such patience in a boy of thirteen.

Almost surreptitiously, he began swinging the metal detector in that slow arc again, in ever-decreasing circles until he seemed to find what he was looking for, almost at his feet. He sidestepped, stooped, and began burrowing in the sand. .

When he stood again, brushing sand from some small object, satisfaction was radiating from him. He stuffed the object into his pocket and went to work with the metal detector again, quartering the relevant area as professionally as a search-party. Clearly, he felt that there was more to find.

From this distance, I could not see what he had uncovered. I could tell, however, that he was very pleased with himself, so it must have been something of value. Intrigued, I watched as his search progressed.

'Oh, Trudi—' I jumped as the unexpected voice spoke at my elbow. 'I'm so glad you waited for me.' Kate was looking down at me eagerly. 'What did you think of the sketch?'

'Umm . . .' I tried to look as though I were considering my answer. Actually, I hadn't given it a thought, but I could hardly admit that. Nor did I feel I could go into the 'Darling, you were marvellous' routine which keeps most performers happy. Kate was a cut above that. True, she wouldn't spit in my eye if I did say it, but she would be hoping for an honest answer. Not quite so honest as the truth, though. Besides, I had been thinking about the act — while it was going on.

'You changed it a bit,' I said slowly. 'Watered it down . . .'

'With that audience, what else could I do?' She heaved an exaggerated sigh. 'I knew they weren't dead — I could hear them breathing. And rattling sweet wrappers. And passing the time of day with each other. I don't know why they bother to pay the admission charge if they're going to ignore the show. It isn't as though it was raining today.'

'They *were* awful.' I was able to agree unreservedly. 'It was the heat, I think. They aren't used to it.'

'It will be better tonight.' She cheered up. 'Cooler. And not so many kids in the audience. I'll let rip then. Too bad you won't be able to see it.'

'Never mind.' I stood and we began strolling back along the pier. 'I'll catch another matinee — after you've broken it in a bit. Then you'll have a better idea of how it's going. By the end of the Season — '

'*If* the Season lasts another month, the way it's supposed to,' she interrupted. '*If* the yobbos don't come back this weekend and burn down the rest of the town.'

Automatically, our eyes turned to the sea front. It looked much the same as usual, except that the crowds were thicker and livelier. It was, of course, impossible to tell whether there was latent hostility and incipient rioting lurking behind the animation. By the time we knew that, it would be too late.

We had nearly reached the promenade when I became aware of that familiar prickling sensation at the back of my neck again.

Someone was staring. At me.

I halted abruptly and Kate stopped, too, puzzled. 'What's the matter?' she asked. 'You've gone quite pale. Aren't you feeling well?'

'No,' I said shortly. Trying not to be too obvious about it, I began scanning the pier, turning slowly. No one in the immediate vicinity appeared to have any interest in me. Very well. I widened the area of my scan.

'Do you want to sit down? I could go over to the café and get you a cup of tea. You're not going to faint, are you?'

'No.' There was no one behind me on the pier, no one ahead on the sea front, who was paying any attention to me at all. Of course, there might be someone watching from behind the curtains at one of the upstairs windows in the self-catering holiday apartments over the shops along the front.

'Well, you're looking a little better now,' Kate conceded. 'You're sure you don't want to sit down and rest for a minute?'

'No. Thank you. I'm sorry, Kate, I just—'

And then I saw him. Standing below on the beach, glaring up at me. Relief flooded me.

It was only Little Johnny Handel. A second later, I wondered why I felt such relief. If it had been an adult staring at me with the same implacable hostility, I would have been frightened.

'That brat again!' Kate followed the direction of my gaze and made a face. 'At least he wasn't at the matinee today. I suppose I should be grateful for small mercies.'

'No,' I said. 'He's been playing on the sands with his new toy, that metal detector.'

'Norma spoils him. Those things are expensive. And he'll only get bored with it before long. It will be tossed aside, just like all his other expensive toys.'

'He seems interested enough in it at the moment,' I said, which was not strictly true. He seemed far more interested in me—but not in any pleasant way.'

'He's glaring at you.' Even Kate had noticed it. 'He seems in an absolute fury. What on earth have you done to him?'

Caught him shoplifting this morning. Or *almost* caught him.

But I could not say that. I had no proof. Only an instinctive certainty which would never stand up in a court of law. Kate would believe me without proof, of course. But she would also talk about it. That way lay trouble — plenty of trouble. Even the dormant Norma could be roused like a tigress to defend her cub against an accusation like that.

'I don't know,' I said feebly. 'He just seems to have a grudge against the whole human race. I suppose you can't blame him too much. Even though Norma seems to buy him everything he wants, he's still getting a pretty rough deal from life.'

'I blame him,' Kate said firmly. 'I'd blame him for anything. After all, plenty of other kids have had a rough deal in life but they don't go around acting the way he does.'

'Some of them act worse,' I defended, although I hadn't really much interest in playing devil's advocate for Johnny Handel. 'Look at the ones who leap on to motor-cycles and ride out and beat up towns.'

'Give him time,' Kate said. 'That will probably be Johnny's next step. I'd say he's well on the way to it now. As soon as Norma is fool enough to let him have a motor-cycle, he'll be hell-bent for leather with the rest of them.'

It was only too probable. Only his age and the laws of the land kept him from it now. As soon as he was old enough, there'd be no stopping him. Where once rebel children dreamed of running away and joining a circus or the gipsies, Johnny Handel would dream of joining Hell's Angels — and he was a prime candidate.

'Come on.' Kate pulled at my arm. 'We can't stand here and hold a staring match with him. Besides, you'd never win, you know.'

'I know.' Johnny could outstare the Sphinx. As I turned away, he moved at last. He lifted his arm, doubled his fist and shook it at my back, not aware that I had caught the gesture from the corner of my eye. It was a pretty international gesture.

Well, okay. What did I care for his opinion of me? He wasn't my favourite person, either.

The quickest way off the pier led through the amusement arcade. It was possible to get on or off the pier without passing through, but it wasn't easy. The alternative route was a long curving detour skirting the featureless outside of the arcade building. No doubt it had been carefully arranged this way, since the City Council had had a great deal to do with the building and siting of the arcade. They weren't ones to let the punters have a chance to keep any change in their pockets.

We strolled through the dark aisles assaulted on all sides by whooping electronic noises. Microchip-powered Space Invaders warred with traditional rifle-shooting booths where the targets were untraditional three-dimensional laser beam projections. All the wonders of modern day science harnessed to a coin pay slot to pull in the suckers' loose cash.

There were also the perennial old favourites, the fruit machines, incorporating the fairly recent innovation of the Nudger button, to give the punters the spurious illusion that skill might have something to do with their chances of winning. If they could just learn to Nudge at the right moment.

A particularly English favourite was the Penny Falls, although few of them could be worked for a penny any more. Two pence was the going sum, with five-pence and ten-pence machines creeping up. It was new to me. The money rolled down a chute to land on a level constantly brushed by an upright partition moving back and forth. If the coin fell in the right position, it was then pushed against the mound of other coins already on the shelf, dislodging some of them to drop down to the next level, where the process was repeated. If the player was lucky, a few coins—or an occasional landslide of coins—fell into the payoff cups at the bottom of the machine.

There seemed to be a constant queue of children at most of the machines, and quite a few adults, too. There was no minimum age limit for players. If a kid was big enough to shovel money into the coin slot at the top—even if it had to stand on its toes to do so—it was old enough to play the machine.

The English were infected with gambling fever at an early age. No wonder there were betting shops on every city street corner.

'Whew!' We emerged into the sunlight, blinking and trying to shake off the semi-hypnotic state induced by the darkened arcade, the weird sounds, the gambling fever all around us. 'There's something frightening about those places.' Thank heaven for daylight again.

'Oh, this one's all right,' Kate said. 'Unlike some I could mention—' She broke off abruptly, as though discretion had suddenly set in.

I decided to let it pass. I was vaguely aware of sinister rumours about a couple of shadier amusement arcades down at the seedier end of the town, but this was not the moment to pursue the matter. So far as I knew, there had never been any open scandal and the march of progress would inevitably take care of such places. When the Marina was completely finished, that sort of sleazy rundown property would be in too valuable a position to be allowed to remain. Some enterprising merchant would take it over, tart it up, and run a reputable line of merchandise from it.

The problem would solve itself, given time. Whereas, other problems . . .

Involuntarily, I glanced over my shoulder. Johnny Handel was following the tide line as the tide went out. He had moved in closer to the metal struts supporting the pier, despite the fact that they seemed to be driving his metal detector haywire. But he appeared to be able to sort out the different messages.

As I watched, he stooped and began digging in the wet sand.

'Come on,' Kate said. 'You want your tea before you go to work, don't you?' She glanced at me anxiously. 'You're sure you're well enough to work tonight?'

'Yes,' I said. 'I'm fine.'

CHAPTER 7

The Phoenix was crowded and noisy. I had been practically standing on the loud pedal for the past half-hour in order to make myself heard over the hubbub. On the off-chance that there might be a few customers who were actually interested in the music. It didn't seem particularly likely tonight.

As usual, the more uninhibited of the clientele were clustered around the piano bar, but even they seemed more interested in each other than in the entertainment. It was Saturday night with a vengeance.

At least, the Saturday-night Starer wasn't here. Not yet. Maybe he wouldn't show up at all. Maybe he'd got his fill of whatever strange kicks turned him on last night. Maybe.

Ted had stationed himself near the door and was inconspicuously vetting the customers as they arrived. He'd refuse admittance to any undesirables—if he could spot them in time. Sometimes they started out all right but underwent a personality change after a few drinks. You couldn't always tell. Most of them just got rowdy, or perhaps extra affectionate, but a few, a very few, turned really nasty.

For the moment, everything was fine. My audience, although not particularly attentive, was appreciative, as the row of glasses ranged above the music rack testified.

Had they really contained Gimlets, I'd have long since been under the piano. But Ted and I had the usual arrangement and no one on the floor could tell that they were only lime juice; what Ted charged for them was his business. It was all part of keeping the customers happy—and some of them watched closely to make sure I actually drank the drink they'd sent up to me.

On the shelf beside the music rack, the pile of paper cocktail mats and napkins was growing. Each had a request for a special number scrawled on it, some written out neatly in ink, complete with 'please' and 'thank you'. Others were written in blunt pencil, the paper caught and torn as someone bore down heavily to make the writing dark enough to be read. A few were from couples who obviously never felt it necessary to carry writing instruments around with them and were scrawled out in eyebrow pencil or lipstick.

I usually managed to play most of the requests during the course of an evening, interspersing them with my regular numbers. This, too, was part of keeping the customers happy.

I picked up the top napkin: some nostalgic customer wanted to hear 'Some of These Days'. That was easy enough. What threw me were the requests for songs from English homegrown musicals which had never reached Broadway or received any American attention at all. Deservedly, I had realized when the local amateur theatrical society had performed a couple of them earlier in the season. Although the lyrics were occasionally sophisticated enough in a would-be Cole Porter manner, the tunes were usually tinkling, simplistic—and unfortunately reminiscent (just this side of plagiarism) of too many American hits of that era. Many of them were also pitched far too high, written for the sort of soprano voice that has disappeared from the modern musical stage.

Of the plots, the less said the better. They all seemed to

be laid in mythical kingdoms so that the principals could
strut around in crowns and jewels, the men in gaudy uniforms, the women in glittering tiaras and dresses with long
trains, with a large cast of jolly adoring peasants dancing
around. Perfect for amateur musical societies, but no
wonder they'd never been seen in the States. American
producers might occasionally be stupid or have lapses into
bad judgement, but they weren't totally suicidal.

Nevertheless, I had begun haunting music shops, book
stores and antique/junk shops looking for old scores and
sheet music to repair the deficiency in my repertoire. It
had become a hobby and I was amassing quite a collection. The old musicals might be inept, but there was the
occasional good song, and a lot of the old Music Hall songs
were quaint enough or funny enough to be good material
for American supper clubs today. The suspicion was
growing at the back of my mind that I was on to something here.

Automatically, I had been rippling from one number
to another, sometimes singing, sometimes just playing the
melody. It was an easy audience tonight, prepared to
treat me as musical wallpaper. Sometimes they were as
fractious and demanding as children wanting Mummy's
attention. Even those sitting up at the piano were
absorbed in each other rather than in me. Almost unconsciously, as I went through my routine, I had been
watching Ted.

Now I saw him twitch uneasily and frown. He was still
watching the doorway and I followed his gaze. The reason
for his unhappiness was quickly apparent.

Councillor Tiverton swept through the doorway as
though he were about to address a political rally. Arm-in-
unwilling-arm with him, pinioned close to his side, was
Norma Handel. For once, she looked almost awake . . . and
frightened.

Lips tightening, Ted moved forward to meet them. His

brother-in-law shook Ted's hand as heartily as though he were a constituent who could throw a few thousand votes in his direction. Ted looked grimmer than ever.

Smiling blandly, Councillor Tiverton started for one of the tables for two in a dark corner of the room. Ted and Norma acted in concert. Ted blocked his path, Norma tugged him in the other direction—towards me.

Giving in with fairly good grace, Councillor Tiverton turned and bore down on the piano bar, tossing me an electioneering smile as he looked for a couple of empty seats.

That was all I needed tonight: the end of a perfect day.

' 'Ere—watch it!' The little blonde Cockney sparrow on the stool nearest the keyboard did not take kindly to having the Councillor's ample stomach rammed into the small of her back. Who could blame her?

'Is 'e givin' you trouble?' Her escort rose and, I was happy to see, towered over Albert Tiverton. He looked as though he might be something in the heftier end of the building trade. 'Just you watch it, mate!'

'Sorry—' Councillor Tiverton turned his vote-catching beam on the man. 'I thought you were just leaving.'

'Well, we're not!' He continued to hover truculently over the Councillor. 'So, suppose you just 'op it!'

I noticed that Ted had turned away and was rather ostentatiously taking no notice of the scene. I got the impression that anyone who wanted to thump his brother-in-law would be able to get in quite a few good punches before Ted was moved to intervene.

'Sorry. No offence.' It wasn't going to happen this time. Councillor Tiverton gave the man a placatory smile and moved back.

Norma sent me a wan smile.

'Good evening, Trudi.' He turned his attention to me.

I nodded and gave a frosty smile. I wasn't going to vote for him, either. One night when the bar was crowded he had tried to come round the barrier and sit beside me on the piano bench. We weren't going to have a repeat of that performance.

'You're in fine voice this evening.' He continued to press, implying an intimacy which didn't exist. 'Just what the doctor ordered. That's why I brought this poor young lady along—' From the pained expression on Norma's face, he had squeezed her arm with more strength than was necessary.

'Can't have her sitting at home brooding on a Saturday night when everyone's out enjoying themselves, can we? Not when she's got such an unpleasant duty ahead of her tomorrow—' He lowered his voice so that the announcement only reached those around the piano bar and at the immediate tables.

'It's the day she goes to see her husband. In one of those places at the top of the hill. Nothing to look forward to, poor child. Ah, it's tragic . . .'

A couple of sentimental idiots got up from the piano bar and gave him their seats. I could have killed them.

'Thank you. That's very kind of you. Have one on me—' He signalled to Ted, who was alert again now that the danger had passed and was keeping a disapproving eye on him.

Trying to ignore all the byplay and give the impression of being deeply absorbed in my work, I picked up the next cocktail napkin, and frowned, trying to decipher it. English handwriting is in a class by itself—several thousand classes, in fact. Americans are taught their nice uniform Palmer Method and have no idea how grateful they should be for it. Over here, every child is left to go its own way and the resultant chaos is somehow considered properly individualistic—even though it might be unreadable. The writing surface of a paper napkin didn't improve matters.

At last the hieroglyphics shifted and formed themselves

into some semblance of order as I blinked at them desperately: '*The Eton Boating Song*'. Good. That was one of the new numbers I had learned since coming to this country. I even liked it.

As the melody rippled from my fingertips, I was prepared to bet that, for every battle won on the playing fields of Eton, several more battles had been lost because no one had been able to interpret the handwritten battle orders correctly.

'Here! What do you want to go playing that rubbish for?' Now that he had his ringside seat, Councillor Tiverton was prepared to take over as Master of Ceremonies. His sort was another occupational hazard. 'Give us something lively, so we can have a sing-song. That's what we want on a night like this, eh? Get the party going!'

He could go at any time and I wouldn't mind in the least. I wouldn't even mind if he took Norma with him. She looked ready to fall asleep sitting upright. Unfortunately, such a means of escape wasn't open to the rest of us.

'Come along now—' Councillor Tiverton raised his voice to rabble-rousing pitch, obviously under the mistaken impression that he was being the life and soul of the party. 'Something bright and jolly everyone can enjoy. Something for all these lovely people who've come to our happy town to have a good time—and the best place in the Kingdom to come!' He raised his voice still higher and broke into song, drowning out the piano completely.

'Oh, I *do* like to *be* beside the seaside . . .'

The Cockney couple closest to me decided to let bygones be bygones and joined in.

'Oh, I *do* like to be beside the sea . . .' Other voices took up the refrain.

If you can't beat them, join them. I fumbled for the right key, then decided it didn't make any difference, everyone was singing in a different key anyway. Loudness was all that was required.

I gave up and tried to throw myself into the spirit of the
song although, strictly speaking, I was not beside the seaside: I had my back to it. The piano was placed so that
the customers would have the view. Everyone could look
out over the promenade, the sea and the lighted pier
except me. I could have been in any bar from here to
Hackensack. Only the accents were different, and I was
noticing those less and less as time went on.

The song came to a rowdy ragged end and there was an
outburst of applause. Well, if that was what the customers
wanted, I'd give them one for the home team. I swung
into:

> By the sea, by the sea,
> By the beautiful sea . . .

They took it up enthusiastically. Looking more
amiable, Ted brought over the drinks for his brother-in-
law and Norma and then took orders for refills from most
of those around the piano. He nodded approvingly at me
and crossed round behind me to stare down at the promenade through the large plate-glass window for a moment
before returning to the bar.

It was time for my break, so I flipped on the tape in the
cassette beside me on the piano bench before I got up and
paused at the window to speak to him before disappearing into the staff room.

'Seems to be going well,' I said.

'Aye.' He nodded, still searching the promenade for
signs of impending disturbance. 'Could be worse. Still
plenty of time for trouble to break out, though. I'll be
glad when this season's over. One way and another, it's
been a bad year.'

There was no answer to that. From what I had heard,
he was right. In any case, I had no previous English

criteria by which to judge it.

I nodded sympathetic agreement and was about to move away when I saw him suddenly stiffen and freeze. At the same moment, the skin between my shoulder-blades began to creep and shrivel. I followed the direction of his gaze and saw that he was staring down at a small slight figure silhouetted against the blaze of lights outside the amusement arcade where the pier joined the promenade.

Not the Starer, though. This figure was female. Blonde. Lost-looking. She might have been a ghost—or a revenant. The victim, returning to the scene of the crime. I knew that thought must, inevitably, be in Ted's mind.

'Perhaps the police are doing a reconstruction,' I said quickly. 'She may be a policewoman they've sent out to try to jog people's memories. In case someone who was here last August—'

'Not bloody likely, darling!' An over-familiar hand descended on my shoulder and began insinuating itself down towards forbidden territory. My flesh crept in earnest now. I moved away abruptly.

'Couldn't possibly do a reconstruction. They don't know what the girl was wearing when she was alive.' Councillor Tiverton seemed to be addressing only his brother-in-law, ignoring me. 'She was starkers when she was found. Only way any of them had ever seen her. Couldn't send a little policewoman out like that, could they? The Chief Constable wouldn't like it. No Lady Godiva monkeyshines here. This is a respectable town. Or was.'

For the first time it occurred to me that no town with him in it could be completely respectable. Especially not one which had voted him on to the City Council.

'No. Only one person could ever say what she was wearing—' Councillor Tiverton shot a sly glance at Ted. 'Her killer. Dirty bugger stripped the clothes off the poor lass and took them away with him. Who knows what he did with them? Maybe he burned them in the furnace — the weather was still cold enough that week for all the fires to be lit. Or maybe he's kept them as a sort of souvenir, to take them out and look at them, maybe stroke them and —'

Ted swung away from the window, hands twitching as though they would like to reach out and close around his brother-in-law's throat. I wondered suddenly what he had done with his late wife's wardrobe.

'Ted!' I spoke quickly, without thinking, but it checked him.

'Yes. All right.' He did not seem to be speaking to me. He let his hands drop, but still faced his brother-in-law with hostility. 'Where's Milly?' he asked.

'At home.' Councillor Tiverton appeared slightly less at ease. 'You know how she is. Wanted to do some cooking, holiday weekend and all.'

'I know how she is.' Ted's voice was heavy with meaning. 'I know how you are, too. Why don't you cut along home to her?'

'Here now, is that any way to talk? When I've dropped in to add to your takings? And brought along a poor creature who needs cheering up?' Councillor Tiverton glanced over his shoulder, then did a double-take.

Norma was gone.

'She's got more sense than you have,' Ted said. He looked down at the promenade, but there was no sign of Norma. The girl who had been standing in the pool of light gave a brief upward glance, as though aware that she was under unwelcome observation and melted away into the shadows.

I caught my breath. For an instant, there had been something devastatingly familiar about her. Not the face — that had been just an indistinct blur as she turned it upwards — but . . . The identification eluded me. She was not anyone I had ever met. Had I seen her picture somewhere? . . . On a police poster?

I gave myself a mental shake. More probably, she was someone who had been into The Phoenix and sat round the piano one evening. That might account for the almost-recognition. How many people had crowded round the piano during the three months I had been appearing at The Phoenix? After a while, they all seemed to dissolve into the same face. Few of them were as memorable as they thought they were.

In fact, their clothes were more recognizable than their faces. Thanks to the multiplicity of chain stores, all carrying the same lines, in every corner of the country, women's wardrobes tended to be nearly identical when there was an especially popular line. Unlike the States, where different stores and designers at least tried to ring a few changes when a fad for a certain garment swept the country.

I realized abruptly that that was why the girl had looked so familiar. It was not her, it was the flowered blouse she was wearing. I owned a blouse like that myself. It had been high style a couple of seasons ago, sweeping all before it, from Paris to Seventh Avenue. It had evidently been a success in this country, too. The best is always international—or almost always.

'Oh Christ!' Councillor Tiverton suddenly went rigid, staring over my shoulder at an apparition in the doorway. 'Christ!' he muttered again.

I turned, half-afraid of what I might see. But it was not the ghost-girl from the promenade standing in the doorway, nor even yet the Starer. The doorway was filled with the all-too-solid form of Milly Tiverton. She was carrying a large covered dish and she turned slowly, looking for someone.

Albert Tiverton cast a guilty, frantic glance towards the piano bar. Norma's seat was still vacant. True, a half-finished drink marked the place, but there was no possible way anyone could know whose drink it had been.

The Councillor relaxed visibly. A slow, sly smile slid across his face as he realized that, no matter what his intentions had been, he had actually been caught doing nothing more incriminating than having a quiet chat with his brother-in-law and the resident pianist.

'Over here, love!' he called out, suddenly brazenly cheerful. He waved extravagantly at his wife.

Milly's face cleared and she crossed the room to us. 'I won't stay, Ted,' she said. 'I know it's a busy night. But I thought I'd just bring these along for you. What with the long weekend, I was afraid you might be running low.' She tipped back the tea-towel to reveal three quiche dishes, set one on top of the other.

'I've done a smoked salmon flan,' she said. 'A spinach, and an egg-and-bacon. That ought to see you through. If you don't need them tonight, you can put them in the fridge for tomorrow.'

'That's lovely, Milly,' her brother said helplessly. The crowd had long since lost any interest in food and settled down to serious drinking, the evening was winding to its close. 'Just what I need.'

'That's what I thought.' His sister looked at the crowded room with satisfaction. 'If you need any more, just let me know.'

'That's right,' her husband said, a trace of rancour in his tone. 'She'll do anything you want. All you have to do is snap your fingers.' He snapped his own, in illustration, then looked over his shoulder nervously, as though he feared the gesture might summon Norma back to his side.

Behind him, the door to the Powder Room opened and a girl came out with a worried expression on her face. She paused and looked around the room, as though seeking help.

'Well, come on, love.' Albert Tiverton took Milly's arm. 'You've delivered the goods. Time we were getting on—' He began guiding her towards the exit.

'Oh, stop a bit,' Ted invited wickedly. 'Have another drink. There's no rush.'

From across the room, the girl's eyes found Ted and she began moving purposefully in our direction.

'No, no. If Milly wants a drink, we'll have one at our next port of call. Farther along the front. I want to check a few more places before closing time.' Albert was pushing Milly towards the door now. 'You're all right here, but there might be trouble elsewhere.'

There was trouble here, from the look of the girl who was almost upon us.

Fortunately, Milly hadn't noticed. She was too flattered and flustered by what appeared to be her husband's sudden desire for her company. 'Albert wants to go,' she informed us unnecessarily. 'Perhaps we can stop another time.'

'That's right,' Albert promised recklessly over his shoulder. 'We'll come by and have that drink and a proper visit tomorrow night.'

'You do that,' Ted said wryly. 'Both of you.' He watched them leave before turning to the girl, who had now reached his side and was silently pleading for his attention.

'Pardon me,' she said uneasily. 'But there's a woman in there—' she waved vaguely towards the Powder Room. 'She's slumped in a chair. She's—she's awfully quiet. I—I couldn't even tell if she was breathing. Perhaps you ought to call a doctor.'

CHAPTER 8

Ted sighed deeply. It was Saturday night and almost closing time. There was always something. We walked over to the door of the Powder Room and he hesitated outside.

'Have a look, would you, Trudi? See what's the problem. I can't go barging in there —' He looked over his shoulder. The girl had gone back to her seat, but was watching us. 'Unless I'm certain it's an emergency.'

'Well, okay,' I said reluctantly. I wasn't so keen to go barging in myself, but I could see his point. It was probably someone who had just passed out. A nuisance, but a familiar nuisance. I took a deep breath and pushed open the door.

It was Norma.

I might have known it. That woman could sleep on a bed of nails, let alone in a chintz-covered well-upholstered armchair. I looked down at her without favour.

'All right in there?' The door opened a crack. 'Nothing really wrong, is there?' Ted's voice was fearful. A death on the premises was the terror of anyone in the trade. It gave a place an uneasy aura, not to mention the difficulties of trying to smuggle out a body unnoticed. And, in a place like The Phoenix, which had already been ravaged once by violence, it could mean the beginning of a reputation as a bad luck place. Not the sort of place the punters would choose for a pleasant evening. No wonder Ted was worried.

'It's all right.' I crossed to the door to reassure him. 'It's only Norma. She's fallen asleep again. I don't know why she bothers to get out of bed at all!'

'Just sleeping?' His face lightened. He turned and gave a thumbs-up signal to the girl sitting at the table. 'That's all right. Leave her be, then. I'll tip her into the car when I take you home. No more trouble to ferry two than one. Cheer up, won't be long now.'

'No.' I glanced at my watch. I was due back at the piano for my final stint; my entire rest period had been wasted with this nonsense. For a moment, I debated covering Norma, then dismissed the idea. If she didn't care, why should I? She was so far out of it, she'd never know the difference, anyway.

Nevertheless, her deep motionless slumber might alarm other customers. It had already frightened the last one into reporting her condition. A covering over her would signal that the situation was known and, hopefully, under control.

I found a blanket in the cabinet concealed behind the ruffled curtain in the corner. It also contained an extensive first-aid box and a sewing kit, in case repairs of any kind were needed. The events of last August had bitten deep into Ted's consciousness.

I tossed the blanket over Norma. She stirred, moaned and frowned, as though resisting any attempt to call her back to wakefulness. Unseen, I frowned back at her, then went out and left her there.

Norma passed me in the hallway the next morning on her way back to her room from the bath. She gave me a vague smile and I wondered if she remembered anything at all about the events of last night. Probably not. Everything must seem to be part of some insubstantial dream to her. She had evinced no surprise — or even interest — when she awoke briefly as Ted carried her down the stairs at The Phoenix and into the car; she had made the later transfer from the car into our lodgings without seeming to attain more than semi-consciousness.

Ted had been quite worried as Daisy opened the door. 'You don't think we ought to call the doctor?' he suggested. 'She hasn't taken pills, or anything?'

'Pills could take *her*,' Daisy said, with rare bitterness. 'I've never seen anything like it. Some days she doesn't surface long enough to have more than a cup of tea. No wonder —' She broke off. 'Where *is* Little Johnny? I thought he must be with her, at this hour.'

'Is he out running wild again?' Ted spoke with heavy disapproval. 'No good will come of that lad. If she doesn't

DEATH BESIDE THE SEASIDE

care for herself, she might spare a thought for him, once in a while.'

Upstairs, as though on cue, a door opened. Too much on cue? Sharp ears listening behind a slightly ajar door, spying on the others in the house?

'Is that my mother?' He appeared at the top of the stairs, deceptively innocent in his pyjamas.

'Now, when did he come in?' Daisy muttered under her breath. 'I never heard him.'

That signified nothing. No one heard Johnny unless he intended to be heard. I had learned that at a very early stage.

He had descended the stairs, the picture of filial devotion and taken my place at his mother's side. 'It's all right,' he said nobly. 'I can manage her.'

I'd just bet he could—in more ways than one.

Norma had smiled in reflex action at hearing her son's voice, but hadn't bothered to open her eyes. She had leaned against Ted heavily as he and Johnny guided her up the stairs and into her room.

We watched them from the foot of the stairs and Daisy turned to me, shaking her head. 'I don't know, dear,' she said. 'I just don't know . . .'

But now it was morning, a bright new day. The crack of dawn for Norma to be up and bathed. Eleven a.m. Of course, it was visiting day at the nursing home for her— and Little Johnny. She'd probably sleep for a week after that.

As I descended the stairs, Robey and Fields stalked out from the kitchen to check on me. If only they could talk, Daisy might know a lot more about what went on in her own house. They kept their eyes on everything and every-one: proper watch-cats. But watch was the operative word. They stayed silent and thought their own thoughts.

Right now, they thought I wasn't half so interesting as

what was going on in the kitchen. They were right. Having registered my presence, they turned and went back to the scene of more interesting activity. I followed them.

'Going out, dear?' Daisy greeted me absently, her real attention centred on the onions she was chopping at the kitchen table. 'Don't stay too long. Lunch at one today, remember.'

'I thought I'd go down to the beach,' I said. 'The weather is so beautiful, I might take a swim.'

'That's right, dear,' Daisy approved. 'It can't last much longer. Enjoy it while you can.'

Fields leaped up on the table to check on what she was doing but leaped down again hastily, nose twitching in indignation at the reek of onions. She sneezed, then leaped up on the draining-board to lap up a bit of water from the sink. It was a sight to chill the blood of anyone who was a purist about hygiene, but we had always had cats at home. I would sooner see Fields's nose poked into things than, say, Little Johnny's.

'I'll be back in time,' I said, starting for the door. 'There's not much else to do *but* swim on an English Sunday—even if it *is* Bank Holiday weekend.' All the tourist traps and catchpenny stalls along the front would be open, but they didn't tempt me; they were for the trippers.

The telephone in the hall rang abruptly. Daisy couldn't have been more upset if a bomb had gone off.

'Oh no!' Her knife went clatering to the floor. She looked at the clock in agitation. 'She's too early today. Norma hasn't left yet. I can't talk to her. I can't!' She sent me a pleading look.

'You take the call, dear. Tell her I'm not here. I've gone out and you don't know when I'll be back. Tell her—' she added, with an air of triumphant improvisation— 'tell her I've gone to church!'

The voice on the other end of the line was cold and remote, with a cut-glass accent. I could understand why Daisy would be reluctant to speak to her at the best of times. Without even knowing her, I took a perverse pleasure in frustrating her attempt to get through to Daisy. She informed me frostily that she'd ring again later.

'Now what was that all about?' I went back to the kitchen. 'Who was that awful woman? And what was all that about Norma?'

'She *is* awful, isn't she, dear?' Daisy brightened at having what was obviously her own opinion endorsed. 'Simply frightful. I feel so sorry for Norma. I'd protect her if I could, but I can't, dear. Really, I can't. That was her mother-in-law. She calls every visiting day to check up on Norma and make sure that she *has* gone to the nursing home with Little Johnny to visit her husband. If she catches her missing a visit, she cuts off her allowance for that week.'

'That's barbaric!' I was shocked. This was the first time I had heard anything about these wheels within wheels. 'Surely Norma is old enough to decide whether she wants to go or not. From what I've heard, it doesn't make any difference. He doesn't recognize them anyway.'

'True, dear.' Daisy sighed. 'And making her drag that poor boy along all the time, too. It's wicked, dear, wicked!'

'I don't see why Norma doesn't rebel,' I said. 'She doesn't have to put up with that sort of thing in this day and age.'

'I'm afraid she does, dear. Mrs Handel has all the money. It's not just the allowance — she'll disinherit Little Johnny if Norma doesn't do as she wants. It's the old, old story, dear. The one who pays the piper is the one who calls the tune.'

'Poor Norma.' I felt a new sympathy for her. She had more to contend with than I had imagined.

'We're all ever so sympathetic, dear, but there's

nothing we can do to help her. I'd lie for her, if I could, but it wouldn't work. Mrs Handel rings the Matron at the nursing home after she's talked to me and makes sure that Norma has arrived and is with her husband. It's a private nursing home and a permanent patient like that means a lot of steady income. Matron tells Mrs Handel everything. *She* wouldn't lie for Norma, so there's no use me trying—I'd be caught out.'

'That's monstrous!'

'Quite right, dear, I do agree. Monstrous. Of course, Mrs Handel *is* rather a monster. I met her when she came to inspect the rooms before Norma and Johnny moved in. She wanted to see what they were getting for her money. And she was the one who insisted that they be served their meals privately so that they wouldn't have to mix with the *artistes*. I was awfully glad to see the back of her. Poor Norma!' Daisy sighed again. 'The worst of it is, dear, sometimes I think Little Johnny takes after his grand-mother!'

'Poor Norma.' I echoed her sigh. Poor, poor Norma, caught between two of them. No wonder she was spending most of her life in Morphean retreat. 'If only she weren't so passive. She's still a young woman. She could get out and find herself a job. There must be something she can do.'

'Oh yes, she used to be a secretary, but it's not that easy for her, dear. Her mother-in-law wouldn't approve of that, either. The Handels don't work for a living, not like the rest of us. Norma's got to be careful for Johnny's sake. There's big money at stake there, dear, really big money. More than anyone could afford to throw away for some whim of independence—not that Norma is the type, anyway. All she has to do is hang on—the old lady can't last for ever. Then she and Johnny will get the money. Well, Johnny will, anyway—and everything will be all right.'

Would it? Little Johnny did not strike me as someone who could be depended upon to be generous to an indigent mother. If he held the purse strings, Norma might find herself dancing to even more stringent tunes. *Takes after his grandmother*, indeed. No matter which way you looked at it, Norma was storing up big trouble for herself in the future.

'Perhaps,' I said.

'Oh, I know what you're thinking, dear.' Daisy shot me a shrewd look. 'I've thought it myself at times. But all we can do is hope for the best. After all, it's nothing to do with us, really, is it?'

'Just as well,' I said. There were going to be an awful lot of pieces for somebody to pick up some day. Meanwhile, I still wanted to get down to the beach this morning.

'I've got to get going—' I started for the door, but stumbled over one of the cats, who ran in front of me, obviously hoping to dart out of the door when I opened it. 'Ooops! Sorry, George—I mean Gracie.'

'Oh, she's a one!' Daisy leaped gratefully to change the subject. 'Deceptive right from the start, she was. We called her Sid, at first. For Sid Field. But then she went and had a kitten, so of course she had to be Gracie.

'We called the kitten Tony Hancock,' Daisy continued, reminiscing. 'He was a sweet little thing and very funny. But he ran right in front of a car and got run over. Perhaps we should have given him a different name. Poor Hancock always was suicidal, dear.'

I closed the door behind me softly, cutting off Daisy's memories. I didn't know whether she meant the kitten or the comedian at the last, and perhaps she didn't, either. As a change of subject, it was only slightly less depressing than Norma and Little Johnny. I felt that another day had got off to a bad start.

CHAPTER 9

The bleak uneasy mood stayed with me all the way down
the hill and along the front. The row of bathing-huts
were on the far side of the Grand Pier and seemed to be
another particularly English institution, probably first
conceived with and intended to be used in conjunction
with bathing-machines. Hence, a Victorian lady could
walk through the town fully and respectably dressed,
change in the privacy of the family bathing-hut and then
be conveyed direct from the door to the water in a bathing-
machine without her more immodest costume being
revealed to any watching eyes.

These days they were fighting for the right to have
topless beaches, even nude beaches. The bathing-machine
had become a complete anachronism, but the huts still
lingered on, too useful to be dispensed with. They were
basically a tiny one-room shack, windowless, but with a
wide barn-like door. Inside there was usually a small sink,
a clothesline to hang wet bathing suits from, and an electric
connection for a hot plate or electric kettle so that no one
need ever miss their cup of tea. After that, the contents
varied according to the requirements and whims of the
hut's owner.

The huts huddled together in a long row with scarcely
an inch between them on either side. Most were rented
out for the season, but some of the townspeople retained
their own for private use.

Ted owned one close to the pier and there were several
communal keys so that the staff of The Phoenix could use
it, if and when they felt so inclined. Usually, I was the
only one to take advantage of the privilege.

The day was colder than it had looked, a brisk wind

blowing in from the sea. I nearly changed my mind, but
sheer bravado carried me through. I could not go back to
the house and admit that I had skipped my swim because
of a bit of a breeze. Besides, there might not be many
more opportunities this season.

I didn't linger in the water. However, I was reluctant to
return to the house. I wanted to wait until Norma and
Little Johnny were sure to have left.

I pulled out one of the deck chairs and set it up outside
the doorway, but changed out of my wet bathing suit
before settling down in it. Behind and above me, I could
hear laughter and splashing from the boating pool on the
other side of the road. The customers were beginning to
arrive and pop their kiddies into the little boats to get
them out of their hair for a few minutes. Although it was
not as popular with the children as the amusement arcades,
it was better value for their parents. At least, the kids
couldn't be shovelling coins into a machine while they
were healthfully occupied in the open air pedalling a boat
around the shallow pool.

I let the tattered paperback fall from my hand and lay
back, closing my eyes against the sun. Whenever the wind
dropped momentarily, it was really quite pleasantly
warm. I felt myself drifting off into a doze.

Suddenly the background sound floating through the
air changed character. The shrieks of laughter were transformed into screams of fear. Sharp as an electric shock,
the change of mood jolted through the atmosphere,
charging it with terror and unhealthy excitement.

I struggled out of the deck chair and hurried across the
road. I was not the only one. Already, crowds were
gathering at the perimeter of the pool, casual strollers
rushing forward to view the sensation promised by the
screams and cries.

I shouldered my way through to the railings where distracted parents were vainly shouting instructions to off-

spring in the boats now bumping together in the centre of the pool where the action was taking place. One and all, the children were ignoring the cries of distress and command. Only the pool staff could force the young mariners back to shore — and they were otherwise engaged, watched by a rapt and breathless audience. Even the frantic parental cries were stilled as the drama progressed.

Two attendants had climbed into the shoulder-high rubber waders they usually wore to clean the pool in the early hours of the morning. Grimly intent, they waded forward slowly towards the cluster of small boats. I noticed that, while the people on shore were looking out to the centre of the pool, the children were staring over the sides of their boats down into the water.

There appeared to be a bundle of rags bobbing up and down in the water. But no one would be so grimly intent upon retrieving a bundle of rags.

The ripples eddied out as the waders advanced, setting the body in motion almost as though it were trying to swim away from them. It bumped up against one of the boats and the children in that boat shrank back, nearly overtipping the craft by the swift movement of their recoil.

One of the men stretched out a hand and steadied the boat. The other caught hold of a handful of wet material and pulled the body towards him.

It rolled over lazily, wet blonde locks gleamed dully in the sunlight. The face was parboiled from overnight immersion in the water and had a pale blueish tinge.

Several of the children who had previously been silent in their boats screamed with terror and began sobbing. Suddenly it wasn't just an exciting adventure any more. Too much reality had crept in.

I felt rather that way himself. This was no unknown groupie left in the wake of a motor-cyclists' invasion. This had been a girl with a definite identity, a personality, a boy-friend who cared for her.

Although I could not put a name to her, I knew her face. It was the Cockney girl who had been sitting up at the piano bar last night.

I stared unbelievingly at the washed-out barely-recognizable face, paralyzed by the horror that seizes us all when we become aware that someone we have known — however peripherally — has been overtaken by a fate beyond our comprehension.

Only last night, she had been sitting at the piano bar, laughing with her boy-friend, annoying Councillor Tiverton, joining in the songs, lively, pretty, having a wonderful time. Today, she was nothing but a — a *thing* bobbing about on the surface of the boating pool while people recoiled from her in horror. Something to be pointed at, stared at —

People were even taking photographs. That was too much! What kind of people would want to capture this on film? And why? As the high point of their holiday snaps? 'And this is the actual discovery of the body. You remember that case —?'

Why was I so sure it was murder? Because she hadn't seemed the sort to commit suicide? Because the boating pond was railed off from the general public and locked at night, which ruled out accident? Because the town had been tense and unhappy all weekend, waiting for something nasty to happen? There was very little that was nastier than murder. Had she been raped first?

I forced my eyes back to the body, but it was impossible, of course, to tell if her clothes had been disarranged. They were a wet sodden mass dragging down the body. Such questions would have to wait for an autopsy.

Suddenly I felt a cold prickle at the nape of my neck. I tried to turn as slowly and casually as possible, knowing what — who — I would find behind me.

It was the Starer. He stood on the fringe of the crowd, those avid staring eyes fixed on the body. He stared as though he were taking in nourishment through his eyes, while the men in the pool towed the body to shore by the boarding platform where a couple of uniformed policemen stood waiting. There was an obscure satisfaction deep in his eyes as they drank in the scene.

I shuddered. They always make me shudder.

What is it with these creeps? Once life was so simple. You became an entertainer because you wanted to make people happy. If you succeeded, Stage Door Johnnies waited for you with diamond bracelets wrapped around long-stemmed roses to whisk you off to champagne suppers at Romano's. If you really hit the top, students and admirers unbuckled the horses from your carriage and pulled it through the streets themselves. Those were the days!

These days they just want to kill you.

Perhaps the human race is evolving a deadly new mutant strain, the flesh-and-blood equivalent of the new technological advances in heat-seeking missiles, designed to home in on brightness and warmth—and destroy it.

I began edging my way out of the crowd, away from him. Performers have always had to cope with the side-effects of being in the spotlight. We've had to learn to deal gently with the problem portion of our audience: the misfits, the loners, the oddballs, the human strays who have somehow equated the spotlight with the party and imagine that, if they can just brush close enough to the lights and the laughter, it will somehow become their passport to everything they've missed in life so far. Some mysterious alchemy—like the Royal Touch which cured disease, or the Philosopher's Stone which transmuted base metal into gold—would inject itself into their bleak lives and transform them into sought-after members of the community. The Beautiful People, living on some unimaginable plateau of glory where the sun always shone, the champagne always flowed and the birds made music all the day.

They would feel short-changed and cheated if forced to realize that we also had headaches, got our feet wet in the rain, sometimes felt lost and lonely, frightened and inadequate ourselves. *If you prick us, do we not bleed?*

There was a splash and a shout from the pool behind me and I wished I hadn't had that last thought.

When I turned back, the Starer had disappeared. Had he stared his fill, or had he noticed my movement and feared I might be heading towards him? He needn't have worried. I was no more anxious to confront him than he was to come face to face with me. If we ever met, I wanted Ted between us, plus a couple of sturdy policemen.

Had the Starer been in The Phoenix last night? The new thought struck me sharply. I hadn't been aware of him, but he wasn't particularly memorable in his own persona. Probably, when he wasn't staring, he was as inconspicuous as ninety per cent of the audience. Would I have noticed him if he hadn't been staring?

Or if he hadn't been staring at *me*?

Had he, perhaps, been sitting at some point in the room from which his direct gaze would fall, not on me, but on the Cockney girl sitting close by me at the piano bar? Had she, by inadvertently intercepting his stare, somehow taken my place in his twisted mind?

Had she intercepted the fate intended for me?

CHAPTER 10

I was late back for lunch, after all, but Daisy forgave me in view of the eye-witness report I was able to give. This led to a lively mealtime debate over whether or not I ought to go to the police with the tiny fragment of information I possessed.

'I'd leave it be, dear, honestly I would,' Daisy advised. 'I mean, you don't even know the poor girl's name. You can't really be much help, can you? And as for reporting a man just because he's got funny eyes . . . Well, they might start looking at *you* pretty funny themselves. And you don't know *his* name, either, do you?'

'No,' I admitted. 'But the fact that the girl was in The Phoenix last night might provide a starting-point for the police enquiries—'

'And wouldn't Ted love that!' Daisy gave a mock shudder. 'They'd go and plaster one of their dirty great posters— HAVE YOU SEEN THIS GIRL?—right in front of The Phoenix. Put the customers off going in, that would. You couldn't blame them. It would be like walking into a place with a Plague Cross on the door. People want to have a good time, not be reminded of any awfulness around.'

'Daisy is right.' Henry Parsons speared another roast potato from the bowl in the centre of the table with the same motion with which Punch bludgeoned Judy into unconsciousness at the end of his show. Daisy automatically passed the gravy boat along to him. 'It can't do any good and it might do a great deal of harm. Keep out of it!'

'I don't know,' Kate said dubiously. 'You'd know him again if you saw him, wouldn't you? You might be an important witness.'

'Witness to what?' Dandini asked. 'Did she see the murder? Did she even see them together? All she saw was a man watching a scene dozens of other people were also watching. We'd be in a fine fix if the police could arrest a man for that. It's all anyone does in this town.'

'Our audience—' Kate lifted her glass in a toast. 'God . . . bless them!'

'Exactly, dear.' Daisy nodded sagely. 'It wouldn't do if it got around that you'd reported a member of your audience just because you didn't like the way he looked at you. Men can get awfully sensitive about things like that.'

'She's right,' Kate said. 'The punter probably thought he was giving you his best Robert Redford come-hither look. He'd be shattered if he knew the way you were taking it.'

I allowed myself to be persuaded. I didn't really want to go to the police with the nebulous fears and feeling I had about the situation. They'd laugh me out of the station.

Well, perhaps not exactly. This was England. They'd be excruciatingly polite to my face and laugh after I was safely out of earshot. The end result would be the same; they would not take my information seriously and, worse, I might become branded in their minds as some sort of eccentric or potential hysteric.

But I made a point of telling Ted about it before I started work that evening. I knew he'd take me seriously — and he did. He'd seen the Starer in action.

Not surprisingly, he agreed with the consensus of opinion. 'I've as much respect for the police as anyone,' he said, 'but it wouldn't be good for business to have them hanging around here. Start the customers worrying about breath tests — if nothing worse — and they'd cut down on their drinking. Then they'd start watching what they were saying and begin wondering if they'd have a better time in some other pub. No, it wouldn't do. The police have their work, we have ours. Let them get on with it and see how they go. You can always mention it later if they don't seem to be getting anywhere with their enquiries.'

'All right,' I agreed, sitting down at the piano and riffling off a preliminary introduction. 'Besides, the information probably isn't worth anything. She and her boy-friend might have been in and out of half the pubs along the front last night.'

Ted nodded, obviously not believing the rationalization any more than I did, but that would be our story in the face of any possible future criticism. Our eyes met in silent agreement and he moved away.

The Phoenix was beginning to fill up but no one had been bold enough to sit up at the piano bar yet. I was just as happy. It gave me a breathing space in which I needn't swap cheery comments or listen to snatches of other people's problems.

I gave the customers a long piano medley without vocal accompaniment and they seemed satisfied. More import-ant, so did Ted. I could continue to save my voice for the moment, this was perfectly adequate music to drink by, soft and unobtrusive, familiar but not demanding, soothing as cool fingers stroking a fevered brow. The conversation level in the room was a hum of contentment. The customers were happy and enjoying themselves — which was just the way it should be.

I exchanged bright smiles with the first brave souls to seat themselves at the far end of the piano. I thought I had seen them here before, but could I be certain? Per-formers saw so many faces in audiences, along the sea front, in casual encounters with friends and acquaintances that, in time, everyone came to look vaguely familiar.

The ice being broken, other couples began to take seats around the piano. I kept a wary eye on them, wondering what I should do if the man who had been with the murdered girl last night showed up again tonight. Especially if he was with another girl. Should I report it to Ted? Would it be time to notify the police then? On the other hand, would I — could I — recognize him? Or had his face already blurred in my memory and mingled with so many others of the anonymous blurs that made up my audience? The girl had been the vivid member of that couple. Perhaps too much so for her own good.

I relaxed as the last seats were taken and it became apparent that I was not going to be faced with any such problem. There was a different problem, of course. It was one of those days.

The seats had been claimed by Councillor Tiverton—who was escorting his own wife, for a change. Milly's presence guaranteed that I would be spared the worst of his leering attentions. He would be on his best behaviour to make up for almost being caught out with Norma last night.

'Now then, love.' The Councillor put an arm around her with an air of demonstrating to all the other women in the place just what they were missing. 'Choose your drinks, choose your songs, anything you like. The night is yours.'

I'll bet she hadn't heard that very often.

'Oh, Bertie!' She was delighted and dismayingly flattered by it all. '*I* don't know.'

'Cocktails? Champagne? Brandy? Anything you like,' he repeated expansively. 'And don't forget the music. She'll—' he nodded his head dismissively at me— 'play everything you want to hear.'

Actually I had a few other requests to fill first. The cocktail napkins bearing their scribbled requests were beginning to pile up beside the music rack. I couldn't devote the whole evening to Milly Tiverton's choices.

Not that I needed to worry about it. Her mind had obviously gone blank under the unaccustomed attention. She would be hard put to remember her own name right now, let alone any song titles.

I smiled at her encouragingly and continued with my usual repertoire.

'Champagne cocktails!' Her husband impatiently decided for her. 'We'll all have one. The piano-player, too.'

Ted materialized behind them to take the order, although a waitress was dealing with the other orders around the piano. He returned to the bar to mix them personally and then served them. I got the impression that he wanted to keep a close eye on his brother-in-law.

Perhaps he mistrusted all the sudden solicitude for his sister.

I lifted the champagne cocktail—it was the genuine article—in salute and automatically segued into the '*Anniversary Waltz*'. I had played this scene so often. Champagne cocktails equalled the '*Anniversary Waltz*'; they were seldom ordered at any other time. It also explained why the Councillor was being so extraordinarily nice to his wife tonight.

It was a mistake. Tiverton's face darkened, even as Milly giggled. I saw Ted repressing a smile.

'No!' Tiverton scowled at me. 'It's not an anniversary. And it's not a birthday, either. Can't a man and his lawful wedded wife have a night out without everyone jumping to conclusions?'

I don't know what he was complaining about. The conclusion might be incorrect but it was a lot more innocent—and complimentary—than the conclusions everyone had jumped to when he was out with a woman who was not his wife.

'There now! You see?' He turned on poor Milly. Suddenly it was all her fault. 'If you don't tell them what you want to hear, they'll throw all this rubbish at you and make us look like a fine pair of fools. Now tell her a proper song to play!'

Only too obviously, Milly went blanker than ever. Her distress was a palpable thing. I could have hurled the champagne glass at Albert Tiverton.

Ted had been standing close enough to hear. He gave his brother-in-law a murderous look and moved forward to his sister's side.

'Oh!' All the seats are taken!' A disappointed voice spoke in my ear, providing welcome distraction. 'Do any of them—' Daisy lowered her voice to a conspiratorial husk— 'look like leaving soon?'

'It doesn't matter,' I said, sliding along the piano

bench. 'You can sit here.' It was a favoured seat, although I didn't offer it to just anyone. Only when customers joined me in a piano duet or wanted to sing the lyrics themselves, did I allow them to share the piano bench briefly. But Daisy was different.

'Thank you, dear, that's very nice of you.' Daisy plumped down beside me with evident gratification. She enjoyed an occasional fling in the spotlight again and her voice, although running towards the breathless, was still good — especially in the old Music Hall numbers.

'Come on,' I said, slipping into a familiar melody. 'Take a turn.'

It was not until her voice rose, sweet and clear, that I realized the song I had subconsciously chosen.

> 'She was only a bird
> In a gilded cage . . .'

Our eyes met and I knew we were both thinking of Norma.

'She hasn't come home yet,' Daisy whispered to me, under cover of the chorus in which the customers had joined. 'Neither of them have. It's not like them to be so late. They usually go somewhere nice to cheer themselves up after the nursing home, but they're back before this. I thought they might have come here . . . Well, Norma might —' She broke off to go back to the lyric.

> 'Her beauty was sold
> For an old man's gold . . .'

But Norma was waiting for an old woman to die before any gold could come to her. Or rather, to her husband. And then what? Would she have him declared incompetent, get control of the estate and, possibly, decamp? But the old lady sounded shrewd and mistrusting enough to have forestalled that possibility. Everything was undoubtedly tied up in an irrevocable trust.

> *'She's a bird in a gilded cage!'*

The song rushed to its crescendo, even Milly joining in happily, her recent embarrassment forgotten. She was another fluttering innocent, imprisoned in a cage not particularly gilded.

'My Old Man!' someone called out from the back of the room. Milly nodded enthusiastic agreement, for once not noticing her husband's frown. He would have preferred her to request something no one else had thought of, so that he could demonstrate his authority by insisting that I play it.

> *'My old man said "Follow the van—*
> *And don't dilly-dally on the way" . . .'*

It was a good rousing old favourite. Daisy did the honours with the lyric again while I concentrated on playing honky-tonk.

As usual, once we began warming up, there was a blizzard of request-bearing paper cocktail napkins passed along to me. I tried to stack them in the order in which they arrived so that I could deal with them in turn.

Out of the corner of my eye, I saw Albert Tiverton frown again and then remove the cocktail napkin from beneath Milly's glass. He hunched over it, scrawling a request without consulting his wife. He passed it to me with an air of triumph.

I smiled sweetly at him and placed it at the bottom of the pile without looking at it. His face darkened.

I thumped down on the loud pedal to drown out any remark he might be going to make. He leaned forward belligerently and opened his mouth, but a sudden commotion at the entrance distracted all of us.

'OH NO YOU DON'T!' Ted thundered at someone unseen. 'You're not coming in here!'

We froze. Had the hooligan invasion started? Several of the local men stood up quietly and moved towards the door to back Ted.

'You stay here,' Albert Tiverton instructed his wife. 'I'll take care of this!'

'Be careful, Bert,' she pleaded.

There was a scuffle at the door and Ted bellowed with outrage as a small, slight figure eluded his grasp and darted into the room. The others tensed and waited to do battle with the rest of the invaders while Ted chased after the one who had escaped him.

After several uneasy moments, it became apparent that no others were involved. The culprit playing tag with Ted was the only interloper and he didn't appear to be much of a threat.

The locals went back to their tables; the tourists hadn't even noticed. Although intent, Ted's pursuit was relatively unobtrusive. The intruder slid like a shadow between tables, always avoiding Ted's grasp. Albert Tiverton had sized up the situation and moved swiftly in an opposite direction to corner the quarry in a pincer movement.

The quarry seemed to be leading the chase towards the piano bar. Daisy caught a glimpse of his face before I did.

'It's Johnny Handel!' she said. 'Whatever is he doing here? No wonder Ted is so upset. It just won't do, dear. It won't do, at all.'

Before I could say anything, Little Johnny gained the temporary refuge of the piano, just ahead of the two men closing in on him.

'Where's my mother?' he demanded urgently. 'She isn't home.'

'Neither were you a little while ago,' Daisy said indignantly. 'How am I supposed to know where you all get to?

I haven't seen your mother since you both went out this morning.'

'Isn't she here?' He turned his fierce gaze on me.

'Not tonight,' I said. 'At least,' I qualified, 'not yet. Did she say she was coming here?'

He ignored my question, turning to glare at the customers sitting around the piano. His gaze fell on the one empty place and he stiffened with suspicion. 'Where's my mother?' he demanded again.

'Gotcher, you little bleeder!' Ted pounced, hands descending on Johnny's shoulder in an iron grip. Albert Tiverton approached from the other side and grabbed at the boy's arm.

Johnny instantly began to struggle, kicking out at the men and wriggling like an eel. He caught both men by surprise. What had been a neat, clean capture devolved into an undignified scuffle, endangering the safety of everyone in the vicinity.

Daisy and I abandoned the piano bench hastily as the battle raged around us. The pile of cocktail napkins went flying, the glasses along the piano top shook and several crashed to the floor. Customers snatched up their own drinks protectively, the girls shrieking out in protest.

I moved forward to try to head them away from the piano before they damaged it. I didn't want an out-of-tune piano when interested parties might be coming down from London to watch my act.

Suddenly, with a loud crashing discord, the battle was over. Johnny was spreadeagled across the keyboard, well and truly captured this time.

'Now out you bloody well go!' Ted pulled Johnny upright with another crashing discord and transferred his grip to the nape of Johnny's neck. 'I could lose my licence if you were found in here!'

Johnny muttered about something else Ted could lose for all he cared and Ted visibly restrained himself from

hurling the little monster down the stairs. Instead, he
slowly and carefully escorted Johnny through the door
and we could hear the heavy tread of their feet descending
the stairs.

'I'd better go too, dear,' Daisy said. 'Really I had. It's
almost closing time, anyway. I'll walk home with Johnny
before he gets into any more mischief. He's really upset
not to find Norma home. I must say, I don't know where
she could be at this hour.'

'Perhaps she's fallen asleep somewhere.' I stooped and
began gathering up the scattered cocktail napkins. It
would be impossible to get them back into the right
order. The best I could do would be to sort through them
quickly, play any duplicated requests in their full version
and run the others together in a long medley in order to
get through them all before Ted called 'Time'.

'Anything's possible, dear,' Daisy sighed. 'Especially
with Norma. I do wish she'd decide to leave, you know.
The money's nice, but it isn't everything. And she's getting worse and worse. She quite frightens me sometimes.'

'I'm not surprised,' I agreed. 'I—'

'What's the matter, dear. What is it?'

'Nothing,' I said. I crumpled the cocktail napkin in my
hand quickly. 'Someone thinks they're funny, that's all.'

'Oh, one of those,' Daisy said wisely. 'Never mind,
dear. This weekend will soon be over and they'll all crawl
back into the woodwork for another year. Don't let it get
you down, dear.'

'I won't,' I said, allowing her to go on thinking that it
was either a proposition or an obscenity. I did not want to
display the actual message, although it was seared into
my mind.

KEEP YOUR MOUTH SHUT OR YOU'RE DEAD!

For further emphasis, it appeared to have been written
in blood.

CHAPTER 11

I was later than usual and the house was dark and silent
when I returned. I snapped on the front hall light, but
nothing happened. I flipped the switch up and down
again and was rewarded by a pale flickering glow. The
light bulb was going fast.

It was indicative of the state of my nerves that I jumped
at the faint sound behind me although I had heard it a
thousand times since I'd been here: the soft thud of a cat
dropping to the floor from some higher perch.

The faint mewling cry of distress was new. I turned to
see Gracie limping into the hallway, favouring her front
left paw.

'What's the matter, Gracie?' I started towards her, but
she backed away. There was no sign of the other cats.

'Come on,' I coaxed, crouching. 'What's the matter
with you tonight? You're usually the friendliest of the lot.'

Gracie circled me warily. There was definitely something
wrong with that paw, but she would not come close
enough for me to take a look at it.

'All right,' I said, opening my handbag. 'I know what
will fetch you.' I brought out the little plastic bag of
cheese cubes.

Gracie began edging closer, as though against her better
judgement. I shook a couple of cubes into my hand and
held it out enticingly. She twitched her whiskers and
settled back on her haunches to think about it.

Just then the hall light gave a final flicker and a loud
'pop' and everything went black. That bulb was definitely
gone now. I heard the scampering paws as Gracie,
already upset and now startled and frightened, darted
elsewhere for safety.

There was nothing more I could do tonight. Even if I knew where Daisy kept her spare bulbs, it would need daylight and a stepladder to change the bulb. Nor did I feel up to chasing a frightened cat through a dark house.

I found the stair rail and cautiously began climbing. There was no light on the first-floor landing either. I wondered if all the bulbs had given out at the same time or whether Daisy had had a sudden attack of economy. Or perhaps she had thought that we were all in for the night and had turned off all the lights before going to bed herself.

Moving carefully, I reached my own room without mishap and thankfully turned on my own light. The sudden brightness made me blink.

I found I was still holding the bag of cheese and dropped it on the desk top. The light thump of the bag hitting the desk was immediately echoed by another soft thump as something leaped out of the shadows and landed on the desk.

Again I jumped, and again there was a soft yowl of pain from a cat. But Robey was made of sterner stuff than Gracie, particularly where food was concerned. He limped determinedly over to the bag and began working it open.

'How did you get in here?' I asked. 'The door was shut. Have you been in here all evening?'

Robey drew his head out of the bag, a square of cheese between his teeth and crouched down to eat in comfort. He kept glancing at me out of the corners of his eyes. Like Gracie, he seemed to be in a mistrustful mood.

'What have you two been doing?' I asked. 'Did you get your paws caught in a closing door, or something?'

Robey gave me a suspicious look as I bent over him and backed to the far side of the desk.

'All right,' I said, 'relax.' I bowled another piece of cheese over to him and he caught it neatly, but still looked at me uneasily.

'Where's Formby?' I wondered aloud. 'Is he wounded too?'

Robey finished his cheese, shot me a dark, unhelpful look and jumped down, crying out again as he hit the floor. He limped to the door and stood there waiting for me to open it for him. His whole attitude proclaimed that he didn't have to hang around here listening to stupid questions.

'Have it your way,' I said and crossed to open the door. It was obvious I wasn't going to be allowed to investigate any sore paws tonight. Not that I'd know what to do about any sores I might discover. Daisy was the cat expert and she probably knew all about it and had already started the proper treatment.

I had problems of my own. I closed the door behind Robey, who was gingerly descending the stairs as though advancing into enemy territory, and went back to the desk.

I removed the crumpled cocktail napkin from my bag, smoothed it out and looked again at the sinister message before transferring it to a desk drawer. My first impulse to throw it away had been superseded by an uneasy recognition that—if anything happened to me—it might just possibly be evidence of some sort.

Against whom? Did I seriously think the Starer had decided to warn me against himself? How did he know how much I suspected? Or was he just guessing? Perhaps the expression on my face as I looked at him had told him more than I thought.

Suddenly I was overpoweringly exhausted, much too tired to stay awake a moment longer, fit only to fall into bed. I would think about the problem further in the morning. Yet I had the depressed certainty that I wouldn't really sleep—not the peaceful dreamless sleep I needed to-night . . . this morning . . .

I was right. I dropped off into nightmares, from which I woke at intervals with a deep sense of relief, only to drift away again into even worse nightmares. It was not until I opened my eyes to see a rim of light around the window curtains and realized that it was truly another day that I could relax.

Then I slept properly—and too deeply—awakening with a start to discover that it was nearly noon. I leaped from my bed. At this rate, I'd soon be challenging Norma for the Sleeping Beauty Trophy.

There seemed to be no one in the house when I went downstairs. The cats who, with the usual curiosity of their kind, normally came rushing to find out who was stirring, were nowhere in sight. The kitchen, always a-clatter with pots and pans at this hour as Daisy worked on lunch, was silent.

I walked down the echoing hallway conscious of an eerie feeling of being the last one alive on board the *Mary Celeste*. The chill foreboding of my unremembered nightmares enshrouded me again. Something was wrong somewhere—perhaps everywhere.

Yet the kitchen looked perfectly pleasant and sunny. Outside, gulls wheeled across a bright blue sky, uttering their plaintive cries.

Lunch had been started, although there was no sign of Daisy. A bowl of scrubbed potatoes stood on the draining-board. A half-scraped pile of carrots was beside it. A paring knife lay on top of the carrots, as though dropped hastily when some emergency erupted. The only sound in the whole house seemed to be the ticking of the clock on the outside wall.

My eyes went to the clock automatically, then were drawn by a flurry of movement at one of the windows flanking it. Formby, urgent and indignant, reared up on his hind legs, demanding entrance.

'All right, all right, keep your fur on!' I crossed to the

window and opened it.

Formby literally fell into the kitchen, complaining and purring in the same breath. He jumped from the window-sill to the floor without wincing and headed straight for his food bowl.

'Well, *you're* all right,' I said thoughtfully. Whatever had happened to the other cats, Formby had obviously escaped. Perhaps because he had been out on the prowl all night.

'If only you could talk,' I said.

He looked up and gave a piercing yowl.

'*My* language, I mean.' How many questions might he be able to answer? How many useful bits of information might he vouchsafe? Like the proverbial fly on the wall, the cats moved everywhere. They watched, listened, formed their own opinions and were—alas—dumb.

'Where are the others?' I asked him uselessly. 'The other cats, the other people? What's going on?'

He raised his head and gave me a long, inscrutable look before turning and lowering his head to the saucer of milk beside his food bowl. Now the loudest sound in the room was an untidy slurping noise as he vacuumed up the milk.

'Oh, George!' I shuddered. 'You might at least be dis-creet about *that*, along with everything else.'

He ignored me, concentrating on lapping up the milk. He had apparently had a long hard night.

As who hadn't? I looked around again, remembering that I hadn't had any breakfast. Not that I wanted much. I crossed to the fridge and poured myself a glass of milk. Formby came over to me and gave me an imploring look. He could get his point over well enough when it was to his convenience. I topped up his saucer before replacing the milk in the fridge.

The slurping noises resumed as I closed the fridge door, competing with the tick of the clock to dominate the silence. I heard nothing else, so it was no wonder I jumped and screamed when I backed into someone standing close behind me.

'You are nervous,' Dandini said. 'The artistic temperament. It claims us all.'

'I didn't know you were there,' I said crossly. 'I didn't hear you come in.'

'Of course you did not. Am I not a magician? Do I not possess the secrets of the Orient?' He had dropped into the voice he used for children's matinees but I was not amused. 'I do not enter rooms in the boring physical way— I materialize in them when I choose!'

His announcement would have been more impressive if he hadn't brought his shopping with him.

'No Daisy?' He began unpacking and stowing away his purchases: the yoghurt and bean curd on his own special shelf in the fridge, the muesli and wheat germ on his own shelf in the cupboard. Even though it was Bank Holiday, the health food store remained open. Dandini wasn't the only customer when the town swarmed with trippers. In holiday mood, few of them objected to paying over the odds in health and speciality stores for items to carry home tonight to tide them over until their own shops were open.

'No anyone,' I said. 'I thought you might know where they'd all gone.'

'I?' He shrugged. 'They do not confide in me. Everyone was at breakfast—' He hesitated. 'Everyone who is usually there,' he clarified. 'How should I know where they have gone from there?'

'I thought something might have happened,' I said. 'An accident or—or some excitement outside. They might have gone out to look . . .' And not come back? Why?

'Henry Parsons will be at work,' Dandini pointed out. 'The weather is good, it is the last day of the holiday, he will be at his pitch to entertain the children and pass the

hat around as many times as possible today. He has probably taken sandwiches with him and will skip lunch.'

'Of course,' I said. 'I'd forgotten that.'

'Why shouldn't you?' He shrugged. 'You do not have
Punch-and-Judy men in your country. You are not accustomed to performers who do not work regular hours.'

Only another performer could speak of our hours as
'regular', but it was true that, in our way, our times of
employment were as routine as any nine-to-five office
worker's. It was even truer that I was not familiar with the
itinerant buskers and entertainers I had found on the
fringe of the English theatrical world. The concept of
someone with no fixed stage, performing a routine when
and where the pickings looked good — and always with
one eye out for the approach of a policeman — was strange
to me.

Of course, here at the seaside, Henry Parsons didn't
have to keep his eyes peeled for the police but, from what
I had seen, he moved on as often as if he did. Perhaps it
was force of habit, or perhaps he didn't want to lose the
knack in case he ever had to go back to busking for theatre
queues. But Our Henry covered the waterfront. You
never knew where you would run into him and his portable
booth next. On really wet days, he favoured a niche on
the Grand Pier itself; on good days, he could be anywhere
along the sands or promenade.

'But that doesn't explain where Daisy is.' Still following
my train of thought, I spoke aloud.

'Perhaps she remembered some ingredient she needed
for her cooking and popped out to get it?' Dandini was
still prepared to be helpful, but I didn't like the calculating look that had crept into his eyes. Nor the knowledge
that we were alone in the house.

'Not today,' I said. 'The stores she uses are shut and
she'd do without before she paid the tourist-trap prices in
the ones that are open.'

'You are a clever girl.' He had obviously decided to try a bit of flattery and see if it would get him anywhere. 'You must be a keen judge of human nature.'

'No more so than a magician.' I turned the mirror back to reflect himself. It hardly ever failed. It didn't now.

'It is part of one's stock in trade.' He preened himself. 'Always it is necessary to recognize the components of one's audience: which will be unbelievers, which will be suspicious, which will allow themselves to be enchanted.'

'I hadn't thought about that.' I gave him an admiring look. 'It's not the sort of problem I have to face.'

'Ah, but you do not require your audience to *believe* anything!'

The hell I don't, I thought, fluttering my eyelashes automatically.

'With magic, so much more is required. All those people out there—' He waved a hand at Formby, momentarily transforming him into an audience of upturned human faces. 'They must *want* to suspend the laws of nature, to believe against sense, against science, that the lady has been sawn in half and magicked back into one piece again. To believe that I can make someone float in the air, that I can say the secret words and turn objects into something different—'

Make believe. That was the name of the game for all of us, only magic was even more so. The beginning of it all, the original enchantment.

'Magic answers the deepest human need—' Dandini fixed me with his glittering eyes, half-hypnotizing me with his intensity. 'It calls out to the deepest instinct, the one that wants to believe there is more than we can see or hear, more than the façade we have been taught to take for granted. Things are never the way they seem—'

His extravagant gesture encompassed the kitchen, the half-prepared vegetables, the cat.

'Is time what it seems or is it a thin veil screening us

from another world? Is that the lunch—or the beginning of a witch's cauldron? Is that cat—' his quivering forefinger pointed directly at Formby— 'is that cat her *familiar*?'

Formby gave him an enigmatic look and disappeared under the stove.

I felt a *frisson* myself and didn't blame Formby. Dandini had a good line in patter. A few decent breaks and he wouldn't be on the end of a pier in a second-rate seaside town many more seasons.

'And *you*?' Dandini turned his burning eyes upon me, trying to devour me. 'Are *you* what you seem? Are you a simple singer wasting your precious talent in licensed premises? Or have you come through the time warp, too? Are you one of the sirens against whom men blocked their ears and lashed themselves to the mast?'

Push over, Formby, here I come! But, although chilling, it was insidious. I never could resist a good cue.

'And you?' I asked. 'Are you a stage magician? Or are you the reincarnation of Merlin, come back through the mists of time to search for Arthur and lead us all into the new Golden Age?'

We stared at each other silently for a moment.

'You see?' Once again, his hand described an indescribable arc. 'There *are* more things in heaven and earth than this world dreams of. Who knows?' He moved a step nearer. 'Who can tell—?'

The front door slammed, breaking the spell, for which I was properly thankful.

It had just occurred to me that Dandini's eyes were more than hypnotic—they were reminiscent.

At another time, in another context, he could be one of the Starers himself.

The footsteps hurrying down the hallway brought back sanity and the actual world, without shadows, without ambiguity. Formby came out from under the stove and darted towards the doorway, meowing a relieved welcome.

CHAPTER 12

'*There* you are!' Daisy erupted into the kitchen with the force of a volcanic lava flow. She swooped up Formby in passing and, cuddling him, turned to face us accusingly, quite as though we had been the ones who had gone missing in the middle of the luncheon preparations. 'I don't suppose *you've* seen that little bleeder, have you? Since last night, I mean?'

Although indefinite, the description was familiar. 'Don't tell me Little Johnny is missing?'

'Bed not slept in — and Norma in hysterics when she discovered it!' Daisy said with relish. 'Oh, what a scene! She's missed her calling, dear. Lady Macbeth wasn't in it! She went rushing out to hunt for him and I had to go with her. I was afraid she might do herself an injury, the state she was in. But I lost her half way along the front, so I thought the best thing to do was come home. I don't suppose you have any idea where he could be, dear?'

'I haven't seen him since Ted threw him out of The Phoenix last night,' I said truthfully. 'I thought you were going to walk home with him.'

'He was gone when I got downstairs,' Daisy said. 'I thought I might catch up with him, but I never did. I assumed he'd run home ahead of me and gone up to his room.'

'How strange,' I said. 'No wonder Norma is upset. Where could he be?'

'*Pah!*' Dandini pantomimed a spitting movement between clenched teeth. 'Who can care about such a one as that? The world would be a better place without him!'

'That's all very well for you to say, dear,' Daisy reproved. 'But you aren't his mother — and she *is* fond of him.'

'All appearances to the contrary,' I could not refrain from commenting. Daisy gave me a reproachful look and I added hastily, 'The last I saw of him, he was out looking for Norma—'

'She explained where she was, dear. After they left the nursing home, Johnny wanted to play Space Invaders, but the noise in the amusement arcade always gives Norma a headache, so she said she'd wait for him outside. She sat down in a deck chair on the sands and—'

'And fell asleep,' I finished resignedly.

'Well, yes, she did, dear. It takes an awful lot out of her when she has to go and see her husband, you know—'

'And that rotten little swine went off and left her sleeping on the beach for hours. No wonder he got upset when he found she hadn't got home. He must have been afraid the tide came in and swept her away—and it was all his fault.' I could picture it only too clearly. 'Or else he thought Norma allowed some tripper to pick her up.' That was more likely, with the nasty mind he had.

'They must have just missed each other, dear. If only he'd waited at home a bit longer, she'd have shown up.'

'But he went out looking for her. And now Norma is out looking for him—' I shook my head.

'*And* she has had you out looking for him as well,' Dandini accused Daisy. 'When you should have been here preparing the meal for the rest of us who have to work today. These people are more trouble than they are worth. They disrupt the whole house!'

'I'm afraid I agree.' For once, I felt Dandini had a good case. We were all wasting far too much time thinking about and worrying about a couple of people who would have to fight their way out of their problems themselves. 'Johnny has probably stayed out all night to pay Norma back in what he thinks is her own coin.'

'It wouldn't be the first time he's stayed out all night, that's true,' Daisy sighed. 'But Norma never even noticed

before. He was always home before she got up. Now she's
found the empty bed and she's frightened. And of course
I can't tell her it's nothing new for him. It would only
upset her more.'

'I don't see why,' I said. 'If he's done it more than once,
then he obviously goes off and stays with a friend. It could
only reassure her to know that—'

I broke off. They were both giving me the sort of look I
hadn't been on the receiving end of for a long, long time.
Years, in fact. It told me I was too young and too dumb to
know what was really going on. Both of them knew a lot
more than I did—but they weren't about to tell me.

'Such a one does not have friends!' Dandini hissed.

'We don't want to go into that, dear!' Daisy's voice cut
like a whiplash. 'Norma would be upset—' she softened
her voice, directing her next remark to me— 'because
Johnny shouldn't be out at all, the hours he keeps. He's . . .
he's still only a child, you know.'

Dandini dipped his head, obscuring his face. He picked
up his carrier bag and headed for the door.

'Lunch will be ready in about half an hour.' Daisy was
not going to forgive his accusation of dereliction of duty.
'Don't you go far—and mind you're on time. It's chump
chops—and I don't want to overcook them.'

That was unusual in itself. Not her desire not to overcook, but the chops. We usually had stewing steak, pie
veal, mutton—things that were cheap and could be
simmered slowly in a casserole until the sum was greater
than its parts. Chops were an extravagance—but quick.

I felt a pang of foreboding as Daisy lowered Formby to
the floor and pulled a bloodstained parcel out of her own
shopping-bag. Had she really gone to that extortionate
butcher who opened today in order to rook the tourists?
She had often opined that, from the prices he charged, he
was a direct descendant of the highwaymen who had once
roamed this area.

Stand and deliver! Had Daisy really stood still for those prices and delivered the cash demanded? Like a tripper?

It seemed that she had—and was on the defensive about it. She did not meet my eye as she crossed to the sink, unwrapping her parcel. Formby twined around her feet, impeding her progress, inflamed by the scent of blood and yowling his hysteria.

Daisy dropped the meat on the draining-board and fended off Formby's hopeful leap before she realized what was wrong and turned to me with a puzzled frown.

'Where are the others?' she asked.

She meant the cats, not the people.

'I don't know . . .' I hesitated. Should I tell her more? Was it possible she didn't know?

'What's wrong?' She picked up the hesitation. 'What is it?' Her voice sharpened in alarm. 'You're going to have to tell me sooner or later, dear, you know. Was it—? Was it the traffic?'

'No, no! Nothing like that. They're all right. They're around here somewhere. Well, they're mostly all right. I mean, they're not *very* hurt—' I knew I was growing incoherent, but I couldn't think of the right words and, far from calming her, I seemed to be adding to her alarm.

'What is it?' She was almost frightening as she advanced upon me and grabbed me by the shoulders. She'd shake it out of me, if she had to. 'What's happened to them?'

'Something's wrong with their paws.' I blurted it out quickly. 'I don't know what. They wouldn't let me get close enough to see. I discovered it when I got in last night. I thought you must already know—'

She released me so quickly that I staggered, off-balance, and stooped to pick up Formby again.

'Not him,' I said. 'He seems to have escaped whatever it was. Of course, he was out all night.'

'Out all night . . .' Daisy echoed. She met my eyes and we both remembered who else had been missing all night.

Only now it seemed that there might be a more expedient reason than mere pique at his mother. Daisy would murder anyone who had harmed her darlings.

'Come along, dear.' Tight-lipped, Daisy led the way to the basement door. 'They'll be hiding down by the furnace. They always do when they're upset. Let's see what's wrong.'

She went down the stairs ahead of me, still clutching Formby and calling out, cooing, to the other cats. A faint uncertain mew from a dark corner answered her.

'Gracie, darling—' Daisy had no difficulty in identifying it. 'Come to mother. Here—' She turned and thrust Formby into my arms. 'Take care of him while I see what this is all about.'

I held the squirming cat and remained at the foot of the stairs. The injured cats had already demonstrated that they were no longer prepared to trust the lodgers. With the suspicion that was forming in my mind, I could not blame them.

'Here, darling, let mother see—' Daisy had captured Gracie, who nestled in her arms mewling querulously while Daisy gently turned her paws over and inspected them. Hearing the loved and familiar voice, Robey limped from the shadows for his share of comfort.

'Oh!' Daisy's exclamation of outrage sent him scurrying back into the safety of his corner. Gracie flattened her ears and began a plaintive sing-song wail. I had the feeling that she was telling us all about it—if only we could understand her.

'What is it?' I let Formby drop to the floor and approached cautiously. Gracie watched me with wary eyes, but was willing to have me near since she had Daisy to protect her.

'Look!' Daisy was shaking with indignation, she could hardly speak. 'Just look at that!'

There was a sharp cut across the soft sensitive pad of

Gracie's front left paw. It looked deep and painful. I winced in sympathy.

'How dreadful! No wonder she cried out when she jumped to the floor. And—' I looked over my shoulder— 'Robey did, too. Do you suppose the same thing happened to him?'

'We'll see about that. George, George, come here, darling—' Cooing, she coaxed Robey from the shadows, ignoring Formby who twined round her ankles, puzzled at the lack of attention.

She couldn't catch Robey while she still held Gracie, and Gracie had put her claws out and was hanging on for dear life, still spilling out her tale of woe.

'I'll get him.' I swooped and captured Robey, who tried, but was too slow and heavy, to escape in time. Gravely we inspected his paws and found the cruel laceration.

'Why?' Daisy was nearly in tears. 'Oh, I know he's a rotten little beast. He always has been and he always will be, dear. But *why* should he hurt Robey and Fields? What have they ever done to him?

She didn't really expect an answer but, as I looked at the narrow encrustation of blood across the little pink pad, one came to me.

'If you'll come up to my room,' I said slowly. 'I think I can show you why.'

'You can?' Daisy looked at me incredulously. She had been thinking along the lines of inherent evil. The idea that there might be an actual reason shook her even more.

'Wait a minute,' she said. 'I'm going to lock the cats in down here where they'll be safe.' She spent a few more minutes comforting them, bringing down a bowl of milk, opening a tin of their favourite cat food and explaining at great length that mother was not abandoning them, but leaving them down here for their own good.

There were tears in her eyes when she closed the door

on them. 'I hate leaving them down there alone in the dark,' she said. 'You should have seen them on stage in the old days. They were giants, dear, giants.'

I patted her shoulder and led the way up to my room. I was thankful that I was at the top of the house. Daisy was too breathless from the climb to give full vent to her feelings when I opened the desk drawer and pulled out the cocktail napkin, but her eyes flashed dangerously.

'That's the napkin I found last night,' I told her. 'I didn't want to make an issue of it then. I didn't know who'd slipped it into the pile.'

Daisy concentrated on breathing deeply. She kept her eyes fixed on the rust-brown message. She was beginning to make me nervous. I hoped Little Johnny wouldn't pick this moment to return — his life wouldn't be worth two cents.

'I can see now,' I continued quickly, 'it's a childish thing. The melodramatic wording, the threat . . . and written in blood—'

'And not even his *own* blood!' To Daisy that was the most heinous sin. 'My poor little Gracie and George! How could he *do* such a thing?'

Because Gracie was too trusting and Robey too portly to get away quickly, as Formby had done. But Daisy wanted the psychology explained to her, not the mechanics, and that I was unequipped to do. I had never encountered a budding monster like Little Johnny Handel before, either.

'And what does he mean by it?' Daisy had progressed to studying the actual wording. '*What* does he want you to keep your mouth shut about?'

'I caught him shoplifting in Woolworth's,' I said. 'At least, I couldn't be sure, I didn't actually see him doing it, but he must have thought I did. Anyway, there's not much room for doubt now.'

'No,' Daisy said thoughtfully, 'there isn't.' She straightened up and glared at some point beyond me, in a towering rage. I could only be thankful that I was not the target for such devastating fury.

'He must have been carrying it with him,' I said. 'Robey was in my room when I got home last night. Johnny must have taken one of the cocktail napkins I have around and written the message up here. Then Gracie got out when he left, but Robey was too slow and got shut behind. Then Johnny came down to The Phoenix and created the scene and dropped the napkin at the same time he knocked the pile of requests to the floor, so that I wouldn't see it immediately.'

'That is enough!' Daisy slammed her hand down on the desk top, making me jump. 'That is too much! I have put up with an awful lot, dear. In all conscience, I have. But I've turned a blind eye because I've felt so sorry for Norma and not wanted to add to her troubles. But this has bloody well torn it! I don't care! They leave tonight! Not one more day do they spend under my roof!'

'Can you do that?' I asked tentatively. 'I mean, I thought the law protected—'

'Damn the law!' Daisy snarled. 'There is no law in the world that can force me to keep those people in my house. If I have to pack their bags myself and put them out on the pavement, I'll do it! If I have to set fire to their rooms—'

'All right, all right,' I placated hastily. 'I was only asking.'

'I mean it, dear,' Daisy said solemnly. 'On my life, I mean it. This time, he's gone too far!'

CHAPTER 13

Of course, Daisy cooled down as the day wore on. It would be impossible for anyone to remain at that pitch of fury. She subsided into a simmering rage, but there was no one to vent it on. Neither Norma nor Johnny returned to the house all afternoon.

Daisy spent most of the day in the basement, consoling the cats. Now and again, she emerged to open the front door and stand looking out, watching with grim satisfaction as the increasing stream of traffic surged past at the end of the street. It was a soothing sight: holiday-makers, heading back to London and their home cities, leaving the town to its own inhabitants again.

She did not, I was relieved to see, march into Norma's room and begin packing, as she had threatened. Protocol demanded that she first announce to Norma and Johnny just what she was going to do—and why. Until both of them turned up, the scene was held in abeyance, although I could hear Daisy rehearsing random lines under her breath whenever I was near enough.

Which wasn't often. Everyone in the theatre develops a healthy sense of self-preservation and I noticed that Kate and Dandini were also keeping well out of the way. It was a quiet afternoon, with everyone lying low. We would have continued lying, if anyone had asked us, by uniformly protesting that we were saving our strength for our evening performances. Fortunately, no one asked us.

By the time I was ready to leave for The Phoenix, Daisy had reached that state of controlled edginess usually associated with an understudy watching the leading lady successfully keeping 'flu and laryngitis at bay. She was keyed up, ready and eager, but it looked as though she were going to be cheated out of giving the performance of her life tonight.

'No Norma?' I commiserated on my way through the hall. I wasn't particularly surprised. At last report, Norma had been searching along the front. Since the search had started at an hour far in advance of her normal rising hour, it was possible that her strange neurotic fatigue had overcome her mother-love. She had probably slipped into a cinema, telling herself that she was looking for Johnny in there, and slept the afternoon away.

On the other hand, it was possible that she had caught up with Johnny and he had confessed what he had done to the cats—although perhaps not the real reason for it. In that case, they might both be fugitives now, afraid— quite rightly—to come back and face Daisy's wrath.

'No sign of her, dear,' Daisy said. 'I wish she'd get back soon. I'd like to give her enough notice so that she has a couple of hours to look around for another place. Not that she'll have much trouble—most of the trippers will be leaving this afternoon. There'll be plenty of vacancies.'

'Not if the landladies have ever run into Little Johnny,' I said grimly. 'She'd have an easier time trying to book in with a coiled cobra in her luggage.'

'I was on the bill with a snake-charmer once.' Daisy brightened, reminded of happier days. 'It's not as danger- ous as it looks, dear. The trick is—there are tricks to every trade—to keep them well fed. That's why Zalia always got a dressing-room to herself, even though she wasn't a proper star. No one was ever willing to share with her. It wasn't so much the snakes, dear, it was the feeding times. Mice, you know, live mice.'

'Ugh!' I shuddered, caught between fascination and horror. But Daisy's reminiscences were unfailingly intriguing, evoking a lost world of music halls and variety stages. Had I been born a couple of generations earlier, it was a world which I might have inhabited myself.

'Yes, dear, but even that wasn't the worst of it. We shared the bill with Saldoni, a conjuror who swallowed a white mouse for the finale to his act. Not the same one every night, of course, he had two—'

'Only two?' I asked. 'You mean he . . . got them back . . . after he swallowed them?'

'He regurgitated them, dear. They were specially trained. You can't go around swallowing strange mice, you know. It would make them very nervous and they'd get all jumpy. Stands to reason, when you think about it, that he'd have to have his own trained mice.'

'I've never thought about it before,' I said faintly.

'Well, you do. It takes ages to train them—he used to tell us about it—but without them, you haven't such a good act. It was a wonderful finale, dear. At least three ladies fainted at every performance.' She sighed. 'We had a great show that year and personally I put the blame for what happened on the management. They never should have put Zalia and Saldoni in adjoining dressing-rooms. It was asking for trouble.'

'And they got it?'

'Exactly, dear. One of the snakes got loose one afternoon, slid into the next dressing-room—and helped himself. Zalia found him because he'd gone to sleep halfway down the corridor, but it was too late for the mouse, of course. It wasn't like being swallowed by a human. Well, poor Zalia was frantic. Did I mention that Saldoni had a terrible temper?'

'And an amazing gullet,' I said weakly.

'That, too, dear. He needed it. Anyway, Zalia took one of the white mice she kept to feed the snakes and put it in the cage with the other one. They all look pretty much alike, you know.'

'You see one white mouse, you've seen them all,' I agreed.

'She was leaving the show that night, so all she needed

was a bit of luck. There was a sporting chance Saldoni wouldn't notice the substitution until she was safely away.' Daisy sighed again. 'She almost made it.'

'But not quite?'

'Saldoni always arrived late and always in a rush, otherwise he might have realized something was wrong. But he dashed in, snatched up what he thought was his mouse, and rushed on stage. Everything went all right—until he tried to swallow the mouse. Then you never saw such a performance in your life!

'They had to ring down the curtain. And, of course, when Saldoni saw Zalia's face—and that snake of hers—he knew what had happened. It was written all over her, dear. She wasn't an actress, just a snake-charmer, you know. Temper! The stagehands had to hold him down or there'd have been murder committed. And language! There's all this permissiveness today, but when gentlemen used to hold it all in, it was quite something to hear when they really let rip.'

'Did Zalia live to tell the tale?'

'Well, of course, she did, dear. The boys weren't foolish enough to let go of Saldoni until she was well clear of the theatre. And her hamper of snakes with her. They took him round to the pub and poured drinks into him. Not that he could drink much that night, with his poor scratched throat.'

I felt my own throat convulsing in sympathy.

'I never saw anything like it, dear, and I thought I never would again, but—' Daisy's eyes narrowed and I had the uneasy feeling that she was reviewing the battle in order to pick up a few pointers for her forthcoming scene with Norma and Johnny.

'Look,' I excused myself hurriedly. 'I've got to get down to The Phoenix now or I'll be late. I'll see you later.' With luck, it would all be over by the time I got back.

'That's right, dear.' Daisy's eyes were turned inward as

she brooded afresh on her grievances—and those of
Robey and Fields. 'I'll see you later . . .'

I headed for The Phoenix, half hoping that I would
run into Norma along the way. If I did, I would suggest
that she stay away from the house until Daisy had gone to
bed. By morning, Daisy might have cooled down enough
to contemplate giving them a second chance—or at least
two weeks' notice to quit.

It was not that I did not have every sympathy with Daisy
and the cats. I did. But I found I still could feel sorry for
poor Norma. It was not her fault that her son had evolved
into a monster . . . was it? Certainly, she could have had
nothing to do with her husband's turning into a vegetable. It
was all in the luck of the draw—and Norma had been
picking up rotten cards all her life.

I didn't see her, of course. I didn't see anyone I knew. A
steady stream of traffic growled along every road,
heading out of town now. Since it was still fairly early,
these were mostly family cars filled with luggage and toys
and children, driven by parents who wanted to reach
home in good time to get the children to bed at a decent
hour. Here and there, an occasional motor-cycle
threaded through the traffic, a grim reminder of the fears
that had been groundless.

Two policemen stood on the corner where the promenade
joined the main road, watching the mass exodus with grim
faces. I realized not everyone was happy to see the trippers
leave. Another Bank Holiday, another dead girl. Was
there a connection? Perhaps even now, in one of those
cars moving past, the killer was escaping . . . again.

The police could not seal off the town and refuse exit to
the thousands of holiday-makers until they had found the
killer. All they could do was appeal to the public for help.
But the public didn't want to get involved, to forfeit the
last hours of their holiday answering questions, divulging
their names and an address where they could be contacted

for further enquiries. They didn't want to get embroiled in something that was no business of theirs.

Powerless, their suspicion and frustration etched on their faces, the policemen stood on the corner and watched their suspects leaving town.

Of course, the killer might have left town already. He could have taken off as soon as he had killed her; hopped into his car or on to his motor-cycle and disappeared into the night.

Or, more practically, he might have left first thing in the morning. If he were staying at a hotel or lodging-house, there would be no surer way of calling attention to himself than leaving in the middle of the night. On the other hand, if he had booked in for the entire weekend, it would also have aroused suspicion to depart a day early, no matter how good a story he told of sudden illness at home. A landlady is suspicious by nature and as soon as news of the murder had reached her, she would have been down at the police station giving them all the details of her late lodger, just in case.

No, the police were right to keep an eye on the departing tourists. There was always the chance that something suspicious might be noted and lead on to something else. Even as I walked away, one of the constables jotted down the licence number of a car. I wondered what had prompted his action. The occupants of the car, two adults, two children and a dog, looked perfectly innocent to me. Just another family party heading home.

It was later tonight when the police ought to be at their most vigilant. That would be when the unattached, or lightly-attached, departed: the ones without responsibilities to take them back early, those joined in weekend wedlock, the chancers, the singles, the loners, the misfits. The Starer and his tribe.

The front seemed as busy as ever when I reached it. Many were staying on until the last possible moment. Of course, some of them might have chosen a late holiday and this weekend marked the beginning of it and not the end.

It was an unsettling thought. I hoped the Starer had used all his annual holiday time and departed. I never wanted to encounter him again.

And yet there were Starers everywhere. The disappearance of one would not ensure that another would not appear. The one I had spotted might be quite innocent of everything I suspected of him. Then again, he might not . . .

I entered The Phoenix with relief, the flock-papered walls seemed to close around me protectively as I went upstairs. I felt safe here with Ted and the staff to deal with any awkward customers.

I was early, but Ted was already on the job, filling small dishes with peanuts, olives and cubes of cheese. Milly must have been there earlier, for there were fresh quiches ranged along the bar counter waiting to be precut into serving slices.

Ted nodded as I crossed to the piano and began sorting out some sheet music. I nodded back silently. I had learned that he liked a quiet hour to himself before the bar opened for business. I was here, but I wasn't going to intrude on his privacy, my nod told him. I liked a bit of quiet time myself.

It was a formula we had tacitly worked out in the time I had been appearing here. I was surprised when he was the first to break the companionable silence.

'Everything all right?' he asked.

Why shouldn't it be? But there was no point in giving that as an answer. The town was like a giant shimmering spiderweb, with the slightest tug on its outermost filaments setting the whole thing a-quiver. Don't ask who knew what — or how. They did — and that was all there was to it.

'Little Johnny hasn't come back yet.' I answered the

question he intended, but hadn't asked. 'Neither has Norma. Daisy is beginning to get awfully worried.'

'Born to be hanged, that one.' Ted kept his head lowered, concentrating on the little dishes. I knew that he wasn't talking about Daisy, or even Norma.

'No one hangs any more,' I reminded him. 'There isn't any capital punishment now.'

'More's the pity,' he grunted. 'Only thing that would do some people any good.'

That was a moot point if I ever heard one and I didn't bother arguing it. I sat down at the piano and began experimenting with some new—or rather, very old, although new to me—music hall material I had discovered but not had a chance to try out before. Perhaps, now that the season was ending, I could find more time for myself and my own concerns. I could take some time off and explore farther afield. There were all those ferries sailing across the Channel every day to all those fascinating and, to me, romantic foreign ports: Dieppe, Calais, Ostend, Zeebrugge, Dunkirk, Boulogne . . .

I played softly, losing myself in reverie. So many places to go, so many things to see. I had the feeling of a world on my doorstep in a way that wasn't possible in the States. Everything here was so near. A few hours and you could be anywhere in Europe. People in these seaside towns popped across the Channel just to do their shopping in French hypermarkets—and the French came over here for English specialities, and of course everyone picked up their duty-free drinks and cigarettes on board the ferries.

'Never mind, eh?' Ted came over and began setting out the dishes of appetizers around the piano. 'We're all right.'

'I hope so.' Then I realized that it wasn't just a general comment, but referred to something particular. 'What do you mean?'

'Haven't you heard?' He seemed surprised. 'They hit up

north this afternoon. Seventeen arrests, so far. Fighting still going on. Police called in from surrounding regions.' He spoke with relish. If it was happening somewhere else, it couldn't be happening here.

'The motor-cycle gang? How do you know it's the same one? I wouldn't relax just yet. There may be more of them around.'

'I'm not relaxing.' His tone reminded me that the events of last August Bank Holiday were just hearsay so far as I was concerned; he had been an eye-witness and deeply involved. 'But I think we're well on the way to being out of the woods. There are preliminary disturbances, you know, if the gangs are around and bent on trouble. I haven't seen any of those signs this weekend.'

Some people might have considered a dead girl in a boating pool some sort of sign of disturbance. However, I knew what he meant. He was talking about mass rioting and looting, not violence on a one-to-one basis.

'No—' A hint of complacency crept into his voice. 'No, we've had our fair share of motor-cyclists this weekend, but they're the respectable ones, like. I don't think we're in for any more trouble this time.'

I nodded, more to keep him happy than because I agreed with him. A mood of gloom settled over me and I could not keep from thinking about the dead girl. I found my fingers straying over the keys, picking out the melody of the 'Dead March'.

Ted didn't notice.

CHAPTER 14

After that, it was all I needed to look up from the key-board later in the evening and lock eyes with the Starer. The music crashed into discord as my fingers stiffened and hit the wrong keys in shock.

He almost smiled, well-pleased with the effect he had made, then he disappeared again. Even as I looked round frantically for Ted, he was gone.

A ghost . . . a wisp of fog . . . a curl of smoke . . . *No smoke without fire*. Where was Ted?

For that matter, where was the Starer. *Now you see him, now you don't*. He could still be here. With that nondescript face and — I couldn't even remember what he was wearing. I hadn't looked away from those eyes. They were his only outstanding feature. If he kept his eyelids lowered, he could mingle with the rest of the people in the room and we would never be able to pick him out. Throw him out. He was the Invisible Man in person — or almost-person.

Automatically, I launched into a livelier song, as though the crashing of keys had been a deliberate prelude to a change of mood. The audience weren't paying that much attention. Some gave a murmur of approval at the cheerier mood, but most just continued with their drinking and conversation.

Ted must be out back. As I let my gaze roam around the room, he was nowhere in sight. Neither was the Starer. Yet the back of my neck crawled in cold and constant apprehension. He was still here somewhere. I knew it.

Just get through tonight, I lectured myself. *Pull yourself together. You can't go to bed and hide your head under the covers just because there are nuts and weirdos in the world*.

Deep down, I remained unconvinced. Huddled into a cave of blankets, unconscious for twelve, twenty-four, thirty-six, forty-eight hours, seemed a consummation devoutly to be wished. *To sleep, perchance to dream* the next few uncomfortable hours or days away seemed the perfect solution.

That must be the way Norma felt.

The realization brought me sitting bolt upright, chilled to the bone, as though a bucket of ice-cold water had just been thrown over me. Shock and pride sent the adrenalin coursing through my veins. I *wouldn't* be like Norma— not in any way, shape or form. I wouldn't give up and turn into a shapeless, spineless amoeba just because the world didn't turn the way I wanted it to turn!

Heads turned towards me questioningly and I realized that my music had become challenging, aggressive. With an effort, I modulated the pitch and tempo of the music. The Starer—the killer?—was somewhere out there within earshot. It was foolhardy—perhaps dangerous—to challenge him. Tonight marked the end of the long weekend; it was time to lie low and keep an even lower profile.

And make sure that Ted escorted me safely to the door tonight.

Momentarily, I wondered what I would find when I got home. Not, I hoped, a pile of suitcases outside on the pavement.

Then I began to wonder where Ted was. If he had been guarding the door, anyone suspicious-looking would not have been allowed entrance. Of course, the Starer probably didn't look inordinately suspicious—unless you caught a glimpse of those eyes. But where was he now? And where was Ted?

Now that I looked around, I noted the growing slackness of the staff, the casualness in the service that suggested the owner wasn't on the premises at all. A table in the corner was signalling for another round of drinks and no one was speeding to fill their order. The barmaid had been lingering beside one customer for far too long. Ted ran a tighter ship than that.

I tried not to be swamped by a wave of panic. The Starer was somewhere in the room— and Ted wasn't. I felt as though my main line of defence was gone.

What if Ted didn't come back before closing time? Would I have to go home alone? Perhaps followed? Perhaps . . . ?

It didn't bear thinking about. Also, there was no point in crossing bridges that might not even exist. If Ted wasn't back, I could call a taxi, that's all. If no taxi was available, I'd simply wait here until one was. If worst came to worst, I could even sleep here. Norma had seemed to find the armchair in the Powder Room comfortable enough.

Wait here . . . ? Sleep here . . . ? With the Starer prowling outside? Those watching, prying eyes would register that I hadn't left the building, that I was still inside . . . alone.

I shuddered myself back into the here and now: the crowded room, the laughing customers, the request napkins being passed up to me. Business as usual, and I must try not to flinch at the requests written in lipstick — especially blood-red lipstick. Not everyone carried pencil or pen with them and certainly no one else would ever write a message in blood.

'*When the Saints Go Marching In*'. I could cope with that. A good rousing number, it ought to get the crowd swinging. They struck me as a trifle subdued tonight, perhaps a bit gloomy at the prospect of going back to work tomorrow.

Or perhaps some of them were thinking about the dead girl discovered in the boating pool yesterday morning. One of themselves, down here for a good time. Happy and laughing one minute, dead the next. Because she had taken up with the wrong person? Or because she had been in the wrong place at the wrong time? By how narrow a margin might it have been themselves?

Or was there some sort of communal sixth sense operating tonight? Perhaps some paranormal emanations given off by the Starer as he moved among them warned the more sensitive that it was best to be quiet, be subdued, lest they attract the wrong sort of attention and find that *they* were perilously close to the wrong person, in the wrong place, at the wrong time.

Against my will, my fingers slowed, dragging across the keyboard in a reduction of tempo that threatened to cast a pall over the room . . . even more of a pall. Perhaps, if Ted were here and the service was operating at its usual brisk speed, the drink flowing, the snack bowls replenished, we might all be more cheerful. It wasn't like him to desert ship at the height of the evening. Had something come up? It was hard to imagine what. In the time I had known him, I had learned that he thought nothing more important than The Phoenix.

So why wasn't he here? And was he coming back? If so, when? Before closing time?

Oh no! I had been watching the door when through it walked the last person in the world I wanted to see — apart from the Starer. I guess that made Councillor Tiverton the second-last person — the one and only time he rose so high in my estimation. All the creeps were out in force tonight.

He looked around, obviously looking for Ted. He didn't find him, but I noticed that the staff abruptly began to shape up. The barmaid straightened, took her elbows off the bar, reached for a glass and began polishing it. A waitress darted forward to the table of gesticulating customers and took their orders.

It reinforced the rumour I had heard that Councillor Tiverton had his financial fingers in The Phoenix pie.

Out of the corner of my eye, I could see that he was bearing down on me. I tried to avoid noticing him until the moment he stood beside me and further pretence was useless.

'Where's Ted, then?' he demanded without pre-liminaries.

'How should I know?' I could be rude, too, but the

trouble with someone like him was that it went right over his head.

'He ought to be here. What's he doing, buggering off tonight, of all nights?'

'He was here earlier.' Even if Tiverton did have a share in the business, he had no right to criticize Ted like that. Ted worked harder and longer hours than the Councillor ever would. 'He must have just stepped out for a few minutes. He'll be back soon.'

'Will he?' He looked down at me with open disbelief. 'Where's he gone, then?'

I gave him a few bars of the '*Colonel Bogey*' march. I'd been over here long enough to catch on to a few things. There's this great national institution called 'dumb insolence'. After all, I hadn't said a word.

There were gleeful catcalls and whistles as the customers took up the refrain. It just suited the mood of people who had to go back to being wage slaves in the morning.

Councillor Tiverton compressed his lips and gave me the sort of look that translated as: *Don't get funny with me, young woman*. But, with the happy satisfied customers all around, he couldn't say anything. All too obviously, I had struck off their mood and was playing just what they wanted to hear. And that was what I had been hired for in the first place.

'I've other calls to make tonight.' He glanced at his watch. '*When—*' he emphasized the word heavily— 'Ted gets back, tell him I want to see him—fast. Tell him there's trouble down at t'mill. He'll know what I mean.'

Even I knew what he meant. The really gripping question was: which mill? Rumour also said that the not-so-good Councillor had interests in half the business in town, both the going concerns and the projected development, the legitimate and the shady.

At least, it wasn't our own dear gin mill. Before leaving, Councillor Tiverton shot a look around the room, over the heads of the customers, that galvanized the staff into frenetic activity.

'I'll be back,' he told me, loudly enough for the others to hear. 'Just as soon as I can.'

I gave him a final chorus of '*Colonel Bogey*' to march him to the door.

Ted grunted unenthusiastically when I relayed the message from his brother-in-law. It seemed he'd heard that song before.

'There's always trouble at one of Albert's mills,' he grumbled. 'He's like a juggler trying to keep too many balls in the air at the same time. Someday they'll all come crashing down on his head.'

It was a beautiful thought. I wished I could be there to see it.

'He said he'd be back as soon as he could but—' It was growing late and he might only have said it for effect, to keep the staff on their toes in Ted's absence. They wouldn't slope off so flagrantly if they thought Councillor Tiverton was going to return unexpectedly and catch them at it. His displeasure was more to be feared. Ted was too easy-going.

'He'll find me if he wants me,' Ted predicted gloomily. He reached out and touched the dimmer switch. The room darkened momentarily. 'Last orders, please,' he called out. 'Ten minutes to closing, ladies and gentlemen. Last orders, please.'

The clock in The Phoenix, like all pub clocks, was permanently five minutes fast. It was really fifteen minutes to closing, although it often took longer than that to clear everyone out.

I slid into '*Good night, Ladies*', always ready to help a good cause along. Some of the customers took the hint and drank up quickly. The diehards crowded the bar to collect one last drink.

It was obviously going to take '*God Save the Queen*' to get this lot to their feet and start them moving. I'd keep it in reserve until Ted called the final closing.

'I'll see you home,' Ted said, just before he went back to the bar to help the barmaid with the last orders.

'Thanks.' I hadn't had time to tell him about the Starer. I'd started off with Our Albert and that had plunged Ted into enough gloom without depressing him further. Besides, I hadn't felt those eyes on me for some time now. Perhaps the Starer had slipped out earlier, when I wasn't looking — not that I knew who to look for. There was every good chance that he had to get back to London tonight and we had seen the last of him.

And, if he was hanging about outside, so what? Ted was seeing me home. I was safe. The weekend was over. The motor-cycle invasion hadn't materialized. We were all safe.

Famous last words.

CHAPTER 15

The house was ablaze with light when we pulled up outside. Ted grunted, swung in to the kerb and yanked up the hand brake with unusual vehemence. I did not need to be told that he was coming in with me.

Silently he walked round, opened my door and took my arm as we walked up the path. I didn't need my key, the door opened to my touch.

The hall seemed curiously deserted as I paused uncertainly, looking around. Voices, one with a rising note of hysteria, babbled in the living-room.

Daisy appeared in the doorway and I realized what was missing. The cats. It was the first time I had ever entered the hall without one or all of the cats coming in to investigate. Daisy really meant it when she swore she was going to keep them in the basement until Little Johnny was out of the house. From the noise behind her, it sounded as though the eviction notice had already been served.

'Oh!' Daisy said flatly. 'I thought you were the doctor.' She turned and went back into the living-room.

Ted and I looked at each other, then followed her.

Norma was semi-reclining on the sofa. Semi, because she was struggling to get up, but every time she tried someone pushed her back down again, murmuring soothingly. Far from soothing Norma, this was, not surprisingly, adding to her mounting hysteria.

'Help me!' Norma called out as she saw us enter. 'You've got to help me. Please!' She struggled to rise again. 'These people don't understand!'

'These people' turned faces towards us which told us that they understood all too well.

'Drink some more of your nice tea, dear,' Daisy said. 'The doctor will be along soon. His answering service is trying to find him now. He'll give you something to help.'

'I don't want the doctor!' Norma's voice rose in a modified shriek. 'I want my son! I want Johnny!'

So he hadn't come back yet. No wonder Norma was so upset.

'He's being very naughty, dear, but he ought to be home soon now.' Daisy's eyes narrowed. 'And then we'll have a little talk with him.'

'Just be calm—' Kate leaned over to push Norma back as she struggled forward again. But Norma pushed first and Kate went flying, collapsing in a heap at the other end of the sofa.

'Calm!' Norma was on her feet, wringing her hands. 'How can you ask me to be calm when my child is missing? Look at the time!' She glared around at us accusingly. 'All your shows are out! It's past midnight and he isn't home. He didn't come home last night, either. And it's the end of the holiday! We've got to find him!'

Since the Handels were permanently—or so they thought—in Daisy's house, I didn't see what the end of the holiday had to do with the case. They weren't trippers who had to be somewhere else in the morning.

'You mean he's been missing for twenty-four hours now?' Ted was incredulous. 'That long? And none of you have done anything?'

'We've been looking for him,' Henry Parsons said defensively. 'All day.' I had a sudden vision of him peering anxiously from behind the curtains of his Punch-and-Judy box as he trundled it up and down the front, pausing occasionally to give a performance.

'Anything official, I mean.' Ted brushed aside the defence. 'He's just a lad, after all. It's high time his mother notified the police.'

There was a sudden curious silence in the room. Even Norma was momentarily still and uncertain, head cocked to one side as though listening for something just beyond the far edge of her consciousness.

'Oh no, dear,' Daisy said softly. 'You don't want to do anything hasty like that. It wouldn't be wise.'

'But—' Ted seemed as baffled as I. 'But it's a long time for a young boy to be missing.'

'He may have his reasons, dear,' Daisy said darkly. She gave Norma a sideways look. 'Good reasons.'

And plenty of them. I remembered suddenly that most people disappeared because they wanted to. Little Johnny was a mite too young to be able to carve out a new life for himself, but the impulse must be there. It was not just that the realization of the enormity of what he had done to Daisy's cats might have suddenly swept over him. It was more likely that that had triggered off his basic dissatisfaction over a life lived in a boarding-house with an absentee father, who might as well be dead, and a mother who was practically an absentee, as well. No wonder the kid had run away.

'And perhaps no reason,' Dandini said abruptly. 'There are always those who go missing. Sometimes they return with stories of visits to flying saucers. Sometimes they never return. They have stumbled through the time warp into the fourth dimension—'

He was off again. I stopped listening, but Norma was on the verge of losing all control. She opened her mouth as though to scream—

'That's enough, dear,' Daisy said firmly. 'We haven't paid an admission fee, so don't waste it on us.'

Although directed at Dandini, that snapped both of them out of it. Norma closed her mouth and shuddered. Dandini glowered at Daisy and gave the wave of his hand with which he caused objects to vanish during his stage act. Daisy, however, stood four-square and glared back at him with the look of a landlady who had just discovered a lodger trying to smuggle out the family silver in his suitcase.

'Come on.' Kate took advantage of the hiatus to grasp Norma's elbow and try to urge her back on to the sofa. 'We'll help you. Just lie down and—'

'No!' Norma shook herself free. 'You're *not* helping me! You're *not* my friends! You're just standing around wasting time while Johnny . . . Johnny . . .' She burst into tears.

'All kids run away at some stage of their lives.' I tried my hand at comfort, but tried to be practical, too. 'Have you checked his room to see what's missing? You might get some idea of where he's gone by the things he chose to take with him.'

'Trudi's right, dear.' Daisy led Norma towards the stairs. 'There's no use ringing his grandmother and getting her all upset if he isn't there, nor likely to go there. Let's take a little look-see in his room first.'

In a body, we ascended the stairs behind Norma and Daisy. We might as well. It was quite clear that no one

was going to get any rest in this house until we found Little
Johnny. I began to suspect that we might soon long for
those halcyon days when Norma went to sleep at the drop
of a hat and remained unconscious for hours at a stretch.

Norma entered Johnny's room as though she hoped,
against all the odds, to find Johnny curled up in his bed
asleep. Daisy pushed the door wide to allow room for the
rest of us to enter. It was a tacit admission that we might
know more about Johnny's clothing and playthings than
Norma did.

'Ohhh . . .' Norma looked around the room helplessly,
obviously not knowing where to start.

'Start with the wardrobe, dear,' Daisy advised briskly,
crossing to one of the hulking oak caverns the English
substitute for closets. She opened the door in a no-
nonsense way and beckoned Norma to her side. 'Now,
can you tell if anything is missing?'

If Norma could, it would be a miracle. She had been in
a semi-comatose state for so long it was a wonder that she
remembered that she had a son, at all.

'I . . . I don't know . . .' Brenda poked her head inside
vaguely. The rest of us looked at each other with exasperation, it was plain that she was going to be worse than
useless. The best we could hope for from her was that she
wouldn't go off into hysterics again.

'Oh!' Kate had pulled back the coverlet of the bed and
lifted the pillow. 'Well, his pyjamas are still here,' she
said.

However well-intentioned, it wasn't particularly helpful.
Johnny was unlikely to have worried about the niceties
of nightwear when packing hurriedly. But her action
seemed to release the others from a spell and they moved
forward, eager to do their part in the search.

Dandini drifted over to the dresser and began aimlessly
pulling out drawers. Henry lifted the lid of an old sea
chest that doubled as a toy chest and looked into it blankly.

Kate wandered around the room, peering into the corners as though they might hold a clue to Johnny's whereabouts. Ted remained frowning in the doorway.

'His best suit is still here.' I heard the rattle of coat-hangers as Daisy carried out an expert check in the wardrobe. 'And those cricket flannels he never did wear anyway. I don't know why he bothered to buy them . . .'

'Cricket flannels?' Norma asked vaguely. 'When did he get those?'

'Oh, um . . .' Daisy seemed oddly flustered. 'Just after his birthday, I think, dear. Probably he bought them with the birthday money his grandmother sent him.'

Meanwhile, I had picked up the *Radio-TV Times* lying on top of the television and begun flipping through it absently. What I saw did not reassure me. Johnny had marked in advance the programmes he had intended to watch. The markings extended through today and to-morrow, to the end of the week. If he had been planning to decamp, he obviously had not been planning it for very long. I dropped the magazine hastily, before anyone noticed and asked me any questions about it.

'I don't know—' Norma keened abruptly. 'I don't seem to recognize anything in there. He . . . he must have bought most of his clothes when . . . when I wasn't around.'

There was an awkward silence which made me suspect that I was not the only person in the house who had caught Little Johnny shoplifting.

'He's growing up, dear.' Norma did not seem to notice the false note as Daisy soothed her. 'Naturally he's going to want to choose his own things. Spread his wings, like.'

There was a muffled snort from someone in the room, hastily stifled. When I looked around, all the faces were carefully expressionless.

'I suppose so.' Norma grasped the proffered straw grate-fully, heedless of undercurrents. 'It's hard to realize that he isn't just my . . . my little baby any more.'

I wondered how old Johnny had been the last time he
had had Norma's undivided attention. Seven years old?
Eight? Perhaps nine or ten? She seemed to have no cogniz-
ance of him as an adolescent—a disturbed adolescent.
Maybe she was too disturbed herself to admit of possible
disturbance in anyone else.

I gradually became aware that my fellow lodgers had
thrown themselves into the search with a subdued but
feverish zeal. At first I thought they were, in that
peculiarly English way, covering their intense embarrassment at Norma's unusual—and belated—display of
maternal devotion. Then I began noticing that there was
a bit more to it than that. I backed up against the window
and watched them dispassionately.

Surely it was excessive for Dandini to burrow down to
the bottom of the drawer and lift up the lining paper?
And why should Kate, having ascertained that the pyjamas
were under the pillow, now be running her hands underneath the mattress? What did Henry Parsons, who had
withdrawn to a corner of the room and was casually and
in a detached sort of way curling back a corner of the
carpet with the tops of his shoe, think he could discover
under there?

It was the first time any of them had breached the citadel
of Johnny Handel's room and they were taking full advantage of it. What did they hope to find? You couldn't tell
me they were just looking to see what clothes he might
have taken away with him. Even the cats would laugh at
that one.

'Here's his school blazer.' Daisy kept up the pretence,
even as she went through every pocket of the blazer. She
pulled a crumpled wad of paper from one pocket, smoothed
it out absently and looked at it. It appeared to be a shopping list—or perhaps a shoplifting list. She crumpled it
again and replaced it in the pocket.

'Here—' Ted crossed over to me and spoke in an undertone. 'What's going on?'

'That's a good question,' I said.

There was no doubt about it, they had all lost sight of
their original goal. I decided to volunteer an observation
which seemed more pertinent than most of their endeavours.

'His metal detector isn't here,' I said. 'He must have
taken that with him.'

'What metal detector?' Norma rounded on me incredulously. 'Johnny doesn't have a metal detector. He wanted
one, but—' her voice broke— 'but I told him we couldn't
afford it.'

Again there was that curious silence in the room.

'Don't brood about it, dear,' Daisy said. 'He got one
anyway. Trudi's right. I've seen it.'

'But . . . how could he?'

'Oh, he was a very enterprising little boy, dear,' Daisy
said. 'And there are all sorts of ways to earn extra money.
Especially in a town like this—' She broke off abruptly. 'I
mean, dear,' she said carefully, 'perhaps he ran errands
for people in the nursing homes. They're always wanting
bits of shopping done for them and they tip well.'

That wasn't what she had started out to say and everyone in the room knew it—except Norma.

'And—over there!' Norma pointed at the television so
suddenly we all jumped. 'That's a video cassette recorder!
Where did he get that? We couldn't afford that, either.'

I had the feeling Norma was beginning to catch on.
Little Johnny would have had to run an awful lot of
errands to earn that kind of hardware—even if the old
dears in the nursing homes tipped like drunken sailors.

'Oh, well, dear—' Daisy tried to field the question, but
a growing desperation on her face betrayed that her in-
ventive powers were beginning to flag. 'After all—'

The telephone saved her. The sharp imperious summons

rang out through the hallway and up the stairs. We glanced at each other uneasily. It was a late hour for anyone to be calling.

'Johnny!' Norma cried, rushing for the doorway.

'*I'll* get it, dear,' Daisy said firmly. She moved quickly, cutting in front of Norma, reminding us that it was *her* house and her right to answer the telephone. There was also the underlying implication that, if it were bad news, it would be better for someone else to learn it first.

Norma plunged downstairs in her wake and, released from the need for discretion, the others went back to their tasks with renewed vigour. Each was so intent on their own preoccupations that perhaps I was the only one who saw what happened next.

Dandini, with a swift furtive look at the others, pulled an envelope from the drawer he was searching and made it disappear into his own pocket so quickly that, if I had blinked, I would not have seen the transfer.

Suddenly it all crystallized, confirming a suspicion I had had before. The atmosphere, the implications, the insinuations, the desperate searching could all be explained by one nasty word.

Blackmail.

CHAPTER 16

'It's for you, Ted.' Daisy came back into the room, Norma at her heels. 'It's Milly.'

Ted grunted with surprise and went down to the telephone.

I leaned back against the window-sill, mentally examining my theory for flaws. I could not find any. As Daisy had said, Johnny was an enterprising little boy. It stood to reason that he would not stop at mere shoplifting. Not when there was so much more—in actual cash—to be swept up in other ways.

He had searched my room. And no wonder he had subsequently displayed so much hostility towards me. I must have been even more of a disappointment to him than I had thought. There I was, an American with, as everyone knew, all the gold in Fort Knox at my disposal—and he had not discovered anything he could blackmail me over.

However, he seemed to have been doing all right with the others. I watched Kate turn from the bed with a baffled, frustrated expression just as Henry Parsons, who was now operating in a different corner of the room, swooped triumphantly on something that lay at his busy feet.

It was dawning on me that practically everyone had ulterior motives for dissuading Norma from calling in the police. If the police searched Johnny's room—as they inevitably must—who knew what they would find? If Little Johnny really was in any serious trouble somewhere, he was hoist by his own petard.

'It doesn't look too good, Trudi, does it?' Kate had come over to me and was absently fingering the curtain.

'No, it doesn't,' I said, more truthfully than she could guess. 'In fact, to borrow one of your English expressions, it looks bloody awful.'

She sighed and ran her fingers down the curtain. I saw her face change.

'Excuse me,' I said, 'I want to talk to Daisy for a minute.' It seemed more tactful to leave her in peace to retrieve whatever she had just found in the hem of the curtain.

'You see, dear—' Daisy was still maintaining the fiction with Norma. 'There doesn't seem to be anything much missing, so he can't have gone far. He's probably just being naughty—' But as she spoke, Daisy's fingers were probing at the inside of a pair of moccasins she appeared to be examining casually.

Daisy, too? It was hard to believe. Somehow, I just couldn't see Daisy as a blackmail victim. She was trying to protect her lodgers, then, playing for time, giving them a chance to retrieve the incriminating evidence Little Johnny had collected. But surely he couldn't have found anything against Daisy.

On the other hand, she had been running her theatrical digs for a long, long time. Over a great many years, any number of awkward incidents might have occurred. Nothing criminal, perhaps — or at least not these days — but things Daisy might nevertheless prefer not to become general knowledge. Had Johnny discovered some of them?

But Daisy was a wise old bird, it was hard to believe she would leave evidence lying around where it might be found and used against her. All her secrets — guilty or otherwise — were buried deep in her mind, surfacing only in anecdotes of the old days. And it was doubtful that she would have spent much time reminiscing with Little Johnny.

'It's too bad, dear.' Daisy shook her head at me, speaking across Norma. 'If he doesn't come back soon, we *will* have to call in the police.'

By which, I gathered that Daisy had seen her friends repossessing their pilfered belongings and felt that the coast was now clear.

'Oh, not yet!' Norma gasped. 'Not so soon!' She looked around the room frantically. 'He'll be back. He must! Where else could he go?'

Where, indeed? And why wasn't Norma more anxious to call the police? Perhaps she was beginning to fear what they might discover about her precious son. Her gaze lingered fearfully on the video cassette recorder and then moved around the room, as though seeking other expensive items that she had never bought for him.

But there was still an evasive look in her eye. She had not yet brought herself to asking the big question: If she hadn't, then who had?

'You know,' Kate said, 'I think Daisy's right. I don't think we can put it off much longer.' Her attitude was carefree, rather than concerned.

In fact, despite Norma's distress, a pervasive air of cheerfulness was spreading through the room. Henry Parsons was leaning against the wall, hands in his pockets, and seemed to just stop himself from whistling. Dandini was still keeping up a pose of helpfulness, but his fingers were giving too many unnecessary flutters. He looked rather as though he were about to pull a long streamer of flags-of-all-nations from the buttonhole he was fingering. He certainly couldn't think he was going to find any clues as to Johnny's whereabouts there.

'I'm sorry—' Ted came back into the room, startling us all. He must have climbed the stairs very silently. 'I don't like to leave you like this, but I'll have to get back to The Phoenix. Someone's seen a prowler.'

Johnny! It wasn't just my idea. I saw the thought pop into all our heads simultaneously.

'I'll come with you.' Hope flared in Norma's eyes. 'It . . . it might be Johnny. And . . . even if it isn't—' her voice broke again— 'I . . . I want to take another look along the front.'

It wouldn't be much use. Everything was closed now. But none of us wanted to voice any discouragement. Norma was too close to cracking up.

'That's right, dear.' Daisy patted her shoulder. 'And I'll come with you.'

'Oh, what the hell!' Kate said recklessly. 'So will I.'

'Wonderful!' Norma said. 'The more of us there are, the better chance we'll have of finding him—'

Or of catching him when we do find him. If he hadn't come home, he was unlikely to rush into his mother's arms just because she went looking for him. Nor did I like the thought of him prowling around The Phoenix. Little Johnny was a nasty bit of work and he had a grudge against

Ted. I wouldn't put a spot of arson past him.

'All right. Why not?' Henry and Dandini moved forward and we went down the stairs in a body. Ted, looking worried, was in the lead.

At the car door, he stopped. 'I'm not sure I can fit you all in,' he said uneasily. 'Wait a minute—'

Norma had started to run. 'Take the others,' she called back over her shoulder. 'I'll get there faster walking.'

Ted cursed under his breath and chased after her. She was in no condition to go running about the front by herself.

'*We'll* walk down.' Kate linked arms with Dandini and Henry. '*You*—' she nodded to me— 'ride with Daisy and help her try to keep Norma calm.' They started off down the street, pausing momentarily to speak to Ted, who had caught up with Norma and was trying to pull her back to the car. She had begun struggling violently.

'It's going to take more than us to calm Norma,' I said to Daisy. 'Where's that doctor you were expecting? He won't know where to find us, if we're gone when he arrives.'

'His answering service can't reach him,' Daisy said. 'He must have gone away for the weekend and his locum is busy with a real emergency.' She sighed deeply. 'It doesn't really matter, dear. *He* wouldn't be able to calm Norma, either. Not unless he gave her a shot of something and knocked her out. You know what the trouble really is, don't you, dear?' Norma and Ted had nearly reached us; watching them, Daisy spoke in a rapid undertone.

'Norma's not just afraid Johnny's run away.' Her eyes were sad and infinitely knowing. 'Oh no. She's afraid the chicken hawks have got him!'

There was silence in the car, except for Norma's ragged breathing, as we drove through the silent, darkened town and pulled up in front of The Phoenix.

'Wait here while I look around,' Ted said softly. 'Don't move until I get back.' He slipped out of the car, then swung the door back quietly, latching it loosely.

Daisy caught Norma's arm as she tried to follow him. 'I wouldn't, dear,' she advised. 'Really I wouldn't. Just let him go his own way. He knows what he's doing.'

Norma subsided reluctantly and that was where Daisy made her mistake. She let go of Norma's arm. Norma was out of the car in a flash and running. I caught the door as it swung back, keeping it from slamming and alerting Johnny.

'Oh dear,' Daisy sighed. 'No good will come of this. I've always said so, and now, here we are. I wish I'd never let Albert and Milly talk me into having them in the house. It's all very well to feel sorry for people, but sometimes it's a mistake to do anything about it. A bad mistake, dear.'

I could only agree with her. Both Ted and Norma had now disappeared from view. The others — reinforcements, as I was coming to think of them — had not yet reached the front.

'Well . . .' Daisy sighed and heaved herself out of the car. 'I suppose we'd better go after her. Ted will be terribly upset if she rushes up and spoils everything just when he's catching the boy in the act. And Norma might see something that would upset her even more. I don't know, dear, I really don't know. If I had it to do all over again, I'd never let them set foot across the threshold.'

I nodded dumbly. It was fairly certain that Norma would be upset if she saw Little Johnny dabbling in arson, or perhaps he had progressed to burglary. Ted was careless about dropping the night's takings in the Night Safe at the bank every night. I couldn't remember whether he'd bothered to all weekend. Things had been hectic and we'd had a lot more to worry about than money.

I joined Daisy on the pavement and we stood listening

for a moment. Norma must have stopped running; there
was no sound of footsteps. Ted would be stalking the
intruder as silently as a Redskin through a forest. Now it
was our turn to become part of the hunt.

'It will be best if we split up, dear,' Daisy said
practically. 'Ted's gone in through the building, so if we
go down to the corners and cut up the side streets and
then turn into the alley, we can meet at the back door and
one of us ought to have collected Norma on the way.'

She moved off without waiting for my agreement. It
did seem a sensible plan of action. Norma wouldn't have
got far, especially if she had stopped running. One or the
other of us was bound to catch up with her. Preferably
Daisy.

It was deserted along the front, the overhead lights
seemed to have dimmed. The sky was dark and cloudy,
the moon sporadically disappearing behind scudding
clouds. I looked up, then quickly looked down again. I
don't like the night sky over here, it's too unsettling. All
the stars are in the wrong places.

The tide was coming in, I could hear the slap of the
wavelets against the pilings of the Grand Pier. The wind
was rising, bringing a breath of dampness. It seemed that
we were going to have that rain everyone had been hoping
for—now that the weekend was over and it no longer
mattered.

By the time I had reached the corner, I had remembered
the Starer. Daisy's idea no longer seemed so bright. I looked
back along the front, but she had vanished. She had already
turned her corner and I was at mine.

I might as well go forward as back. With Johnny, Ted,
Norma and Daisy, the alley ahead was more populated
than the front. And Kate, Dandini and Henry Parsons
would be along at any moment. I would look foolish if
they found me hanging around on the corner, waiting for
company like a frightened child.

I turned the corner and walked down the little side-street to the narrow alley. I thought I heard voices ahead of me and, emboldened, I stumbled in. The only light was from the moon.

The alley was something I had only seen from the back window of The Phoenix and I had not taken much interest in it. The Phoenix and every establishment along the front and the street parallel with it, had a small back yard which, with the English passion for privacy, was walled off, fenced off or railed off from each of the neighbouring yards and from the access alley itself. The alley was just the passageway running between the back yards where the dustmen could collect the rubbish and the various deliverymen could make their deliveries without disturbing the holiday-makers.

As I moved along the alley, I was increasingly conscious of those yawning yards behind the flimsy wooden fences or more solid brick walls. Occasionally, there was a gap where some establishment had done away with the wall in order to provide parking space. They were even more unnerving, providing as they did, direct access to sheds or sheltered doorways where anyone might be lurking.

I found I was tiptoeing, not wanting to make any sound that might draw attention to me. The comforting voices I thought I had heard ahead were silent now, not even murmuring.

I had lost track of the distance I had travelled; none of this territory was familiar. I realized, with a faint sense of rising panic, that I could walk right past The Phoenix without knowing it. I had never used the back entrance — not even in the daylight.

Where had everyone gone? I halted and strained my ears, but I could only hear the wind and the incoming tide. Some stealthy silent plague might have wiped every human inhabitant off the face of the earth. Except me.

My heart thudded loudly, my breath rasped even more

loudly, I felt that I was making enough noise for at least a dozen people. And a herd of elephants. I took a step forward, my foot came down on a large loose rock which rolled away taking my balance with it. Involuntarily, I cried out as I fell. My hands caught at the nearest fence — a wooden one.

I managed to stifle my cries as splinters dug into the palms of my hands, but the fence was an old and half-rotten one. It swayed and creaked under my weight. For a moment, I thought it was going to collapse.

Surely all that noise must have attracted some attention. Surely it should have brought Daisy — if no one else — rushing to help me. But nothing happened.

I pulled myself upright and stood there trembling, a new fear supplanting the earlier ones: Was I in the right alley? Had I mistaken the turning in the darkened sidestreet? Was I now stumbling along some strange alley, wondering where everyone was, while the others were congregated outside the back entrance of The Phoenix wondering where I was?

It seemed only too likely in that nightmarish moment. Anyone who had travelled about in England soon realized that the English were far more interested in — and better at — laying out mazes than laying out towns. Streets changed names half way along, the better to confuse innocent strangers, or they took off on doglegs running miles in the opposite direction to that expected. 'The rolling English drunkard made the rolling English road.' And that went double in spades for mews, squares, places, lanes, rows, gardens, alleys and any and all subsidiary thoroughfares.

I did a few exercises to control my breathing while I tried to think out my next move. Not that there was much doubt about it. A quick backward glance confirmed that I had passed the point of no return. It would be quicker to go forward than to go back.

Cautiously I moved my foot, finding and rolling aside

the treacherous rock. On firm footing, I pushed myself away from the wooden fence, my palms still smarting, and tried to move soundlessly.

Was there a muffled sound — a smothered laugh — just ahead?

'Johnny?' I called softly. 'Johnny, is that you?'

It wasn't Johnny. I realized that with a sudden deadly clarity. It was something wickedly amused — and evil — just ahead of me. I drew back instinctively, but uselessly, just as the new sound floated back to me.

It was whistling. Not the happy carefree whistling I was accustomed to hearing from my audience, but a nasty insinuating arrogant whistle. It was telling me, defying me, mocking me.

After a long moment, my brain supplied the words to that familiar nursery tune:

> Oh, dear, what can the matter be?
> Oh, dear, what can the matter be?
> Oh, dear, what can the matter be?
> Johnny's so long at the fair . . .

CHAPTER 17

I stood frozen, trying to determine whether the sound was advancing towards me or retreating; whether attack was imminent or only intimidation was intended. I could not decide. The sound seemed to be all around me. He could be at the far end of the alley ahead; he could be at my back.

There are different kinds of terror. Some people are terrified of snakes or spiders; some of wide-open spaces or closed-in spaces. People have often said to me, 'I could never do what you do. Get up in front of all those people and play the piano and sing. I'd be terrified!' I usually smile and say confidingly, 'I often am.' It's all part of the patter, and sometimes stage fright does resemble terror. At least, I had always thought so until this moment.

This was an icy brain-numbing terror, triggered by the hatred and malevolence behind that vindictive whistle. My worst nightmare had come true. I was alone in the dark with the Starer and all the unspeakable things that were seething around in his disordered mind.

My past life didn't start unreeling behind my eyes, but then, I wasn't drowning. Not yet. Who knew what ultimate fate the Starer had in store for me? My mind dodged that bit of unpleasantness nimbly and darted ahead into a future in which I would not exist—except as an inanimate object.

Presumably the local authorities would know that the US Embassy ought to be notified about the death of a citizen abroad, but what about the rest of it? Would they bury me in England? Would they send my body home to Mother? What would happen to my clothes and the collection of sheet music I had been building? And my piano bar—would Ted send it away, or keep it for someone else to use? And Daisy, left with the job of clearing my room and disposing of my effects. What would Daisy do?

She'd probably name the next cat after me.

The caustic thought snapped me back to life—and a fighting mood. I wasn't going to stand here and wait to be murdered. If I went down, I was going down fighting, but it would be better not to go down at all.

Very slowly and cautiously, I began to move forward again. Every step I could gain was one less step I might have to run, with the Starer in pursuit. With luck, I might make it to a place of safety—perhaps even The Phoenix itself. It must be just ahead somewhere.

Meanwhile, if I couldn't place the Starer from the sound of his whistling, the chances were good that he wouldn't be able to locate me, once I had moved away from the spot where he had last pinpointed me.

I kept edging forward, aware that the whistling had stopped and unable to decide whether that was good or bad. Perhaps he was gathering his energy to spring; perhaps he had tired of the game and disappeared like a wisp of fog once more.

Then suddenly it came again, more faintly, just the last line echoing along the alley in a ghostly reprise:

Johnny's so long at the fair . . .

The whistle faded out on a dying fall. I knew I wouldn't hear it again. The message had been delivered. Or was it a warning? Or just sheer vindictiveness? Someone was playing with me . . . with us.

The agonized scream tore through the night and I knew that I was not the only one who had heard the whistler. Perhaps I was not even his target . . . his victim.

No longer afraid for myself, I ran. Ran towards that terrible screaming and the hubbub that surrounded it. As I drew closer, incoherent words began to emerge.

'Johnny . . . Johnny! . . . Johnny, where are you?' It had to be Norma. She was the only one who would care that much.

'Here, steady on—' More voices became identifiable as I got nearer. That was Ted's. 'Steady on—'

'All right, dear, all right. We heard it.' Daisy might just as well be cooing into the teeth of a hurricane. 'Pay no attention. It's just a nasty joke, dear, that's all it is. A nasty joke . . .'

'Take it easy, Norma!' So Kate was there, too. The re-inforcements had arrived. But what good were they doing?

'Johnny . . . Johnny . . .' The demented screaming went on.

And then I screamed myself as steel fingers caught my

arm, tightening in a cruel relentless grip.

'Oh, sorry, sorry.' The hands let go, the voice went babbling on. 'Terribly sorry, Trudi. I didn't know it was you. I thought . . .' Henry Parsons let his voice trail off. We both had a pretty good idea of what he had been thinking.

'It wasn't me,' I said. 'I can't even whistle. Sing, yes — but not whistle.'

'Sorry . . . ' He seemed prepared to go on apologizing endlessly. He made little dabbing motions at my arm, as though to brush off any marks his hands might have made. I had the impression that he was as startled as I was.

'You don't think . . .' He lowered his voice as we walked towards the others. 'You don't think it was Johnny himself whistling, do you? It was so senseless and cruel to upset Norma like that. It was just the sort of thing he might do.'

It was. I hadn't thought of it before, but Henry was right. The random frightening malice of that taunting whistle was just like Johnny. Especially if he knew his mother was within earshot — and that a whistle was essentially unidentifiable.

The thought that I had not been the target relieved me immensely. It also dissipated my irrational fear of the Starer. Of course he could not have been the whistler. He could not have known — or even guessed — that we were out looking for Johnny, so how could he have tried to taunt us with that tune? It had to be someone closer to the situation. And who closer than Little Johnny?

'Where is he?' Norma shrieked. She threw one sharp disinterested look at me, marking only that the person Henry had gone off to capture was of no consequence. She cared for no one except her Little Johnny. It was a pity the concern wasn't mutual. 'Where's Johnny?'

'We'll find him, dear,' Daisy said helplessly. 'Don't worry. You're among friends. We're doing all we can.'

And that wasn't much. There wasn't much anybody could do. One thing though, we wouldn't need to worry about calling the police ourselves. If Norma kept on screaming like that, the neighbours would soon do it for us. Some of the people around here had flats over their shops and already lights were flashing on in previously darkened windows.

'Come inside,' Ted begged desperately. We were disturbing the peace, if not conducting an affray or creating a public nuisance. Not the sort of commotion a publican wants outside of his premises. 'Come along, Norma. We'll all go into The Phoenix and have a drink. It's after hours, but it will be a private party, just a few friends having drinks. The police can't say anything.'

'Party!' He had used the wrong word. Norma turned on him, spitting fire. 'You'd hold a party while Johnny is— is—' She couldn't bring herself to finish the sentence. She looked as thought she might physically attack Ted.

'I didn't mean that kind of a party.' He raised his hands defensively, as though to ward her off. 'I just meant— Look, come inside. We'll talk it over and—'

Farther along the alley, a window was raised and a head popped out, turning angrily in our direction.

'Come on.' Kate placed firm hands on Norma's shoulders, propelling her through the back yard and into The Phoenix. 'It won't do any good to get half the neighbourhood out here with us. It would only complicate matters.'

We crowded into the back entry of The Phoenix behind Kate, cutting off Norma's line of retreat. Kate pushed Norma up the back stairs. She seemed to be encountering less resistance now and I cherished the faint hope that Norma might relapse into her normal state and fall asleep once we got her sitting down. She'd been expending an unaccustomed amount of energy over the past few hours. No such luck, however. Norma refused to sit down at all. She paced the floor while Ted went behind the bar and got drinks for us. Dandini drifted over to stand near the door in case Norma made a sudden dash for it. Daisy sank thankfully into a chair; there were darkening circles under her eyes.

I found that I had automatically seated myself at the piano and I pulled my hands back sharply as they began wandering towards the keyboard. This might be the place but it certainly wasn't the time for background music.

Most certainly not for the music still echoing through the back of my mind, music my traitorous fingers might translate into audible sound if I wasn't careful:

Oh, dear, what can the matter be . . . ?

I turned away from the piano to look down on the front. The pier was dark and ghostly, jutting out to meet the advancing mist and disappear into it, giving the impression that it might stretch out endlessly across the water, perhaps reaching into space itself.

'It's beginning to look pretty spooky out there, isn't it?' Kate came over to stand beside me and look down.

'The dark before the dawn,' I murmured, not very hopefully.

'It's a long time till dawn,' Kate said.

'We can't just sit here—' Norma's voice was rising again. 'We've got to get out and find Johnny—' She started for the door. No one else moved, except Dandini who shifted fractionally to block her way.

'You don't care!' Norma whirled back to face us. 'You never liked Johnny! None of you! You don't care what happens to him! You sit there drinking—'

'Oh, give it a rest, dear, do,' Daisy said wearily. 'We'll go out and look for him again. Just let us have a few minutes of peace first. The rest of us need a drink, even if you don't.'

'I don't!' Norma's glare halted Ted in his tracks. He had been heading for her with a large brandy. Now he stopped and took a deep gulp of it himself. 'But the rest of you go right ahead. Have your drinks. Have your rest. It's nothing to you! And you needn't worry about me. I'll be all right. I'll find Johnny myself. *I'm* his mother! *I'm* the only one who cares about him—'

She had us dead to rights. We didn't like Little Johnny and we didn't care what happened to him. We glanced at each other guiltily.

'Oh, come *on*! Let's go and find the little . . . darling.' Kate set down her glass with a thump. 'You win, Norma. We'll go out and scour the whole damned town. We won't rest until we find him! We'll bring him back to you, de—' She broke off abruptly, but it was too late.

Dead or alive. The unfinished sentence hung in the air and every one of us was able to supply the ending. Even Norma. She paled visibly.

'Come on, Trudi!' Kate caught my arm, hauling me to my feet. 'You and I will check the pier. He might—' she threw out an implicit apology to Norma— 'he might be camping out in one of the dressing-rooms. Kids have sneaked into the theatre before this.'

'Here . . .' Ted followed us to the door and handed me a key. 'Go through the Fun Palace. This will let you in. You might take a look as you're going through. He . . . might have got in . . . somehow.'

Our footsteps echoed as we crossed the deserted amusement arcade to the entrance to the pier. It was especially eerie to walk through the place without hearing the electric bleeps and whoops that were usually almost deafening. The dark oblongs of the machines loomed like the sentinel stones of a pre-historic age. (Would, someday, archaeologists unearth an amusement arcade and declare it a late twentieth-century Stonehenge?)

The booths were deep and shadowed, rustling with sounds that might be the wind stirring the plastic curtains partitioning off the backs — or might equally well be the surreptitious movements of late hidden revellers indulging in some secret frolics that would not stand the light of day.

Johnny's so long at the fair . . . But not this particular fair.

Then Kate pushed down on the crash bars of the emergency exit and the door opened out on to the pier itself. I hurried through it after her, breathing deeply of the dank sea mist — almost, but not quite, released from the dark spell that had curled around me as we passed through the arcade.

'I don't like the mist.' Kate shivered as we walked forward into it. 'It makes me feel . . . disembodied, somehow. Almost a ghost myself.'

Like the Starer. The thought came unbidden and unwelcome. I thought I had shaken free of my fear of that insubstantial figure. It was disconcerting to realize that he was still lurking at the back of my mind — if nowhere else.

'I know what you mean,' I said uneasily. 'It seems almost as though we could dissolve into the mist ourselves. If we weren't careful.'

'Perhaps that's what happened to Little Johnny.' Kate gave a not very successful laugh. 'He forgot to look over his shoulder and the fog got him.'

'Dandini favours the Fourth Dimension,' I said. And then, because it was dark and we could not see each other clearly through the mist, and because everything seemed slightly unreal anyway, I asked softly, 'What was he blackmailing Dandini about?'

For a long silent moment, I thought she was going to pretend that she hadn't heard the question, then she sighed softly. 'He had a photograph . . . taken on the promenade . . . photography was his hobby last year. And . . .

and Dandini . . . used to be a pickpocket before he went
legit. He used to have times when he got bored . . . wanted to
see if he could still do it. So he'd walk along the promenade . . . dip into the pocket of a likely tripper . . . get
his wallet . . . then come back the other way and replace
the wallet. He always replaced it. Except he had no way
of proving it because the tripper never knew it was gone.
Little Johnny got a picture of him in the act. Not the sort
of publicity photo you'd want featured in the local
newspaper.'

'I see.' Very carefully, I left it at that.

'And me . . .' Kate answered the unspoken question.
'When I first came here . . . nerves on edge . . . trying out
the show . . . I smoked occasionally. He got hold of one of
them. Stupid . . . it could be traced back to me easily.
Last year's lover . . . little present of monogrammed
filters. Only hand-rolled joints in town with monogrammed
filters. It was a laugh at the time . . . not after Johnny got
one. Town fathers would be very stuffy about it . . . if
they knew. He was clever, he never asked for more than
we could spare. And we could always tell him where to
go. But . . . it would be such a nuisance, talking our way
out of it . . .'

'I see,' I said again. Clever Johnny, indeed, battening
on the peccadilloes that could be made to seem more for-
midable, given the bright beam of publicity. And never
asking for more than the traffic would bear, but collecting a
tidy sum for nuisance value when it was all added up.
'What about Henry Parsons?' I asked.

'I don't know and I don't want to know!' Kate shrugged
irritably. 'I just want to get away from this show and this
town and forget about the whole thing. It's so annoying to
think a little . . . *twit* like that could disrupt everyone's
lives . . .'

The echo of our footsteps changed as we crossed the
drawbridge and moved out on to the wooden planks of

the pier. I didn't mind it so much here where the planks were neatly aligned. But farther out, there were spaces between them, some nearly an inch wide. I dreaded that stretch of the old pier, but there was no avoiding it, not if we wished to reach the theatre.

Kate wasn't wearing heels, she strode forward confidently. More cautiously, I picked my way along. The fog swirled around us, the sea soughed beneath us. I didn't like this part of the pier, but it was worse in daylight when I could look straight down through the gaps and see the water swirling below.

There were lights along the length of the pier, but the main lights had been extinguished and only tiny pinpoints glowed here and there like the night lights in a child's nursery. The encroaching mist dimmed and blurred them. We kept well to the centre of the long walkway and I instinctively tried to walk lightly in order not to make so much noise. In another minute, I'd be tiptoeing.

Kate felt it, too. Her steps slowed and were quieter. From a sense of duty, we split up as we came to the sheltered benches, each of us taking one side of the shelter. I walked more quickly then and could hear Kate doing the same on the other side. We met at the end with relief and shook our heads.

'Do you really think we'll find Johnny in the theatre?' I asked Kate softly.

'No,' she said. 'Do you?'

'No.' We walked side by side, moving closer as the tentacles of fog reached out to coil around us. Below us, the sea was rising as the tide flooded in. Considering that we were out in the open air, it was curiously claustrophobic.

'I suppose we ought to go round the outside first,' Kate said, as we reached the theatre. 'Make sure all the doors are locked before we go in.'

I nodded silently. This time, by tacit agreement, we did not split up. Together, we began circling the building, Kate trying the exit doors as we passed. They all seemed to be locked. We were at the very end of the pier now, behind the theatre, where the most determined and hopeful anglers fished all day with their rented fishing rods. They weren't allowed to fish at night after the pier had closed.

The sea sounded different out here. For a moment I thought the tide might have turned, but the waves still seemed to be rushing towards the shore. There was another sound . . . fainter . . . almost lost in the endless muted roar of the sea.

'What's that thumping?' Kate heard it, too. 'It must be a piece of driftwood caught under the pier,' she answered herself without conviction.

We moved to the railing and stood looking down into the water — or trying to. The fog was so thick we could not see the water. But there was something down there. It thumped softly, persistently, against one of the pilings, a piece of flotsam trapped by the tide.

Then, briefly, the fog lightened and drifted aside. The small dark form could have been a bundle of rags floating there, but rags wouldn't thump when they hit against a piling.

As we strained our eyes, the form took shape, pale white hands at the ends of outflung arms, a head curiously twisted to one side. Just before the fog closed in again, I saw that the body was tethered to some cross-section underneath the pier by the noose around its neck.

We had found Little Johnny after all.

CHAPTER 18

It was well after dawn before we got to bed. By that time, there didn't seem much point in bothering, but we withdrew to our own rooms as much to get a few hours alone with our thoughts as from any hope of sleep.

Only Norma slept, sedated, for once, into the state that had previously seemed natural to her. I wasn't looking forward to the moment when she woke. None of us were.

Kate and I had quite frankly taken the coward's way out after discovering Johnny Handel's body. We had remained on the pier and used the telephone in the theatre to call the police. They had told us to stay where we were, which was precisely what we had had in mind anyway.

'After all,' Kate had said defensively, 'it isn't as though Norma were a relative of ours—or even a very close friend. Let the police break the news to her—they have lots more experience doing it than we have.'

She was preaching to the converted. I would sooner walk into a tigers' den and try to remove the one-and-only cub from the particularly nasty-looking tigress in the far corner than face Norma and tell her about Johnny. It amounted to much the same thing.

We were too restless to stay in Kate's dressing-room, so we went outside and waited in front of the theatre for the police to arrive. Silently, we had watched the flashing blue light speed along the promenade towards the pier. We were both conscious that Norma and the others were somewhere along the promenade and would know what the police car portended.

The car had just drawn up at the entrance to the pier when, carried clear and ringing over the water, we heard Norma's scream of anguish.

I didn't really sleep and every time I dozed off, the events of the previous hours returned to haunt me. I drifted in and out of consciousness to the echo of distant screaming and the dull metronomic thumping of something soft and inert bumping against pilings in the wash of the tide.

Faces, too, loomed and receded: Norma's, mouth open

in an everlasting scream like someone trapped for eternity in a Francis Bacon canvas. Johnny's, as I had last seen it in life, taut and hostile, defying the world to penetrate his secrets. Even the Cockney girl's, carefree and laughing over her drink, joining in the singing around the piano bar.

Then the sound of water lapping again, and the bodies broke to the surface of my nightmares as they had risen to the surface of the water, rolling over to reveal blueish-white faces. The girl's body in the boating pond, Johnny's body beneath the pier. They floated, twisting with the current, side by side, bumping into each other and seeming to merge until Johnny's body and the girl's became one and the girl was Johnny and Johnny was the girl. And, over it all, the sound of Norma screaming.

The final scream in that sequence was so loud it brought me upright, blinking and groggy, convinced it had been real. It took a few moments of listening to the silent house to persuade myself that the scream had been part of my nightmare. I started to lie back again but changed my mind. I might as well be up and doing as sink back into the kind of dreams that were haunting me this morning.

The cats came to meet me as I descended the stairs. If it weren't for the circumstances, I would have been glad to see them free again. They had no such reservations, however. The concept of protective custody was unknown to them and they had obviously been deeply upset by being shut away from everyone. They were sociable cats, fond of company, and overjoyed to have regained their proper place in the world.

They twined and rollicked around my ankles, throbbing with delight and nearly tripping me as I went down the hall to the kitchen. I could have done without the guard of honour, but I appreciated their feelings.

I pushed open the door, helped myself to coffee from the pot bubbling on the stove, and joined Daisy at the kitchen table. She smiled wanly at me. The circles under her eyes were darker than ever.

'You haven't slept at all, have you?' I accused.

'Plenty of time for that now, dear.' Her face brightened as Fields jumped into her lap and chirruped at her. Formby, not to be outdone, followed suit. Robey looked with disgust at the crowded lap and deliberately walked over and climbed into my lap. From their vantage points, the cats surveyed the table with dissatisfaction. Nothing on it but cups of coffee. They looked hopefully at the cream jug.

'Poor darlings,' Daisy cuddled Gracie and Formby. 'They've been neglected lately. But— ' she brightened even more— 'that's all over. They can have the run of the house again.'

'Nice for them.' I doubted if Norma would be able to find the silver lining so easily.

'Oh, I don't mean to sound heartless, dear.' Daisy was instantly contrite. 'But it *has* been very difficult lately. And now I won't have to give Norma notice, after all. I doubt that she'll want to stay on after this.'

'Don't be too sure of that,' I said. 'Her son may be dead, but that doesn't change the fact that her husband is up in the nursing home. Her mother-in-law will still insist that she stays near and visits him, won't she?'

'Oh dear! I hadn't thought of that.' Daisy went pale. 'I hadn't thought of that awful woman at all. She'll have to know, won't she?'

'It would be hard to keep it from her,' I agreed. 'I imagine it will be in all the newspapers by the evening editions.'

'Oh, poor Norma!' Daisy's eyes filled with tears. 'As though she hasn't enough on her plate. It isn't fair, dear, it isn't fair at all.'

'I don't know,' I said. 'It seems to me that Norma may have brought at least part of this on herself. You can't exactly say she brought Johnny up to the best of her ability. Not unless her ability was zilch to start with.'

'I can't deny she let the boy run wild,' Daisy sighed. 'But what she was like before they came here, I can't say, dear. They moved in three years ago — and I rue the day. It seems to me they went to rack and ruin from the moment they got here. Both of them.'

Daisy slanted an oblique look at me. She seemed to expect some reply I was unqualified to make. I could not decipher what question had been asked behind what had seemed, on the surface, a simple statement of a known fact.

'It's a shame,' I said ambiguously, stroking Robey under the chin. He turned his head and stared up at me. His look was easier to interpret: a chuck under the chin was all very well, thank you, but there were times when a cat preferred a more practical demonstration of affection.

'Sorry, Robey,' I murmured. I removed my cup from the saucer and reached for the cream jug. Across the table, the other cats watched jealously.

Robey blinked his thanks to me and smugly lowered his chin to the saucer. Gracie could stand it no longer. She struggled out of Daisy's lap and marched across the table-top to dip into the saucer from the other side. Daisy's attempts to restrain Formby were only perfunctory; he darted across the table to get his share.

'I *wish* they wouldn't do that.' Daisy glanced at the door guiltily. 'I suppose it's all right, as long as no one sees them.'

'My fault,' I said. If Daisy thought she was kidding anyone, I might as well humour her. But I doubted if I'd ever been the only one to remove a few hairs from the rim of the cream jug before I poured. I suppose it didn't really matter; the cats were clean and Daisy would never allow any cat-hater to lodge with her in the first place. 'I should have put the saucer on the floor.'

'It's all right, dear, I understand.' Daisy forgave me graciously. 'They're dreadful little beggars and they've had *such* a bad time lately. They deserve to be spoiled a bit now.'

Daisy needed a bit of spoiling, too, I thought. She'd been having a pretty rough time herself — and it was going to get even rougher when Norma woke up.

'Well . . .' I drained my coffee and set down the cup. I had already decided to escape while I could. 'I think I'll get a breath of air.' I removed Robey from my lap and placed him on the table with the others. He didn't miss a lick during the operation.

'Don't you want some breakfast, dear?' Daisy offered. 'Or will you have it when you come back?'

'Don't bother about me,' I said. 'Nor for lunch, either. I'll pick up a snack along the front. I'm not really hungry.'

The door of the bathing-hut swung open as I began to fit the key into the lock. I *had* locked the door the last time I used it, I assured myself against an uprush of guilt. Someone else must have been here. I was so accustomed to being the only one who took advantage of Ted's open invitation that I tended to forget that I did not have exclusive rights to the hut.

Really, Ted was far too easy-going. He ought to make sure that people would take care of his property before he let them use it. It was unspeakably careless to go off and leave the door unlocked. I grew indignant on Ted's behalf.

True, there wasn't much worth stealing in the hut, but vandals might have got in and smashed up the place. Perhaps everyone had let down their guard now that the Bank Holiday weekend was over.

I looked around carefully, taking stock. The place was messier than it had been when I last saw it, but there appeared to be no actual damage. The deck chair was stretched out in the centre of the floor, as though it had been too much trouble to refold it properly. The light blanket had been tossed on top of a cardboard box in the corner, all wadded up. Something long and sticklike leaned against the wall behind it. No, nothing had been taken. In fact, things seemed to have added; someone seemed to be using the hut for storage purposes.

It was really none of my business. I pulled the deck chair into the open doorway and stretched out in it, knowing that I would not be able to sleep, but hoping that I might get a bit of rest.

I couldn't. Perhaps it was a mistake to have come down here. It was too close to the Grand Pier and I had too clear a view of it, even lying back in the deck chair. I got up and turned the deck chair to face in the opposite direction — and that was worse. Now I had the feeling that something frightful was creeping up on me behind my back. I could hear the waves slapping against the pilings of the pier and could not shut out the picture of Johnny floating on the tide.

It was better to face the pier and keep my imagination at bay. I got up again, returned the deck chair to its original position and slumped back into it. Now I realized how chilly I was getting. There was quite a brisk wind coming in off the water and the sun had disappeared behind gathering clouds.

Jumpy as a cat. Muttering to myself, like a cat unable to settle, I got up again and went into the hut for the blanket to throw over me.

I shook the blanket out and inspected it carefully — no telling where it had been. It seemed all right. A bit sandy, but that was only to be expected around here. I took it to the door and shook it vigorously to get the sand off, then draped it across the foot of the deck chair.

Something stopped me from getting back in the deck

chair. Something I had seen but not properly registered when I picked up the blanket, I turned slowly and retraced my steps to the far corner of the hut to investigate.

The box was an ordinary cardboard carton, flaps folded down loosely to close it, some meaningless commercial code stencilled on the outside. The box appeared to have been closed in some haste—a corner of flowered material protruded from beneath a flap. There was something strangely familiar about that flowered material.

I opened the box and pulled out a flowered blouse. The feeling of familiarity intensified, triggering off silent alarm bells at the back of my mind. Who had I seen wearing it?

Then I remembered: the ghost-like girl who had stood on the promenade across from The Phoenix on the night of the Cockney girl's murder. Even then, I had recognized something familiar about the blouse, but put it down to the fact that I owned a blouse like it myself.

Now I had the growing suspicion that this *was* my own blouse. I inspected it carefully and the last doubt vanished. It bore an inconspicuous ILGWU label. No one else in this town was likely to own a blouse made by the International Ladies Garment Workers Union. Only exclusively American garments bore that label. For further confirmation, another label said 'Ohrbach's'.

I stared at the blouse incredulously. It had been in my closet when I last saw it. What was it doing here?

And in such a condition? Torn at the neckline, buttons missing, sweat-stained under the arms—and reeking of that sweat and some cheap scent. No wonder I had not recognized it immediately. It looked as though it had been through the wars, as though it had been torn off someone. It had never got into that shape when I was wearing it.

Abruptly I dropped the blouse back into the box and rubbed my hand on my skirt. I felt dirtied—contaminated.

Who could have taken—stolen—my blouse from my closet and used it like that?

I wouldn't find out by turning my back on the problem. I forced myself to pick up the blouse again and put it to one side and go through the rest of the box.

A sleazy slit skirt—not mine—also bearing signs of wear . . . and tear. Grimly, I began checking the rest of the contents of the box. Something that looked like pale yellow bedraggled rats'-nest, but turned into a blonde wig when I shook it out. A wig that, curiously, reminded me of Daisy.

A few pieces of costume jewellery—again, reminiscent. Hadn't I once seen that necklace—looking a great deal smarter—around Kate's neck? . . . Items of chain store cosmetics. A Woolworth's lipstick, still bearing the price sticker . . . It all began to add up to a frightening, unthinkable whole.

I let everything fall back into the cardboard carton and stepped back, as though to dissociate myself from it. But I could not.

My mind, once set in motion, would not stop rushing along that dark, dangerous, forbidden track. Something in me knew more than my conscious mind wanted to admit and was going to face me with it. I managed to block it off for a few final peaceful moments.

Then, incautiously, I raised my eyes. They fixed on that strange stick-like object half-hidden behind the cardboard box.

Against my better judgement, which seemed to have abdicated for the duration, I moved the box. The object stood revealed for what it was. The flat disc hovering just above the floor was unmistakable.

A metal detector. One I had seen before, under different circumstances. Owned by . . . wielded by . . .

Little Johnny!

'I'm sorry dear, dear—' Daisy would not stop apologizing. 'But I *had* to bring her along. I didn't know what else to do with her. I was afraid to leave her alone in the house, and that's the truth of it, dear—'

'It's all right,' I said unconvincingly. It was not all right. Norma sat at the piano bar like the proverbial skeleton at the feast. She did not look as though she had so recently been sedated; she did not look as though she had ever slept at all. She sat staring out at the vista of the Grand Pier, lighting one cigarette from the stub of another. Why should she fear the spectre of cancer? What did she have left to live for?

I found I was playing Ravel's *Pavane for a Dead Princess*. Or did my subconscious interpret it as *Prince*? Perhaps it didn't matter. The operative word was *Dead* . . .

'And that terrible telephone call was the last straw, dear,' Daisy continued airing her own grievances. 'I couldn't believe she'd have the nerve! I said to her, "I'm sorry, Mrs Handel, I just don't have a room to spare." And I don't, dear. I could hardly believe it when she said she'd take Johnny's room! I mean, how unfeeling can one get? I said to her, "Mrs Handel," I said, "that is quite impossible. The police have sealed Johnny's room and I don't know when it will be free again." '

'And they have, dear, and I don't. I asked, but they wouldn't tell me. I don't know what they think they'll find—' a trace of complacency crept into her voice. 'There isn't anything *to* find. I'm sure of that.'

I didn't look at her, I just went on playing softly. She didn't seem to need any encouragement, which was just as well, for I had none to give her. She had not confided in me, none of them had. Everyone in the house knew — or had had a pretty good idea — what was going on with dear Little Johnny. Except Norma, of course. But they had chosen to keep it a secret. Now I had secrets of my own.

I had not gone back to the house after making my discovery. I had crossed over to The Phoenix and called the police from there. They had come and removed the material from the bathing hut and sent in technicians to measure, fingerprint and run all sorts of tests. They had taken a statement from me after hours of polite but firm questioning, which betrayed the fact that they believed Johnny had been killed in the hut while wearing the female clothing and his body then carried to beneath the pier.

I was not surprised that they had gone to the house and sealed Johnny's room. Daisy, who had watched her lodgers remove the incriminating evidence relating directly to themselves, might think there was nothing else to find. I was not so sure. Neither were the police. Little Johnny's activities had been wide-ranging.

'There is *no* way, dear, I'm going to allow another of those Handels into my house.' Daisy's brooding gaze rested on Norma and slid away again. 'As soon as it's decent, after the funeral, I'm going to suggest Norma goes away. Oh, I won't give her notice — I'm not that brutal, dear. But someone needs to talk to her and remind her she still has a life of her own. That husband of hers can live for another forty or fifty years and his mother will never let her get her hands on that money. Johnny was her only chance and now he's gone. She might as well go back to London and get a job.'

I just kept playing softly. Daisy's view of the world was too simplistic for me to cope with.

'I've had enough. Just let me get Norma away — and never again, dear. Not under *my* roof. No more Handels. I swear to you, dear, if I even so much as hear the opening

bars of *The Messiah* or the *Water Music*, I'll switch off
the radio so fast it would make you dizzy!'

Was Daisy really that naive or simply an accomplished
liar? And what of the other people in the house? Had
Johnny really been blackmailing them for the fairly innocent reasons so artlessly admitted by Kate? Had they really
retrieved all the evidence? Or had something been overlooked? Perhaps something relating to other people? It
was an arresting thought.

Would Johnny have stopped at blackmailing only the
people in this house? He had lived in the town for three
years. What might he have discovered about the shopkeepers along the front? The people in the nursing home?

And there were all those shady amusement arcades at
the disreputable end of the promenade. It was now obvious
that Johnny had been no stranger to them. No wonder Daisy
had whispered so furtively about chicken hawks. There
wasn't much she didn't know — or guess — about the people
under her roof.

As Daisy had said, Johnny was an enterprising little
boy. No wonder he had had money to squander.

The Phoenix was beginning to fill up. The audience
was mostly locals tonight, shopkeepers who no longer had
to keep open late to catch the holiday trade and wanted
to relax. I wished them luck. Norma's presence was not
going to be conducive to relaxation. I noticed that none
of them wanted to sit near her.

Henry Parsons had been sitting quietly in a corner since
the place had opened. This had not escaped Daisy. She
frowned as Ted brought him yet another whisky.

'Oh dear! I hope *he* isn't starting up again. It's more
than I can stand, dear, really it is.'

I began to realize why Henry hadn't risen any higher in
show business than a Punch-and-Judy exhibition wandering
along the sands.

'I suppose I can't blame him tonight,' Daisy sighed. 'He

wouldn't want to stay in the house alone. It's all too depressing, dear. As soon as ever I can — ' she brightened —
'I'll have that room redecorated. Painted a nice cheerful
colour with pretty wallpaper and new pictures. I'll have
Norma's room re-done, too, as soon as she leaves.'

Norma lit another cigarette. I hoped she wasn't going
to continue like that. The way she dropped off to sleep,
she'd constitute a major fire hazard. I found myself more
sympathetic to Daisy's desire to get her out of the house as
soon as possible.

Not that Norma showed any signs of sleepiness now.
On the contrary, she seemed preternaturally alert. Now
that it was too late, Norma was wide awake. Her eyes
darted everywhere and she could not sit still. She left her
place frequently to walk over to the bar and back. Or to
pop into the Powder Room where, to judge from the
length of her absence, all she did was run a comb through
her hair. Or to walk to the long plate-glass window
behind me, where she stood silently gazing out on the
pier. That was the most unnerving of all. She was no joy
to look at, but I'd rather have her in plain sight than
prowling around behind my unguarded back.

The evening wore on and I was not surprised when Kate
and Dandini arrived. Now that the main part of the season
was over, the Mad Manic Music Hall was down to one performance a night, at 7.30 instead of 6.30 and 8.45, which
meant they were over in good time for the performers to
enjoy an hour of peaceful relaxation before the pubs
closed.

Kate and Dandini headed for the piano bar, but veered
away when they saw Norma was sitting there. They joined
Harry Parsons at his table. He did not seem pleased to see
them, nor did he seem particularly displeased. He nodded
to them expressionlessly and went on drinking.

Almost on their heels, Councillor Tiverton entered —
once again escorting his wife. She must have come into

money recently. Or had great expectations. Even Ted's eyebrows tilted upwards, although he gave an approving nod.

Never one to shirk the limelight, Albert Tiverton steered his wife direct to the piano bar. With his usual inflated ego, he thought I was smiling at him when he sat next to the empty place with the drink in front of it. He discovered the reason for my amusement when Norma reclaimed her seat and he had to sit there with Norma on one side of him and Milly on the other.

Hail, hail, the gang's all here . . .

It was too good to resist, and I didn't. Our Albert gave me a poisonous glare, turned away from Norma and concentrated on Milly.

At least, he tried to. But Milly leaned across him to do the decorous thing to Norma.

'I was so sorry to hear of your . . . your trouble,' she began, in the usual massive English understatement.

Norma looked at her as though she had just crawled out from under a rock and lit another cigarette. It was a moment when I could not entirely blame Norma.

'Here, that's enough of that,' Albert said. 'She doesn't want to be reminded—' He gave Norma an uneasy vote-catching smile. 'She's here to try to forget and enjoy herself a bit, like.'

Even Milly knew that was the wrong thing to say. She sank her elbow into Albert's ribs.

'*Ooomph!*' But he took the reprimand in good grace, for him, and set about trying to retrieve the *faux pas*. 'I mean to say, she's in a state of shock, yet. What with the boy not only dead, but all those things coming out about him— *Ooomph!*'

Norma turned away as though she had not heard a word he'd been saying. Perhaps she hadn't. Her burning eyes moved to scan the room. What was she looking for? Whom did she hope to find?

'Would you like another little drink, dear?' Daisy asked her uneasily. 'It will soon be Last Orders. Something a bit stronger, perhaps? Something to help you sleep, dear.'

Norma looked at her unseeingly, eyes so wide they might have been lidless. She was never again going to escape into sleep so easily, so effortlessly. Sleep was an unknown word to her now. 'No,' she said flatly. After a long moment she added, 'Thank you.'

'Oh, well, suit yourself, dear. I just thought—' Daisy met my eyes over Norma's head and shrugged helplessly.

'I'll find him!' Norma spoke suddenly, vehemently, in answer to some conversation being waged only in her own mind. Her voice was deep and hollow, sounding curiously disembodied, but it carried a deep conviction. 'I'll find the devil who killed my Johnny. And, when I do, *I'll* kill *him* . . . slowly.'

It was a real conversation-stopper. She had leaned over close to my microphone and her words boomed out through the room. I was so startled, I forgot what I was playing and lifted my hands from the keyboard. The sudden silence emphasized her vow.

After a moment someone gave a nervous laugh and conversation resumed. I dropped my hands back to the keyboard. I couldn't remember what I had been rendering. It didn't matter . . . play something quickly . . . anything . . .

I'll see you again . . .

No, no, that wasn't right. Fuel to the flames. I broke off abruptly, my mind a blank. Something else . . . what?

'Yes.' Norma turned her burning eyes on me. '*You* know. You understand . . .'

'No,' I denied quickly. 'I'm sorry. It was a mistake. I—

I'm sorry . . .' My hands fell to the keyboard again, vamping a bridge. But a bridge to what melody? Every tune that sprang to mind seemed suddenly fraught with *double entendre*. I dared not let my fingers rove at will among the keys—they had already proved too untrustworthy.

'Come along, dear,' Daisy said practically. 'It's time we were getting home. They'll be closing here, anyway, any minute.'

'Not for another half-hour.' It was clear that Norma wasn't going to budge. She turned again and scanned the room, leaving a ripple of shudders in the wake of her gaze.

'Have it your way, dear.' Daisy shrugged and seemed to surrender. Perhaps I was the only one to notice the quick sweep of her hand. Her drink went flying into Norma's lap.

'Oh! Oh! I'm so sorry, dear! How clumsy of me!' Daisy caught up some of my pile of paper napkins and dabbed ineffectually at the pool of gin and tonic.

Norma leaped to her feet, the glass hit the floor and rolled away from her. She shook her skirt and brushed at it.

'Come along, dear.' Daisy took her arm. 'We'll go to the Powder Room and get you tidied up—'

Unresisting for a change, Norma allowed herself to be led away. Daisy looked back at me with a meaningful nod. Obviously, she was going to whisk Norma straight home as soon as she was dried off.

'Whew!' Councillor Tiverton pulled a handkerchief from his pocket and mopped at his brow. 'That was tricky! Getting real nasty, that was. Someone's going to have to do something about that woman. She's going straight off the rails—'

'Some people might think she had good reason.' I tried to keep my voice steady, tried to look and sound normal. Above all, I tried not to let him see that I had noticed the tiny object that had dropped from his handkerchief and skittered across the piano top. He must not guess that I recognized it and that it conveyed any meaning to me.

It was a flower-shaped button. One of the buttons from my blouse. The blouse Johnny Handel had stolen and worn.

The blouse he had been wearing when he met his killer.

CHAPTER 20

Under the guise of sorting through the request numbers on the cocktail napkins Daisy hadn't used in her mopping-up process, I managed to drop a couple of napkins over the button. I could retrieve it later, it wouldn't be wise to try right now under Albert Tiverton's watchful eyes.

I looked around for Ted, but he was gone. The police were never around when you needed them, either. I bit down on a slightly hysterical giggle. That was something else that wouldn't be wise.

There was a more-or-less-private public telephone in the back hall, at the top of the stairs. I could call the police from there. All I had to do was get to it.

Carefully arranging a smile on my face, I slid off the piano bench. 'Just taking five,' I said airily, to no one in particular, and walked off without looking back.

I threaded my way through the tables, ignoring Kate's wave of invitation. For as long as possible, I headed in the direction of the Powder Room, in case I was being watched. At the last moment, I changed direction and slipped through the emergency exit to the back hall.

The pay-phone hanging on the wall shone like a beacon. It was not in use. I lifted the receiver and heard the comforting purr of the dial tone. I had a five-pence piece clutched in my hand and I balanced it in the slot, ready to ram it home when the police answered at the other end of the line. I began to dial the number I had unconsciously memorized earlier in the day.

'Now then, you don't want to do that!' A hand slammed down on the hook, cutting me off. 'Now, why don't we go downstairs and—?'

I eluded his descending hand and rushed back through the emergency exit into the saloon bar. I knew I wouldn't be able to make it in a straight dash back to the piano. The thing to do was to appear calm and unhurried. I had to act as though everything was normal and the worst I suspected of the Councillor was that he was making yet another boring pass.

A small nondescript little man sat alone at the table just inside the door. I had not noticed him on my way out — he was not the noticeable type. Never mind, any port in a storm. I stopped at his table and pulled out the chair facing him.

'The line was busy,' I said chattily. 'I'll just sit here, if you don't mind, and try again in a minute—'

He raised his head and those pale smoky eyes transfixed me. The Starer.

I stood frozen, unable to move or even to continue speaking. He was no port—and the storm was all around me. I was truly caught between the devil and the deep blue sea.

'That's right.' Hands like iron bands grappled me from behind and pulled me backwards. 'We'll try again.' I was pushed through the emergency exit before I could catch my breath to scream.

At the top of the stairs, he changed his grip. One hand clamped across my mouth, too quickly for me to bite. Twisting my arm behind my back, he propelled me down the stairs at top speed. I caught at the stair rail with my free hand to keep from falling. He would not care if I hurtled headlong and broke my neck. It would save him the bother of breaking it himself later.

He had to let go of my arm to open the back door. Before I could catch my balance, he had reclaimed the arm and bundled me out of the door and into the back yard.

The door swung shut behind us and we both hesitated at the sudden darkness. Then he began pushing me forward again, he was more familiar with the area than I was and, presumably, he had some destination in mind.

I dug in my heels and resisted. He was not going to get me out into the alley without a fight — preferably a noisy one. Once we were out of the backyard, he might go anywhere. No one would be able to find us. If they came looking, that is.

With a muttered curse, he brought his knee up into the back of my knees and they buckled under me. He held me upright as I sagged and kept moving forward inexorably. We were at the gate now, another moment and we would be out in the alley and I would be lost.

He cursed again as he realized the gate opened inward and he would have to free one hand to open it. I could feel his mental turmoil as he tried to decide whether to uncover my mouth or free my arm.

He opted for the arm, ramming me against the gatepost with his hip to hold me immobilized. If he got me through that gate, I was as good as done for. It was agonizing to think that just behind me and up one flight of stairs friends were laughing and talking, unaware of my peril. Surely someone must soon notice that I had been gone longer than usual and begin to wonder.

Daisy must soon shepherd Norma out of the Powder Room and start for home. Would she glance towards the vacant piano bench and wonder where I'd gone? Ted must be back by now. Wouldn't he be surprised — and perhaps indignant — not to find me there playing the 'drinking-up music' as he called out for last orders? Wasn't Milly getting jealous as she realized that the pianist and her precious husband were both missing? Had Kate and the others noticed that I had gone through the back door with the man I most despised? That must have occasioned some surprise — especially as I hadn't returned. What did they imagine we were doing? Even if they thought we were burying the hatchet, they must think we were taking an unconscionable time about it.

But perhaps no one had noticed anything at all. I had probably not been gone all that long. Even though my life-expectancy had telescoped down to its last few moments, in terms of actual time consumed, the whole process had not taken more than three or four minutes.

Albert Tiverton uttered a wordless snarl as he discovered the gate was locked. He suddenly hurled me from him, slamming me against the fence and pinioning me there by the throat with one hand as he fumbled for something in his pocket.

My throat was dry and my lips numb from being ground against my teeth, but I could speak again. Not too loudly. That hand around my throat had only to press a bit harder to crush my windpipe. I wanted to begin a dialogue, not startle him into killing me instantly.

'Ted locked it last night,' I whispered. 'There was a prowler — ' Realization struck me belatedly. He knew all about it. 'It was you!'

'Just doing my rounds.' He spoke with suppressed fury. 'Some fool saw me but didn't recognize me. Tried to telephone Ted, but couldn't reach him. Telephoned my home, knowing I was part-owner of this place. Milly took the call. I wasn't home, so she managed to find Ted and send him off on the wild goose chase — '

He found what he wanted and pulled a large bunch of keys from his pocket. Enough keys for half the premises in town. I began to realize what he meant when he spoke of doing his rounds. He must have a key to every place in which he owned a financial interest. He would have access to most of the buildings along the front . . . And the boating pool?

'It was you . . . that terrible mocking whistle. You killed Little Johnny. But why . . . ?' It was an unnecessary question. I was in a situation that concentrated the mind wonderfully. I caught the distant whiff of civic corruption. Little Johnny had gone everywhere along the front, prying and spying. 'I suppose he knew too much?'

'That, too.' He was trying to sort out the keys one-handed to find the right one for the gate. 'More reasons than one, the little bastard had it coming to him.'

'How could you?' I choked. 'He was just a little boy—'

'Oh no.' He gave a grim laugh. 'No, he wasn't. I don't know what he was, but a boy he was not. Little—' He broke off tried to fit one of the keys into the lock.

'Just the same—' I tried to distract him, to keep him from realizing that some strength was returning to my aching arm— 'it was unnecessary. No one would have taken his word against yours—' No, but it might have started them wondering. There was more to it than that, though. The torn clothing, the taunting whistle, bespoke a more personal malice. 'What had he ever done to you?'

'Done? Done?' I shrank back from his explosive fury. 'I'll tell you what he done! Luring me on! With his painted face and his female clothes. I didn't recognize him. How could I? Who'd have expected—?'

'Even so . . .' I said.

'I'd had a hard day.' He was momentarily plaintive, the need to justify himself was strong. 'A man's entitled to some fun. I took Milly home and came back to the front that night. Middle of a holiday weekend, lots of trippers around, girls looking for a good time on a Saturday night . . .'

Saturday night . . . my mind filled in the gaps. That was the night Norma had escaped him . . . and his wife had caught up with him. He must have been seething with frustration.

It was also the night a pretty little ghost-girl had been loitering alone across the street from The Phoenix. Johnny . . . keeping a jealous eye on his mother? Or looking for a pick-up? Or perhaps a bit of both.

'So I came back to the front and met up with this *girl* — this *tripper* —' He was swept along on a tide of righteous indignation, but it didn't stop him from trying another key in the lock. Any moment, he was bound to find the right one.

'How was I to know? How could any normal man expect —? He led me on, then he began to laugh at me. He thought I *did* know — or pretended he thought so. Then he broke away and ran — still laughing. I chased him — what else could I do? He ran down the dark alleys — he knew them all. He would. I followed the laughing until it stopped. And then I heard it behind me and I thought he'd doubled back. I swung around and caught him — her — by the throat. I'd teach the little sod to laugh at me!'

His hand tightened convulsively on my own throat. My blood thrummed in my ears, rays of light exploded behind my eyes. I clawed at his hand desperately, but he didn't seem to notice. He was reliving the recent past. It had happened then, too.

'He stopped laughing, all right. I held on to him for a minute longer, to teach him a lesson, like. Then I gave him a good shaking and dragged him under the street light to frighten him some more. But when I looked down, it wasn't him — it was her. And she was dead —' His voice hardened. 'But she'd laughed at me, too. She'd seen what happened with Johnny and she thought it was funny. She'd laughed earlier, too, around the piano —'

The girl in the boating pond. His hand was too tight for me to speak. He had found the right key and was fitting it in the lock absently, his mind still going over the scene he had been describing. He'd have the key to the boating pond gate, too. Would he risk dumping another body there?

'He got away—that time. But he'd watched what had happened to the girl. After the police discovered the body, he rang me, wanted money. He was a fly one, but he still had to arrange to collect the money—'

Oh, Johnny, Johnny, I thought sadly. *If only you hadn't been so greedy . . .*

'He had the gall to wear that outfit again—' Tiverton's voice choked with righteous indignation. 'To come mincing along like—like a woman of the streets! He looked around, but he didn't see me where I'd hidden myself. I watched him pick up the parcel and I followed him back to the bathing-hut where he'd been hiding out. And I—' He broke off, turned the key in the lock, and pulled the gate inward.

'You killed him there,' I managed to whisper.

'Aye—and I stripped the deceiving finery off him before I strung him up under the pier. Born to be hanged, that one was, and he made it. I washed his face off, too, before I left him. It was the least I could do for poor Norma.'

'You're all heart.' I no longer cared whether I antagonized him. I braced myself for the final struggle.

'And now you—' He wasn't going to waste any more time. Still holding me with one hand, he drew back his other hand to knock me unconscious. I tried to scream, but all that came out was a whimper of alarm. I closed my eyes against the blow.

There was a crunching noise. He gave a strange grunt and then I heard a thud.

I opened my eyes to find him in a heap at my feet. Half of a heavy glass ashtray lay beside his head.

I looked up and straight into the eyes of the Starer. I found my voice then and began screaming.

The light over the back door went on abruptly, flood

lighting the back yard. The back door burst open—it had already been opened once. I realized that was the source of the light rays I had thought were due to my having been half-strangled.

Then they were all around me. Kate and Dandini supporting me, Daisy holding Norma back. Ted stood looking down at his brother-in-law with horrified resignation.

'Are you all right, Miss Kane?' the Starer asked earnestly. 'I heard everything he said. It was awful. I hope you don't mind that I had to resort to violence—' He was still clutching the other half of the glass ashtray. 'But he was going to hit you and I couldn't let him do that. So I hit him first with the ashtray. I—I'm sorry. I know it wasn't cricket, but he's bigger than I am—'

Upstairs, after the police had come and gone, he was still contrite. 'I'm sorry I broke the ashtray—' He looked around to apologize to Ted, but Ted had taken a dazed Milly and Norma to a nursing home and wasn't back yet. We were down to a private party again, a few friends drinking after hours.

'It was such heavy glass,' he said. 'I didn't think it would break so easily—'

'Never mind the ashtray! I'll buy you another.' I threw my arms around him wildly and kissed him. I'd been doing rather a lot of that in the past couple of hours. To everybody. It was so good to be alive. 'I'll buy you a dozen ashtrays!'

'Oh no, thank you,' he said primly. 'I don't smoke.'

'That Albert Tiverton always did have a head that could break a cement block,' Daisy said.

Sidney, ex-the Starer, turned his large eyes towards me. They were really rather attractive eyes, now that they were focused properly. There was nothing to fear from him. There might be, probably would be, other Starers, and one of them might be deadly one day. It was the fear every performer had to learn to live with, especially in these times. But Sidney was all right.

'Actually,' he said, 'I've been following you about for days. I hope you don't mind, Miss Kane—'

'Trudi, please.'

'Trudi—' He blushed. 'I've been trying to get up the nerve to speak to you. I saw you in the music store buying some old sheet music, so I knew our interests were similar. Then I found you were appearing here and I came every chance I could get—'

Thereby nearly reducing me to a nervous wreck. But I couldn't say that. I must never admit it. He'd be horrified.

Meanwhile, I was beginning to get a bit nervous about the way the conversation was going. I hoped he wasn't about to make a Declaration. I was grateful to him for saving my life, but I didn't feel like consigning the rest of that life to his care for evermore.

'It was so marvellous when you came to sit at my table tonight,' he went on. 'It was like the answer to a prayer— and I knew I could talk to you then. But that man came up and took you away. I didn't have the feeling that you wanted to go—'

'You were *so* right, Sidney,' I murmured.

'I thought it over for a bit—I'm sorry I took so long. And then I followed you. I don't know why I took the ashtray with me. I—I guess I felt something might be wrong—'

'Well, thank heavens you did,' Daisy said warmly. 'Let me get you another drink.'

'No, thank you,' he said. 'I don't drink much. What I'd really like . . .' He hesitated.

'Go on,' I said cautiously.

'What I'd like— I mean, I wouldn't bother you *every* night . . . perhaps not even every week . . . but once in a while . . . if you'd be so kind . . .'

They were all watching him with fascination. He became conscious of this and blushed.

'You see,' he explained earnestly, 'my mother doesn't approve. She says I'm driving her crazy. The neighbours don't like it either. And I thought perhaps you wouldn't mind—'

'Go on,' I said again . . . This had begun to sound familiar. Only the accent was different.

'I'm not bad. I assure you, I'm not. And I wouldn't get in your way . . . drown you out. Just softly . . . in the background . . .'

'Drums,' I said. 'You play the drums.'

'That's right.' He beamed at me. We had achieved a meeting of minds. 'I've got my own set. I thought I could leave them here. And . . . and perhaps we could even work out some arrangements together. Oh, not if it's too much bother—' He was apologetic again. 'I just thought—'

'It's a lovely thought, Sidney,' I said. The price could have been a lot higher. 'You've got yourself a deal.'